KEEPER OF SHADOWS

LIGHT-WIELDER CHRONICLES, BOOK 1

BRIDGETT POWERS

Map illustrations by: Matthew Thomas. http://www.mthomascomics.com/

Cover design by: Kirk DouPonce, DogEared Designs

ISBN: 978-0-9996506-0-8

TALES
OF THE
SEVEN
LANDS

KEEPER
OF
SHADOWS

LIGHT-WIELDER CHRONICLES | BOOK ONE

BRIDGETT POWERS

Light's Scribe
Books

To Mom, faithful companion through all my journeys. Thanks for always helping me find my way out of the Shadow Mist.

For Avery and Xavier, who insisted that I never stop making up stories.

CONTENTS

PREVIEW: DARK PRISM

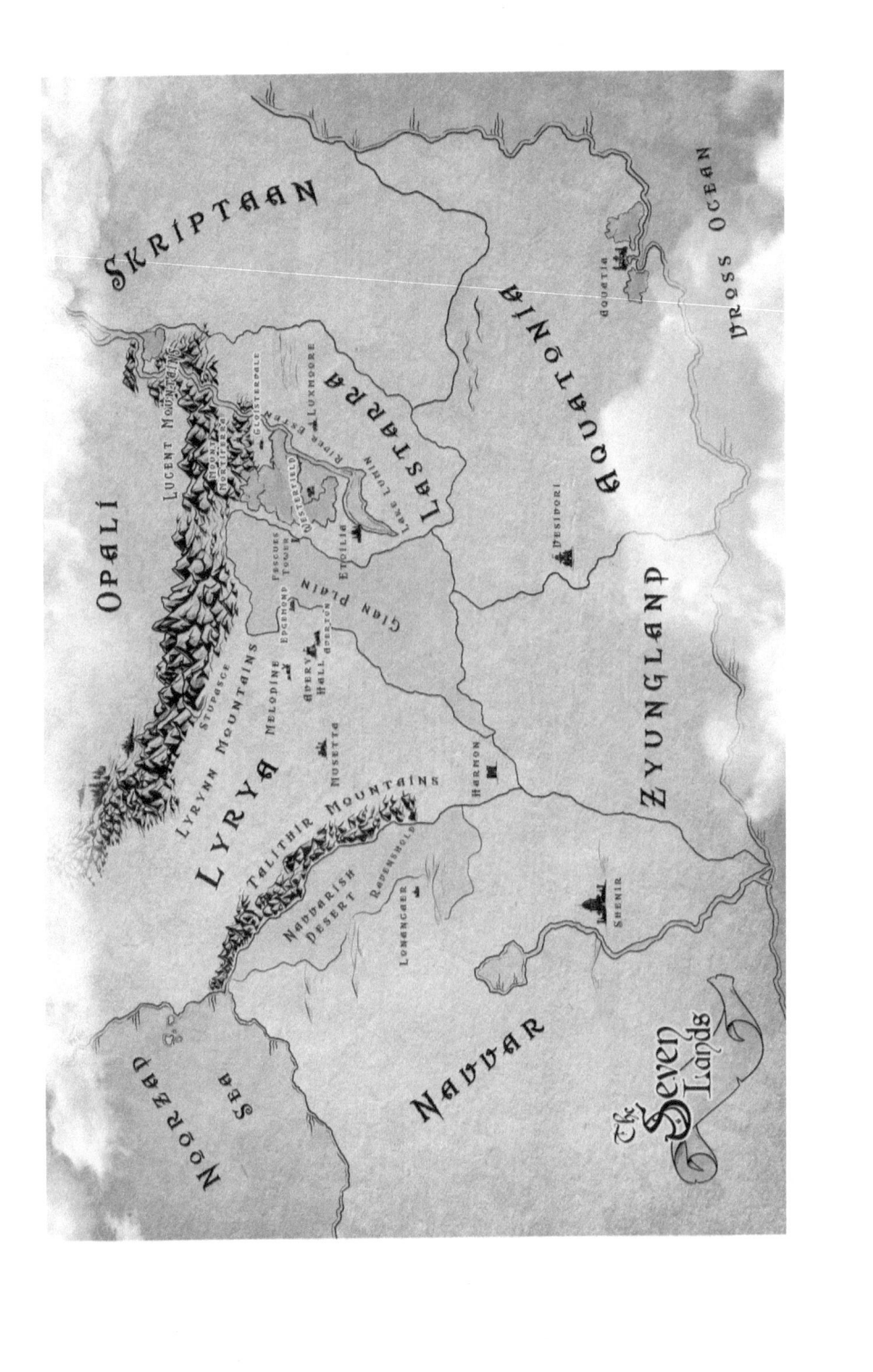

LUCENT MOUNTAINS
STUPASCE
OUNTAINS
MOUNT MORTIFERRA
GLOISTERVALE
MELODINE
EDGEMOND
FESCUES TOWER
WESTERFIELD
AVERY HALL
AVERTON
LUXMOORE
RIVER ESTEN
TA
GIAN PLAIN
ETOILIA
LAKE LUMIN
LASTARRA

CAST OF CHARACTERS

Major Characters: (in order of appearance)

Noire: a raven on a quest to break a family curse and free his people from tyranny

Lyssanne Caelestis: village teacher in Cloistervale, Lastarra

Jarad: an orphan boy from Cloistervale, one of Lyssanne's students.

Lady Venefica Mortifer: Keeper of the Shadow Mist, last descendant of Cloistervale's nobility

Sir Brennus Xavier: a disillusioned knight in service to no realm.

Citizens of Cloistervale:

Madam Blythe: nervous mother of six, including twins who love Lyssanne's tales.

Brianne & Lysander Caelestis (deceased): Lyssanne's parents. (mentioned)

Kevan Clayton: grain farmer/wood carver, Aderyn's suitor.

Mr. & Madam Colby: an older couple who look after the orphans.

Mr. Cutler: the butcher.

Mr. Gierre DeLivre: scribe originally from Lyrya, Lyssanne's mentor.

Mistress Evlia: village healer.

The Furins: (Hugo & Teremiah): feuding father and son. (mentioned)

Mr. Irvin: vegetable farmer whose land borders that of Mr. Riles.

Mr. Murrough: village miller.

Madam Murrough: sister to Mr. Whiskin.

Elaiza Murrough: miller's six-year- old daughter.

Elward Murrough: miller's son, in his early teens.

Madam Nettleworth: sour-faced elderly farmer's wife.

Niklette: nearly grown orphan girl, takes over teaching during Lyssanne's illness.

Councilman Ratomer: second-highest ranking member of the Council of Cloistervale.

Mr. Riles: farmer attacked by the Shadow Mist while plowing. His lands border those of Mr. Irvin.

Madam Sewell: weaver, seamstress, and chief gossip.

Chief Councilman Torin: Head of the ruling Council of Cloistervale.

Madam Torin: Chief Councilman's wife.

Aderyn Torin: Chief Councilman's daughter, Lyssanne's dearest friend, the beauty of the village.

Adalbin Torin: Chief Councilman's son, farmer.

Arron Torin: one of Adalbin's teenaged sons.

Mr. Whiskin: village baker,

Gavan Whiskin: baker's son, age eight.

Mistress Flora Whitfield: chandler who specializes in scented candles and soaps. (mentioned)

Willem: Village carpenter, and Aderyn's suitor.

Faeries:

Alvar: captain of an attack forces detail in the Offensive Warfare branch of FAE Division.

Cusith: Alvar's giant, green faerie dog.

Jada: warrior faerie, Olivia's subordinate.

Olivia: captain of Protection Detail in the Royal Elfin Army, FAE division. (Faeries Against Evil)

Princess Tria (deceased): daughter of the queen. (mentioned)

Miscellaneous:

Brija Vivva-Beh: Innkeeper of Fields End, Westerfield.

Luteson: king of Lyrya. (mentioned)

Magda: elderly maidservant of Venefica Mortifer.

Seanan Fescue: (a.k.a Shaman of the Wood.) Hermit living in a tower at the edge of Gian Plain.

Stella 11: reigning queen of Lastarra. (mentioned)

Talisman peddler: a strange man selling charms and amulets in Westerfield, former student of Seanan Fescue.

Mr. Waxford: a scribe in Westerfield.

Inhabitants of Avery Hall:

Lord Duncan Avery: Lord of Avery Hall & Averton, Lyrya. Best friend of Sir Brennus, His father trained them both in knighthood.

Lady MeMe Avery: wife to Duncan. Maiden name, Cintilla.

Lady Noel Avery: Daughter of Duncan and MeMe. Age 10.

Madam Bedford: chief housekeeper of Avery Hall. (mentioned)

Clark: blacksmith, was once a foot soldier, nearly seven feet tall. Wife: Carol.

Emma: Lady MeMe's personal maid.

Sir Fenard: Baron of Harmon, Lyrya. Duncan Avery's cousin.

Countess Fynette: young widow of a minor Lyryan earl. Sir Fenard's sister.

Captain Gunther: captain of the guard.

Lily: housemaid assigned to serve as lady's maid for Lyssanne. Emma's sister.

Non-human Characters:

Amphisbaena: two-headed serpent. One of its heads must always speak truth, while the other can lie.

Bob: assassin resembling part hermit crab, part man. Skilled in knife-throwing.

Diornian: deadly creature with the wings of a dragon, body of a spider, tentacles of a sea creature, and a lethal third eye.

Neigeans: (a.k.a. Snow Men of Lyrynn) creatures with alabaster skin and elongated bodies. Their music has magical and coercive properties.

Oni: faceless, silvery creatures resembling liquid pewter or cloaks hung on pegs, with clawed hands. They rob victims of will and emotion.

Reina: unicorn, guardian of Lastarra's forests.

Seianelle: a simurgh: creature with the body of a bird, head of a dog, claws of a lion, tail of a peacock, and copper wings.

Serena: a small, white dove that befriends Lyssanne during her illness.

LIGHT-WIELDER PROPHECY

Child of Light
Of Heaven born,
Trapped within
Her mortal form,
Through Mist of doubt
And Shadow rise,
And bring release
To a land that cries.
One hidden gift
To dispel the night,
Destroy the Darkness
And bring forth the Light.
No common pow'r
This strength she wields,
When to the King
Her weakness yields.

— AISLIN, SEER OF THE F.A.E.

SHADOW'S OATH

Spring, year 1121 After the Dawning

The watcher clamped his beak tight, as needle-laden branches parted to allow him passage through the mountainside thicket. His lifelong quest had come to this, playing spy —and now carrier pigeon—for a sorceress with an overblown desire for vengeance. Still, if he succeeded their bargain would be struck. Nothing, not his strength, his dignity, or even his life, was more important.

He broke free of the treetops, startling a flock of common ravens into flight. Though his likeness in every outward fashion, they fled in his wake. Ah, but 'twas not he they should fear.

A dark mist seeped from the trees at the base of the mountain, his would-be liege lady's favored weapon, loosed so it might reveal the origin of the force blocking her power. A force she required his eyes to perceive.

He followed the Shadow Mist down into the valley. It slithered over the tips of the grass without benefit of breeze, boiling with a black life of its own. Sorcery! His talons curled around empty air.

After so long compelled to stalk the skies, how had he sunk this low? Perhaps he no longer deserved to see his quest fulfilled.

A shiver ran beneath his feathers, and he snapped his gaze to the Mist. One plume curled higher, as if reaching for him. Uttering a caw, he shot upward. He *must not* become ensnared.

His ebony wings assaulted the air, propelling him beyond the Mist and over the balding head of a farmer, who hummed as he trudged behind a hand plow. The man's toe caught on a stone, pitching him forward and forcing his plow deep into the soil. With a single grunt, he tugged at the handles. His attempts to wrest the blade free gave the Mist ample time to reach him.

The watcher circled as tendrils of black fog snaked around the farmer's legs. The man's only reaction was to pull harder at the plow. One of the handle rods snapped, and the blade broke free of the soil with a jolt, forcing him to stumble backward. The Mist clung to his trousers, wisps curling up his body. His face contorted into a grimace, and he slammed the plow down so hard it bounced on its wheel. He lifted it again, angled the blade, and slashed at the neat furrow he'd created. Clouds of dirt mingled with the Mist as he kicked, banged, and gouged, mangling wheel, blade, and soil alike.

As his rage grew, so thickened the Mist, but the farmer's gaze slid past it, unseeing.

The watcher flew lower. So, the sorceress had spoken true in this; mere human eyes could not perceive the Mist's presence.

Spewing forth a string of venomous words, the farmer flailed the splintered wood from which his blade now dangled. His eyes widened in a crazed gleam, as his mad motions slashed blade and wood across his arms and torso. He flung the remnant of the plow from him then stalked off, wisps of Mist slithering over the blood trail in his wake.

When the man neared the edge of the field, the Mist clinging to him halted as if it had slammed against an invisible barrier. He staggered on a few more paces, leaving the Mist behind, then stopped to shake himself. Frowning, he glanced down at the blood dripping from his sleeve and torso, confusion replacing the mad gleam in his eyes. Pressing a wad of torn tunic to the worst of his wounds, he turned back to the wreckage of his plow and field, and he swayed.

The watcher spun midair to stare at the Mist. It surged toward the farmer, molding against its unseen barrier as if to a domed shield. The Mist pressed harder, and the barrier shimmered into prismatic light—at once containing all the colors of the rainbow, yet pure and clear as glass.

At last! Now to find the source of this light that so weakened his lady's power. The watcher sharpened his avian gaze, as any raven might to trace the iridescent leavings of distant prey. The barrier, an intricate weaving of fine filaments of light, curved upward and stretched out over the small village ahead. As the farmer staggered toward his house, the watcher fixed his gaze on a single thread of light and followed it.

Golden earth and emerald slopes blurred beneath him as he sped over the tidy rows of cottages peppering the small valley. He shot toward the heart of Cloistervale, the shimmering thread he stalked growing brighter. Its source must be near, but where? The watcher angled his wings to swoop lower, as his strand of light converged with others and formed a carriage wheel pattern, centered...there!

From a chandler's shop window in the market square, a glow spilled forth like water bursting a dam. A radiance that had nothing to do with candle or lamp.

The watcher settled on a rooftop across the square, just as a petite peasant maid exited the shop. As if she'd cloaked herself in every flame the chandler's wares might someday produce, the glow exited with her. She hoisted the handle of her basket higher on one arm then tugged a lock of copper-streaked hair free of a snag. With a swing of her head, her unbound curls flowed around her shoulders like those of a child rather than a girl of marriageable age.

She wove between milling townsfolk, the crowd swallowing her tiny form. Ah, but they could not conceal her light from the watcher's view, though everyone surrounding her remained heedless of its multihued brilliance. He clacked his beak. The toll that light had taken on his lady's power, and on her ability to grant what he sought, would soon be remedied. He launched into the air to better stalk his prey.

Above the din of creaking carts, neighing horses, chatter, and general market bustle, several children's voices rose in a sudden shout. Four small bodies broke away from a knot of women and hurled themselves at the peasant maid, staggering her backward several steps. The children hugged her waist and tugged at her homespun skirts.

Two of them, twins in appearance, cried out in unison, "Tell us a story, Lady Lyssanne!"

Lady? Ha! Sorceress, perhaps. The watcher suppressed a shiver. Two magic-wielders in close proximity? He would fulfill his part in this sordid bargain and leave them to their war.

"Children!" a woman shouted nearby. "Let Lyssanne pass Marketday in peace. She just spent an entire week telling you stories. You'll see your teacher again soon enough."

Lyssanne squinted, fixing her gaze a bit to the woman's left. "'Tis no bother, Madam Blythe."

The older woman's mouth drew into a thin line. "Madam *Murrough*...dear."

Flushing, Lyssanne ducked her head. "Oh, of course. Your pardon."

Circling overhead, the watcher narrowed his eyes. Was the girl daft? How else could she fail to recognize a neighbor in so small a village? A daft sorceress, a danger these people would be well rid of.

"No harm done," the other woman said. "If you're certain you don't mind, I shall send Elward to collect the little ones when he finishes unloading flour at the bakery."

Lyssanne nodded and led the children to the scribe's shop across the square from the bakery. She sat upon the steps and leaned against the door, the children gathering around her like fledglings to a mother sparrow. The smallest, a fair-haired girl, climbed into her lap.

The watcher flew to one of the eaves above the teacher, his will bent on his single remaining task; procure an object of value from his would-be liege lady's enemy. He peered into Lyssanne's basket. Nothing of use there. The object must not only be dear to her but also have prolonged contact with her person. What was he to do, swoop down and snag a lock of her hair? A stunt like that could get a bird shot in this crowd.

"For you, Mistress Lyssanne," said the child in her lap, handing her a flower.

"Thank you, Elaiza." Lyssanne held the bloom near her nose, but instead of sniffing it, she peered at it as if inspecting its petals for insects. "Oh, a rowan blossom? My favorite." The shimmer pulsed brighter around her as she threaded the stem into her hair.

The watcher sharpened his gaze. What in the Seven Lands was the meaning of this? Before he could consider it further, Lyssanne launched into her tale, her lilting voice ensnaring even his thoughts. His mission half-forgotten, he permitted his mind to wander through far-off lands and fanciful quests, until a lanky youth rushed up to the teacher and her rapt audience.

"Madam Murrough asked me to collect Elaiza and the twins," the youth said. "C'mon." He plucked the little girl off Lyssanne's lap and hoisted her onto his shoulders, then turned to the other children. "Gavan, your father's waiting for ya at the bakery."

"No, Jarad!" Elaiza said, tugging at the youth's ear. "I wanna wait for Elward."

"Your brother's too busy being useful," Jarad grumbled.

Elaiza pouted. "I wanna be useful."

"As do we all," Lyssanne murmured, rising from the steps. "But you've brought me great joy. A most useful task. Now, we must let Jarad fulfill his."

The watcher dug his talons into the eave. Oh, what his kin would give for such petty concerns. If, to free them, he must consign these peasants to the Shadow Mist, so be it.

"Wait," Elaiza said, tugging at Jarad's ear again, "what happened to the princess?"

"Well," Lyssanne said, smiling, "the tiny flame from that single candle banished fear from her realm. You see, light not only dispels darkness, but reveals each shadow for what it truly is." As she bent to embrace the children, the blossom fell from her hair. Heedless, she strode off along the street.

The watcher sprang into the air. At the height of his ascent, he flipped, tucked his talons beneath him, folded his wings at his sides, and plummeted beak-first toward the flower. Just in time, he snapped his wings open, arched his back, and snatched up the blossom. His belly skimmed the ground, stirring the loose dirt just before he angled upward.

He clamped his beak tighter on his prize. If this flower sufficed, Lyssanne's shield of light would soon shatter, no more a hindrance to his path than had been the mountainside trees.

~

Cradling a large piquantine fruit in the crook of one arm, Lyssanne opened her cottage door and squinted at the familiar figure silhouetted against the waning sunlight. Tall, slender, a red-gold glow outlining her fair hair. "Aderyn?" Lyssanne asked.

"Lyss, thank the King! I need to…" Aderyn drew a shaky breath and sniffled. "Oh, there I've gone and interrupted your work!" She gestured at the fruit. "I shall go."

"Nonsense." Lyssanne stepped aside. "I was just set to brew a pot of flyl, but this will make more than I could drink. Come, help me see it doesn't go to waste." She closed the door behind Aderyn. "What's amiss? I thought you were to dine with your brother's family tonight."

"I was…I did," Aderyn said, flailing her hands as if searching for words. "But he…it…"

"Oh, Aderyn." Lyssanne wrapped her free arm about Aderyn's waist, her own throat tightening. "Has something befallen Adalbin or the boys?"

Aderyn shook her head. "Nothing like that. 'Tis Father and Willem and…"

Lyssanne backed away, one brow raised. "Willem? The builder's son? What has he to do with your distress?"

"Everything!" Sobbing, Aderyn crossed the sitting room in three long strides and sank onto a kitchen chair.

Frowning, Lyssanne followed her into the alcove that served as kitchen and dining area. She placed the fruit in a large bowl then handed her friend a cloth.

Aderyn dabbed at her eyes and slumped, her long, slender body folding in on itself. "Father says the daughter of a councilman must choose wisely whom she weds."

Keeping her gaze fixed on Aderyn, Lyssanne feathered her fingertips over the cutlery and crockery littering her scrubbed-wood countertop. "Surely everyone should take care in such a choice." At the touch of cold, smooth porcelain, she slid the bowl containing her fruit forward.

"Yes, well," Aderyn said, "*I* think Father lets his position go to his head. After all, it isn't as if I'm a lady, or even a merchant's daughter."

Lyssanne's lips twitched as she pressed the tip of a knife to the fruit's orange hull. The hull resisted. "I'm certain he merely wishes you well-settled. He loves you."

Aderyn sighed. "Yes, but he can be so...so *fierce* with it! You know what I mean."

"I can imagine it, somewhat," Lyssanne said, angling her knife and pressing harder.

"Oh, Lyss, I'm sorry. I sometimes forget...but surely your mother was just as irritating?"

"She could be protective," Lyssanne said, careful not to squeeze the fruit as she worked her knife, "but she was more likely to push me out the door than shelter me." She smiled as the stiletto blade finally pierced the hull. "Good thing, too, as it turned out."

"Well and I suppose she wanted to be sure you could survive on your own. Losing your father the way she did, so young." Aderyn let out a shaky breath. "What am I to do, Lyss?"

"Do?"

"About Father, and Willem, and...everything!"

Lyssanne set her knife aside, brushed a fingertip over the hull to locate the puncture she'd made, then guided it over her bowl. "What has Willem done?" she asked, squeezing the fruit.

"Adalbin says he plans to speak to Father. *Of me.*"

Lyssanne dropped the fruit. "Willem told your *brother* he intends to offer for you?"

"Yes, tomorrow, after Father concludes the Kingsday celebration." Aderyn sighed. "I think Father favors him."

Lyssanne rescued the fruit from the bowl of juice. "Do *you* favor him?" she asked, pouring the juice into a copper kettle, which she then hung on its hook over her fire.

"I like him well enough, but…I don't know! What would you do?"

Choosing her words with care, Lyssanne began snapping honcin sticks and dropping the spicy twigs into a mortar. "I shall only marry for love," she said at last.

Aderyn huffed. "Love like in your books doesn't exist."

"No…" Lyssanne said, drawing out the word as she worked the pestle. She pressed with all her strength, chasing as often as crushing the rolling honcin.

"Here, let me grind the rest of that," Aderyn said. "Give my hands something to do."

Lyssanne passed her the mortar then gathered the juiced piquantine, knife, and bowl and sat next to her. "I wouldn't settle for simple storybook love, even should it exist," she said, sliding the tip of her knife along the smooth hull until the blade slipped into her original puncture. "I desire a love like that of my parents. Not untroubled, but undying. Love that defies time and circumstance."

"Even should you find such…" Aderyn groaned. "Oh, what does it matter? 'Tis not Willem I love."

"Ah," Lyssanne said, "but there is someone?"

Aderyn's voice thickened. "Kevan."

"Truly? He's a good man." Lyssanne smiled and continued turning her fruit, slicing through to its spherical core. "And he seems a more even-tempered sort. I'm certain your father would not disapprove."

"But Willem is his family's sole heir," Aderyn said. "Kevan's only a grain farmer's son, and with two elder brothers, he'll inherit but a small parcel. Father says, since Kevan will have so little to tend, he should find another trade, lest he be tempted to idleness."

Lyssanne tensed. "I've never known Kevan to be idle." If Councilman Torin thought this of him, how could she ever prove herself useful to the village?

"It is of no consequence," Aderyn said. "Kevan hasn't offered for me." She leaned forward. "How do you do that?"

"What?"

"That!" Aderyn gestured at Lyssanne's hands. "You aren't even looking at the knife!"

"Oh. My hands know where to go," she said, separating the piquantine halves. "I trust them more than my eyes."

"Humph. Mr. Riles could do with such a skill."

"Mr. Riles?" Lyssanne asked, removing the core. The vengeful fruit spat forth a stream of juice, and she sprang to her feet, spreading her fingers to minimize contact with the stickiness.

"He cut himself something fierce while plowing today," Aderyn said. "Mother helped Mistress Evlia patch him up. Said he looked like he'd been attacked. Nearly bled his life away before he reached home."

Gasping, Lyssanne turned, her hands deep in her washbasin. "Is he—"

"Fine as flyl. His wife ran for help in time. *He* has that love you spoke of."

Lyssanne dried her hands, reeling at the abrupt change in topic. "Does Kevan know of your affection?"

"I suspect so, though we haven't spoken of it." Aderyn dropped the pestle and jumped to her feet. "He made this for me, from the heel of the shoe I broke at the Celebration of Lights."

Lyssanne leaned closer to peer at the little figure Aderyn held. "It is lovely." She dropped her cloth to run a fingertip over the wooden charm. The bird, carved in intricate detail, hung from a chord of fine, braided threads. "He must have spent a great deal of time on this."

"I think he did," Aderyn said.

Lyssanne returned to her chair and began scraping pulp from the piquantine hull. She then mashed it with a spoon to extract more tangy juice. As the sounds of grinding resumed from Aderyn's end of the table, Lyssanne cut the hull into slim strips.

"You think I should tell Kevan how I feel," Aderyn said. "Do you not?"

Lyssanne drew a slow breath. "Well, if you—"

"What if he doesn't share my affection?" Aderyn's said. "Am I to accept Willem?" The pestle clattered against the mortar, and she let out a groan. "Oh, why must life be such a trial?"

Lyssanne bit her lip. "Mother always said a difficult choice is better than no choice at all."

"Sure, but..." Aderyn drew in an audible breath. "Lyss, I wasn't thinking! I am so selfish. But you still have time. Perhaps Adalbin or Father could speak to...someone on your behalf."

Lyssanne laughed. "Oh, I'm not troubled by my lack of offers." She stood and carried the pulp and peel over to the pot of bubbling juice. "I've enough to do just preventing the Council from thinking *me* idle. All I meant was, your fortunes far outweigh your trials."

"You have it aright, of course." Aderyn joined her to toss in the pinch of honcin powder that would add a sweet bite to the brew. "Of your many, useful talents, this is the greatest."

Lyssanne raised a brow. "Flyl?"

Aderyn laughed. "No, this...us. You always know what to say."

Lyssanne shook her head. "I merely know how to listen."

The watcher perched on a step just below the uppermost landing of his lady's winding tower staircase. The sun's burnished eye winked at him through an arrow-slit, bathing the surrounding stone in an orange glow. If the acrid steam seeping through the open doorway of the chamber above was any indication, he'd find no hidden exit point here. No matter; his thorough search of the secluded manor and the mountainside on which it stood had yielded several options—should the need for secret entry or escape ever arise.

"Are you certain, milady?" an ancient voice croaked from within the chamber. "Can your spy be trusted?"

"The water mirror never lies, Magda," a younger woman said, her melodious voice cold as the Lyrynn Mountains in winter. She glided into view, her emerald silk gown glimmering.

Lady Venefica Mortifer—dark enchantress, Keeper of the Shadow Mist—the watcher's soon-to-be liege lady.

"Besides," she said, setting a black basin on a wooden stand in the center of the room, "his findings leave little doubt. That girl bears the marks of my first attempt to vanquish her."

"Marks?" Magda asked, shuffling forward to mop spilled water from the stand.

"Diminished sight and stunted stature," Venefica said. "Meager substitutes for my intended ends."

"Still, a grand show of power, that was, milady."

"A grand *failure*," Venefica said, spinning away from her wizened maidservant with such force, tendrils of ebony hair escaped their jewel-spangled netting to spill over her shoulder.

The watcher sidled along the stair to keep her in view through the doorway.

"Failure? Humph," Magda said. "Fire so hot it fused even the smith's hearthstones? You would've succeeded if not for those faer—"

"Do not speak of them!" Venefica swung back around. "Their prophecies and interference cost me everything."

Magda cringed, sloshing more water from the basin. "I thought 'twas the villagers who stole your birthright."

"Indeed," Venefica said, "but robbing me of my betrothed? The fullness of my power?" She flicked a wrist, igniting candles in several wall sconces. "Seventeen years, wasted! I travel the known realms to gain more skills than all my ancestors combined, and does the remnant of my attack draw the Mist to that girl like iron filings to a lodestone? No, this… Light-Wielder grows more dangerous than ever I imagined possible."

"She's no match for your greatness, milady," Magda said, slinking from view.

"Perhaps," Venefica said. "*All* who stole from me will soon lament their existence." She glanced down into the basin then whirled to face the door, dark eyes flashing. "Noire?"

The watcher bent his head, acknowledging the name he answered to only in this place and company.

"Cease lurking among the other shadows and join us," Venefica snapped. "If, that is, you still desire this bargain."

He hopped onto the landing, where he could stretch his wings, then fluttered into the circular chamber and alighted atop a worn table near the entrance.

Magda set a tea tray beside him. "Couldn't do this below?" she muttered, massaging her lower back.

"No," Venefica said, striding over to a brazier beside Noire's table. "The newer portion of the manor house wouldn't withstand what I have planned." She stirred the coals, intensifying the sulfurous atmosphere. "Ancient magic as much as mortar seals these walls. Besides, this remnant of the old fortress was constructed to the perfect height for accessing the elements."

"It is to be a dangerous spell, then?" Magda asked, handing Venefica a crystal goblet.

Venefica nodded, glaring at the vessel. "Mugwort tea, a crutch for amateurs. Still…" She downed the black liquid. "This night's work will require every ounce of my remaining power."

Noire narrowed his eyes. For that reason alone, this had better work. A sorceress without power was about as useful to him as a feather without a wing.

"But, milady," Magda said, taking the empty goblet, "if the Light has so weakened you, how can you be certain this curse will do what your full power could not?"

Noire hopped back a pace, away from the crone and out of range.

Venefica shrugged. "Because, this time, I do not mean to slay the girl."

Magda's eyes widened so, their surrounding wrinkles smoothed out.

"Taking her life would only increase her influence in *my* village,"

Venefica said. "Nor do I possess the power to destroy her Light. Perhaps I never did." A slow smile stretched her lips. "I've found another way."

"I shall leave you to it, then." After a stiff-kneed curtsey, Magda scurried from the tower.

Perhaps Noire would be wise to follow, but if this dark deed succeeded, Venefica would again have the power to fulfill their bargain. Thus, he would remain—and track her every move.

Venefica lifted the long-handled bronze pan onto which Noire had placed Lyssanne's Rowan blossom earlier. "Now, let us see if you are worth the time I've invested, my pet."

Pet? His wing twitched. That pretentious peahen had the nerve to call him such? His feathers stood out in grand disarray. *If* he chose to render service to any creature, it was by his will and for his ends. He was no one's pet.

Ah, but he had need of her skills. He forced his wings to his sides and ducked his head.

Venefica set the pan atop the coals in the brazier. "If these fragments have absorbed the girl's essence," she said, "behold what shall become of her health, influence, and power!"

The rowan blossom fell to instant ash.

Venefica raised her hand, fingers hovering over the ash. She closed her eyes, and the shadows thickened in the chamber, creeping inward from the far edges as if drawn to her.

"This will do," she said. The shadows and the chill that accompanied them receded as she fixed her obsidian gaze on Noire. "Yes, this will do quite well. You have proven your worth."

She stepped forward and trailed a fingertip down the center of his head, from between his eyes to the first joint of his wings. Noire shivered.

"I accept your oath," Venefica said. "Our bargain is sealed."

With all her theatrics, she could have found a home among a troop of Skriptaanese players. Still, he bowed low, the very semblance of a faithful servant awaiting instruction.

Smiling, Venefica placed the pan on a metal rack to cool, then turned to stir the contents of a small kettle suspended above the brazier. "A strong infusion of chamomile, to induce prolonged lethargy." From a nearby jar, she extracted a pinch of yellowish powder and dropped it into the bubbling kettle. "Saffron to carry my spell upon the wind."

Did she really think Noire cared what the ingredients were to do? Her one-sided war with that peasant girl was no concern of his, nor was he a lackey paid to simper at her every word.

Gathering a dark green, slimy-looking weed and a square of fine-meshed cloth, Venefica returned to the cooling rack. After placing the rowan ashes at the center of the cloth, she folded its corners to form a pouch.

"Knotweed to bind her gift," she said, tying the makeshift bag with the stringy plant.

Noire fluttered to the opposite edge of the chamber and crouched beneath a bench. He was no coward, but neither was he a fool. The final steps in her spell were sure to be the most violently magical. Who knew what a stray spark of power might do to a feathered fellow?

The dying sunlight shot a red beam through the chamber's slit window. Venefica raised her hands high, and shadows pooled about her. Icy wind roared through the room, pulling her ebony hair loose and whipping it around her shoulders. Noire tucked his beak behind one wing, as she began to chant.

"In weakness you will wander,
All stamina shall fail.
With pain as your companion,
No wind shall stir your sails.
Alone and without aid,
You'll face this silent thief.
For none shall comprehend,
This curse that lies beneath.
No respite shall you find,
No way to spread your Light.

Your gift I seek to bind,
Succumb to my true might!"

Noire peeked over his wing; hoping a spell's effectiveness didn't depend on the quality of its poetry.

Lifting the pouch of ashes toward the heavens, Venefica uttered ancient words. The last beam of sunlight caught on the pouch, and she shrieked, "Join in the death of this day's light, and surrender to the dawn of night!" With a flick of her wrist, she flung the pouch into the kettle, shouting, "*Adficio!*"

The fire blazed up, engulfing the kettle in a shower of green and orange sparks that obliterated the feeble beam of sunlight. The wind inside the chamber intensified. Sharp, pungent smoke curled outward through the single slit-like window set high into the tower wall.

Aderyn lifted her cup of flyl toward Lyssanne as if in salute. "I shall speak with Kevan. You've convinced me."

"You should follow your heart—and the King's leading—not mine."

"Sure and I shall. Only, what am I to do about Father?" Aderyn held one fist near the neckline of her dress, perhaps clutching the charm Kevan had given her.

"What if," Lyssanne said, "Kevan were to carve small trinkets, boxes, that sort of thing?"

"Oh, I can hear Father's response to that!" Aderyn said, flipping her fair hair over one shoulder. "Frivolous waste of time and good wood. Useless excuse to shirk real chores."

"Useless here, perhaps," Lyssanne said, "where we do not prize such things, but elsewhere they are highly valued."

"You jest! Valued and *sold?*"

"'Tis no jest. My mother told me of it." Lyssanne hurried to a table near her settee and retrieved a trinket box. "She said this cost what a merchant might pay for a bushel of Kevan's wheat. And that was years ago."

Aderyn took the box. "For this, they traded…what, coins?"

"Yes." Lyssanne leaned against the table and sipped her flyl. "I am no judge of such things, but I think Kevan is more skilled than the one who carved the box."

"That, he is," Aderyn said. "His detail is finer."

"His carvings could provide the extra trade your father mentioned," Lyssanne said. "He can store up his wares and, in summer, sell them to the merchant who accompanies the tax man. Your father may even prefer him to Willem once he sees Kevan's rare talent."

"Would the merchant give Kevan coins?" Aderyn asked. "Father says people elsewhere trade in such a way. 'Tis baffling. Coins are nice to look upon, to be sure, but they can't be eaten, or used as tools, or…anything."

"True, but outsiders prefer them. They can be used to pay the village taxes or—" Lightning-bolts of pain stabbed through Lyssanne's temples, ripping all thought from her mind. "Oh!" The word, half gasp, half scream, tore from the pit of her stomach.

An explosion of pressure within her skull drove Lyssanne to her knees, her cup shattering beside her. Clutching her head in both hands, she struggled to focus on Aderyn's voice, muffled as if from a great distance. White light filled her vision, darkness lurking at its edges.

"Lyss! Lyss, what's befallen you?"

Lyssanne couldn't speak, couldn't *think*. Pains stabbed her temples, as pressure built in her head. Her ears rang louder and louder. Her skull would surely burst! She sank onto her side, then darkness consumed her.

Noire lowered his wing a feather at a time. How would they know if it worked?

A plume of gray smoke rose from the blackened kettle. Blinking, Noire edged from the shelter of the bench. The smoke thickened and formed into the shape of a many-pointed star. Sparks danced upon its surface, giving the star the illusion of a twinkle.

The star expanded until a dark cavity opened at its center. Within it, an image formed—the peasant girl, Lyssanne. Her face paled, as jagged fingers of power stabbed through her temples, driving her to her knees. The cup she held dropped to the floor, and she clutched her head in both hands as if to prevent its explosion.

A shriek tore from the image, so sudden and terrible Noire flinched. The girl collapsed. The star burst apart. The fire died. The last remnant of sunlight vanished...and all was silence.

"It is done," Venefica said.

Noire shifted, just as Venefica's triumphant laughter rang throughout the manor.

Outside the slit window, no star pierced the newborn night, and even the moon dared not show its face.

2

FALLEN STAR

*T*he darkness encasing Lyssanne's mind thinned like river fog burning off beneath the rising sun. Oh, if only it hadn't! Voices—Too loud, they pounded against her skull like hammer blows—and light. Daggers of it pierced her eyes when she tried to open them. Groaning, Lyssanne raised a trembling hand to block the burning brightness. Not even her lids could protect her from it.

"Mistress Evlia," a familiar voice whispered, "I think she's awake."

"Good," another woman said. "Douse one of those lamps, will you? And shoo that bird out the door. Humph, what a dove's doing followin' folks indoors…"

That brisk voice, too near Lyssanne's ear, tore another groan from her throat.

"Lyssanne," the woman said, "'tis Evlia, dear. Can you hear me?"

What a question! "Yes," Lyssanne whispered, her own voice thunder inside her head.

"I know it is difficult, but you need to open your eyes. I must look at them."

Lyssanne forced her lids open fraction by fraction. Even dimmed, the light stung.

"That will do," the healer said. "You can close your eyes."

18

Lyssanne sighed.

"'Tis obvious you're in pain, dear. Can you tell me where?"

"My head." If only Mistress Evlia could have heard Lyssanne's thoughts. Speaking was just too exhausting. Jagged bits of memory pierced her mind, and she gasped. "Aderyn?"

"I'm here," Aderyn whispered from her other side. "You collapsed. What happened?"

"'Twas so…sudden," Lyssanne said, still trying to recall what had preceded this pain that had struck like a blow from within. "So sharp…here." She touched her temples.

"Sharp? Like a knife cutting your skin?" Evlia asked.

"No, like…lightning inside." Lyssanne had to pause for breath as if she'd run all the way from the meeting hall. "Hard, fast pains…only seconds at a time, but…so many of them."

"The pain is only in your temples?"

"No, they're striking everywhere, now," Lyssanne whispered. "And the pressure, it won't stop growing…like a water-skin that's being filled to bursting." Strength leeched out of her like moisture from a wrung-out dishrag. Her voice, too, grew weaker. "What's happening to me?"

"I—I am not certain, dear," Evlia said. "I shall brew you some mourning-tree tea for the pain. Then, we shall see."

Gasping, Lyssanne struggled to sit up. "The flyl!" She fell back to her pillow in a wave of dizziness.

"You took it off the flame ages ago," Aderyn said. "Just rest and wait for that tea."

Lyssanne struggled to comply. As hours slipped by, the fog of agony numbed her mind to all else, including the time of day. Yet, it kept her too alert for unconsciousness or even sleep.

Six months thence, Lyssanne pushed open the shutters on her north-facing window. Light filtered through the filmy curtains like feathers borne on the soft autumn breeze. Its heat and the coos of the dove perched on the sill warmed her more than the mourning tree tea she sipped. After drinking the bitter brew thrice daily for half a year, she barely tasted it anymore.

Leaning against the window frame, she stroked the dove's feathers and gazed out at the lush grass sloping down Rowan Hill, but only remembered darkness filled her view. "I had the dream again, Serena," she whispered. "But you knew that, didn't you?"

Serena tilted her snowy head into Lyssanne's hand.

"You always seem to know." Lyssanne closed her eyes, but couldn't banish the image of the nightmare that had haunted her since her illness began. "Had you not awakened me…" She shivered. "What is this shadow that stalks my slumber? From whence stems this certainty that, should it ever reach me, that shadow will destroy me and all I love?"

Serena ceased her cooing.

"What answer can I expect from a dove?" Lyssanne's shoulders tightened. "Still, to speak of such things with anyone else…not even Aderyn or Mr. DeLivre would understand."

Shrill voices drew Lyssanne's gaze across her lawn. A smudge moved just beyond the hedge bordering Broone's field. The children! To avoid the pain their knocking would inflict upon her skull, she strode to the door and stepped outside to await her former students.

A swarm of small bodies rushed up Rowan Hill toward her. The children took turns embracing Lyssanne or offering shy greetings.

"Niklette made us a kite!" little Elaiza Murrough said, tugging at Lyssanne's skirt. "It's got six sides. Just like me…six years. Gavan, show her."

Elaiza's cousin held up the kite for Lyssanne's inspection, then the children rushed off down the lawn.

Niklette laughed. "I told them they'd only have a few days to fly it before the winds grow too gusty, but they insisted." She gestured to the cottage. "Would indoors be better for you?"

"No," Lyssanne said. "The cottage walls would amplify the children's voices." She smiled at the younger girl. "How are you faring with the teaching?"

"A bit flustered," said Niklette. "Jarad's been rather troublesome. Caused Madam Colby some bother at the orphanage, too." She lowered her voice. "This morning, he threw his bowl of porridge at a smaller boy after a simple jest. Almost came to blows."

Lyssanne shaded her eyes and searched the lawn for a glimpse of Jarad. "I've never known him to show such violence," she muttered, "especially toward a younger child. He has always treated little ones with gentle protectiveness."

"Think it has anything to do with his accident?" asked Niklette.

"That was months ago," Lyssanne said.

Niklette sighed. "It has changed him. He used to climb anything that could be scaled, but after that fall from the oak in Market Square, he won't even go near the dais in the meeting hall."

Across the lawn, several children squealed in laughter, as the kite caught the wind.

Lyssanne pressed her fingertips to her temples, smiling through the pain in case a child should glance her way. "Fear can lead to worse things," she said.

"I suppose." Niklette glanced skyward. "Time I'm off to assist Madam Colby…if you're certain you feel up to this."

"A few hours shouldn't prove too taxing," Lyssanne said. "I must ease back into life, lest I become a useless lump, of no benefit to anyone."

"I'll return before noon," Niklette said, then she hurried off toward the village.

Lyssanne called the older children to meet her and the little ones on the hillside near the rowan grove. Once they'd all gathered, she explained the many ways renowned men of science had used kites in their endeavors to predict weather patterns. As the children's questions and Lyssanne's strength waned, she gave her students permission to enjoy the cool, autumn day as they willed. After helping Elaiza untangle her kite's string for the third time, Lyssanne grew unable to bear the increasing weakness in her limbs.

She snagged a passing boy. "I must request a favor."

21

The boy stopped and turned. His features blurred, as if a dark haze lay over Lyssanne's eyes. "Favor?" he asked.

"Jarad," Lyssanne whispered, his familiar voice revealing what her eyes had not. "Indeed a favor, or rather a quest," she said, drawing inspiration from the tales he'd always admired. Perchance she could turn this to good purpose and lighten his melancholy, at least somewhat. "'Tis nothing as grand or dangerous as your beloved *Epic of King Aleric*, but it will save a lady from distress."

"I can do a quest," he said, his voice brightening. He leaned down, already having exceeded her height at eleven years of age. "Even if it is dangerous."

Lyssanne smiled. "I've no doubt of it. What I need is a place to sit, where I can watch the little ones."

Jarad glanced about. "One of your kitchen chairs!" At her nod, he ran toward her cottage.

"Can I have a quest too?" Elaiza asked, twirling with her kite string held high.

"Quests are for boys," Gavan said.

Raised voices cut off Lyssanne's intended response.

"I said, stand aside," Jarad shouted. "I'm on a quest for Lady Lyssanne."

"You? Ha!" said Elward Murrough, his voice coming from the vicinity of Lyssanne's porch. "You'll never even see a knight, let alone go on a quest. None of us will."

"You wanna make our teacher stand all morning when she's ill?" Jarad snapped.

Lyssanne trudged up the hill toward her cottage, calling, "Boys!"

"Maybe it is a quest, to him," Aderyn's nephew Arron said as he and Elward descended the porch steps and passed Jarad. "Such a dangerous climb, all the way to the top step."

Jarad swung around and slammed his fists into both older boys' backs. With an explosion of flailing limbs and shouts, all three landed in a writhing heap on the ground.

The mist in Lyssanne's eyes thickened, forcing her to wipe them. Gooseflesh trickled along her arms and down her back like water from a frosted-over washbasin. "Cease!" she cried, pressing her hands to her temples as she rushed to the boys. "Elward, Arron, stop this at once. Jarad, get up from there. Now!"

Still blinking against the ever-darkening haze obscuring the boys, Lyssanne glanced about for some way to stop them, and the blur dissipated. A thin, fallen limb stuck out from her neglected flowerbed. She snatched it up and returned to the scuffling boys.

Dodging boots and elbows—and blinking against the returned blur, she thrust the limb between two of the boys. Arron scooted backward, staring down at the limb, then looked up at her. He pushed to his feet and shuffled past her, still a bit hazy, but the blur remained darkest around Jarad.

Lyssanne squinted, as the pain in her temples grew. "Elward Murrough, I said cease!"

Elward glanced up and received a blow to the jaw for his distraction. Shoving Jarad aside, he lurched to his feet. Jarad lunged for his legs, but Lyssanne blocked his way, again brandishing her limb.

"Jarad, enough!" Keeping her gaze fixed on his blurred form, she said, "Elward, Arron, report to your fathers. Tell them I've sent you to make better use of your aggressions for the rest of the day."

"What about him?" asked Arron. "He has no father to work off steam with."

Jarad lurched forward, but his chest met Lyssanne's outstretched branch.

"You'd best concern yourself with what yours is going to say," Lyssanne said, still eyeing Jarad. "And if you fail to do as I ask, I shall hear of it."

As Arron followed Elward down the hill toward Broone's field, Lyssanne sank onto the steps and waved Jarad over. He slumped on the lawn, arms folded, face averted.

"Were you harmed?" she asked, struggling to assess his condition through the haze surrounding him.

"Nah."

The crunch of footfalls on grass drew Lyssanne's gaze to a small figure approaching. She raised a hand to forestall the child then turned back to Jarad. "That was unwise."

"Arron called me a coward, and—"

"I heard," she said. "His words were out of place, but did your actions disprove them?"

Jarad held his silence, his face turned toward the stone exterior of her cottage.

She swept a hand over her eyes. "Sometimes the most valiant course is to stand in the face of ridicule and not let it sway your actions."

A sudden, shrill cry cut off her next words. Lyssanne pushed to her feet and rushed toward the sound. The child who had sought her attention beckoned her to a rowan tree halfway down the eastern slope of the hill. Children clustered around it, pointing.

"What's amiss?" Lyssanne asked. "Is someone injured?"

"Gavan went up the tree to save our kite!" Elaiza cried. "Now he's stuck, too."

Lyssanne shaded her eyes. "Gavan," she called, focusing on a lump of brown and white among the branches that must be the small boy. "Just ease back down the way you went up."

"C-can't." His voice was a mere squeak. "Dizzy. D-don't wanna let go."

"Don't be silly," one of the Blythe twins said. "You got up there. You can get down."

A whimper was his only reply.

"Scolding will not help him," Lyssanne said. To Gavan, she shouted, "Hold fast. We shall get you down."

"What's to be done?" asked the other twin. "You can't climb up there in skirts."

"Jarad!" Lyssanne called. "I shall need your assistance."

Gasps and whispers surrounded Jarad as he pushed through the group. Though Lyssanne couldn't determine his expression from his distance of several paces, his shuffling footsteps shouted his reaction.

"Shouldn't someone else do this, mistress?" Jarad whispered.

"On the contrary. As the oldest boy still here, it falls to you to rescue him." She fought to ignore the haze darkening around him. "Such delicate work requires utmost skill, and I happen to know you're the village champion at picking skyberries, without bruising a single fruit."

"But that was before." Looking away, Jarad muttered, "I cannot. What if I...?" He scuffed the toe of a worn boot in the dirt then stared at the shallow hole he'd made. "I'm not brave like the knights in your stories."

"True courage cannot exist except in the presence of something worthy of fear," she said, her soft words filling the hush that had fallen. "Consider a candle. Lighting it would serve no purpose if there were no darkness for it to brighten. The knights of old weren't unafraid. They ventured forth nonetheless, the quest more important than the fear." She grasped his shoulder. "You are no different. Gavan needs you. Now, go!"

Huffing, Jarad jerked away from her hand. He shuffled over to the tree, along the way kicking something that smacked against the base of the trunk.

Noire glared down at the peasant girl standing beneath his perch. That night in the tower was to have changed everything; yet, here he sat, half a year later, spying for the sorceress. *Still.*

Venefica's enemy shivered, her fair skin paler than ever; her iridescent shimmer dim but not extinguished. How could her Light yet blanket the village, albeit threadbare and riddled with holes, when she was thus weakened and, most days, confined to a darkened cottage?

Noire squeezed his talons around the branch, piercing its bark. As long as Lyssanne's Light denied the Shadow Mist free rein, Venefica would lack the power to fulfill their bargain.

He leaned forward. Perhaps the dark fog was gaining ground. For, a mere five paces from Lyssanne and that infernal Light, one of her precious charges stood swathed in the Mist.

The boy Jarad leapt at Noire's tree and caught hold of the lowest branch. He planted his feet against the trunk, gripping the thin limb so tight the wood creaked. The boy reached for the next branch then froze. He lifted the palm of his hand, then the fingers.

Shards of ice lanced Noire's spine, the chill that always preceded a burst of Venefica's power. Words whispered through the roiling Mist, sibilant susurrations of fear and failure, of falling and fatal injury. Shadowy tendrils slithered over Jarad, up the tree, reaching for the smaller boy he'd been commissioned to rescue, and climbing toward Noire.

With an undignified squawk, Noire sprang into the air, raining leaves over Jarad and causing him to all but lose his hold. Landing in an adjacent tree, Noire glanced at the cottage roof. The Mist was still too close, but he dared not venture nearer Lyssanne's home, after almost having his eyes pecked out the last time.

Sure enough, the dove, which had claimed Rowan Hill Cottage as her exclusive territory since the onset of Lyssanne's curse, peered up at him from the windowsill. Smaller she might be, but fast as a mountain storm and just as fierce. Well, this branch would afford him a better vantage anyway.

Lyssanne stepped nearer to Jarad's tree, blinking and swiping at her eyes as if—Could she see the Mist? Impossible. No mere human could perceive its presence, let alone one with such poor sight. Still, what he'd observed earlier seemed to confirm it, and she *was* a sorceress.

"Jarad," Lyssanne said in the hushed tone one might use with small, frightened animals, "focus on the bark in front of you. Look at the colors in the wood, the direction of the grain. Can you describe it to me?"

"Well," he said, "there's a big knot right in the middle of the trunk."

"Good." She hugged her upper arms as if chilled. "Keep your eyes on that knot and pull yourself upward until you can see only the next change in the wood. Forget all else. Nothing matters now but the tree."

As Jarad stared at the bark, his lips compressing in a thin line, the whispers in the Mist grew fainter. He hoisted his lanky body upward with agonizing slowness. Lyssanne's praises rose with each successive branch he gripped.

Threads of Light streamed from Lyssanne and pierced the Mist, reaching for Jarad as he neared Gavan. The Mist recoiled, then surged into the breach with renewed vigor. Jarad faltered as he reached for the branch on which Gavan sprawled. He closed his eyes for an instant, then grasped the younger boy's leg.

"C'mon, Gavan," Jarad said. "Scoot backward toward me."

Gavan shook his head and gripped the limb tighter.

Jarad tugged at his foot. "I'll help you."

Was that a flicker of light from *within* Jarad? The flicker sputtered then died.

"You're s-scared too," Gavan said.

Jarad bit his lip. "Yeah, well, not if we do it together."

"Wh-what if we fall?" Gavan asked. "You did. B-broke your arm and—"

"That's because I didn't have *me* to help," Jarad said. "I'll hold you steady. You heard Lady Lyssanne. I'm the best climber in the valley."

As Gavan inched toward him, the flicker within Jarad flared again and held. He kept a firm hand on the smaller boy and led him in a painstaking descent, while Lyssanne and the children offered encouragement.

Waves of Light, tinged with green and silver, flowed from her to Jarad, and from within Jarad back to her, reflecting and intensifying the brightness. Noire struggled to focus on the Shadow Mist through the glare. The dark fog lurched away from the boys as if in pain, broke apart, and whisked away, despite the absence of the slightest breeze.

Jarad delivered Gavan to the embraces and cheers of his friends, then backed away and offered Lyssanne a sheepish grin.

Smiling, she rested a hand on his shoulder, no longer swiping at her eyes. Then, she swayed.

"Lady Lyssanne?" Jarad said, struggling to steady her.

She pressed a hand to her brow, her other arm winding around the boy's middle. "I must sit. I'm...Find Niklette. She needs to...return for you."

Jarad helped her to the ground then glanced around at the younger children. "Don't just stare like that. Somebody get her some water or something. I'm gonna get Niklette."

~

Lyssanne set Aderyn's basket on the table and lifted the cloth, releasing a savory aroma that set her stomach to rumbling. "Spiced meat pies?" she asked.

"That, and a treat as well," Aderyn said, stomping her boots on the mat in front of the cottage door. "I bargained Mr. Whiskin out of his last unicorn horn pastry for you."

Lyssanne replaced the cloth and turned to her, smiling. "You do know me well, my friend. I've not had one of those since..." Her smile wilted at the recollection of the day her illness had begun.

"Lyss," Aderyn's said, "the air in here is as frigid as outside." She made a shivery sound as she hung her heavy winter cloak on a peg. "And no wonder. Your fire is almost out."

Lyssanne strode over to the fireplace to toss more peat moss onto the coals. "I suppose it dwindled during my unexpected nap. Those overtake me rather too often, of late."

"Well..." Aderyn's voice took on a cheery tone that sounded forced. "This weather is apt to send us all into hibernation."

"I suppose." Lyssanne plucked the quilted sackcloth mitt her mother had made from its peg beneath the mantelpiece, slipped it over one hand, and grasped the lever hidden along the inner wall of the fireplace. Gritting her teeth, she pulled it toward her with all her strength, and the firewood basket swung outward. She lifted a small log from the meager stack in the corner and dropped it into the iron basket. With her protected hand, she pushed the lever toward the back wall then pulled down, opening the basket to drop the log into the trench-like rack over the coals.

As Lyssanne reached for another log with trembling hands, Serena fluttered over and perched atop the mantelpiece. Aderyn let out a squeal so sudden, Lyssanne dropped the log.

"You let that bird inside?" Aderyn said. "Feeding her on your sill is one thing, but is this not unhealthful?"

Lyssanne braced a hand against the mantelpiece and smiled up at the dove. "Serena never leaves a mess indoors. She pecks at the window frame when she needs to go out." She turned back to the fallen log. "I think she must have been trained, but no one has claimed ownership."

"Let me finish here," Aderyn said, joining her at the hearth. "You've gone pale. Go, enjoy your dinner."

"If you're certain..."

Hefting the log, Aderyn chuckled. "Do you know how long I've wished to test this marvelous device your father invented? You'll be granting me a boon."

Lyssanne handed Aderyn her mitt and wiped moisture from her brow before returning to her dining table. She wrapped a meat pie in a cloth and carried it to her settee.

When the dove flew to the end table beside Lyssanne, Aderyn asked. "Why call her Serena?"

Lyssanne swallowed the bite she'd just taken. "It was the name of a relative Mother once mentioned, I think. A grandmother or aunt or..." She shrugged. "It just seemed to suit her."

"This is ingenious!" Aderyn said, a thump punctuating her words. "The basket's arm positions the wood into just the right spot. And that curved rack! How many times have I fought logs back into our fireplace when they shifted and fell? Your father must have been brilliant."

Lyssanne paused with a morsel halfway to her lips. "Mother called him an artist with metalwork. He invented this while they awaited my birth, so she wouldn't have so far to bend." She grinned. "I daresay he'd be stunned to learn how it has aided me."

"Such a thoughtful husband," Aderyn said, straightening, "as Kevan is sure to be." She dropped the mitt and rushed across the room, words flying from her almost too fast to comprehend. "He and I are to marry! Father has given his consent. Kevan had such success with the merchant this summer. The man simply adored his wood carvings!"

Lyssanne arose and embraced her. "That's wonderful! When?"

"Next month. We want you to stand with us, as my Pillar of the Marriage."

"Oh, Aderyn!" Lyssanne pulled away. "I would be honored, of course. Only...I've not had strength to walk into town for months. I don't know if I can even hold the ceremonial pole aloft long enough for the hand-fasting ritual to—"

"We've worked it all out." Not to be denied, Aderyn rushed on. "Kevan's eldest brother has agreed to let us use his gentlest plow horse. He's to stand with Kevan, you know. He'll carry you...the horse, I mean...to the village. You can rest at my house—*Father's* house." She giggled. "I shan't call Father's place mine for long. Kevan used all his earnings to commission a fine little cottage for us." She grasped Lyssanne's hands. "Sure and it'll be just like when we were girls! You'll stay with me the night before and....Oh, Lyss, you simply *must* be there!"

"Very well," Lyssanne said, laughing. "If Kevan's brother has to tie me to that horse and pull me the entire way, I shall be there."

Aderyn bounced like bubbles on the surface of boiling flyl. "Can a heart burst from joy?"

A bolt of pain struck just behind Lyssanne's ear. She forced a smile for Aderyn's sake, pressing her fingers to the side of her head.

"Are you unwell?" Aderyn asked. "Do you need to lie down?"

"No. It always does this." Lyssanne closed her eyes as more lightning bolts streaked through her temple.

"Let me see." Aderyn leaned close. "You know, I think your head is swollen right there." She moved Lyssanne's hair aside. "It even feels a bit spongy. What makes it do that?"

"Mistress Evlia has no explanation." Lyssanne sank back onto her settee. "She says these ridges—the ones that often rise when the fast pains strike—carry blood across the surface of my skull. She says they shouldn't be so hard or so enlarged, though."

What would happen if one of those fragile blood-carriers grew too large? Might it break? If it did, would she die? Lyssanne refrained from voicing such thoughts.

"A cool cloth might help." Aderyn scurried off to Lyssanne's kitchen alcove.

That would do little good, but Lyssanne held her silence. During her mother's final months, she'd had far too much experience with the helplessness of watching a loved one endure pain. "You could distract me," she said over the sloshing from the kitchen. "Have a meat pie and tell me of your plans for the wedding."

"I've eaten," Aderyn said. She returned with the cloth but hesitated before handing it to Lyssanne. "I must confess, there is another reason for my visit."

Lyssanne closed her eyes and pressed the damp rag to her temple. "More happy news?"

"I fear not." Aderyn sat at the other end of the settee. "I was helping Mother serve the Council refreshment yestereve and heard a bit of their meeting. Not a-purpose, you understand, but...well, they were discussing you."

Lyssanne lowered the cloth. "Me?"

Aderyn leaned closer. "They raised concerns about, well, you no longer taking charge of the children. They didn't sound pleased, Lyss."

Lyssanne's stomach lurched. "I've tried. Surely they realize this? Your father, at least—"

"All I know is, it sounded most serious, and not at all good."

"What would they have me do?" Lyssanne fought to keep her voice level. "When I attempted teaching on my own, I grew so weak, Niklette had to return. Despite her aid and Jarad's, I could hardly stand, let alone walk to my cottage. I caught a fierce chill that night and was confined to bed for an entire week."

"That was before harvest. I thought your pain had lessened since then."

Lyssanne shook her head. "Only at times. Just last Kingsday, I was near certain another head was trying to grow through the back of my skull. So strong was the pain-induced fog shrouding my mind, the cottage could have caught fire, and i wouldn't have noticed until the flames licked at my toes. I couldn't rise for days."

"Oh, Lyss, I had no idea 'twas still so awful."

Lyssanne sighed. "Some days, I feel as if I've become pain. It has swallowed me whole and is my only sign that I still live. Too often, I can only lie in bed, entombed in torture, wishing for oblivion." She shrugged. "Yet, as you said, it is no longer constant. For that, I am thankful."

"Perhaps…if Niklette stayed on and assisted you? She could take over when—"

"The Council would never agree to spare two people for a task one alone could perform." Lyssanne cleared her throat. "Besides, we tried that, each taking charge of a small group of children. I can share tales well enough, but to engage the children in a new or difficult task? 'Tis too taxing." She lifted her pie but merely stared at it. "Then, there is the preparation for lessons. Reading even short passages exhausts me. That is, when I can read at all. And that's not to mention the torture so many excited voices bring."

Aderyn cleared her throat. "'Tis just, some people worry that you've, I don't know…" She fidgeted with a lock of hair. "Given up."

Lyssanne's breath hitched, and she had to force words out. "Is that what you think?"

"Well," Aderyn said, "it's not like you." She twisted her hair around her fingers. "You never quit anything once you've started. I just worry for you. One of the councilmen mentioned the…invalids' home."

Lyssanne gasped. "Live with the elderly who lack family? They think me so useless I'd require that?" She went cold. "Lose the cottage? No, worse. I…I've not stored up enough credit in service to warrant a private room. I'd have no more than a straw pallet in the common area."

"Nothing's decided," Aderyn said. "I shouldn't have mentioned it. 'Twas only one man's random notion. The others gave it little thought." She squirmed as if she sat upon a stone instead of cushioned cloth. "We just need a way to get you back to teaching."

Lyssanne stared at the pastry in her hand as if it were an odd creature in one of Mr. DeLivre's books. "Tell me, what does one do when their greatest joys become the source of greatest pain?"

Aderyn's silence suffocated the air in the cottage.

Lyssanne turned toward the mantelpiece above her fireplace, where her father's iron sculptures cast eerie shadows akin to those in her persistent dreams. Was it this the nightmares had foretold? All this talk of her attempts at teaching brought to mind a shadow more disturbing even than those that stalked her slumber. A sight she'd spoken of to no one, not even Serena.

"What's amiss?" Aderyn asked in a subdued tone. "That haunted look results from more than illness."

"'Tis nothing," Lyssanne murmured. "The memory of unpleasant dreams."

"You've never given credence to such fancies." Aderyn snagged her hand. "If you're concerned about what I said—"

"I've seen something," Lyssanne said before she could prevent herself. She drew a slow breath and told Aderyn of the dark mist that had surrounded Jarad when she'd attempted teaching. "It seemed to incite his anger, or perchance the reverse. It thickened as his ire grew."

Aderyn gasped. "Like sorcery? Here? Have you told anyone? The council, or elders?"

Lyssanne set her uneaten pastry crust before Serena. "No. It may be nothing."

"I don't know." Aderyn folded her legs beneath her and turned to face Lyssanne fully. "As I said, you're not one to jump at shadows. Who do you think caused it?"

"Aderyn, I'm not even sure it *is* sorcery. Magic hasn't tainted this valley in over a century."

Aderyn leaned forward. "Yes, but if this is like the Noble Oppressors...we must not keep silent. The council—"

"Will, I daresay, think it an excuse for my idleness, or worse, that I've gone mad."

"Nonsense," Aderyn said. "Father will need to root out the cause and—"

"No!" Lyssanne struggled to slow her racing heart as ice coursed through her. "They may accuse Jarad or one of the other children. No one else was there. Aderyn, we mustn't say anything." She fixed her gaze on her friend's face, struggling as best she could to stare into her eyes. "Promise me."

"Very well. You have my word." Aderyn slumped against the settee's cushioned back. "You doubtless have it aright. Could be just the illness causing your vision to blur."

Lyssanne's every muscle released its stranglehold. "Let us turn our thoughts to happier things," she said. "Your wedding and, perchance, a new, useful employment for me."

3

THE PHANTOM FOE

Summer, year 1122 After the Dawning

A maelstrom of sound, scent, and color assailed Lyssanne's senses as she crossed Market Square. Chatting townspeople wafted through the fragrances of spicy sauces, perfumed candles, and fresh-baked bread. Up the street, two men's voices boomed, debating the price of a saddle. Lyssanne tried to ignore the noise as she made her way toward the scribe's shop.

Despite her weariness after another failed attempt at a new trade, she needed a bit of cheer. Brooding alone in her cottage would gain her nothing but an energy-stealing melancholy she could ill afford.

As she forced one footfall to follow another, wagons creaked, horses neighed, and people whirled by in a kaleidoscope of color. The chaos of Marketday would have overwhelmed her, had she not visited this square a thousand times or known the exact location of each stall. Even now, her feet carried her without need of thought toward the doorway at the corner.

Just inside, she paused, letting her eyes adjust to the scant light from the shop's two small windows, which peeked like heavy-lashed eyes through the bookshelves lining the walls

"Mr. DeLivre?" she said, placing her basket on the nearby table. "Are you here?"

She scanned the rows of shelves that marched down the left side of the room. Squinting, she peered into the lantern light dotting the ceiling, toward the back wall. Nothing stirred behind the scribe's massive desk.

Something shuffled amid the shelves, followed by a muffled, "*Fii. Over here!*"

Lyssanne hurried toward the sound, the scribe's series of Lyryan exclamations hastening her pace. She rounded the next shelf and froze, gaping.

On the floor lay a haphazard mound of books—and poking up from it, a head, white hair sticking out in every direction.

She rushed to remove books from the trapped man. "Are you injured? What happened?"

"Oh, those dreadful old books!" Mr. DeLivre said, pushing aside several volumes. "I should take them out more often. One was stuck, you see—and when I pulled, the whole bunch came crashing down on my head."

She helped him to his feet, and they began re-shelving the offending volumes. "You're certain you are unharmed?" she asked, handing him a stack. "You only lapse into your native language when things are dire."

He chuckled. "Dire? No, a knock on the head is good for us once in a while." He stared at a slim book. "Keeps us on our toes. Besides, I think I just found the one story I've never shared with you."

Laughing, Lyssanne bent to gather up more books. Pain pressed against her brow as if her head were a jug tipped onto its side, all its contents sloshing into its weakest spot. Fighting a wave of dizziness, she braced a hand against the bookshelf.

"Oh, *Shirii*, you are unwell," said Mr. DeLivre. "Leave those. Come, you must rest." He grasped her arm in wrinkled but strong fingers and pulled her toward the table.

Lyssanne's chest tightened. "You are too kind to me. How can you still address me as beloved daughter when I've become so useless?"

"Useless? Bah! Is that why you're here so early? Your work with Madam Sewell was unsuccessful?"

Slumping into a chair, she struggled to steady her breathing. "My future…as a weaver…is about as promising as my prospects as a candle-maker." She closed her eyes. "I tried to finish some of her work while she readied the shop for market. How all those threads got tangled in the spinning wheel, I cannot fathom."

Mr. DeLivre uttered a little squeak as if stifling a laugh. "Perhaps you'd fare better at the loom?"

She started to shake her head, but thought better of it. "I attempted that yesterday, worked for hours to produce a tiny square of cloth. It looked fair enough in my sight, but some threads were too tight, others too loose. With practice, I'm certain my hands would learn to detect what my eyes cannot, but Madam Sewell hasn't the time to waste on such."

"Humph. Just means a better apprenticeship awaits you."

"Where?" Lyssanne asked. "I've attempted every trade and craft anyone will permit me to try. My supplies are all but depleted, and I'm running out of things to trade for food."

"You will adapt, as always. If an old ink-wielder like me could adjust to life here, you'll find a way." He stared beyond her as if gazing into the past. "Imagine my surprise when I first arrived, a bag of coins in my fist and nowhere to spend them! Still baffles me, this trading goods for labors and labors for goods. Would've left straightaway, had those poor people not been so desperate in need of someone to read royal proclamations and keep the traveling merchants and tax officials honest."

"I am glad you stayed," she said. "If not for you, who would have taught me to read?"

"Your mother."

"Only in Starransi. She didn't know Lyryan or the bits of other languages you taught me."

"Well, speaking of mothers, Madam Blythe could certainly use a hand with that new infant. Her seventh, isn't he? Have you thought of assisting her?"

Lyssanne nodded. "I watched him for her a fortnight ago. His cries so wearied me; my arms grew weak and shaky. I feared I might drop him, so I lay with him on the floor. Then, exhaustion dragged me into slumber while he was awake." She ducked her head. "I even sat up trying to prevent it, but couldn't."

Mr. DeLivre gasped.

Lyssanne looked up, her eyes stinging. "What if something had befallen him on my watch? I couldn't have born it!" She turned away. "I dared not tell his mother."

"Certainly not. Madam Blythe is a nervous woman in the best of circumstances."

"What am I to do?" Her voice quavered. "How can I be useful to the village in such a state? The Council is already vexed with me. If I don't find suitable work soon..."

"They are good men, the Council," he said, "but I shall never understand this obsession with usefulness. Who is to judge what is useful?"

She glanced about the shop and lowered her voice, though no one had entered since her arrival. "I have wondered, at times, whether the King of All Lands truly approves of such a law. It seems contrary to all I know of His nature." She sighed. "But the Council is far wiser than I."

"Debatable," he said. "Has Evlia any notion what is causing your weakness?"

"No." Lyssanne's voice thickened. "She's plied her healing arts to no avail. My home is in constant disarray. My flowers are choking with weeds, I can make only the most basic meals, and to do laundry depletes all my energy for two days. I can't even brew flyl anymore. I haven't the strength to grind the honcin."

"Now, that *is* a shame," he said. "Your flyl is the best I've ever tasted."

"'Tis as if something inside me has broken, and I know not how to piece it together." Her throat constricted. "My mind and spirit cry out to stretch their wings and soar. I ache to run with the children, to fulfill the tasks, the adventures, my mind continues to conceive, but..."

"Oh, *Shirii.*" Mr. DeLivre rested a hand atop hers. "If the wings of your soul and mind yet stir, there is hope."

"Oh, they flutter, but *I* am bound. Trapped in this…cage my body has become, a prison from which I cannot, even for a moment, escape." She swallowed, struggling to hold back tears. "'Tis no prison of solid walls, but a cage of iron, beyond which I can still see, hear, and smell…*life.*"

Mr. DeLivre slid his chair in front of hers and took her face in both hands, as he had when she'd been a child.

"That's…the greatest torture of all," she whispered, the tears breaking the last of her resistance and flowing over his gnarled fingers. "At times, a wisp of life brushes my hand as I reach for it through the bars of fatigue that hold me captive. Yet, it eludes my grasp."

Lyssanne rested her head against his shoulder, his arms wrapping her in grandfatherly comfort. "I just can't bear to lose the cottage, but the councilmen don't know, can't see this enemy I battle every day."

Was it not enough that she must suffer this pain in her head; must she also endure pain of the heart? What was she to do?

Dragging in a breath, she pulled away. This wasn't helping. One could not open a cage by huddling in its corners. "Forgive me. What was that story you wished to share?"

At the western edge of the village, Noire alighted on a woodshed roof. The current target of his espionage stood ten paces away, hacking at a log, strands of Shadow Mist snaking around his feet. The man, Willem, one of the first to fall beneath Venefica's power, had become central to her latest strategy to destroy the Light-Wielder.

Noire dug his talons into the roof. If her scheme to infect the children hadn't succeeded, why should this one? Now, he was to act as a conduit of her power, but how would gaining control over this man give her the leverage to ensure the chief councilman fell to the Mist? Venefica's cryptic vow to use the villagers' own laws against them made no sense. Well, let her keep her secrets. Noire certainly had his.

He stiffened as Venefica's taunts whispered through the Mist—no, through *him*—into Willem's mind. How could this be? Did observing through Noire's raven eyes give her a deeper connection to him than he'd suspected? He must guard his thoughts, just in case.

"Ignored once again, while all Cloistervale celebrates Kevan's success?" Venefica's voice whispered, as if springing from Willem's own thoughts. "He sits whittling at slivers in his spare time, while you bend your back, sweating beneath the sun to build the homes they live in, the furniture they rest upon, and the carts and tools that make their work possible."

Willem's knuckles whitened around his axe handle.

"Oh, your grand Council claims all in Cloistervale are equal, but you know it isn't so." The Mist around Willem's legs began to thicken and rise. "You are heir to a noble trade, the only man in the valley with the skill and right to carry on the building that keeps this village alive. And this *Kevan*, what is he? Youngest son of a common farmer! A man with so little inheritance, he turned to carving frivolous wares for profit."

Droplets of sweat poured from Willem's brow to mingle with the rising darkness.

"And yet, this trinket-carver has taken the one thing you most desired."

A chip of bark flew toward Noire's head. He ducked just in time.

Willem's chopping grew erratic. He swung his axe harder and harder, gouging the log in random places, oft missing the notch he'd labored to carve. Still, Venefica taunted, her voice growing stronger with every passing moment.

"You repair the sagging beams of the very hall in which the Council meets, and does Chief Councilman Torin grant you his only daughter's hand? No. A merchant shows a little interest in Kevan's useless trinkets, and Torin weds the most beautiful girl in the valley to him! Oh yes, Kevan has stolen what should have been yours by right."

Willem's blade stuck fast in the wood. He braced a foot against the log, struggling to free it.

"The land is parched from drought," Venefica whispered, "yet Kevan's meager fields flourish. What will happen when harvest is done? Will the village hold a feast in his honor?"

Willem swung his axe free in a high arc over his head then buried the blade, to the haft, in the log. He stood motionless, fists clenched, eyes squinted shut.

Noire's vision wavered. Instead of gazing upon the angry young man in front of him, he found himself staring into the face of the sorceress. She leaned forward, her image shimmering as if he viewed her from the bottom of a clear pool—or the water mirror she used when observing through his eyes. After a dizzying moment, the world righted itself.

Venefica smiled, looked into his eyes, and whispered, "It is time."

She raised a fist to her lips then eased it open, blowing across her palm. Her image rippled, and a smoky darkness crept over everything in his sight.

Noire blinked. Again appeared Willem and his unfortunate log. Shadow Mist gathered about him from all directions, coating him in a sooty blackness he could neither see nor feel. Willem opened his eyes. They blazed with the heat of a forge fire.

Willem stalked into the shed. Moments later, he emerged carrying a burlap pack, skirted a stack of planed boards, then began rummaging in a box of scrap wood. Into the pack, he tossed bits of dry wood and straw. After tying its straps, he stormed into his large house, sparing not a glance for the work he'd left unfinished.

Within moments, a second door slammed. Noire flew to the front of the house just as Willem stalked off up the road.

Venefica's command vibrated through Noire, more sensation than sound. *Follow him.*

He needed no encouragement, however. Already, he was soaring over Willem's head.

The man halted at the edge of a field. Stalks of grain grew tall and golden, and a quaint little cottage guarded the far end of the plot.

Dropping his pack, Willem crouched beneath a tree at the end of a row.

Noire perched atop a scarecrow, as Willem pulled brush from beneath the nearest stalks and crushed it in his hand. The dry vegetation crumbled away like dust. Willem nodded then began emptying his pack—two long sticks, a flinty stone, and bits of wood and straw—all the while surrounded by a thick cloud of Mist.

Venefica's laughter rang through Noire's mind.

"What shall we read next?" asked Mr. DeLivre, placing his book back on a shelf.

Lyssanne glanced to the far wall where he kept scientific volumes. "Have you anything on the workings of the eyes or the kinds of things that can go amiss with them?"

"Mm, not that I recall." He strode past her. "Why do you want such a book?"

"I think my sight has grown worse."

"Oh, *Shirii*, no!" He rushed back to his seat. "You can still read, yes?"

She nodded. "But…there's this…blur."

"Ah, just your eyes growing weary."

"I don't think so," she said. "Sometimes it happens when I've hardly used them. This is unlike in childhood, when I tried to read text that was too small. That's why I fear I'm losing what sight I have. That, and…'tis dark."

"Dark?"

"Like a black haze. Foggy. I can see a person through it, but only just. 'Tis as if night has taken on solid form and wrapped itself around someone."

"Someone? Is it only people who are blurred?"

"I…Yes! I hadn't realized until just now."

"Let us list the times this has happened, determine what is

common among them." Mr. DeLivre fetched parchment and a quill from his desk, then settled across from her.

"Well, the first time was..." Lyssanne closed her eyes and took a slow breath. She could trust him with this. He would never say or do anything that might endanger Jarad or the other children. She told him of the incident at her cottage, leaving out Jarad's frightful rage.

"When was this?"

"Last autumn."

"Ah, so it began after you'd been ill for some time."

Lyssanne's eyes flew wide. "Do you think the two maladies are connected?"

"Impossible to know. Go on. Perhaps we shall discover the answer."

"Hmm." She spoke as if half in dream. "Early this spring, Mr. Riles and the Furins' sons—oh, and Mr. Cutler last week."

"So, this comes and goes. Several months between incidents, but now more frequent?"

"Yes. Strange, it didn't plague me all those months I was most ill. Of course, I rarely left the cottage except..." She gasped. "At Aderyn's wedding. Aderyn said Willem looked furious, and...he was covered in the dark haze."

"That was at the close of winter, yes? Perhaps—"

Bells rang out in three sudden peals, cutting off his words. Their clangs vibrated through Lyssanne's head as if she'd become the bell tower atop the meeting hall.

"They're summoning the fire brigade!" Mr. DeLivre shouted.

Clamping her hands over her ears, Lyssanne followed him to the door.

After long moments and several attempts to gain information from passing townsfolk, Mr. DeLivre at last snagged Madam Sewell's attention.

She met them on the steps. "Half the men are helping put out the fire," she shouted, her high voice almost as painful to Lyssanne's ears as had been the bells. "Tell ya the rest inside." She pushed past them, her ample girth pressing Lyssanne to the doorframe. "Oh, the Chief Councilman's poor daughter!"

"Aderyn?" Lyssanne asked, as Mr. DeLivre closed the door, muffling the clamor outside.

Madam Sewell shook her faded, red hair from her eyes. "House and field blazed up like a feast day fire."

Lyssanne's heart forgot to beat. "Is she—?"

"Safe," Madam Sewell said. "She wasn't home. Was with Evlia when it happened, receiving joyous news. But now, with that new husband of hers gone..."

"Kevan, gone?" Lyssanne's throat seized.

"Neighbor saw him fall tryin' to put out the blaze. Went to help but, well, good thing Evlia was with Aderyn when they came to tell her. Poor man never knew he was to be a father."

"Oh, Aderyn!" Lyssanne rushed back to the table to grab her basket. "I must go to her."

"The real mystery is," Madam Sewell said, "what caused that fire." She lowered her voice. "Some say—and I'm not tellin' who—but they say Willem was lurkin' where he ought not be."

Willem.

"What is it, *Shirii?*" Mr. DeLivre asked. "You've gone pale."

"I—I'm just worried for Aderyn." She snatched up his list. "May I keep this?"

"Of course."

Lyssanne hurried from the shop. As she made her way toward the healer's door, faces obscured in shadow raced through her mind. Chief among them, the man who had once sought Aderyn's hand.

Noire perched in the rafters of the meeting hall just as the last villager entered. Once again, Venefica claimed the events about to unfold would rid them both of the obstacle to their goals. Well, he would swallow *that* meal when it landed in his beak.

The obstacle in question stood near the back of the crowded hall, one arm looped about the waist of the woman whose husband they'd buried earlier that day. Lyssanne flinched each time the chief councilman banged his cobbler's mallet like a gavel for order.

Noire dug his talons into the rafter. Venefica's plan had failed. The chief was yet free of the Mist.

"Citizens of Cloistervale," Chief Councilman Torin said, his voice resonating through the hall, "we call this meeting to address an urgent concern. Crops are failing, the mountain wolves have grown bolder, and"—he cleared his throat—"crimes are increasing, all at levels we haven't seen since the Days of Noble Oppression." His gaze swept the hushed crowd. "I submit to you, this is no natural occurrence."

"Some say as how smoke's been risin' above the trees o' the North Forest," said a withered old man. "Some say from Mount Mortiferra. That ain't no natural occurrence neither."

Noire folded his wings tighter to ward off the chill of Venefica's displeasure.

As the townspeople's murmuring increased, Lyssanne glanced from her friend to the crowd and back again. She pulled away and inched toward the dais. Color drained from her cheeks, then they flamed a vivid rose. Her wide eyes darted about as if she were a deer preparing to bolt. Instead, she lifted a hand.

"Lyssanne?" said the chief councilman. "You have something to share on this matter?"

"Y-yes." She cleared her throat. "Yes, Councilman Torin. I've seen something that may be causing all this. Or, at least, I think it is somehow connected to the trouble."

The villagers jostled Lyssanne until she stood before the Council's table.

"What have you seen?" asked Torin.

"'Tis difficult to describe...like a black blur, a fog. It hovers around people, just before some misfortune befalls them or they cause such for others."

The Mist. The chill air surrounding Noire grew teeth of ice.

The chatter rose again, this time with a distinct air of irritation borne on wisps of shadow.

45

Councilman Torin raised a hand for silence. "This...fog? What do you mean it hovers around people?"

"It surrounds someone like a dark, filmy curtain, making it difficult for me to focus on that person. If I look away, the blur dissipates."

"'Tis just your poor vision, dear," said the healer. "Doubtless acting up because of your illness."

"I thought so, at first." Lyssanne's eyes scanned the crowd as if searching for the healer, who stood mere paces away. "Then, I realized trouble always follows in the wake of the fog."

"We're wasting time," said the councilman at the chief's right hand, eddies of Shadow Mist swirling about his feet. "Let's get on with the reason we called this meeting."

"In a moment, Ratomer," said the chief, waving away further protests. "Trouble? You'll have to be clearer, Lyssanne. Give us an example."

"Well, I don't like to air other people's misfortunes—"

"This is pointless!" Ratomer rapped a fist on the table, Mist crawling up his legs.

Lyssanne fidgeted, glanced back toward her friend, then sighed. "Just before Mr. Irvin's daughter fell ill and his well was found fouled, Mr. Riles came into Madam Sewell's shop to pick up something for his wife. He was covered in the fog. Every time I've seen him or Mr. Irvin since, they're shrouded in it."

Still Mist-cloaked, the men in question glared at each other across the hall.

"That was during their dispute over property borders," said the chief councilman. "Did you know they were feuding at the time?"

"No, I hadn't seen either of them in months."

"Surely, this fog has nothing to do with that," said an elder councilmen. "Madam Sewell doubtless told you of their dispute, so they caught your attention."

"She didn't, I'm sure of it," said Lyssanne. "Besides, that wasn't the only time I've seen the black mist precede trouble. Just yesterday, Madam Nettleworth—"

"There was nothing there, I tell you!" A wiry matron shouted, pushing to the front of the hall. "This girl comes up to me in the middle of the market, after all that fuss with the fire, and starts brushing at my skirts. Says I must get away from the fog before some ill befalls me. I told her then, and I say it again"—she jabbed a finger at Lyssanne, wisps of shadow dancing about her feet—"there... was...no...fog."

Lyssanne stared into the woman's face. "But later, at the butcher's stall—"

"Coincidence!" the woman snapped. "That pig was worth more than all those chickens combined, and Cutler knows it. Serves him right if the pig went amuck. Calls himself a butcher, humph. No magical mist made him cheat me."

"Has no one else seen this, er, fog?" asked Councilman Torin.

Negative murmurs swept through the room.

"Like Evlia said, her eyes are deceiving her," said a junior councilman.

"In any case," said the chief, "our village cannot continue in such a state, especially with the time of the queen's tax soon upon us." The room fell silent. "We, the Appointed Council of Cloistervale, have been meeting of late to determine the cause." He paused as if to ensure he had their full attention. "Our conclusion? Someone has violated one of our sacred laws."

Gasps rolled through the chamber like whitecaps on a roiling sea.

"We're suffering because we allow this person to go unpunished?" asked the miller.

"That is our suspicion, yes."

A groan filled the room.

"Our task tonight is to identify the offender and decide how to proceed," said Torin. "This requires a consensus of the entire community. To avoid swaying opinion, I'll not voice the Council's conjectures until you've discussed this among yourselves."

Neighbors began whispering against neighbors, every eye regarding with suspicion those standing near. As insult and anger rose, the sparse tendrils of Shadow Mist throughout the hall coalesced and thickened. Noire flexed his talons and prepared to spring, searching out every available exit. Venefica had sworn the Mist wouldn't be permitted to touch him, but could she wield such precise control while her power was still diminished?

"Which law has been broken?" asked the baker, his head towering above all others. "Determine that, and the offender shouldn't be difficult to find."

A junior councilman began reciting the five sacred laws of Cloistervale—superstitious drivel forbidding blasphemy against their invisible King of All Lands, along with statutes prohibiting theft, violence against people or property, self-importance, and finally, sloth.

"Each citizen of Cloistervale shall perform such useful tasks as enhance the lives of all," quoted the councilman. "Thus, none shall burden his neighbors. Sloth is akin to pride, and pride is an abomination against the King of All Lands."

"That's it!" shouted a farmer near the back. "The law that's been broken."

"This was the predominant suggestion among the Council," said Chief Torin. "Others, theft and such, also arose, but appear symptoms rather than the root of our problems."

"Those crimes only began after Lyssanne abandoned her duties," said Ratomer.

Stares and whispers focused on Lyssanne, and a space widened around her.

"Abandoned?" Lyssanne said, her voice raspy. "What are you saying?"

"You've broken the Fifth Law," Ratomer said. "You are guilty of sloth."

～

Lyssanne stared at the councilman. "Sloth?" Surely she'd misheard.

"You haven't performed your duties in fifteen moons," said Councilman Torin.

"I've been ill!" Heat flooded her face, as she turned to Aderyn's father. "You know me," she said, forcing a calm tone. It wouldn't do to let anger rule her tongue while addressing the Council. "You all know me. Never have I shirked duties or tasks, even when they were difficult." She paused for breath. "If I had, I could never have accomplished anything."

"Everyone gets headaches," said Madam Nettleworth, her face growing less distinct. "If I stopped bailing hay every time I have a wee pain in the head, my animals would starve."

"But I've tried—"

"Your illness has ended, has it not, Lyssanne?" asked Councilman Torin.

"The pain is no longer as constant or severe, but it hasn't ceased altogether."

"Doubtless a curse laid upon you by the King," said Madam Nettleworth. "He knows the hidden truths of the heart." She turned to the Council. "Girl's been lazy all along, playin' with children like some lady of leisure."

"Leisure?" Madam Sewell snorted. "Herding children's not as easy as slopping pigs."

"She just got used to not doin' anything, sick for so long," a woman said.

"I'm glad she isn't watchin' over my boys anymore," said Aderyn's brother, Adalbin. "Those stories she was always tellin' filled their heads with fancy ideas and foolish dreams. They talk nonsense about leavin' the village and havin' adventures!"

"Yeah, she poisoned their minds against our customs," said a stout man several feet away, "ones that have been good enough for Cloistervale since our ancestors rid us of the Oppressors. Why, my boy says he doesn't want to be a farmer!" He shook his fist at Lyssanne. "What's *want* got to do with it? I'm a farmer, he'll be a farmer."

"She's brought disaster down upon our heads!" Mr. Riles shouted. "And if we let it continue, we're just as guilty."

"She's already suffering punishment," said Madam Nettleworth. "Fer lolling away her time with frivolous reading and such."

"Not even Mistress Evlia knows what caused the illness," Lyssanne said.

Madam Nettleworth huffed. "You squander what the King's given you, it's bound to displease Him."

"He wouldn't do such a thing." Lyssanne hugged her arms and shivered.

"Now, you claim to know the mind of the King!" a woman shouted. "Blasphemy!"

"No, of course not, but the *Kingsword* says—"

"Enough!" Councilman Torin rapped his cobbler's mallet against the table.

No one was listening. Chatter and haze swirled around Lyssanne, building into a frenzy.

"The poor dear has attempted several trades," Madam Sewell said. "Last week, she nearly collapsed helping Mr. Whiskin at the bakery. She just hasn't found anything she's suited to."

"More like nothing suits her high-minded taste," said Madam Nettleworth, her voice dripping venom and her body engulfed in shadow.

"'Tis the fog again," Lyssanne said. "You would not say such things, else."

"Trying to deflect blame, girl?" said Madam Nettleworth.

"Can you not feel it?" Lyssanne glanced around. "Can none of you *see* it?"

"She's gone daft!" a man shouted.

"Making up phantoms to excuse her sloth, more like," Mr. Riles said.

"She isn't making anything up." Aderyn squeezed between two women and stepped to Lyssanne's side. "She's seen this fog thing for months."

"And this is the first we hear of it?" asked Councilman Ratomer. "Convenient."

"Explain," Aderyn's father said in a calmer tone.

"Well, there was..." Aderyn turned to Lyssanne as is seeking release from her promise.

"Willem," Lyssanne said. "At Aderyn's wedding. She'd declined his offer of marriage, you see, and..." Under the weight of Aderyn's stare, she had to fight back tears. "I'm so sorry," she whispered. "Had I spoken sooner, Kevan—"

"You dare accuse me?" Willem's voice boomed from the back of the hall. "Of what?"

"I accuse no one," Lyssanne said. "I merely answer the Council as to what I've seen."

"Yes, let us discuss that wedding," said Councilman Ratomer. "You stood as Pillar of the Marriage, did you not? Dropped the ceremonial pole during the vows."

"Ill omen, that," an old woman said. "Didn't I say as much then?"

"Ridiculous," said Aderyn, one hand pressed to her stomach. "She's brought us only joy and prosperity. Her encouragement got Kevan started in his new woodcarving trade."

"Oh, and how did that turn out?" asked his mother. "Your fields and house burned, and my Kevan, dead!"

The light in the hall dimmed, and Lyssanne rubbed her arms for warmth as blood beat against her temples. "You can't possibly think me responsible for that."

"She's cursed!" said a reedy voice. "Everything she touches goes foul. Just look what happened to her own poor father—and Brianne, dying so young."

"*Hoola gah ri!*" Mr. DeLivre shouted. "This is foolish talk. She wasn't even born when Lysander's forge exploded!"

Had the townsfolk known how colorfully Mr. DeLivre had just insulted them, they would have doubtless called him into judgment beside Lyssanne.

"Th-there's another sacred law she's broken," said Madam Blythe.

"Which law is this?" asked Councilman Torin.

"Self-importance."

"Preposterous!" said Mr. DeLivre.

"Truly, and worse, she has involved the children. They call her lady...Lady Lyssanne."

"No, it isn't like that." Lyssanne said, wiping moisture from her eyes. Everyone, *everything*, remained blurred through a sheen of tears and darkness. "It is just a game they play, a name of affection *they* gave me. I never..."

The noise of the crowd drowned out her words, the frenzy rising to a frightening pitch. Her shoulders bowed like metal that had been drawn from a fire then thrust into icy water. Such an act would shatter un-tempered steel, and she feared she was made of even less durable stuff.

"This is a serious charge," Councilman Torin said, his voice booming above the clamor. "Not only does elevation of self contravene our most basic ideals of equality, it is against the laws of Lastarra to present oneself above one's station. If the queen's man heard even a child address you as a noblewoman, you could be sentenced to prison, or even death. The royal court would not care that it was a game."

"Worse still," said Councilman Ratomer, "it would bring too much notice to us. For years, the royal house has allowed us to govern our valley as we see fit, but if such an incident were brought to Queen Stella's attention, she might reestablish an overlord in Cloistervale."

The entire hall gasped.

"And if she is seein' a fog 'round people right before trouble happens," Mr. Irvin said, "perhaps she's causing it."

"Sorcery!" someone shouted.

"What's to be done?" asked Mr. Murrough.

"The penalty for sorcery is death," Mr. Riles said.

Lyssanne's vision lurched, and Aderyn caught her elbow.

Aderyn's father held up a hand, and the crowd hushed. "We have no proof of sorcery. The only certainty is crimes against the Fifth Law. Like a fever, sloth can infect an entire village. So, the offender,"— he looked at Lyssanne—"must be removed. Permanently."

"R-removed?" Aderyn said.

"As in banishment."

"Leave?" Lyssanne's voice squeaked. "Wh-where would I go?"

"That is not our concern."

Aderyn's voice shook. "But, Father, she's ill. She—"

"You can't!" Jarad shouted from the rear of the room. "She...she won't survive!"

"Remove that boy from the hall!" Councilman Ratomer shouted. "No children allowed."

As the door slammed, drowning out Jarad's shouts, Lyssanne turned to Councilman Torin. "You always say families take care of their own."

"I am not your family, girl. Your father left no living kin, and your mother—"

"Was an *outsider*!" Ratomer shouted, spitting the word.

Lyssanne flinched as if spittle might reach her all the way from the dais. "But you are...Cloistervale *is* my family. You said so at Mother's graveside." Recalling the chief councilman's exact words suddenly seemed the most important task of her life. "You said, 'When one member of a body suffers, all suffer. If a foot is injured, the other members must take up the lack until it recovers.'"

He sat motionless as stone, voiceless for the first time in Lyssanne's memory.

"And if that foot is infected with gangrene," said Ratomer, "you... cut...it...off!"

"The Council shall hold a vote," Aderyn's father said, holding up a strip of bark. "White side, innocent, Lyssanne stays. Brown side..." He didn't need to finish.

Lyssanne's gaze swept the councilmen. Oh, if only she could see as others did. If she could have looked each in the eye, perhaps they would recognize the truth in hers. "Please..."

Fire roared in her ears, though ice coursed through her veins as, one by one, the councilmen placed their pieces of bark in a box before Aderyn's father.

The ground shifted beneath her. No one took notice. The world was shaken, and only she could see. Ironic, that.

The pounding of the gavel was a blow that all but knocked her to the floor.

4

SHATTERED LIGHT

"*E*xile!"

The word filled the hall—pressed into every corner, beneath every surface, around every beam—leaving no room for air. Lyssanne's stomach fell into her feet, and the Council swam before her eyes.

"Lyssanne E. Caelestis," Aderyn's father said, "by decree of this Council, you are hereby commanded to vacate your home and leave Cloistervale—never to return."

The ringing in Lyssanne's ears grew deafening, yet his every word boomed distinct.

"Sentence to be carried out in one week." The chief councilman gestured to encompass the room. "Citizens, Lyssanne of Rowan Hill is henceforth shunned from our midst. She has seven days to trade for provisions, but outside those transactions, she no longer exists among us."

The gavel pounded again, and someone announced the close of the meeting. Lyssanne could not move, could not think. She hardly breathed.

A loud sob wrenched her from her frozen state. Had the cry issued from her own throat? But no, Aderyn uttered another, quieter, sob as she struggled against Madam Torin's attempts to usher her away from the dais.

Lyssanne stumbled to the council table, which, resting on its platform, stood level with her nose. She stepped onto the thin strip of dais in front of Aderyn's father. Her voice quavered. "Please, you must help me."

His head jerked up. "Lyssanne..."

"You can't let them do this," she whispered. "You know these charges can't be true."

Why was he shaking his head? "It is done. The decision was not mine alone."

"But you could speak for me. On your word, they would surely reconsider."

"Even if I could..." He sighed. "As much as it pains me, I am not entirely convinced they're wrong."

What was he saying? "Sorcery? You can't possibly think..." She took a slow breath. "You're like an uncle to me. I've slept in your home, dined at your table."

"Not sorcery," he murmured. "Such is foolishness."

"Please," she said. "I—I know I'm not good at things...things other women find easy to do, but *sloth*?"

"For months I've watched, hoping you would get yourself together," he said. "You have not." His voice softened. "I partly blame myself for that. I favored you. We all sheltered you because we've pitied your...condition."

"I never wanted your pity." Nausea rose into her throat at the very thought. "All I ever desired was to live a useful life." Her voice trembled along with the rest of her body. "People assumed I wouldn't be able to do things," she said, "cooking and...things, because of..." She waved a hand in front of her eyes then smacked it onto the table. "My life has never been easy, but I always found a way. Maybe a different way from others', but one that worked. You know this. You've seen me struggle."

But had he? Had anyone ever truly realized the time and effort simple tasks required of her? Or had she been so skilled in adapting, her self-sufficiency masked its cost?

"No one disputes your past accomplishments." He snatched up the box of bark fragments and pushed back his chair. "That only makes your present inaction worse."

"Please!" She couldn't let him leave like this. "I'll do whatever you wish." She gestured to the rest of the table. "Whatever work *they* want. Anything. I'll…I'll find a way." She didn't know how she could do more than she already had, but she would try if it cost her last breath. "Just give me a chance."

"Lyssanne, it is too late for that. The word of the Council is final."

"But—"

"Save your strength for the days ahead. The King knows, you're going to need it." He stood. "Go home, get your affairs in order, and may the King grant you mercy." He turned away.

Mr. DeLivre strode toward her, but Councilman Ratomer barred his way.

"Gierre, you heard the verdict. That girl is to be shunned."

"But this is ridiculous!"

"You chose to live here," Ratomer said, "so you must obey our laws. *If* you wish to remain."

Mr. DeLivre peered around Ratomer's restraining arm. "Very well, but I shall record my objections in the chronicles. This is not the last you will hear from me." He stomped off, colliding with Madam Sewell in his haste.

Madam Sewell! Perhaps she could reason with the Council. But when Lyssanne drew nearer, the weaver shook her head, wiped her eyes, and turned away.

Hers was the friendliest response Lyssanne received. Her briefest glance prompted turned backs and icy silence. Even Mr. Whiskin and Madam Murrough withdrew at her approach.

"I'm sorry," Lyssanne said in a small voice. "I never wanted to be a burden."

Dizziness overtook her, and her knees buckled. She sank onto the edge of the dais. For what seemed hours, her surroundings faded into a jumble of noise and nothingness. 'Twas as if, as the Council had decreed, she'd ceased to be.

Noire dug his talons into a branch at the edge of the wood behind Rowan Hill Cottage. Sent once again to peer in windows like a common thief! At least the dove hadn't bothered him.

Like she had since the town meeting, the little pest remained indoors, her violet eyes fixed on Lyssanne as if the girl were an egg waiting to hatch. Could the dove sense Lyssanne's distress, or was she, like Noire, avoiding the Mist?

Venefica's favored weapon lay like a malevolent second skin over the little stone house, yet the Shadow Mist hadn't penetrated the once tidy interior. Noire's tree afforded him an excellent view through both rear windows of the cottage, each flung wide as if the Mist rendered the air within those shrouded walls as oppressive as it did its victims' spirits.

Why hadn't Lyssanne used her strange magic to dispel the Mist? Perhaps she didn't yet know how to control it. Or had she used it unawares? Her Light certainly hadn't saved her from the sentence Venefica had orchestrated. Still, if she survived, she was sure to learn of its existence in due course. Noire didn't want to be near if ever she did.

Light or Shadow, magic was magic.

Lyssanne passed her kitchen window, sorting items into piles, some to trade and others to take with her. As she worked, she held a one-sided conversation with the dove.

"Too heavy," she muttered, placing a large cooking pot on her overcrowded dining table. "I must bring at least one pan, assuming I can find anything to cook in the wild." Sighing, she glanced toward her kitchen counter. "If only I could hunt like you, Serena. Had I even a measure of your swiftness and keen vision, I might h-have a...chance." She closed her eyes and clamped her lips shut, then pulled out the only unburdened chair and sat, elbows on knees, chin in hands. "How shall I have the strength to carry all this?"

How, indeed, when even the walk to the village left her weak-kneed and winded? Perhaps Venefica's plan would succeed in ways Noire hadn't envisioned. As the boy Jarad had said, Lyssanne would doubtless be dead within the month.

Lyssanne at last abandoned her ransacked kitchen to rummage through her bedchamber's armoire. She pulled out several blankets and plopped them onto her bed, selecting only two for her journey.

"Where shall I sleep, Serena?" she asked, tracing the delicate pattern sewn into her pale blue coverlet. Tears splashed onto the hand-stitched cloth as she lifted a pillow and cradled it against her cheek. "Where will I go?" Her voice hitched, and she stared at the fluffy pillow. "I don't suppose I should…" She sighed, replaced it on the bed, and turned to her meager assortment of clothing.

Her fingers grazed the four gowns hanging above a single pair of shoes in her wardrobe, then she withdrew a folded bit of cloth from the upper shelf. She shook out the shawl, the one she'd worn to her friend's wedding and to every weekly ceremony honoring their fabled King.

Lyssanne's repeated folding and unfolding drew Noire's focus to the cloth. A mixture of snowy white and a blue as deep and brilliant as a king's cloak, the entire shawl was shot through with shimmering threads of gold. How had a peasant girl obtained so fine a garment? Only court weavers had access to thread-of-gold, and the villagers' attire proved no craftsman in Cloistervale possessed the skill to produce so intricate a weaving.

Lyssanne held the shawl to her chest and squeezed her eyes shut. She sank onto her bed, shoulders shaking. "Oh, Mother."

More tiresome tears? How much longer would it take the girl to sort her possessions? Noire widened his beak in a yawn so deep, his throat emitted an undignified croak. He glanced toward the other window, through the dining area to her sitting room. Not much left there.

A furtive movement caught his eye.

A thin trail of Mist seeped beneath the back door. Noire leaned forward then took to the air. He flew as near the cottage as he dared, determined to witness what progress the Mist made.

Lyssanne sat, oblivious, as the smoky tendril drew nearer her bedchamber door. So often, her Light had barred the intrusion of the Shadow Mist. This time, however, the semi-blind teacher with the ability to see darkness took no notice of her own peril.

Ironic, just as Venefica found a way to rid herself of the girl, Lyssanne might at last surrender to the Mist. The one thing the sorceress wanted all along.

Lyssanne shivered. "No—no!" She rose and thrust the shawl onto the pile of items she would take on her journey, as if thrusting dark thoughts from her mind. "All will be well," she said. "The King will turn this to…to something good." She spun to face the dove perched on her headboard. "Like Mother always said, it's in the *Kingsword*, so it must be true. It just must." As she wiped the tears from her red-rimmed eyes, the Mist shrank back beyond the cottage walls.

On the last of her trips to the square, Lyssanne risked a visit with Mr. DeLivre under the pretext of returning a book of Navvarish legends he'd given her in childhood.

"Nonsense," he said. "This was a gift. It will keep you company in your new home."

"And I cherish it," she said, "but I fear I shan't have strength enough to carry what provisions I shall need, let alone such a thick book."

"Ah, *Shirii*, I would've taken you in, if only I could," he said, "but you heard them. The Council would exile me too. *Fii*, that would please Ratomer." He slammed a book shut on his desk then sighed. "If I were a younger man…but I am too old to go through such again."

"Is that what happened to you? Why you left Lyrya?"

"That tale is too long and much too boring." He waved a hand and said in perfect Cloistervalean practicality, "Now, you require a cart. The builders can fashion you one."

"I passed their stall this morning," she said. "They...they wouldn't look at me—Willem or his father. When I spoke, they kept talking to Mr. Furin as if I weren't there."

"Did no one witness this?"

"Several. They turned away, pretended not to see. I think it embarrassed them."

"Humph!" said Mr. DeLivre. "Well, there is more than one way to bait a unicorn, as they say. Have you anything dear to you that you must leave behind?"

"I can bring little," she said, struggling to decipher his odd change in subject. "All I have left of my parents are Mother's shawl and Father's iron sculptures. The shawl, I can take, but—"

"Perfect. I shall commission a cart, as if for myself. In exchange, allow me to keep your father's ingenious mettle-works safe for you." He gestured to a seat. "When do you depart?"

She sank into the chair. "I'm allowed three more days, but still have much to do."

"So soon," he murmured. "You must also rest, *Shirii*. Take at least that last day to do so."

"Rest?" She raised a brow. "Sleep eludes me. My thoughts churn with ways to persuade the Council to reconsider." She laughed. "'Twould be easier to swim upstream in the River Esten after a storm."

"Do you have everything you need for the journey?"

"I've traded for salt-meat, bread, water-skins, other things. I've no idea if it will be enough." She clasped her hands to keep them from trembling. "What I'll do if it runs out..." She shook her head. "I've no wish to spend my last moments with you bemoaning my fears."

"I'm certain it will be enough," he said. "Have you decided on a destination?"

She sighed. "I know nothing of what lies beyond the boundaries of our valley."

He rummaged in his desk then began scribbling on parchment. "What of Brianne's family?" he asked. "Her father was a traveling merchant, yes? Perhaps you could go to him?"

"Mother said they never stayed anyplace longer than a winter.

That's why she loved our cottage so. She'd always longed for a stable home, and now, I…" Lyssanne cleared her throat. "Even if my grandfather still lives, I've no idea where to search for him."

"The King will lead you," he said, handing her the parchment. "I cannot recall distances, but this map includes every town I passed when I first came to Cloistervale. It will give you some direction, at least."

"Thank you," she whispered.

"Now, you truly must rest, *Shirii*. Leave the cart and that…*Willem* to me." He leaned against his desk. "When they said you were to be shunned, I never thought anyone would actually do it. Then again, Willem has changed."

"'Twas not only him," Lyssanne said, the shards of broken trust honing her words to a cutting edge. "Cloistervale abounds with dutiful citizens." She softened her voice. "Just for a moment, I thought I'd become one of them—useful, wanted."

An ache built behind her brow. *Perfect!* She pressed her fingertips to the area, kneading her skin. Now that she must leave, would pain cage her once again? She could have borne even this, had her prison not grown so cold. Exiled, *shunned*, she must fight this insidious foe alone.

"What did I do, Mr. DeLivre?" she whispered. "How did I make them hate me so?"

"Oh, *Shirii*, 'twas not your doing." He stood to pace the bookroom. "It is all a mistake. A foolish mistake. You and…sloth? I've told them it is madness, but…well, I'm an outsider, and not even Torin understands the importance of what you've done for the children."

"Maybe they're right," Lyssanne said. "'Tis true I've never labored on a farm, sewn until my fingers cramp, or risen before dawn to bake bread. Perhaps my work was too easy."

Their accusations throbbed inside her head even now, each word a sword that cut to the depths of her soul. She pressed a palm against her brow, longing to staunch the pain, but how was she to staunch the agony that flowed from a wounded soul?

"None of them really know you, *Shirii*," he said. "If they did, they

61

would see that giving up is a thing so opposed to your nature as to be impossible."

That revelation struck as sudden and sharp as the first pains of her illness. They never *had* known her. She was more alone than ever; betrayed, abandoned, worse than orphaned.

～

An hour later, Gavan and Elaiza ran up to Lyssanne as she passed the bakery on her way home. Neither Elaiza's mother nor the baker turned when the cousins shouted her name.

"Jarad said you're going away," Gavan blurted. "I told him he's daft. You wouldn't."

"I fear it is true, Gavan," Lyssanne said.

"Why, Lady Lyssanne?" Elaiza whimpered.

Lyssanne glanced about, wide-eyed. "Shh, you mustn't address me thus."

"Why're you going away?" Elaiza's voice shrilled. "Don't you love us anymore?"

"Oh, Elaiza." Lyssanne hugged the child to her. "Always. Wherever I go, whatever I do, I shall love you."

"Then, why are you leaving us?" Gavan demanded.

"I…" What could she say? Your parents don't want me in the village? She fought the hot tears clogging her throat. Then, inspiration struck. "I must begin a new adventure. I'm counting on you to keep our old ones alive, to help everyone remember all the stories and fun we've shared. Can you do that for me? Can you be brave enough? Strong enough?"

"Yes, yes!" the children said.

Lyssanne hugged them both then hurried around the corner, no longer able to stifle tears.

～

Two days later, Noire circled high overhead as Lyssanne emerged from the rowan grove and stepped onto a wide patch of charred earth at the bottom of her hill. She knelt before a mound of blackened rock, so misshapen it resembled stones that had melted and fused. She unclenched her short fingers from around the few scraggly blooms that had survived the chokehold of weeds in her flowerbed.

"Father," she whispered, laying a red blossom upon the ground. "My last tribute to you, in honor of your fiery craft. Even after twenty-some years, no grass grows where once your forge stood, as if the earth refuses to yield anything fruitful in this place that stole you from us."

She rose and brushed off her skirts, gazing down at her offering. "I wish I'd known you," she said. "Our hero, Mother called you. Strong but gentle, a man of great courage." She smiled. "I always imagined you astride a fiery steed like a warrior from tales of old."

Lyssanne strode several paces away and propped the remaining flowers against the marker identifying her mother's resting place. "A poor tribute to such a beautiful person," she murmured, running a hand over the rough stone, "but 'tis all I have, Mother."

The dove landed near her fingers, and Lyssanne jerked them back to clutch at her bodice.

"Serena!" she said. "Always near, are you not?" She sighed. "Oh, I shall miss you."

With a scrape of talons and flutter of wings, the dove took to the air and sailed toward the wood behind Lyssanne's cottage. She paused, darted back toward Lyssanne, then resumed her path to the trees. Lyssanne followed, an odd look in her eyes, as if unsure why she did so.

Noire pursued Lyssanne into the trees—until the dove reversed course and rushed him. They grappled, talons piercing, wings beating, feathers falling. At last, his superior strength prevailed, or so it seemed. As sudden as it began, Serena's attack ceased, and she flew off.

Noire landed on a branch to steady his heartbeat and shook out his feathers. Venefica would hear about this. He'd narrowly escaped disfigurement! Now, where had that girl gone?

~

An odd sensation filled Lyssanne's mind. Hadn't she done this before —followed a flying creature this direction? She'd lost sight of Serena, but instinct drove her on. Somehow, she knew where she must go, though not toward what she ventured.

Then, she came upon the circle of moonflowers.

A shiver ran up her spine. "I've stood here," she whispered. Only, hadn't the circle of flowers been larger? The surrounding trees taller?

As she lifted one foot over the flowers, images flitted through her mind, blurring past and present. This clearing in darkness…a pink firefly floating ahead…

Voices whispered from the ring's empty center, drawing her back to the present. She paused, half in, half out of the circle.

"She must face what is to come," hissed a small but gruff voice, its words too clear to be a swish of wind in the trees, or Lyssanne's imagination.

Yet, where was the speaker?

"There will be time enough for that," murmured a second voice, higher and softer than the first. "Gentleness is required at present. I shall handle this."

The instant Lyssanne brought her other foot into the circle, wind whooshed in her ears, and a wall of brilliant white light shot upward from the ring of flowers. The glowing wall grew until it obscured the treetops then dimmed to a shimmering blue barrier. The sun-dappled wood beyond appeared distorted, as if viewed through painted glass.

Further disorienting her, Lyssanne's vision again flickered between the sight before her and images of a larger, moonlit clearing. No, 'twas the same place, only she'd been smaller. She clutched her midsection and closed her eyes, but the dizzying images alternated faster, then melted together as one.

At last, the onslaught of sight ceased, and she opened her eyes. An unnatural quiet had descended over the wood.

Like glowing insects, two green sparks flitted to and fro in front of her, trailing smaller bits of light. The deeper, jewel-toned spark zipped off toward the barrier and vanished. When Lyssanne looked back toward the other, leafy-hued light, it, too, was gone. In its place floated a miniature woman. *Floated?*

"Greetings, Lyssanne of Rowan Hill," the woman said in the soft, high voice from moments before. "I am Olivia." She bowed. As she straightened, light shifted behind her—through fluttering, translucent wings. "Fear not. We serve the same King."

"You're...but you can't be..." Lyssanne rubbed her temples. Perhaps her sight *was* going, conjuring wild images in a last, crazed effort to remain.

"Can't be what? Real?" Olivia said. "Oh, I'm as real as you, and yes, I am a faerie."

The memory that had been dancing at the edges of Lyssanne's mind slammed into focus. "Then, it was true?" she whispered, more to herself than to the tiny, green-clad woman. "The pink firefly? I thought it a childhood fancy or—"

"That was no dream," said Olivia. "The *firefly* who led you here in your fifth spring was one of my kind. You've visited this place twice, in fact. Though, you'd only remember the second. A visit in which you had the honor of meeting my queen."

A musical voice from the past echoed through Lyssanne's thoughts.

"Fear not," a lady clad in glittering pink had said. "You are safe here. You will *always* be safe here. You possess a great and precious gift. It is like a light inside your soul, which shines on those around you. There will be others who need the warmth of this Light to survive. You alone can pass it on to them. You alone can teach them to find the Light within themselves."

Lyssanne's eyes flew wide and locked onto Olivia. "The lady in pink, with the violet eyes—she's your queen?"

Olivia nodded.

"And my first visit?"

"Shortly before your birth, your mother trod the same path that brought you here today." Olivia glanced about. "But we've no time to discuss that now. Already, we risk discovery."

"Who would notice us here?" Lyssanne asked. "Only my cottage is near."

"This place is protected, true, but there are watchful eyes lurking about. No time to explain. We must speak of your journey."

"How do you know—?"

Olivia waved away the question. "You must throw off your cloak of sadness. Its weight will hinder you in following your new path. Embrace your newfound freedom."

A half laugh escaped Lyssanne's throat. "If you knew anything about me, you'd not say I'm free." She wasn't even free to live in her own home.

"You have your burdens, true, but you are now released from the chains of obligation that bound you to this place and its people."

"My people, an obligation?" Lyssanne said. "Never!"

"I speak not of your love for them," the faerie said, "but of freedom from the notion that you must remain here to serve them in repayment for what they've given you."

"That's not freedom. 'Tis…" Lyssanne's throat closed in on her words.

"What may feel like a punishment is but the opening of a doorway." Olivia floated closer, her voice urgent. "We've little time. Tell no one of your destination."

"I have no destination. Even with a scrap of a map, I've no idea where I can go."

Olivia's voice softened, a warmth flowing over Lyssanne's skin. "Follow the road to the river's bend. There, take the faint track into the forest."

"What about Merchant's Bridge? Mr. DeLivre's map shows Trader's Road crossing the River Esten by—"

"No. Take the forest path." Olivia took Lyssanne's hand in both of her tiny ones. "You will not journey alone." The faerie fluttered backward, glancing over her shoulder. "Go now, Lyssanne. We will find you and explain what we can."

After another flash of brightest white, Lyssanne stood alone in the clearing. Sound returned so suddenly, the soft rustle of leaves boomed in her ears.

~

At last, the day had come. Noire could have crowed as Lyssanne and her two companions emerged from her cottage, a boxy cart in tow. Instead, he remained silent as shadow, huddled atop her roof. No one must see him; nothing must distract him and incite Venefica's ire this time.

Still, had it been his failure that angered her? Or was it, as Venefica's questions indicated, something about the direction Lyssanne had wandered? Venefica's preoccupation with the dove, too, made no sense. What did it matter how long the pest had been lurking around Lyssanne, or the shape of her violet eyes? The girl was leaving.

Narrowing his eyes, he glanced about then leaned over the edge of the roof to peer at the windowsills. The dove...where was she? For more than a year, she'd scarcely left Lyssanne's side. Perhaps Venefica's muttered pledge to take care of the pest hadn't been idle ranting.

"I have something for you," said the old coot who called himself a scribe, releasing Lyssanne from a fatherly embrace. "I put it in your cart earlier." He removed the lid from the tall, two-wheeled box, then withdrew a thick leather-bound book and handed it to her.

"*The Kingsword?*" Lyssanne held the book to her chest, eyes drenched.

"You will not have services to attend," he said. "My old friend Fescue copied this version in a larger hand than usual, perfect for you. I know it is heavy, but you have the cart now."

"This is too much, too valuable for you to part with," Lyssanne whispered.

"I have others. Read it with joy." DeLivre took the book and plopped it back into her cart, then grasped her hands. "Be careful, *Shirii*. You are very trusting. The people out there..."

"We are all children of the King," she said. "I'm sure I shall be safe."

"Not all outside this valley honor or believe in the King. You must be cautious."

Her brow furrowed. "How could anyone not believe in the King? 'Twould be like not believing in trees or...the sky."

"Such faith is a credit to you, *Shirii*. May you never have cause to lose it." He hugged her again. "The King's love will not desert you. You'll never walk alone."

"I almost forgot my gift," Lyssanne's friend Aderyn Clayton said. She held out a star-shaped, wooden pendant. "Kevan..." She drew in a shuddering breath. "He carved this during winter, and I painted it— blue to match your eyes, and these flecks of gold at the edges remind me of the sunlight in your hair. I was saving it for the anniversary of your birth, but..."

"Oh, Aderyn!" Lyssanne embraced her, both women in tears. "I've a gift for you as well," she said as they broke apart. "I wish you and the babe to have my cottage."

"What? Lyss, no."

"Please, Aderyn." Lyssanne donned the pendant. "'Twould comfort me, knowing it is filled with love. I ask only that you tend Mother's grave. I would not have weeds overtake it."

Aderyn nodded. "Don't go!" she cried. "You can hide here in the cottage. I shall move in like you asked and, and no one will ever know you're still here." She clasped Lyssanne's arms. "You don't have to leave."

Lyssanne shook her head, her lips parting, then closing.

"Mr. DeLivre won't say anything." Aderyn sniffled. "Will you?"

"I would not." He laid a hand on Aderyn's shoulder. "But you wouldn't wish such a life for her. To never leave the house, to live always in fear?" He stepped away and faced the village. "Besides, it would not work. They are coming later, the Council, to make certain she has gone."

Aderyn's shoulders shook with silent tears.

"How does one revisit a lifetime of friendship in a few stolen moments?" Lyssanne said, embracing her friend once more, heedless of the wisps of Shadow Mist swirling around Aderyn's feet and gathering in increasing density atop Rowan Hill. "I must go now, or I shall never have the strength." She drew back, one hand over her heart. "I shall hold you here, always."

Lyssanne turned away and fixed her watery gaze eastward, toward the steadily rising glow Noire so despised, the longing in her tremulous sigh so deep, he could have drowned in it.

"I love you," she said, glancing over her shoulder, "both of you." Her voice hitched. "My dearest and truest friends."

The Light Venefica loathed wavered around Lyssanne, a dim reflection of its former glory, while the radiance that plagued Noire's existence intensified—the light of day—a constant reminder of his unfulfilled quest.

Lyssanne's back straightened, her chest rising on a shaky breath. She released the starburst pendant she'd been clutching and wiped her eyes. Gripping the cart's handle, she kicked at its bottom to tilt it onto its two wheels, and started down the hill.

"Never will you be forgotten, *Shirii*," DeLivre called, as Lyssanne walked alongside her beloved rowan grove. "That, I promise you."

Lyssanne covered her mouth with her free hand and quickened her pace.

Aderyn let out a wail akin to the lowing of cattle.

Noire shook out his feathers. Such an undignified display!

Aderyn's keening trailed after Lyssanne as she followed the path her eyes had taken—an unmarked route down the hill toward the River Esten and the road out of Cloistervale.

5

SINKING

*L*yssanne reached the bridge as the sun's descent drew shadows across the water like half-closed curtains. Here, the River Esten took a sharp turn to the Southwest, slashing across Trader's Road. The ground before her dropped away in a steep slope to wide wooden planks and the rushing water beneath them.

She'd made it. Now, she needn't fear sharing sleeping quarters with whatever wild beasts rustled within the forest to her right—if she could descend that embankment and cross Merchant's Bridge before full eventide.

Gripping her cart handle for balance, she slid the toe of one shoe along the slope. A few loose pebbles and clumps of dirt clattered to the bridge. The dark waters churned in a dizzying swirl that seemed to lurch toward her. She backed up a step, tightening her hold on the cart. Her legs, already wobbling from a half-day's intermittent walking, threatened to fold. She released the cart and sank onto the road, staring out at the river.

"How shall I have the strength?" she whispered. A tremor ran through her body as she glanced over her shoulder toward home—her *former* home. The tears that had ceased hours before threatened to resurface. She waged a brief but valiant battle to hold them at bay, and lost.

How long had she traveled since her last rest? An hour? Half that? Perhaps she should have brought an hourglass. Still, what need had she to mark the time in this wild place? No one, now, cared where she was at any given moment or whither she should venture.

She closed her eyes, and the weeping of the river along its rock-strewn banks filled her ears, the perfect accompaniment for her mood. The mourning-trees that framed the Esten to the north would have made a more fitting backdrop, though, than the forest stretching beside her.

Soon, she would leave even that behind, along with the sheltering valley she'd always thought so akin to a house, walled in on all sides by river, mountains, or forest. Had she the courage to take her first tottering steps through its only door? She had no choice but plunge a-purpose into a wild openness as wide and turbulent as the waters churning below, setting herself adrift on a fathomless current of alien shapes and unable to see clearly past the few paces ahead.

A passage from the *Kingsword* echoed through her mind for the tenth time that day. *Though all others abandon me, the King's hand shall direct my path.*

"Where are you?" she whispered. "Please, let me feel your hand leading me."

Overhead, a raven cried, and something rustled the leaves several paces from where she sat. She folded her arms against the prickles that shivered over her skin. The sounds of the forest couldn't frighten her half as much as this...lost-ness clutching at her heart.

At least she had the road to follow. That lifeline offered some sense of where she was and would lead someplace, eventually. Sitting here wouldn't get her there. She climbed to her feet, ready to venture on— one footfall at a time, her toes feeling the path for holes or lumps.

She stared toward the forest. Words buzzed like fireflies through her mind—warning words spoken in a ring of flowers by an impossibly real creature of myth.

Was there a path into the forest as Olivia had suggested? Lyssanne drew closer to the trees. Could that patch of deeper green be a slight break in the foliage? Still, no trail caught her eye. All was darkness and shifting shadow. How could she find her way through that tangle? With identical trees at every turn, she would doubtless end her days wandering in circles.

She hesitated only a moment longer. Faeries of legend were notorious for leading travelers astray, after all. Besides, Olivia had mentioned nothing of what lay within or beyond that forest. And where could she cross the river, if not at Merchant's Bridge?

She turned from the trees, resumed her grip on her cart, and edged closer to the embankment. As a filmy mist settled over the river, she set her jaw and, toes and stomach clenching, picked her way down to the bridge.

The weight of her cart threatened to push her too rapidly downhill, and her feet slipped several paces. Weather-painted planks stretched before her, wide enough to hold a wagon and team of horses; but with no railings or rope handholds on either side. She adjusted her descent toward the middle of the bridge, lest her inability to judge distance or depth put her off balance.

The shadows of trees and approaching dusk darkened the river fog, calling to mind the black mist that plagued Cloistervale. If only that fog, too, had been as simple to explain as the collision of heated air and cold water that brought the clouds to earth this evening.

As Lyssanne planted her right foot onto the bridge, her left sank into the dirt. Wood groaned as she eased forward. The boards shifted to take her weight, and she flung her free arm out for balance. She took another step. With a thunderous crack, wood snapped beneath her foot. Before she could retreat or even scream, the world fell away.

Lyssanne fell with it.

Mud reached for her, a gaping maw sucking her in, as if she were water in a funnel. Splintered wood broke free of the bridge to rip at her skirts and bite her legs. Letting go of the cart, she flailed for something solid to hold. She only sank deeper. Lyssanne struggled to free her other arm from the mire, but the greedy suction held it fast.

Tongues of slime snaked up around her arms and neck. She was being swallowed whole!

River water flowed in around her, filling the gap her body was creating in the mud. Its icy chill knifed through her sun-warmed skin, forcing her to draw a sharp breath. A gastric belch of rotting vegetation and fish rose up from the mud to clog her lungs. She clamped her mouth shut against the stench; so dank she could taste it. Her scrabbling grew frantic. The mud merely oozed between her fingers. Thick lumps of decaying plant life, and she knew not what else, slithered like snot over her fingertips. She fought down burning nausea—and slipped deeper.

The mud oozed over her shoulders, and she could no longer move. Water filled the space her body had occupied, sloshing past her clamped lips and into her nose. Holding her breath only amplified the soft burbling of the mud and water swirling around her ears, an oddly gentle sound like distant laughter.

As mud squelched around her chin, and water covered her face, Lyssanne opened and closed her free hand above her head. If only she could clasp the sky as she had grasped the handle of her cart.

Then, something clamped down hard upon her exposed wrist.

Lyssanne struggled anew. She could *not* let this…thing hold her under. All reason fled as blood drummed in her head, and her ears rang out the need to breathe. Her struggles grew weaker as she fought the burning in her chest that compelled her to gulp in air. 'Twould be only water and death she swallowed.

The vice around her wrist tightened, sending sudden pain down her arm, then…pulled.

Her arm threatened to slip free of its socket as she was hauled upward, fraction-by-fraction. Unwilling to relinquish its meal, the mud tugged at her limbs, sucking her skirts against her legs. Her face broke free of the water, her mouth flying open to take in such a great gulp of air she choked on it. Fang-like wooden teeth snagged in her hair and grazed every inch of her skin through her clothing, as she was jerked past them.

At last, she lay gasping and coughing on solid ground. Awareness of her surroundings seeped through the haze her starved lungs had conjured. She must be lying at an angle on the slope of the riverbank. How close to the water she still was, she couldn't determine; for, she had no strength to open her eyes—hadn't strength or will to do anything but breathe.

A wet cough racked her body until she turned toward the downward slope and spat out half the River Esten. She lifted her un-muddied hand, throbbing wrist and all, to wipe river water and tears from her eyes. Blinking, she searched for her rescuer.

A huddled shape, silhouetted against the water, began to rise, resolving into the back of a person near the shattered end of the bridge. The shape turned.

"You're unharmed, then, Lady Lyssanne?"

"Jarad?" She levered herself up onto one elbow, still panting.

"I got your other shoe. It was hung on one of those broken boards."

"Jarad, what…" She cleared her throat to rid her voice of its watery croak. "What are you doing here?"

"Well, pulling you out of the river, mistress," he said.

"Yes, but—"

Suddenly, a shape swooped low over Lyssanne's head, fluttering her hair into her eyes. She flattened herself against the ground. A gruff caw split the air just off to her left. A raven? Lyssanne's shoe thumped to the ground as Jarad reached over his shoulder to pull something from his back. The raven cast its shadow over her again, flying a bit higher this time. A creak in Jarad's direction drew her eye. He held a bow aloft, aiming at the retreating bird.

"Let it be," she said. "It has done us no harm."

He lowered the bow but shouted at the bird as it flew toward the trees. "You'll have no dinner here! She's alive." He looked back at Lyssanne. "Did it claw you?" When she shook her head, he replaced his arrow in its quiver and moved closer. "Must've been drawn to the blood. You have lots of cuts."

"I'm beginning to feel them," she said.

Jarad brought her the wayward shoe. "I rinsed out the mud."

"Thank you," she said, forcing her sodden foot into the even wetter shoe, "for this and for, well, you've saved my life this day."

He ducked his head, then held out a hand to help her up. "I don't think we should try to cross that," he said, looking back at the remains of Merchant's Bridge.

"No."

They made their way up the bank, Jarad pulling her cart behind him. Lyssanne leaned against a tree beside the road. From her cart, she withdrew a cloth and began mopping up the blood from the numerous small cuts stinging her arms and legs. Every moment or so, she glanced up at Jarad, his presence as unaccountable as that of a faerie.

"Jarad," she said, "I am glad, and grateful, to see you, but why are you here?"

"Um, I followed you."

"You...? Why?"

"Well," he said, then blurted all in a rush, "they made you leave and you didn't do nothing wrong and you always help us when we can't do somethin', and I can hunt and..." He took a breath. "I figured, maybe I could help."

"Oh, Jarad, that was very kind of you." Lyssanne said, her knees shaky. "It is growing dark. Let us find a place to camp. You can return home on the morrow."

"I'm not going back," he said. "I'm going with you." He held out a bundle. "See, I've brought all my stuff."

"You've run away from the orphanage?" At his grunt, she dropped her cloth into the cart and slumped against the tree. "You can't do that. 'Tis the only home you have."

"Sure I can. I'll be with you."

"Jarad, you do realize, I can never return to Cloistervale?"

"Yeah."

"I don't know where I'll sleep or what I'll eat," she said. "I can't provide for you out here. There may be wild beasts and any number of dangers. I have no way to keep you safe."

"That's why I must go with you," he said. "Everyone says I'm a good

75

hunter. I can shoot or scare off wild things, like I scared that raven." His teeth flashed in the fading light. "You told Gavan you have to go on a new adventure. Well, us orphans should stick together." He lifted his chin and raised a fist. "Twill be like your stories, a lady and her knight off on a grand journey."

"This isn't—"

"I'll do whatever you tell me," he said. "I promise. Besides..." He looked over his shoulder at the river. "I think I was s'posed to come with you."

Perhaps the King of All Lands had indeed sent Jarad to save her. Lyssanne shivered. Her sodden clothes would give her a chill if she didn't warm herself soon. "Come along. We'll set up camp and save this discussion for morning." Tilting her cart, she walked toward the gap in the forest she'd seen before trying to cross the bridge.

"I'll just follow you again, y'know," he said. "If you make me go back."

Lyssanne sighed. "We shall work all that out later. Let's get moving."

"Can't we just camp here?" he asked. "I could build a fire, and we can dry your clothes."

"I do need to wash." Lyssanne turned to gaze out at the river that had nearly claimed her life. The fog clinging to its surface darkened and boiled. Despite the summer warmth, a damp chill stung her skin like cold words spoken in anger.

Her ruined clothes dragged at her waning strength. The slimy sludge caking her skin tightened as it dried, itchy, cracking, unbearable. And her hands! She kept her fingers splayed, lest the slick residue of decaying vegetation that coated them slide against itself and loose the bile so near to erupting. She fair twitched with the need to wash.

"But not here," she said, shivering again. She longed to be far from this place of cold, grasping death—or, failing that, concealed from the invisible eye of the fog. "We must go into the forest...now. We can find our way back to the Esten farther south. It shouldn't take long."

"There's a sandbar a little way downriver," Jarad said. "I saw it when I was looking for your shoe. The Esten bends a little, and I bet there's a shallow spot where you could bathe. I'll test it first, to be sure it's safe."

"Good. Let us be off." She turned and pulled her cart behind her, already missing the packed dirt road that had made keeping it upright easier. "I should have heeded the faeries," she muttered, stepping among the trees. Olivia had known, somehow, about the bridge.

"Faeries?" Jarad hurried to catch up and reached for her arm. "Lady Lyssanne, you should sit down. You must've hit your head on the bridge."

"No, my head is well."

"Or, or maybe you got too much sun today," he said, lifting a hand to her brow.

"What are you going on about?" she said, chuckling.

"You were just talking about faeries."

"Oh." He'd heard. Well, if he insisted on accompanying her, perhaps she should tell him. "Yes, I saw two of them yesterday. Or, I heard two, I only saw the one."

"Yesterday? You must've been dreaming or something, right?"

"No. I spoke with them in the wood behind my cottage. One of them told me not to cross Merchant's Bridge, but go into the forest instead."

"It had to be a dream," he said. "Unless—Everybody says you've been upset. You must've imagined them. I did that once, cried so hard I sort of fell asleep and saw weird things."

"I was perfectly calm, Jarad." As calm as one *could* be when having a conversation with a myth. "A dream couldn't have warned me about the bridge."

She turned to trudge deeper into the forest. Indeed, a narrow track of smoothed ground lay ahead. Whatever Jarad believed about the faeries, he followed.

As he landed, the clack of Noire's talons reverberated through the cavernous chamber. Twenty chairs surrounded the glossy dining table on which he stood, only one of them occupied.

"If I may be so bold," Magda said, setting a yellowed dinner plate before Venefica. "You shouldn't expend so much strength all at once. Five days of pooling all your power into one trap? You've circles under your eyes, Effie-girl, and I can see your veins."

Shadow and ice crackled around Venefica. "Never," she said, "address me thus."

Noire flapped a hasty retreat to the other end of the long table, as Magda went rigid, her face white as the towel she choked between her gnarled fingers.

"Do you think it so easy to manipulate nature?" Venefica said, her voice bouncing off the dark paneled walls, rattling dinnerware in cabinets and setting crystal droplets to tinkling on the chandelier. "The power required to alter the flow of that river would crush you to dust!"

"F-forgive me," Magda whispered. As if released from a puppeteer's hold, she slumped. She turned and rummaged at the sideboard, then dropped a pewter trencher at Noire's feet. "It nearly worked, milady."

Noire tilted his head, narrowing his eyes at the trencher. His senses detected no poison, and he'd consumed far less pleasant fare, but that crone was not to be trusted. She'd spoken true on one matter, though. Venefica's plan nearly *had* worked—until Jarad appeared.

"I had to change the course of the current to wash out that cursed bridge," Venefica said, snatching up a heel of bread. She squeezed it, letting a few crumbs fall. "The Shadow Mist isn't a solid hand, you know. An entire month's collected fury and fear was barely sufficient fuel to churn those waters and create that sinkhole. Weakening the consistency of earth from this distance isn't as simple a matter as crushing bread."

"Yes, but you knew it was a risk, milady," Magda said. "There was always the chance the girl wouldn't even go that way."

"There is no other path out of this pathetic village," Venefica said, "except the forest, and she'd be a fool to travel through that tangle. She'd never survive on her own."

Ah, but Lyssanne wasn't on her own. Not any longer. Noire's tail feathers twitched, silent in the ominous stillness that filled the dining hall.

Venefica swung her gaze to him. "The forest—that is the only choice left her. Find her. Follow her. I want to see every twig she snaps." She opened her hand, eyeing the mangled bread as it rolled to the floor. "I want to watch her die a slow death in that wood."

Noire bowed, his beak grazing the tabletop. He would do her bidding, but at a distance this time. He'd not risk becoming a target of Jarad's heroics or the Shadow Mist, as he had at the bridge. Foolish, straying so near the Mist and being swept up in Venefica's fury! If he became nothing more than one of her puppets, he'd never force her to fulfill their bargain.

"Do not let her leave your sight," Venefica said, piercing him with eyes of liquid night. "But should her steps turn back toward Cloistervale, inform me at once." She swirled the wine in her crystal goblet. "I want her dead or so far from my village, she has no hope of returning."

A fortnight later, Noire sidled closer to the trunk of a plateris tree twenty paces from Venefica's prey, rendering himself invisible amid the shadows. Lyssanne's rests had grown longer with each passing day, while the distance she and the boy covered grew shorter. Now, she sat curled between two large roots, her face drawn and pale.

"Jarad?" she called, pulling her blanket and cloak tighter around her shoulders.

A rustle and muffled grunt from the upper branches of the tree in front of Lyssanne's resting place were the only reply.

Still, Noire permitted not a feather's twitch. The dove, who'd rejoined Lyssanne sometime that first evening, lurked nearby. Besides,

Jarad was too good a shot with his arrows, felling other birds and small game from impressive distances for their daily meals.

"Do you see anything?" Lyssanne asked, shivering despite the stifling summer heat.

Branches creaked, leaves plunged, and Jarad shimmied partway down the tree. "I wish you could see this!" he yelled. "The treetops look like lumpy green clouds from up here. There's a clearing not far south. I saw a flash of light down there. Could be sunlight reflecting off a pool or stream."

"Thank the King," Lyssanne muttered, eyeing the half-full water-skin beside her, the last of the rainwater she'd collected in her cooking pot during an afternoon shower. "Will it take long to get there?" she asked, her voice a mere rasp.

"What was that?" Jarad yelled.

She cupped her hands to her mouth and drew in a deep breath. "How far?"

"Um…" Jarad shimmied back up the tree.

Lyssanne rested her head on folded arms.

Moments later, Jarad dropped to the ground in a flurry of leaves and twigs. "Looks like a couple hours' walk at most."

Lyssanne sighed and fixed her glassy eyes upon the afternoon sky. "We shall set out first thing on the morrow."

"But we still have several hours of daylight," Jarad said, "and we really need fresh water. Who knows when it'll rain again, and that's the only water source I've seen since the Esten spilled over that cliff. Even I'm not crazy enough to climb down there." He peered down at her for long moments then shook his head. "You're right, we should wait. I'll find some firewood."

As Jarad retreated into the trees, Lyssanne lay on her side, curling into a tight ball as if attempting to warm herself. Her eyes closed, and her breathing slowed, but her shivers did not.

Noire took to the air and found Jarad's clearing in short order. The travelers could have reached it long before nightfall, had Lyssanne possessed the strength. Ah, but the signs were clear. She had contracted a fever. With no shelter and only a stagnant pool awaiting her in the clearing—even should she last the night to reach it—she would not long survive.

Noire aimed his beak toward the North, toward his bargain's overdue fulfillment.

~

Lyssanne trudged behind Jarad as if slogging through syrup instead of air. He stopped to hack at a net of tangled vines with his hunting knife then broke through to paradise. Gentle beams of sunlight streamed through the surrounding trees. A soft breeze swished the leaves, stirring Lyssanne's hair like a wildflower-scented breath from the King's Shining Land.

Jarad whooped, and Lyssanne smiled despite the war of heat and chill raging beneath her skin. Freeing her hair from the snag of prickly vines, she blinked at a flash of sunlight across the glade. A small pool reflected the wavering light, clear as mirrored glass.

Serena soared off across the clearing, perhaps to hunt. Lyssanne took a few steps onto the thick, sun-dappled grass then swayed.

Jarad rushed to her side and grasped her arm. "You're on fire."

"Only...on the...outside," she whispered. "A block of ice set aflame —'tis no wonder my legs feel watery." As Jarad helped her settle in a spot of shade, she attempted a small jest. "Should I melt, you can refill the water-skins."

"You're shivering, mistress," Jarad said, his tone grave. "Should I get you a blanket?"

"Yes, thank you."

Draping the cloth over her, he murmured, "What should I do? How do you stop a fever?"

"Perhaps you might test the pool for freshness? I am dry as kindling." Had any mourning-trees been near, she would have bidden him make a tea from their bark. She closed her eyes as the coolness of Jarad's shadow left her.

He returned minutes...or hours...later. "The water isn't foul, but rather stale," he said. "I'd bathe in it and perchance use it for cooking, but don't think we should drink it."

Lyssanne fought the urge to weep. Doubtless, she hadn't even enough moisture left for tears. She must think of something, but her fevered brain was as sluggish as water refusing to boil. "That's it!" she whispered. "Boil it. When it cools, we can drink it."

"Do you think it will be safe?"

"We have no choice."

While Jarad bustled around the campsite, Lyssanne stared ahead in a daze. Her skin grew hotter, yet ice rushed through her veins, violent shudders rocking her body. Strength fading, she lay on the ground. She bade Jarad pile her blankets, their cloaks, and half her outer dresses atop her—then wished she could shed even her skin to escape the raging heat.

"The water's starting to boil," Jarad said at length, resting a cold hand against her brow. "You're getting worse. You need Mistress Evlia."

"I can't go back," she whispered.

"I could go get her," Jarad said. "If I ran all the way, I'd get there in half the time it took us. I know how to make a trail, too, so I could find you again."

"She wouldn't come," Lyssanne said. "No one would come."

The Council would never allow it. Besides, by the time Evlia could reach her, Lyssanne feared she would be beyond the woman's skill to heal.

Lyssanne shuddered anew. She should tell Jarad to leave her, spare him what would doubtless come. She couldn't force herself to say it. Selfish as it was, she didn't wish to die alone.

Jarad strode over to the campfire as Serena returned and set to pecking at the ground nearby. Sunlight streamed through the dark trees, dazzling beams shooting down to the pool. Lyssanne blinked. A brighter flash shone in front of the water; so brilliant it hurt her eyes. When she opened them again, the whiteness had moved closer, out of the glaring sunshine.

She must be hallucinating. The whiteness shining in front of the trees resembled a horse. A shaft of light shot upward from its forehead—a thin silver-white point like a shard of glass or…a horn. The creature stood motionless, appearing to stare right at her.

"Jarad?" Lyssanne whispered.

Either he hadn't heard or was too spellbound to speak. Tempted as she was to turn to him, she couldn't take her eyes from the beauty before her.

The horse took several silent steps forward. It bent its head toward the ground. The silvery beam jutting from its brow moved with it, attached. "Lyssanne," the creature said.

6

CLOSE ENCOUNTERS

*N*oire slowed his flight over Cloistervale, peering down at the Shadow Mist. In his brief absence, it had spread across more than half the village. He glided lower over a pocket of the valley yet free of the fog. Even there, eddies of darkness appeared, swirled about, then faded. With Lyssanne's odd magic removed, nothing could hold it back.

The market below bustled with activity, only the children yet shimmering with Lyssanne's influence. The Mist enshrouded many adults and touched the others on occasion. Even those who'd once reflected Lyssanne's glow unawares had forfeited that protection the instant they'd embraced belief in the charges laid against her. Grief over her exile would doubtless draw the Mist to the few still loyal to her.

Venefica would soon have all she desired, and Noire would be free.

He found the sorceress in her dusty music room, staring at a portrait miniature atop the pianoforte as her fingers drifted across the keys. Haunting notes filled the chamber with a melancholy as fathomless as the longing in her eyes. Her gaze shot to Noire as he landed, and she flipped the portrait facedown, ending her tune before he could identify its familiar melody.

"I know what you seek," she said, her voice for once lacking its haughty aloofness.

～

Lyssanne stared at the creature. Her fever must be worse than she'd thought. Now, she was hearing things that weren't there, as well as seeing them.

"Joyful greetings to you, Lyssanne of Rowan Hill," said the horse-hallucination. "And to you, Jarad of the loyal heart."

Lyssanne rubbed her scorched eyes. This *must* be a dream.

"I am no phantom, daughter of the King," the figment of her imagination said, stepping closer. Her words washed over Lyssanne, soft as a mare's coat, yet rippling as if a whinny bubbled just beneath the surface. "Like you, I was created at the word of the King of All Lands."

Lyssanne's lips parted, but her burned-out brain supplied no words.

Jarad didn't share the affliction. "You're a unicorn!"

"That, I am."

"And," Jarad said, "you can talk."

"Yes, with those who have ears to hear."

"Wait," Jarad said, a thump punctuating the word. "How'd you know our names? Are you some kind of spirit or something?"

"Were I a spirit sent by the Deceiver, your arrows would avail you nothing."

Lyssanne eased her swimming head toward Jarad. He held his bow trained on the unicorn.

"Your lady and I have a mutual acquaintance," said the creature.

"Who?" Lyssanne whispered.

"The King's faeries are well-traveled. I believe you have spoken with Olivia?"

Lyssanne nodded. A fever dream might know that.

"I do not ask you to take me at my word alone." The unicorn

stepped alongside Lyssanne and bent her forelegs. "Come, test my coat and horn. See that I am what I say."

Lyssanne inched a hand toward the creature's gleaming side, then jerked away from its warm, living softness. The unicorn extended her horn to the ground. Lyssanne traced a trembling finger along the smooth, shining surface, then the unicorn backed away.

"'Tis true," Lyssanne whispered. If only she could muster the strength to rise. Even sitting upright would feel safer than lying prone at the feet of a looming horse—unicorn.

"Sorry," Jarad said. His bowstring relaxed with a protracted creak.

"I am Reina, guardian of this forest," said the unicorn. "And you, child, do not look at all well."

"She has a fever," Jarad said. "I'd planned to go for help but…Oh!" He rushed forward. "Maybe you could bring me. It would be much faster." His steps faltered. "Or don't unicorns do that sort of thing? Carry people, I mean?"

"No," Reina said. "It is rare for us to show ourselves to humans, rarer still that we speak. To do as you suggest…" A tremor ran like a wave from Reina's mane to her tail. "What I can do, though, I shall."

"Do you have magic?" Jarad asked. "Can you heal her?"

"The King of All Lands granted me many gifts," Reina said, "but alas, the healing art is not among them. Though, I have some small knowledge. Your lady needs water. Her lips crack."

"I boiled some," Jarad said, "but it's still too hot to drink."

"Boiled? Why would you…?" The unicorn turned toward the pool and sniffed. "Oh, dear," she said, trotting over to its edge. "Why was I not informed of this?"

Reina touched her horn to the surface of the water. Ripples of light spread out from the horn's tip. Once the shimmering swells reached the far edges of the pool, Reina lifted her head and shook it, luminous droplets splashing into the water. Then, she trotted up to Jarad.

"The water is now pure and fresh. Its coolness will be much more soothing than what simmers in your pot."

Jarad went to the pool, and something sloshed. "Mm. This is the best water I've ever tasted!" he said. "How did you do that?"

"It is my gift to purify the waters of the forest," Reina said.

Jarad knelt beside Lyssanne, holding out a water-skin. She struggled upright and drew it to her lips. Oh, of all the gifts the King had bestowed, none could be sweeter.

"This water now holds healing properties of a sort," Reina said.

"Like medicine?" Jarad asked.

"Not precisely," Reina said, "though it can be made such. Alone, it can temporarily restore one's strength. Useful, but far from adequate to Lyssanne's needs." She trotted toward the edge of the glade. "Come, Jarad. Gather what herbs I shall tell you."

"Leave Lady Lyssanne? With you?" He remained crouched.

"I cannot gather them," Reina said. "My teeth would mulch them beyond usefulness."

"I'm not leaving her," he said.

"Unless we act soon," Reina said, "she will not survive."

As if to prove Reina's point, Lyssanne's arms gave way, and she sank back to the ground.

Jarad fixed his gaze upon her and sighed. His boot leather squeaked, and the warmth of his nearness dissipated.
"What herbs?"

Lyssanne slipped in and out of awareness while Reina told him what she needed.

Lyssanne blinked awake in darkness. Jarad withdrew his hand from her shoulder and stepped back. Firelight and Reina's moon-bright coat illuminated the shadowed glade. Jarad helped her sit up and handed her a steaming cup.

Lyssanne sniffed its contents. "What is it?"

"Forest herbs, feverfew, other medicinal plants," said Reina, "mixed with my refreshed water to strengthen its potency. You must drink this tea four times a day until you have strength enough to walk thrice around this clearing without stopping."

Praying the tea was safe for human consumption, Lyssanne sipped.

Her eyes widened at its sweetness. She drained the cup, set it aside, and melted back to the ground.

Within the hour, her fever broke. Throughout the night and most of the next day, she drenched the ground in sweat. She slept fitfully, fever returning for short periods then breaking again. Each time she woke, either Jarad or Reina hovered near.

Noire idled in the shadows of Venefica's tower chamber, while the sorceress sifted through one of her ancient books of witchery. Each page slid with a prolonged hiss across its fellows, until it had no choice but flop over and reveal the next. Perhaps Venefica didn't find removing a curse as entertaining as casting one. Her frenzy to devise the enchantment she'd laid upon Lyssanne had nearly ripped those same spell-laden leaves from their spine.

As long as her lackluster mood was no reflection of the power she would pour into the spell, Noire cared not whether she enjoyed the exercise. Persistence had its reward. At last, she would fulfill their bargain.

"Ah, this should suit my—*our* purposes," Venefica said. "Now, don't move, my Noire, not a feather." She smiled that deceptive, alluring smile which had first ensnared him. "That is, if you wish to keep all the wondrous parts of you intact."

He stiffened. What had he agreed to? But then, he'd had little choice. He braced himself as Venefica began chanting so low he couldn't make out what strange words she uttered. Didn't she need to brew a potion, or fling colored dust into the fire, or draw the Mist, or...something? This monotonous mumbling seemed rather anticlimactic after all his years of waiting.

Needles of fire stabbed every inch of his skin. Night coalesced around him, ignoring the fact that it was just past noon in all the land. His bones stretched, threatening to rend his joints asunder. Then, his fire-riddled skin simply melted away, leaving him standing taller than before, with no sensation whatsoever.

The last night-black wisps faded, only natural shadows remaining to shroud his tortured form. He looked down at his hands, his *human* hands, and could have crowed. His elation died in his throat, though, as he ran his fingers down his torso. The fabric of his tunic caused no sensation against his fingertips, nor did his stomach register his hand's pressure against it. Fighting his first pang of true fear in years, he flattened his palm against the stone at his back.

His hand passed through the wall like smoke.

"What is this, witch?" he said, his voice a hoarse croak. He cleared his throat. "What have you done?"

"You are displeased?" She spread her arms. "Is it not day, and are you not a man?"

"The shadow of a man!" He coughed, but couldn't rid his voice of its hollow croak. "I can feel nothing, touch nothing. Have you destroyed my body entirely?"

He lunged toward her. He would force that cool indifference from her face. He would...

The instant his outstretched hands pierced a sunbeam streaming through the slit window, his phantom bones constricted. Where the impression of arms had been, wings beat the air. He shouted, but only a caw filled the tower. Talons raked the ground as his body, a raven's body, rose in furious flight.

No! He longed to rage, to scream. He settled for slashing at Venefica's face.

She ducked, his talons inches from her cheek.

He circled the chamber—faster, faster—as if he could shake loose this feathered body. He'd been so close!

His frantic flight brought him back to the shadowed edges of the room. The moment the feeble sunlight left the tip of his last tail feather, he dropped without sound or sensation to the ground. He fell silent, for there in shadow, he'd once again become something less than a man.

"Is your little tantrum quite done?" Venefica said, smoothing her hair.

"Can you remedy this?" he asked, his voice roughened with remnants of the raven.

"This is…unfortunate." She peered down at her book and sighed. "It seems we were mistaken. I still lack sufficient power to do as you ask."

"You sound unsurprised." He schooled his hollow voice to show no emotion. "What's to be done? Am I to remain thus, caught between bird and man, insubstantial as a shadow?"

"What is wrought cannot be undone," said Venefica. "I must gain more power if you wish me to complete the transformation."

"If!"

"Until then," she said, "this…development may be turned to our use."

"How? I am little more than a wisp on the wind. This ghost of a body is worthless."

"Ah, but it will enable you to spy for me as never before."

"What? You dare—"

"I no longer require your eyes in this village," she said, "but 'tis obvious the girl yet lives, and you are my only link to her. Until she is dead or sufficiently far from this place, I cannot fulfill the terms of our bargain." She closed her book and looked up at him with a seductive half-smile. "So, my pet, it seems you must serve me a while longer."

And this was her price.

～

"Are you sure you're strong enough to leave the glade?" Jarad asked, handing Lyssanne one of the water-skins he'd refilled at Reina's pool. "It's only been a week since the fever left."

"I believe so," Lyssanne said, nestling the water-skin atop a folded blanket in her cart.

Reina trotted up to them, eyeing their preparations. "My waters will help you avoid a return of the fever you have conquered," she said, "but I sense your body battles a greater foe. Not even my small gift can afford you strength enough to reach the nearest town afoot. Exhaustion will make you ill again. Thus, should you wish it, I shall carry you as you journey."

"But how?" Lyssanne asked. "Legends say a human's mere touch is painful for you."

"True," Reina said. "Carrying most humans would cause unbearable torment, to say nothing of the indignity." She tossed her head. "I am no common horse, you know. However, you remain pure in spirit and in deed, a rarity among your kind." She brushed Lyssanne's shoulder with her muzzle. "Besides, I have grown quite fond of you, and it would be my honor."

"I'm fond of you, as well," Lyssanne said. "I know not how to thank you."

"Yet, you hesitate?" said Reina.

"'Tis just, I have no saddle, and in skirts I—"

"Oh, if that's what prevents you," Reina said, chuckling, "ride sidelong. My magic will hold you in place. The blanket Jarad last washed will suffice as a saddle. Jarad, if you please."

He slung the blanket across Reina's back, keeping his hands well away from her side.

"Now hop up, child," Reina said.

Lyssanne reached for the blanket, inches above her head. How was she to do this?

"My, you are a wee thing," Reina said, laughing. "Step back." She bent her knees as if taking a bow then lowered herself to the ground. "There we are. Now, up you get."

After traveling farther west along the cliff top for several days, Reina led Lyssanne and Jarad to the one place where they could descend. Lyssanne dismounted and, with a hand on Jarad's shoulder, picked her way down the steep incline. Jarad retraced the climb for their cart, helped Lyssanne set up camp, then left for his evening hunt.

Standing in a little patch of moonlight, Reina shook out her silvery mane. "What tale will you share with us tonight?"

Lyssanne shrugged. "I daresay, at my slow rate of travel, I shall need to repeat every story I know or start inventing new ones before we reach a town. Though your assistance has tripled our progress, despite my frequent rests."

Reina chuckled. "I can scarce fathom what wisdom you would infuse into a tale of your own invention." She tossed her head. "Might I request your help in removing these tangles from my mane? That wind was welcome today, but it does play havoc with one's hair."

Lyssanne laughed, shaking her own locks free of the scarf she'd tied over them that morn. As she reached toward the unicorn, the fine hairs at the nape of her neck prickled. Reina's ears flattened, and she raised her head, scenting the air. Had she, too, caught that whiff of mint?

A sudden, metallic swish rent the night, a sound akin to a knife drawn across a whetstone.

A flash caught the corner of Lyssanne's eye, and something sharp stung the base of her throat. As if to swat an insect, she raised a hand toward the spot. She glanced down and froze, staring into the slim, mirrored blade of a sword.

Gasping, she traced the edge of the blade with her eyes—to the tall man at its other end.

The campfire blazed behind him, casting him in shadow. "Step away from the unicorn," he said, his voice as hard and cold as the steel he held to her throat.

She backed away, nearly tripping on her hem in her haste. "Please, sir, I have nothing of value." Her words shivered between dry lips. "But what I have is yours. Only leave us in peace."

He made a derisive sound deep in his throat. "I have need of nothing you might possess."

"Then, wh-why—?"

"I will not allow you to harm or corrupt this noble creature." He pressed her farther back.

"What?" she whispered.

Muscle undulated along the man's black-clad arm as the tip of his blade followed Lyssanne's unsteady retreat. After half a dozen more steps, she stopped. It was that or risk losing her balance. The flat of the sword pressed against her neck, and she hardly dared breathe.

She was a flower in the shadow of an oak. The man stood taller than Mr. Whiskin. His hair, black as a raven's wing, swallowed the firelight, leaving his features indistinct.

His head snapped up, and he peered past her. "Lower the bow, boy."

Oh no, Jarad. Great King, protect him!

"Loose an arrow, and she'll be dead before the fletching leaves the bow," the man said, pressing the tip of the sword harder against Lyssanne's skin. Warmth trickled down her neck and ran under the collar of her chemise. "Now, put the bow on the ground and step away. Over by the fire." He jerked his head toward the flames.

Reina's voice filled Lyssanne's ears, so close it might have spoken within her mind. "Tell him to back away from you, child."

Lyssanne flinched. Reina had been so still, she'd nearly forgotten the unicorn was there. And Serena? That frantic fluttering overhead must be she.

The man glanced toward Reina, his blade unflinching.

"He can't understand me," Reina said. "You must interpret."

Lyssanne struggled to keep her throat motionless as she mouthed each word. "She, the unicorn, she says you must back away, sir."

"Am I to believe that one such as *you* can converse in the language of unicorns, when, conveniently, I cannot?" he said. "Do not think me so easily deceived."

"I am only understood by those worthy to hear," Reina said.

"I can't tell him that," Lyssanne whispered, shifting only her gaze toward Reina.

"I can," Jarad said. "Reina—that's the unicorn's name, you know—she says you don't understand her because you're not worthy to."

"You dare?"

The blade twitched, reducing Lyssanne's knees to water.

Reina loosed a shrill whinny, rearing up on her hind legs. She lowered her hooves and head, pointing her horn at the man. Pawing the ground and snorting, she inched toward him.

"Truly, sir," Lyssanne whispered, "sh-she insists you move away from me, or...or she'll attack." Clutching at her skirts, Lyssanne willed her hands' tremors not to travel up her body and cause more damage from that sword.

The man stared at Reina for an age. Then, he backed away a pace, lowering his sword a fraction. Reina stopped pawing the ground but continued eyeing him.

"Peace, Shining One," he said, retreating farther. "I sought only to protect you." He spread his arms as if to show he intended no harm. "I would not have you lose your immortality on my account. If this woman is your friend, I have no quarrel with her."

Reina nodded, then trotted to Lyssanne and nuzzled her shoulder.

"Your pardon, madam." The man sheathed his sword and swept Lyssanne a grand bow, firelight reflecting off shiny threads at his cuffs and along the edges of his tunic.

Jarad rushed to her side and grasped her arm. "Are you injured, Lady Lyssanne?"

"No." She raised a hand to her throat. The cut was small, not even as deep as those she'd sustained at Merchant's Bridge, but it stung something fierce.

"Lady?" the stranger said.

Gooseflesh followed the passage of his gaze from Lyssanne's head to her hem. Jarad's hand flexed around her arm.

"You will forgive my skepticism," the man said. "A bit odd, is it not, a noblewoman traveling unescorted through the forest? Arrayed in such...modest attire."

"She isn't unescorted," Jarad said. "I'm her escort, me and Reina." He stepped in front of Lyssanne. "And no lady would travel these woods in her best clothes."

The man sniffed. "Of course. With such a seasoned warrior as escort, the lady could hardly want for safety."

Jarad straightened to his full height, his fist clenched at his side. "And just who are you?"

"Jarad!" Lyssanne grasped his arm.

"Either you have a great deal of courage, boy, or very little sense," said the man.

"You must forgive him, sir," Lyssanne said, pushing in front of Jarad. "He is merely being protective. Like a, a younger brother."

"Indeed," the man said. "Brennus Xavier, at your service." The bow he executed this time was little more than an inclination of head and shoulders.

Lyssanne curtseyed as Mr. DeLivre had taught her, praying she did so properly, since life in a village devoid of rank or nobility had afforded no chance to test her skill. "Lyssanne," she said, "of…" Her throat closed on the name of Cloistervale. She swallowed and whispered, "Rowan Hill."

"Are you a knight?" Jarad blurted.

"I am." The man folded his arms, his dark mantle flowing about his shoulders as only thick, richly woven cloth could.

That he carried a sword at all proved him no peasant farmer or common shopkeeper.

"Brilliant!" Jarad said. "With the Starguard?"

"I do not ride for the queen of Lastarra," the man said. "I travel wherever I find the need."

"A knight-errant!" Jarad all but bounced on the spot.

Or a mercenary. Lyssanne flicked a cautionary glance at Jarad, but his wide eyes remained fixed on the stranger—whom, moments before, he'd wanted to pepper with arrows.

"I believe, young Jarad," said Sir Brennus, "your rabbit begins to attract flies."

"What? Agh!" Jarad ran to where he'd dropped his bow and, it seemed, their supper.

"My lady," Sir Brennus said, drawing Lyssanne's eye.

"Sir, you should know, the only place I've ever been lady of is Rowan Hill Cottage."

"Mm, a fine domicile, I am sure."

Did his neutral tone signify sincerity, or was he mocking her again? Oh, if only she could discern facial expressions!

"Perhaps," he said, "you will permit me to lend my services to your night's watch?"

The man had threatened her life, now he wished to share their camp? Lyssanne's chest tightened, and she squeezed a handful of skirt. "Thank you, but that kindness is unnecessary."

"I insist, milady." He softened his tone. "I would make amends for our unsatisfactory introduction. You wouldn't deny a knight the chance to set a wrong to rights?"

"No, of course not," she said, her mind racing for a way out of this. "Yet, we are strangers. 'Twould hardly be proper."

"I am oath-bound to guard the honor and safety of any innocent lady I encounter," he said. "Besides, what better chaperones could you wish than a unicorn and your brave escort?"

"He may share my watch," Reina said.

"Very well," Lyssanne said. What choice had she? Refusal would insult *his* honor.

As Jarad and Sir Brennus skinned and prepared the rabbit for supper, Lyssanne worked the tangles from Reina's mane. Jarad peppered the knight with questions, which he answered with minimal information.

A slight accent enriched his deep voice, one unlike Mr. DeLivre's. Something in the way *r*'s rolled off his tongue and vowels took on more depth conjured images of grand halls and glittering gowns.

After a meal eaten in near silence, Lyssanne fought to prevent nodding off.

"Fear is an exhausting business," Reina whispered. "Come, child, stretch out beside me."

Lyssanne hesitated. When Sir Brennus began arranging his bedding near Jarad's on the opposite side of the fire, she at last stretched out her own blankets.

She awoke late in the night to find Sir Brennus pacing the perimeter of the camp, seeming deep in thought. At the chatter of a night bird, he swiveled, his eyes and blade catching the firelight. Lyssanne turned and met Reina's shining gaze, then relaxed again into dream.

When she next woke, 'twas morning, and Sir Brennus was gone.

"He left before sunrise," Reina said, "insisting he must be on his way. He said my friends didn't rest well in his company. I daresay, he was right."

~

The following evening, Lyssanne shook damp hair from her face and tossed more brush onto the fire. Who would guess a bath in a sun-warmed spring could refresh the soul? She glanced in the direction Jarad had taken to search for firewood, but only the shadows of garments hanging to dry in the trees interrupted the light of the full moon. Dusting off her hands, she sat beneath a tree to watch shimmers dance across the spring and glitter off Reina's horn.

Moments later, leaves rustled and twigs snapped amid the trees opposite the fire.

"It would seem you are trailing me," said a deep, somewhat familiar voice, sending an inexplicable chill up Lyssanne's spine.

Jarad's laugh accompanied the creak of branches, as two figures burst into the clearing. "Look who I found!"

"Well," said the taller of the two, "I'll not quibble over who did the finding." When Reina stepped across their path, the man bowed. "A good evening to you, Shining One."

Lyssanne gasped. "Sir Brennus?" She rearranged her skirts to rise.

"Keep your seat, milady," he said. "You couldn't be more surprised than I at our meeting again. While scouting for a campsite south of here, I heard a ruckus and backtracked. I came upon young Jarad making more noise than a bear."

Lyssanne laughed, and even Reina's whinny held a note of amusement.

"We appear to be traveling in the same direction," Sir Brennus said. "Perhaps—"

A hiss shook the branch over Lyssanne's head, silencing the knight.

Her eyes snapped to the limb. Black against the moonlight, the ends of a rope dangled, its middle hanging sling-like just above her face. Then, it hissed again. Not a rope, a snake!

"Don't move," Sir Brennus said, his voice low. "Sudden motion could provoke it."

Lyssanne flinched despite her attempts to *become* the tree trunk behind her.

The serpent dropped onto her shoulders, its middle forming a loose coil around her neck, draping down her back. "Greetingss, Light'ss Daughter," it hissed in her left ear.

Then, the serpent spoke into her right ear. "We wissh to aid you."

"It has two heads!" Jarad said. "Can *everything* in this wood speak?"

"It is an amphisbaena," Sir Brennus said. "Heed not its words. It can't be trusted."

"Iss it we, who can't be trussted?" asked the snakehead over her right shoulder.

Then, the other hissed, "One of uss musst always sspeak truth. The other may deceive, but at leasst we are honesst in our deception. Unlike humanss."

"Yess," said the right-side head. "We would be a good companion for you. We can ssensse deceit in any creature."

Shivering, Lyssanne whispered, "How can one know which of you speaks true?"

"That iss the price." The head to her left wriggled, pinned beneath its coil. "You cannot be ss-certain which iss which."

"You need uss," said the other end of the creature, its voice soft, lulling. "You are too trussting. Your dessire to ssee the besst in otherss blindss you to their true natures."

"Beware falsse friendss," said the head on the left. "For, to trusst these, your companionss, could mean your life."

"My friends would not betray me thus," Lyssanne said, her voice growing heavy.

"No more than would I," said the head to her right.

As the creature spoke, something slid up her back. The tickling sensation relaxed her tensed muscles and sent a pleasant shiver along her skin. Her eyelids drooped.

"Ssleep…" hissed the serpent.

Had the creature's voice spoken near her right knee rather than in her ear? Its cold coil suddenly tightened around her neck. She gasped, lethargy evaporating. Breath refused to squeeze through her throat. She clawed at the icy coil with numb fingers, then her hand fell, limp, to her lap. Reina's distant whinny faded beneath the roaring in her ears.

THE NATURE OF THE BEAST

*D*ark spots danced before Lyssanne's eyes as she widened her jaw in a frantic bid for air.

With a sudden hiss, the serpent's head still pinned to her left shoulder struck at her throat—and missed. Its constricting coil stopped it just short of its goal.

A swift, metallic ringing pierced the roar in Lyssanne's ears. Air gusted past her cheek, an icy droplet slid down her collarbone, and the pressure at her throat eased. The cold body of the serpent, now two serpents, slid down her arms to the forest floor.

Gasping to fill her starved lungs, Lyssanne raised a trembling hand to her bruised throat. As involuntary tears spilled down her cheeks, she parted a rip in her collar that hadn't been there moments before. Cold moisture met her fingertips, and her breath hitched. Blood? She swiped at it with her sleeve and found the skin beneath unscathed. Not her blood, the serpent's.

She blinked up at Sir Brennus, who stood scant paces away, sword outstretched. So swift had been his blade, she hadn't seen it move. "Th-thank you," she said.

He remained silent, his gaze and the tip of his sword trained on the ground at her feet.

Lyssanne glanced down. To either side of her, lay the halved body of the creature. The next instant, the severed serpent slithered away from the tree!

A sudden, green glow engulfed the two segments of serpent, and they slid toward one another. The heads reared, tails writhing, and the green light flashed between them. The light dimmed, and Lyssanne blinked. The amphisbaena lay at her feet, intact.

"Beware your hero, Light'ss Daughter," it hissed. "Lesst it be your head nexst he sseverss."

"Yess," said the creature's other half. "And your head will not sso easily reattach."

"You should be dead!" Sir Brennus said, raising his sword for another blow.

The serpent took its body into one of its mouths, forming a circle, and rolled out of reach. "We can only be sslain beneath the eye of a full moon," said its free head, dangling like a charm. "By a man with pure heart and noble intention."

"The moon *is* full," Jarad said.

"Notice, we are sstill alive."

"You were cut asunder," Lyssanne said, heart pounding. "I felt your blood. How—?"

"Magic," Sir Brennus said between his teeth, the word a curse upon his lips.

He chased the rolling amphisbaena around their campsite, his sword gouging up tufts of grass with every swing. Serena joined the hunt, diving in to peck at the serpent then fluttering out of reach of the knight's blade. Lyssanne forgot to breathe as the dove narrowly escaped the flailing sword. The chase might have been comical, were it not so deadly.

"We are ssorry to have harmed you, Light'ss Daughter," the amphisbaena said, dodging the flashing blade as Sir Brennus swung from a different direction. "You are the truesst human we have met, though you are not alwayss honesst with yoursself."

"Then why'd you try to kill her?" Jarad shouted, letting fly an arrow. It sailed through the middle of the serpent-ring, only to plant itself in the grass.

"No one can change his true nature," said the amphisbaena. "Not even we." As the sword came closer than ever to striking, the serpent uttered a long, indignant hiss, then rolled into the nearby shrubbery. "Let thiss be a lesson to you, Light'ss Daughter," it said. "Trusst no one."

After a fizzing sound and another flash of green light, the bushes grew still.

"It vanished!" Jarad said. "One second it was there, then...nothing."

Serena pecked at the shrub then fluttered to the branch above Lyssanne.

"Infernal magical beasts," Sir Brennus muttered, sheathing his sword. He stared at the bush where the serpent had disappeared then flung his cape back over one shoulder as if tossing away an unpleasant thought. "Should be blotted from the face of the realm, the lot of them."

"*I* am considered a creature of magic, Sir Knight," said Reina.

He stilled then turned to her. "Your pardon, Shining One, but you are the sole exception."

Reina snorted.

Jarad ran to Lyssanne, dropped his bow, and knelt beside her. "Are you hurt? Did it bite you?" He gave her time only to shake her head. "I'm sorry. Everything happened so fast. I didn't dare shoot it in case I missed and hit you." His voice shook. "If Sir Brennus hadn't been here..."

"But he was here." She rested a hand on Jarad's shoulder then pushed to her feet. "Sir Brennus," she said in a small voice, "I—I know not how to thank you. You saved my life."

"Well, the unicorn appeared a bit distressed watching that serpent make a meal of you." He turned to Reina. "It seems I've acquired new linguistic skills since last we met."

"Such a worthy deed as you performed tonight deserves a reward," said Reina.

"Yes," Lyssanne said. "Gratitude may be a poor offering, but mine shall be eternal."

"Just don't expect a repeat performance." He stalked off toward the trees beyond the fire.

"Perhaps I was a bit hasty," Reina said. "Still, if you insist on hanging about, my speaking to you directly does make things easier."

"Touché." Sir Brennus swept Reina a deep bow. "You seem to be traveling south. A town lies a few days' journey in that direction. As I have business there, perhaps it would be prudent to pool our resources for the remainder of the trek."

Lyssanne stared at him, eyes wide. "You wish to travel with us?"

He nodded. "Bandits are rumored to lurk about the fringes of this forest."

"I have heard such rumors," Reina said. "Perhaps what you suggest is wise."

"After that snake," said Jarad. "I'd sure sleep better with an extra pair of eyes around."

"Doubtless, I shall find sleep elusive tonight," Lyssanne said. "I can assist in the watch."

"And risk exhausting yourself as you did last time?" Reina said. "Or worse, trigger a recurrence of that head pain? Absolutely not. The young men and I shall do well enough."

"It is settled then," Sir Brennus said. "I shall ride ahead each day to scout the terrain. What with one of you afoot at all times, my greater speed shall be to our advantage. I am skilled in blending into my surroundings and can avoid notice, should I come upon outlaws."

Before anyone could respond, he slipped in among the trees. Moments later, he emerged, leading a massive horse. He passed Lyssanne and Reina, guiding the dark steed to the spring.

Lyssanne suppressed a shudder. She would have found Reina's height imposing if not for her gentleness, but Sir Brennus's horse… Doubtless, such animals were bred to intimidate as well as bear the weight of armored knights into battle.

Why had she not seen the steed when they'd met Sir Brennus the previous night? The limits of her sight notwithstanding, surely even she couldn't have failed to notice something as large and clamorous as a horse.

Sir Brennus looped his reins over a low branch. "You will see little of me during the day," he said, "but I shall leave signs to indicate whether the way ahead is safe." He turned to Jarad. "Come, boy. Let us catch our dinner, and I shall teach you the rudiments of tracking."

Jarad glanced from the knight to Lyssanne, unmoving.

She nodded. "Go on."

He shouldered his bow but still hesitated.

"All is well, Jarad," Reina said in that rippling voice which, even now, eased Lyssanne's tight muscles. "The amphisbaena is far from here. We are quite safe."

The following evening, Noire stood in the shadows of the forest just beyond Lyssanne's campsite, his form that of neither bird nor man. Would he ever accustom himself to this wispy body the absence of the sun's touch forced upon him? At least the effects of Venefica's botched spell were confined to the hours of daylight.

"Have you seen Sir Brennus?" Lyssanne asked, grasping Jarad's arm.

"I caught a glimpse of him from far off this morning," Jarad said. "He was in the shadow of some trees, but it had to be him. That horse of his is enormous."

She nodded then gathered up the dry limbs and bits of wood Jarad had dropped in the center of the clearing. As the boy disappeared into the trees for his evening hunt, she sighed, setting her burden next to the fire he'd started.

"Something troubles you, child," said the unicorn.

"I think I offended Sir Brennus somehow," Lyssanne said. "He seemed so aloof, almost angry, all last evening."

"I sense our noble friend has fought many battles," Reina said, "not least of which, the one he fights within himself." She tossed her head. "I am no seer, nor privy to any creature's precise thoughts, but I suspect his anger had little to do with you…at least, not with anything you've said or done."

Lyssanne eased a splintered limb onto the dwindling fire. "Why did that serpent attack me?" she asked, backing away as the flames licked at the wood, consuming their newest prey. "I did nothing to threaten or harm it."

"I suspect, only part of the amphisbaena meant you harm."

"Oh, I don't know," Lyssanne said, "a great portion of it was intent on choking me, and the rest thought it quite amusing to bite me. Thank the King, that didn't go as planned."

"It was not you the amphisbaena tried to strike," Reina said. "Rather, that head was aiming for its brother, but the weight of its own midsection hindered it. I believe, in the last instant, the creature attempted to protect you from itself."

"How could it have two utterly opposing wishes at once?"

Reina tossed her head. "Is such not the very bane and nature of mankind? Why should a creature of legend be any different?"

Noire slipped a pace closer, but they'd lapsed into silence, Lyssanne resuming her work on the fire. Holding her breath, she eased a shard of wood toward the burning logs as if unsure just how close her hand was to the flames. Sparks shot upward, and she snatched her hand away. The wood balanced on the stack of logs for a moment, then slid off.

"Try that long limb," Reina said. "Lay it atop the others a little to the right…No, too far."

Lyssanne repositioned the limb as directed. When she released it, this one remained in place. "Thank you," she said. "I just can't stand near enough to see where the logs should go." She dragged a sleeve across her brow. "How do you know so much about building fires?"

"I have watched Jarad."

Lyssanne smiled. "I know not how I would manage without the two of you."

"It is unnecessary to wonder such, for you are not without us." Reina's fathomless gaze rested upon Lyssanne for a long moment. "Something more weighs upon your spirit, child."

"I can't stop thinking of that strange mist. You know, the darkness I told you of?"

The unicorn nodded.

"It may sound foolish, but I cannot erase the feeling they are all in danger, Aderyn and Mr. DeLivre, and...everyone. That mist," she whispered, "'tis not natural."

"There is nothing you can do for them at present," Reina said. "You do well to think of others, but you must see to your own needs, else you will be of help to no one."

Lyssanne sighed. "I'm certain you are right." She walked over to her cart, where the dove had perched. Gazing off into the distance, she stroked Serena's head. "I'm having the dreams again," she murmured. "Two nights, now. That probably accounts for these dark thoughts."

Noire folded shadowy arms across his chest. She should heed the unicorn, unless she wished to endure much worse than she had thus far. "Forget the Shadow Mist," he whispered, "and pray it forgets about you."

Lyssanne's head swiveled, as if she sensed someone near.

Noire slunk deeper into the shadows. He needn't have concerned himself, though. She wouldn't be able to see him at this distance, even should she look in his precise direction.

She hastened back toward the perceived security of her fire's increasing brightness.

Increasing? Noire glanced up at the sky and tensed. Sunset approached. The boy would soon return from his hunt, and so must the knight who traveled with them.

Noire slipped from the shadows, unseen and unheard. The moment waning sunlight fell upon his travesty of a body, he took to the air, feather-clad and again in possession of all senses.

Lyssanne lowered her ceremonial shawl from her hair while Jarad struggled to read a difficult passage in the *Kingsword*. After hours of travel, she longed to pass this Kingsday evening in prayer and rest. If only she hadn't come to dread the awkwardness of night.

Sir Brennus sat on the other side of the fire, as he had each evening for the past week, sharpening his sword or tending other weapons. He spoke little upon his returns from scouting, and that, often in mocking tones. Though Lyssanne insisted Jarad read aloud each night, she refrained from doing the same, lest she give the knight further fuel to ignite his sarcastic tongue.

"Why do people make words so long?" Jarad asked, sighing. "Everybody knows, if you string up too many fish, your line'll break. So, why stick so many letters together?"

Hiding a smile, she folded her shawl. "Sometimes, a long word can say much more than several short ones." A thought struck her. "Jarad, how long has it been since you've written?"

He handed her the *Kingsword*. "Don't think I've wrote anything since...well, since you got sick." He looked off toward the fire. "Yeah, ain't had a reason since then."

Lyssanne frowned. "Well, we must remedy that." How could Niklette have neglected such a vital skill? "We have no parchment," she said, "but a good stick and this loosened dirt will suffice. Why not begin with that inconveniently long word? See if you can better convey its meaning with others of your choosing. I shall return in a bit to admire your progress."

She stood and strolled between the thinning trees. After several successive nights' poor slumber, privacy and prayer might restore her spirits. Though she struggled not to show it, especially in front of Jarad, fatigue was draining more than her physical strength. Yet another reason to thank the King for Jarad's presence. If pretense prevented her giving in, so be it.

"Always the teacher, even in this uncivilized place?"

She jumped at the sound of Sir Brennus's voice so close behind. Her right heel landed on a root, folding her ankle like the pages of a book. Sir Brennus caught her arm, interrupting an unintentional curtsey that doubtless would have been less than graceful.

"You startled me," she said, breathless.

"Obviously."

She pulled away. "H-how do you know I was a teacher? I don't recall speaking of it."

"Perhaps the boy mentioned it," he said, glancing toward their camp. "Or was it the unicorn?" He turned to face her. "What does it matter?"

"It doesn't, I suppose," she said, her voice steadier. "I was only surprised you'd learned of it, while I know next to nothing about you."

"There is next to nothing to know," he said. "I am as you see me."

"A lone knight," she intoned, as if reciting an ancient tale, "wandering the wilds, searching…For what? Himself?"

"Perhaps, in a way," he said. "Though, my life is far less than the grand adventure your words would make of it."

"Oh, I don't know," she said, enjoying their conversation's light turn—and, for once, his presence. "You narrowly escape crossing swords with a unicorn, run afoul of inept travelers, save me from a two-headed snake—a *talking* two-headed snake," she amended, "and endure the torture of evenings spent listening to my dull stories. Surely, such is the stuff of legend."

He laughed. "I wouldn't call your tales dull. Fanciful, perhaps, but your own enjoyment compels one to listen…for a time." He leaned against a tree, arms crossed, surveying her.

Never comfortable with close scrutiny, she looked away.

"As to the rest," he said, "I'd be mad to want Reina as an enemy, and the boy has increased much in skill since first I met you."

"Yes, Jarad has a sharp mind. He has always learned quickly, whatever the task."

"We are nearing the fringes of the forest," Sir Brennus said, his usual gravity returning. "It continues its southward march alongside the trading village I mentioned."

"How far do you suppose that village is?" she asked. Might she at last find a home?

"You should reach the forest's edge before nightfall on the morrow, but the village is a few miles beyond. I would advise camping under cover of the trees and starting for the town the following day. It would be safer."

She tensed. "Have you seen signs of trouble? Perhaps we should change direction."

"I've surveyed the area thoroughly," he said, straightening. "If there were outlaws in these parts, they've long since gone."

He moved past her, toward their camp. Lyssanne followed close at his heels.

"It shouldn't take you more than another half-day to reach the town," he said as they emerged near the campfire. "I shall go on ahead in the morning. My business can't wait."

"You're leaving us?" Jarad asked, looking up from his work.

"You'll be safe enough," said Sir Brennus, "even if you camp one more night."

After dispensing with supper, they all settled around the fire. Lyssanne folded her legs beneath her skirts and propped her elbows on her knees. Even days after the amphisbaena's attack, she remained wary of reclining beneath trees. Quite inconvenient, that, since weariness made sitting unsupported a trial. She rested her chin in cupped hands and closed her eyes.

Reina settled at Lyssanne's back, laying her head upon outstretched forelegs. "Lean against me, child," she said. "The company will do us both good."

Serena landed in Lyssanne's lap, as Jarad asked Sir Brennus what noble quest he pursued.

"There are no noble quests," said the knight. "The time for such ended long ago."

Jarad poked at the fire with a long stick. "We're on a noble quest."

"Seeking what?"

"A new home for Lady Lyssanne."

Why must he mention that to this relative stranger? Lyssanne sensed eyes boring into her. She kept her own averted, pretending to pluck nonexistent debris from Serena's feathers.

"Once this...quest is at an end," said Sir Brennus, "where will *you* make your home?"

Jarad hesitated. "With her, I guess."

"That is no noble quest."

Jarad jumped to his feet. Lyssanne tensed, but Sir Brennus merely lifted a hand.

"Do not mistake me," he said. "Your search may be necessary, but to truly be noble, a quest must hold no benefit for the one embarking upon it."

"Then, what do you get out of yours?" Jarad snapped. "You *are* on a quest?"

"I am," Sir Brennus said, his tone darkening. "The lady for whom I journey has promised a boon. As I said, there are no noble quests." He fixed his gaze upon the fire. "I should know."

"Have you even tried to find one? Isn't that a knight's job?"

"Jarad!" Lyssanne said. "Let him be."

"You have much to learn, boy," Sir Brennus said. "There is far more to being a knight than what you've heard in tales." He crossed to the other side of the fire and bent over his belongings. "Yes, I once searched for such a quest. As did my father and his father before him, for as many generations as years you have lived." His blanket snapped as he whipped it open. "I'll take second watch." He stretched out upon his bedding and turned his back to them.

8

WESTERFIELD

"*L*ooks like a market," Jarad said, as he and Lyssanne approached the center of the town, "but it can't be Marketday already. We just celebrated Kingsday."

"Perhaps we were mistaken," Lyssanne said. "We've lost track."

"Nah, I've been countin'. It's been six weeks since we left Cloist–, uh, the valley."

That was the closest either of them had come to speaking the name of their erstwhile home in a month.

"Six weeks," Lyssanne said, expelling a breath. She turned, shielding her eyes in an attempt to glimpse the outline of the trees against the afternoon sky. "'Tis little wonder no one ventures to the valley through the forest."

"Yeah," Jarad said. "Can you imagine having to climb that hill west of the cliff?"

"You did."

"Sure, but I wasn't carryin' nut'n—"

"Anything."

"*Anything*, when I went back up for our stuff. And I'd been drinking Reina's water." He sighed. "Wish we had more of that."

"As do I." She turned, and they resumed their pace.

"Think Reina really can disguise herself as an ordinary mare like she said?" he asked. "I mean, she didn't seem happy about us leaving her and Serena behind."

"I suspect we've seen but few of her gifts," Lyssanne said as they neared the throng cramming the streets ahead. "Perhaps this town holds a midweek market."

"Why would they do that?" Jarad asked, then he called to the man nearest. "Pardon, sir, but is today Marketday?"

"Every day is market day in Westerfield!"

Lyssanne and Jarad waded into the sea of people. Lyssanne squeezed past a woman, who turned at the same instant, her elbow shoving Lyssanne into the back of the man ahead of her.

She freed her nose and mouth from his rough tunic, muttering, "I beg your pardon, sir."

Soon, the abundance of elbows, shoulders, and upper arms vying for a perch atop Lyssanne's nose forced her to walk with her chin tilted toward the sky.

At last, she broke through the press of bodies and inhaled as if emerging from deep water. Never had she imagined her slight stature could render the simple act of breathing difficult.

The square opened up before her, and she stared, wide-eyed. A plethora of stalls lined both sides of the street, their vendors crying out to passersby.

"Fresh bread! Just baked this morn!"

"Get your saddle oil here. Best in the West Country!"

"Cloth for sale! Cheap or fine, we got it all here."

The street was awash in color. A mixture of brightly- and plainly-dressed patrons swirled by on all sides. Goods hung from lines above stalls, overflowed from baskets, and covered tabletops. The multitude of colors and the chaos of rapid movement made her head swim. Cloistervale could be a busy place on Marketday, but there, she'd known what she was seeing. Besides, this place had to be four times the size of Cloistervale's Market Square.

"Look," Jarad shouted into her ear. "A man just gave that woman three copper coins for a peach!"

She leaned closer, struggling to make out his words above the shouts of peddlers, chatter of townsfolk, and various animal noises.

"So odd," he said, "givin' somebody bits of metal for food. Is that a lot to pay?"

"'Tis more than we can spare," she said. The little bag of coins Mr. DeLivre had slipped into her cart might have to last them days, or even weeks, if she didn't find employment soon.

As if to mock her thoughts, her stomach rumbled at the mouthwatering aromas of spiced meats, herbed sauces, yeast, and tangy fruits surrounding her. Then, the breeze shifted, and the vinegary scent of dye stung her nose and eyes. The odors of sweating men and horses, oiled leather, and some bitter stench mingled with the dye, stirring her stomach's rumble into an unpleasant churning. She couldn't have eaten at that moment even if she'd had the coin to spare.

Her overwrought senses needed a point of focus. She squeezed Jarad's arm. "This way," she said, pulling him toward the first open space she spotted.

A rainbow of shawls hung from poles at one end of the stall. Lyssanne ran a finger down the nearest. It was finely woven, but not as intricate as her mother's.

"Two silvers for that one, dear," the vendor said, "but I don't think yellow suits you." Her head bobbed as if she were examining Lyssanne for flaws. "Oh my, you are in need of a better fastener for that cloak. A stickpin!" She shook her bright red curls and placed an intricate, ivory broach before Lyssanne. "You'll not find one finer, or for a better price, in all of Westerfield."

"I'm certain you are right, madam," Lyssanne said, "but what I am really looking for is employment. Might you know of anyone in need of an extra pair of hands?"

The woman replaced the broach among other trinkets whose use, aside from pleasing the eye, Lyssanne couldn't fathom. "Farmer Crowder was looking for someone to man his vegetable stand, just up the street there, with the sign of the open hand hanging in front."

"With the red awning?" Jarad asked.

"That's the place. He just hired someone, but that's the sign you'll want to look for."

"Thank you," Lyssanne said.

"Well, if anyone hires you, just you be sure to come back here for that cloak pin."

Lyssanne and Jarad made their way back into the bustling street, Jarad promising to keep watch for more signs of the open hand advertising a position for hire.

Just then, a man's voice called something Lyssanne couldn't make out. The sudden rush of people jostling to get to his stall nearly knocked her over. Only the vendor's arm remained visible, raised high above the heads of the pressing throng. A frenzy of hands grabbed for whatever he held aloft.

Across the way, two men bellowed at each other over the price of a hunting knife, and farther up the street, a woman screamed.

"Stop him!" a man shouted. "He cut my wife's purse."

Several men rushed past Lyssanne in the direction of the shouts.

As the afternoon wore on, Lyssanne and Jarad passed countless stalls, some selling familiar goods, others offering items they'd never seen. A woodcarver's stand conjured thoughts of Aderyn and brought the sting of unshed tears to her throat. So many people grappled over the wares, she was certain Kevan's talent would have flourished in this place.

Everywhere, angry voices argued over costs. Lyssanne's shoulders tensed and threatened to remain thus for eternity. Even in the past year, such hostility had never plagued Cloistervale.

Twice, her cart was overturned. The second time, a man helped her right it. "You should mind your things more closely, mistress," he said. "A cart like this is easy pickin's for a thief. A boy could lift yer belongings, and you'd be none the wiser."

"Thank you. I shall remember that."

'Twas a strange feeling, this need to guard one's possessions against theft. Lyssanne longed to leave this place, but what would become of them if she failed to find employment?

She glanced around to ask Jarad if he'd seen any more postings for hire, but he had vanished. Turning on the spot, she searched every face, every swirl of color. Her throat seized up. Where was he? She called to him, straining her eyes to their limits.

A man moved aside, revealing the curve of a bow silhouetted against a light-gray tunic. Lyssanne rushed forward. Jarad stood before a stall, head tilted as if in concentration.

"Jarad," Lyssanne said, "I thought I'd lost you."

"I was here," he murmured. "Can you believe there are so many kinds?" He stared at the knives and daggers arrayed atop the black cloth covering the table before them.

Lyssanne glanced at the swords bristling from stands behind it. "We should keep searching," she said, her strength fading as the hour grew later. She pointed to a nearby intersection. "Have we gone down that end of the square?"

"Don't think so," he said. "Oh, there's a scribe's shop halfway along that street."

Lyssanne's spirits rose as they neared the shop. From all she'd seen, she suspected few in Westerfield could read or write. Even their scarce signs bore pictures to convey their messages.

A bell tinkled as Lyssanne opened the door, and the scribe glanced up from behind a table littered with piles of parchment, inkwells, and candlesticks.

"I'll get to your needs as soon as I can," he said. "I'm only one man, after all."

"There's no hurry, sir," she said. Ah, a chance to catch her breath and rest her tired eyes!

"Well, I *am* in a rush," said a woman leaning over the scribe's desk. "I want to send this message with the courier to the royal city. He says he'll leave for Etoilia tomorrow, early."

"You'll just have to wait, madam," said a man lounging against the wall beside the scribe, his dark cloak and hat blending with the dimness. "I've waited a week for Mr. Waxler to have time for me and my letter. Now, if you'll excuse us, I'd like him to read it to me in private."

"I beg your pardon, er, Mr. Waxler, is it?" Lyssanne said. "Perhaps I could be of service."

"How's that?" the scribe asked, rubbing the bridge of his nose.

"I'm skilled in reading and writing. If you are interested in an apprentice or assistant, I'd be pleased to work with you."

"An assistant," the scribe said, "hmm." He eyed her for a moment. "*You* can read?"

"Yes, sir, and write as well."

"I've no time to test your word at present," he said. "Come back first thing on the morrow. If what you say is true, we shall discuss terms. If not, the magistrate can sort you out."

"As you wish." She hastened from the shop, uncertain what to make of the scribe's abrupt manner and allusion to the magistrate. Still, she grinned. Had she found a place at last?

～

As Lyssanne exited the scribe's shop, Noire squeezed into the gap between two buildings. The space was little more than a slash of shadow—but then, so was he.

Slipping along the street behind Lyssanne and Jarad, he took care to keep even a hint of sunlight from touching his nebulous body. This proved difficult, often forcing him to melt partway into the façade of a building, but he wanted no one aware of his presence —yet.

Lyssanne rounded the corner, and a squat, bedraggled peddler called out, "Oy, mistress!"

Jarad nudged her. "That man's waving at us."

Her glance was all the encouragement the peddler needed. "Fine trinkets, I have. Talismans to ward off illness, to draw love, to bring luck."

Lyssanne seemed keen to pass on by, but Jarad stopped to stare at the carved lead charms, graven bronze discs, assorted animal teeth, bones, claws, packets of pungent herbs tied with thongs, and other sundry trinkets littering the peddler's table.

"Taught by the Shaman o' the Wood, was I," the peddler said. "You've heard o' him, I'd wager."

"I've not had the pleasure," Lyssanne said, her tone polite but cautious.

Noire slithered into the shadow of a low-hanging awning behind the peddler.

"Oh, he's powerful wise, is the shaman," the man said. "Lives t'other side o' the forest, at the edge of Gian Plain. At the edge o' this world an' the next, if y'ask me."

Something shifted in Lyssanne's eyes. She tugged at Jarad's elbow. "We must be going."

"Can I show the young miss nothing?" the peddler asked. "An amulet, perhaps, to preserve your ethereal beauty?"

Lyssanne shook her head and moved past the stall.

The peddler fumbled among his wares, snatched up a carved bit of wood, and ran to Lyssanne. He thrust the trinket toward her then froze. "What charm is this?" His fingers hovered over the star-shaped pendant she always wore. "'Tis you," he said on a breath, "the fallen star who shines!" He glanced at Jarad. "And her stalwart protector. I've a message for you."

"For us? Here?" Lyssanne said. "From whom?"

"The one who causes you to shine." The peddler fished in a belt pouch then passed Jarad a tiny roll of parchment. He turned to Lyssanne and took her pendant in his grubby hand. "This is a powerful talisman," he said. "Aye, it carries the love of dear friends. Potent magic, that."

Lyssanne stepped back, wresting the pendant from his grasp. The instant her fingers brushed his, the peddler jolted. His eyes widened until only their whites showed.

"Darkness stalks you," he whispered. "A powerful darkness has already touched you. Beware the Shadows that take fog as form. The weapon of your enemy...shadow and spirit, are they. Anger, fear, despair—such are their sustenance and secretion."

Lyssanne backed away several paces, her face pale.

"You need protection. Aye, powerful protection." The peddler's ominous demeanor changed to brisk businesslike excitement. "I have just the thing!" He pulled Lyssanne toward his stall. "It'll only cost you one silver." He snatched up a rather foul-looking claw on a chord. "The talon of a griffin, sure protection from all manner o' calamity."

Griffin talon indeed! That was nothing more than a lion's claw painted red with a poisonous-looking green vein running down it. Noire had seen this man's like in dozens of towns throughout the Seven Lands, selling worthless trinkets and fueling obscure superstitions.

"No, no, thank you," Lyssanne said, backing away from the peddler. "I don't believe in such things. Your concern is kind, all the same."

The peddler's face grew livid. "Don't believe, eh?" he shouted. "You'll believe soon enough. Then, you'll wish you'd accepted a poor peddler's generosity!"

Taking advantage of the distraction the man's shouts caused, Noire eased from the shadows, allowing the waning sunlight to touch him and embracing the raven within.

Lyssanne hurried farther into the busy marketplace, pulling Jarad along with her.

"Did you see the stuff that man was selling?" Jarad asked.

"Not so closely as to tell much about it," Lyssanne said. "I'm not sure I'd wish to."

They moved on, away from the addled talisman peddler and heedless of the shadow that stalked them by air.

Night had fallen by the time Lyssanne and Jarad neared the last stalls and shops. He suddenly clasped her arm, cutting her yawn short. "I think that's...It is! Sir Brennus!" He ran to meet the tall figure striding toward them.

"A good evening to you, Jarad." The knight's deep, familiar tones washed over Lyssanne like a welcome rain. "It is unwise to linger in the marketplace after dark," he said. "I doubt your lady would wish to keep company with anyone she'd meet here at this hour."

As he and Jarad drew near, Lyssanne curtseyed. "Sir Brennus."

He inclined his head to her. "This market can be taxing. Have you procured lodgings?"

"Not as yet," she said. Was her weariness so evident?

"If you like," said Sir Brennus, "I shall show you to an inn I discovered yestereve. The innkeeper seems honest and serves a passable supper."

"The supper part suits me," Jarad said.

His stomach chose that moment to voice its agreement, and they all laughed.

Sir Brennus led them through a maze of streets that seemed designed to get one lost.

When they stopped before the inn's wide door, Jarad peered up at its sign. "Field's End?"

"I've seen more peculiar names for an inn," Sir Brennus said, ushering them inside.

Scattered candles and oil lamps shed watery light through the dim interior. Slowly, tables and a long counter solidified out of the gloom. Glasses clinked, men laughed, wood scraped on wood, and voices rose and fell in conversation.

A slight woman bustled up to them, her grey hair pulled back so severely, Lyssanne at first thought she had none. "Sir Brennus, back for another night, eh? And who is this you've brought me? More guests?" She looked Lyssanne and Jarad over. "Just meals or lodgings, too?"

"Both," he said. "Lyssanne, Jarad, may I present the owner of this fine establishment."

"Oh, you do flatter, but your courtly ways won't reduce my fee." Laughing, the innkeeper turned to Lyssanne. "Brija Vivva-Beh, at your service. We're nearly full, but for friends of Sir Brennus, I'm sure we'll find something. Now, follow me. I'll get you a table."

"What does the name mean?" Jarad asked. "The one above the door?"

"A place of rest after a long day's toil," Madam Vivva-Beh said. "I changed the name after my husband died. Thought it more appealing than 'The House of Beh.' Here ya are, then." She swiped a cloth from her shoulder and passed it over a table.

"Brija, love!" a man said from across the room. "Forgotten me already?"

"Get yourselves settled," said the innkeeper. "I'll be back in a moment."

They sank onto sturdy, wooden chairs, Lyssanne and Jarad glancing about. The room was full to bursting with people, rattling dishes, and pipe-smoke. Raucous laughter spilled from one corner, and a man yelled for more ale. So drippy was his voice, he'd likely consumed several flagons already. A younger woman with thick, dark hair wove among the tables, filling cups and jesting with the patrons. Two men began arguing nearby. One fell from his chair, then stood unsteadily and punched his companion.

"Angus!" Madam Vivva-Beh shouted from another part of the room.

A man the size of Lyssanne's storage cupboard lifted both the yelling patrons by their tunics and dragged them from the inn.

"The way you two stare," Sir Brennus said, "one would think you'd never seen an inn."

"One would be correct," Lyssanne said, her cheeks aflame.

"Where, then, did you sleep during your previous travels? Surely you do not always journey through forests."

"This is the farthest I've ventured from my home. I've never before had the need."

"Yet you travel all but alone?" he said. "Odd that so sheltered a *lady* should do so."

"I must apologize for the delay," Madam Vivva-Beh said, coming up behind Sir Brennus. "We're short-staffed tonight. May be a bit of a wait for your supper." She wiped her hands on the cloth draped over her shoulder. "Now, you'll be wantin' rooms for yourself and the boy, eh, mistress? Supper and breakfast, as well? That'll be three silvers and two coppers for the lot. I'll collect and find you rooms after you've eaten." She bustled off without awaiting a reply.

"How much do we have?" Jarad murmured to Lyssanne.

"Ten silvers and a handful of coppers."

Something must have shown on Sir Brennus's face, for Jarad asked him, "Is that not worth much?"

"How can it be, that you do not know the value of coins?"

"They are not used in our village," Lyssanne said. "Rather, we trade in goods and labors. Only the traveling merchant ever pays us in coin. That, we trade to the Council, who use it to pay the annual tax to the realm."

"How, precisely, does this trading in labors work?"

"Well, I might, let us say, grow flowers," she said. "These I may trade to the chandler for candles or soap. She, in turn, uses them to scent her wares."

"What, then, if you have all the candles you need but no bread?"

"Perchance the baker needs candles, so I'd trade my extras with him," she said, "but it isn't always a one-to-one exchange. As long as we do our part to serve the village, citizens may have whatever we need."

"So, everything is, what, rationed out?"

"Not exactly," she said. How could she explain this? "Over the years, the Council has determined how much bread or how many eggs might be needful to sustain a person in good health for the week. Still, let's say I've a desire for a sweet pastry. I might perform an extra deed for the baker or trade something for it."

"That seems a strange life," Sir Brennus said.

"Not as strange as thinking bits of metal are as valuable as food," Jarad said.

Their supper arrived, and Lyssanne could have wept at the aroma. Pan-seared chicken crusted with herbs, green beans, boiled potatoes, and a thick slice of apple tart greeted her ravenous eyes. Never had she been so pleased to see green beans, the first cooked vegetable she'd eaten since leaving Cloistervale.

Jarad must have felt much the same, for he ate without pause. Only after devouring his tart did he draw breath. "D'you think that man, the one selling all those charms and stuff, d'you think he was right about your pendant being magic?"

Sir Brennus set his fork down, slowly, the touch of his gaze boring into Lyssanne.

"No, Jarad," she said. "That sounds too much like sorcery."

Jarad reached down beside his chair, where he'd stashed his bow and quiver. He straightened, holding a slender tube. "Been wondering what this is," he said, untying the string binding the rolled parchment. He eyed the contents then whistled. "Looks like a riddle."

"It is best we entertain no thought of that man or his offerings," Lyssanne said.

"You must hear this, though," he said, then began to read. "Seek out the bird whose bark is the soul of wisdom, that lion who has flown through every age. The copper wings that unite earth and sky carry words to set the Darkness ablaze. Seek out the King's message where the sun lays its head in snow and sea. For you and all, one hope remains. Seek it beyond the granite tree."

"The *King's* message?" Lyssanne reached for the parchment.

As she read and reread the odd lines, Sir Brennus excused himself, and Madam Vivva-Beh returned to fill their juice goblets.

"Can our horse stay in your barn tonight?" Jarad asked.

"If there's an empty stall. You'll have to buy your own feed. I don't supply that."

Once the innkeeper was out of earshot, Jarad said, "I figured we should let Reina know we're safe. I can go get her and Serena. Uh, if that's your wish."

"Do you know the way?" Lyssanne asked, dropping the odd riddle into her cart.

Jarad nodded then hurried off.

Lyssanne stacked their plates and carried them to the front of the room. As she neared the long counter, her arms threatened to give way. She caught the plates against her stomach.

Suddenly, a pair of arms encircled her from behind, strong hands covering her own. She flinched, again almost dropping the plates.

"Easy," Sir Brennus murmured into her hair. "Allow me to assist you." He took the plates and set them atop the counter.

"Thank you."

"You're nearly asleep on your feet, Lyssanne," he said. "Why are you doing this? It is the duty of the inn's staff to clear the dishes."

"Oh," she said. "I suppose 'tis the fault of long habit, cleaning after one's own mess."

"That may be, but I'm certain the innkeeper wouldn't take kindly to broken dishes." He inclined his head. "I bid you a good night. I must be about business quite early."

An hour later, Jarad returned, and Madam Vivva-Beh escorted them down a corridor to a door, which opened onto the rear yard. The barn stood in the left corner, but the innkeeper led them to a small shed beside it. As they crossed the yard, wings beat overhead, stirring Lyssanne's hair. Serena settled on her shoulder. Stroking the dove's feathers, Lyssanne followed Jarad into the shed.

"I use this room for storage," the innkeeper said. "There's still enough space for you to bed down." She turned to Lyssanne and held up her lamp. "The boy'll have to sleep in the barn. Your bird, too. I'll have no animal indoors to spill its droppings on my goods. When you get that settled, come back up to the inn, and I'll give you a clean straw mat."

"A straw mat?" Jarad said. "For all those coins, she should have a real bed."

"All my *real* beds, as you call them, are full," said Madam Vivva-Beh, "with people of rank or means. What, you want I should kick one of them out so you can sleep indoors? Humph." She handed Lyssanne the lamp and walked to the door. "Why a fine young knight like Sir Brennus associates with the likes of you, I can't fathom. Mayhap, part of his knightly oath—mercy and charity and all that rubbish."

"The likes of what?" Jarad snapped. "Anybody'd be lucky to have—"

"Hush, Jarad," Lyssanne whispered. "Madam Vivva-Beh is being most generous."

The innkeeper made a noise in her throat and stomped from the shed.

"I'll get that mat," Jarad said. "I'd take Serena, but she won't go to anyone except you."

"Be civil," she warned as they left the shed.

In the barn, Lyssanne coaxed Serena to perch on Reina's stall, then she returned to the shed. Setting her lamp on a crate near the door, she surveyed the room. A pile of old clothes lay in one corner, between the crates stacked along the walls. She walked over to a bare spot beneath the shuttered window opposite the door. She would sleep there. Any number of foul things might be nesting in that pile of rags, and who knew what was in the crates?

"This isn't much better than sleeping outside," Jarad said from the doorway. He held out the mat. "And there, you don't have to pay for your straw bed."

"This will suffice," she said, taking the mat. "I daresay I'm weary enough to sleep on the bare floor. Besides, here we needn't worry about forest beasts."

After Jarad left, she fell fully clothed upon the straw. So swift was slumber's descent, she failed to extinguish her lamp.

In the depths of night, something startled Lyssanne awake. She sat up, listening. The lamp had burned low, casting shadows from the crates along the wall and something darker at the foot of her mat. Wait, nothing had been in that corner when she'd lain down.

Then, the shadow moved.

Something stung her leg, and she yelped. Two enormous, wing-like shapes unfurled from the shadow. It moved into the light, and she screamed.

A human-like head hovered over her—red, hairless, and glistening. Black, dragon-esque wings curved around Lyssanne's mat like a dark tent. She couldn't see the monster's eyes in the gloom, but was almost certain it had three of them.

Lyssanne tried to back away. She couldn't move! Fire coursed up her legs from the spot where the creature had stung her, and her muscles wouldn't obey her thoughts.

The beast leaned over her, the fin-like ridges on its back silhouetted against the lamplight. She shrank against the straw, struggling to escape its fetid breath.

The fire in her veins coursed up past her waist. The creature's fangs clicked like knitting needles, and something cold and sticky tickled her ankles. If she could still feel her limbs, why couldn't she move them?

Two tentacles twined around her ankles and lifted them high. Lamplight glittered off a shimmery...something...wrapping itself around her legs. The burning sensation and paralysis moved up to her neck, constricting her throat and cutting off her attempted scream.

Her heart hammered as the shimmery wrap spun up her body. Its sticky fibers pinned her arms to her sides, up to the elbows. Tears ran down her cheeks as she struggled to move or to call for help. What would that creature do once she was completely encased in its cocoon?

Oh, King of All Lands, deliver me!

A creak drew Lyssanne's eyes—the one part she could still move— toward the door. It stood open. Was that...Jarad? *No! Go back! Oh King, keep him safe.*

Jarad held up a hand, waving it in broad motions, then he *left.*

The monster's great wings beat the air, distracting Lyssanne from her irrational sense of betrayal. The creature soared above her, blocking the lamplight, then settled near her head. A dark purple tentacle lifted her limp upper body, and the beast wrapped her in more sticky fibers.

She caught a fleeting glimpse of its bulbous, insectile torso, covered in glistening red scales, then her head lolled back on her limp neck. The room flipped upside down. Her stomach flipped with it. The creature's rancid, fishlike stench drew bile into her throat, but her constricted airway wouldn't let it pass. At least she wouldn't be sick on herself, however much her head might bounce.

Just beyond the tip of her nose, three hairy, jointed legs wriggled like those of a grossly enlarged spider.

And she was to be its fly.

That thought was her last before the shimmery threads covered her nose and eyes.

9

DIORNIAN

Breathe. That one thought whispered past the pounding in Lyssanne's ears. *Just breathe.*

The cocoon's threads molded to every dip and curve of her face, pulling at her skin with each breath she managed to squeeze in or out. She forced herself to inhale slowly, lest she draw the fibers into her nostrils. As it was, the damp heat of her exhalations was the only air available. Each recycled breath left her more lightheaded than the last.

The web surrounding her body had hardened, and she no longer struggled to move, saving all strength for breathing. How long would the fibers covering her face remain pliant?

With a sudden jolt, her head and shoulders dropped to the mat, the straw no cushion from the impact. Then, something yanked at her hair. Her heart pounded against her chest, as she longed to beat at the cocoon. That creature was wrapping the top of her head in the web! Soon, she'd be entirely encased in it. Her scant remaining breath evaporated.

A muffled sound reached her ears. Voices? The tugging at her hair ceased, then air whipped at her scalp, as if the creature had rushed past.

Someone screamed, a dull thud jolted the ground, and another voice cried out. Jarad? Then came a scuffling noise, the ring of metal, and—Was that a man's voice?

Jarad shouted near her ear, "Just hold on, Lady Lyssanne. I'll cut you out of there. Don't move."

As if she had a choice. She prayed whatever had distracted the monster would continue to do so, long enough for Jarad to get to safety.

With a deafening *scrape, scrape*, a sawing sensation vibrated the cocoon over her right arm. Then, Jarad shouted, "Sir Brennus! I can't cut through it!"

Sir Brennus? Well, that explained the ringing metal. Whatever the knight might have said, Lyssanne couldn't hear for the ringing in her ears. She must be running out of air. Her gasps grew shallow, and she was losing the thread of her thoughts. A jolt and loud clang shook her prison. More shouts, and then, and then…

A bang roused Lyssanne from her black daze. A sudden crash rolled her onto her left side. Something sharp pierced her right arm.

The cocoon softened and squished against her skin. Nausea rose into her throat as the sticky wetness slid against her face, her lips, everywhere. The sharp object wrenched free of her arm, and hands began tearing at the cocoon over the wound.

At last, she could breathe! Her eyes flew open. A shadow loomed over her. Through the haze of her terror, it slowly resolved into Jarad. *Not the monster.*

"She's alive!" he shouted over the scuffling noises filling the shed. "Are you injured?"

Lyssanne tried to answer, but the invisible vice remained around her throat. She settled for rapid blinking.

"Can you hear me?" Jarad asked, rolling her onto her back. He began prying the remnants of the cocoon off her. "What's wrong?" He lifted one of her hands then let it fall.

"Poison," said Reina, her head lowering into view between the window's broken shutters.

Jarad gasped. He shook his head, muttering frantic, unintelligible syllables.

"I do not believe the venom is lethal," Reina said. "If it were, she'd be dead by now. The toxin is doubtless used to immobilize prey. Help her sit up. That may allow the venom to work its way out faster."

Jarad lifted Lyssanne beneath the arms and propped her against the wall with a crate for support. She must look foolish, her head lolling to one side like an under-stuffed rag doll's.

"I'm sorry I injured you, child," Reina said. "It was the only way to free you."

'Twas Reina's horn that pierced her arm? Sir Brennus was right; the unicorn would make a formidable enemy.

"Cut a strip of cloth from her gown to bind her arm," Reina said.

Jarad complied, gripping his knife in an odd fashion. As he tied the strip around her wound, Lyssanne searched for the source of the clamor that filled the room. Jarad moved aside, and the sight before them fair stilled her heart.

The monster skittered about on its three, claw-tipped legs, wings flapping and tentacles flailing. And circling it, bobbing and ducking like a cork on rough water, was Sir Brennus.

"We should be out of the way here," Jarad said. "Wish I had my bow." He bounced on the balls of his feet as if itching to jump into the fray. "This thing's useless now."

Something clanged between them, drawing Lyssanne's gaze. The blade of Jarad's hunting knife lay on the floor, its handle nowhere in sight. She looked up again toward the creature and knight, still locked in their deadly dance.

Jarad gasped and tugged at her arm. "I almost forgot! Don't look into that beast's eyes." He slid to a sitting position. "Sir Brennus said they could kill you."

No chance of that. She couldn't even tell the beast had eyes from here. It swatted at Sir Brennus with a long, lethal-looking tentacle. Was any part of that creature *not* deadly?

"How's he gonna get close enough to kill that beast?" Jarad said. "Even his sword's too short to get past those tentacles, and who knows what those sucker-things on them would do to you." He drew in his feet as the knight sidestepped a blow, coming too near to where they sat.

Lyssanne strained with all her will to move her outstretched legs, lest Sir Brennus trip over them. Her toes twitched! As she kept trying, they wiggled with more and more freedom.

"Fear not, young Jarad," Reina said. "The knight is quite skilled."

"My bow would still be better than a blade," Jarad said. "I could shoot that monster from here." His next words snapped out, harsh and defiant. "But I'm not leaving you to go get it."

Lyssanne glanced his way. He was staring at her. She smiled, attempting to reassure him.

"I started to go for it, you know," he said, looking back at the combatants, "when I saw that *creature* attacking you. I knew I couldn't fight it and get you out of that cocoon at the same time, so I went to find Sir Brennus."

The creature's shrieked as it lunged and struck at Sir Brennus, distracting Lyssanne from Jarad's tale and her attempts to coax the muscles in her feet and legs to respond.

"We ran into the innkeeper on our way here," Jarad said, as if no interruption had occurred. "She pushed past us to reach the doorway first, and..." He gasped. "Watch out!"

Lyssanne snapped her gaze back to Sir Brennus, just as a tentacle swept toward him. He ducked and rolled out of reach. Before his body had made a full revolution, he swung his sword upward. With a squelching thud, the severed tentacle fell to the floor.

The monster shrieked and took to the air, dripping dark liquid. Its wings thrashed, stirring up a rush of wind that slapped at Lyssanne's face, before they stretched out, nearly the width of the small room. Then, the creature dove.

With surprising grace, Sir Brennus leapt. For a moment, he, too, seemed to soar—his black mantle, dark wings billowing out behind him; his up-thrust sword, a deadly talon that pierced the underbelly of the monster, even as it swooped down upon him.

Then, both man and monster fell to the ground—one panting as he wrenched his blade free, the other writhing in the throes of death.

"Yes!" Jarad said, jumping to his feet, fist raised. "That was brilliant!"

Sir Brennus spun in a slow circle, sword extended, as if searching for more foes. His gaze passed over Lyssanne and the others. Finally, he lowered the blade. "Is everyone intact?"

'More or less," said Reina.

As the knight poked at the remnants of the cocoon with the tip of his stained sword, Jarad lowered his fist and jabbed it toward him. "She almost died in that thing!" he shouted. "Why didn't you help me cut her out?"

"In case you failed to notice, boy," Sir Brennus said between breaths, "I was a bit busy at the time." He looked up and said in a voice every bit as lethal as the creature he'd just slain, "Or would you have preferred I allow the beast to kill us all?"

"That web could not be severed by mortal weapons," Reina said. "Only an object of powerful magic could have freed her, young Jarad."

"So, that's why my knife broke," Jarad muttered.

"The cocoon would have broken a sword just as easily," Reina said. "Has there been any change, Lyssanne? Can you move at all?"

Lyssanne drew up her knees then straightened her legs again. While Reina explained the situation to Sir Brennus, she managed to lift her fingers from the floor.

After the death of the monster, the effects of its venom faded more rapidly. As Lyssanne continued to regain control of her limbs, Sir Brennus cleaned his sword. Then, he motioned Jarad over to the body of the creature.

"Help me drag this out behind the barn," he said, sheathing his blade. "Between Reina smashing through barn doors and windows and the shrieks of the beast, some of the inn's patrons have doubtless been roused."

"Strange," Jarad said. "With its wing folded over its lumpy body like that, it almost looks like a pile of clothes."

Lyssanne squinted at the monster. It lay on its back, one wing outstretched, the other flopped over its midsection, exposing the wing's mottled, black and grey exterior. Her breath stilled as she glanced toward the corner where old rags had lain when she'd entered the shed. The corner was empty.

Jarad gasped, pointing to the corner. "That beast was in here the whole time! When the innkeeper brought us, it was waiting!"

"An ingenious disguise," Reina said. "I doubt even she was aware of its presence."

"I don't know…" Jarad said, drawing out the words. "You didn't hear the way she talked to Lady Lyssanne. She didn't like us much."

"Perhaps," Reina said, "but no sane human would willingly consort with such a beast. It was no creature of nature. Such abominations cannot be reasoned with, nor controlled without the aid of powerful dark forces. You should burn its body."

"Where," Lyssanne whispered. She coughed to clear her throat. When again she spoke, her voice was raspy and weak, but audible. "Where is she?"

"Who, child?" Reina asked. "The innkeeper?"

Lyssanne nodded, able to move at last. Her entire body remained limp, however, as if she'd drunk too much mead like those men in the common room. She looked up at Jarad, as he rushed over to her. "You said…she came with you?"

Jarad turned toward the door, his abrupt silence closing over Lyssanne like a shroud. Why was he avoiding her question? She followed his gaze, and her heart skittered.

Across the doorway, lay a human-sized lump of shadow.

"Madam Vivva-Beh?" Lyssanne whispered. "She's injured!" Bracing her palms against the mat, Lyssanne pushed herself up. Her arms trembled then gave way, and she slumped back against the wall, spent.

"You can't help her," Sir Brennus said. "No one can. Madam Vivva-Beh is dead."

"What? How?"

"Slain by the creature."

"When she came in just ahead of us," Jarad said, "she screamed. That creature looked up, right into her eyes, and"—he snapped his fingers—"just like that, she dropped dead." He sighed. "Sir Brennus pushed me out of the way—I was right behind her—and yelled at me not to look at the monster. He attacked it, and I ran to you. Dunno how he knew about the eyes, though."

"Many lands hold legends of beasts that can kill with a stare alone," Sir Brennus said. "The innkeeper was too strong to die of mere fright. The explanation was obvious."

"But how'd you fight it?" Jarad asked, helping the knight remove the innkeeper's body from the doorway. "You never looked at it, but you always knew where it was."

Sir Brennus dropped Madam Vivva-Beh's feet and tapped his sword. "Reflection," he said, "and sound. Sight isn't the only sense useful in battle." He strode toward the monster. "It is no great feat; I spent part of my earliest training wearing a blindfold."

"A fortunate thing, for all of us," Reina said.

"Yes," Lyssanne whispered, a tear trickling down her cheek. "Thank you, all of you. I—" Her throat constricted. If Madam Vivva-Beh hadn't attempted to come to her aid...

"There, there, child," Reina said. "You are pale as the moon and limp as water-weed." She bent to nuzzle Lyssanne's hair. "You should lie down and get some sleep."

"No!" Lyssanne said with force that surprised even her. She tried again to push herself from the wall. "I, I can't stay here." She looked first at the body of the creature, then at the innkeeper, and shuddered.

"You can take my room," Sir Brennus said, stepping back to the doorway, carrying one end of the creature. "I'll be up most of the night disposing of this."

"She'd never make it up the stairs," Jarad said with a grunt, shifting his burden. "She can't even stand."

"I'll see to that once we return," said Sir Brennus.

Moments later, the knight strode back into the shed and sank to one knee in front of Lyssanne. "You are still unable to stand." It wasn't a question. "I shall have to carry you. Jarad is gathering his things and will bring yours up when he's done."

Before Lyssanne could protest, Sir Brennus snaked one arm behind her back and the other beneath her knees. He lifted her and strode into the night.

Just as they left the light of the doorway, voices reached them from the inn. Sir Brennus slipped into the shadows beside the shed, and Reina met them at its corner. Footsteps pounded across the yard, then onto the dirt floor that had almost been Lyssanne's deathbed.

"Madam Vivva-Beh?" shrieked a woman's voice. "She's dead!"

"Someone slept here," a man said. "Who?"

"That peasant girl who dined with the knight," said the woman.

"Alert the magistrate," commanded the man. "We must form a search party."

"Shining One," Sir Brennus whispered.

"Place her on my back," Reina said, her voice echoing his urgency. "My power will hold her.

"Head due west into the forest," he said, settling Lyssanne into place.

"Jarad!" Lyssanne whispered. "If he's gone to the barn, he won't know—"

"We will follow. Go!"

As Reina flew through the streets, buildings and trees blurring past, Lyssanne managed, somehow, to keep her seat. When they reached the forest, Reina stopped just inside the tree line, insisting Lyssanne stay put until the others joined them.

Once Jarad and Sir Brennus arrived, Lyssanne's cart and the knight's stallion in tow, they all moved deeper into the forest. Sir Brennus cleared away brush and laid a fire, while Jarad helped Lyssanne dismount and settle against a tree. Serena alighted on the ground beside her.

Sir Brennus rose, flames dancing at his feet, and called to Jarad. "We haven't much time. They're looking for us," he said. "For you, rather. Already men comb the village, convinced the two of you were involved in the innkeeper's death."

"Us?" Jarad asked.

"Indeed," Sir Brennus said. "I must return and drag the monster into the wood before anyone sees it. Those people are a superstitious lot. Suspicion I can deal with, but a witch-hunt?" He strode to his horse and retrieved a rope affixed to its saddle. "Your lady is too weak to outrun or outride that kind of frenzy." He issued his next orders like a general commanding men on a battlefield. "Finish laying this fire, but use only what you can find in the immediate area for fuel." He turned to Lyssanne and Reina. "I shan't be long. Stay here...and stay alert."

With that, he melted into the trees like a shadow.

An hour later, Lyssanne stood alone beside the fire, grateful for a moment's privacy. Though her silent tears had subsided, she still trembled. She'd nearly died, again.

Craving warmth and light after the darkness of this night, she inched so near to the whispering flames, the taste of wood smoke coated her every breath. No flame or cloak could ward off a chill from within, however, nor quell this shivery weariness of spirit and body.

How could the others remain so unshaken? Sir Brennus had been gone an age, unflinching in his disposal of that creature. Jarad gathered wood as if they'd merely stopped to camp, while Reina scraped her horn against a rock some yards away, cleaning it, she'd said.

Lyssanne rubbed her arms then extended her frozen hands toward the flames. Would she never be warm again? At least the venom's effects had faded, leaving behind the tingling numbness one might feel when a foot has rested too long in the same position.

A shiver ran along her spine, a subtle shifting and solidifying of the air at her back. Something, someone, was behind her...watching.

She froze, trying to coax herself to look over her shoulder. Her back's vulnerability to the unknown at last forced her to turn. Flinching, she all but stumbled into the fire.

Sir Brennus stood three paces away, imposing and silent as the shadows flitting across his face. "You fear me," he whispered, "don't you?"

She shook her head, her cheeks rivaling the hissing coals for warmth.

"The truth." He stepped closer, forcing her to tip her head up to avoid staring at the middle of his chest. Any nearer, and she might fall over backward.

"You, you startled me. That's all."

"Lyssanne," he said, her name both caress and command.

"Perhaps...a little. Sometimes." She resisted the urge to duck her head, just.

He nodded. A gleam of white flashed in the firelight. A smile? "Good."

"What? How can that be good?"

"It shows you have at least some wisdom. You should be wary of those things capable of causing you harm: fire, wild beasts..." He gestured in the direction he'd taken the body of the monster, then he stared back at her. "Me."

"You? But you wouldn't...would you?"

He laughed, the sound far from merry. "If I intended you harm, would I admit to such?"

"Well, no. I suppose not."

"Remain wary, Lyssanne. The amphisbaena spoke true in this, you are far too trusting."

He brushed past her and...tweaked her chin!

Lyssanne's cheeks flamed anew. The citizens of Cloistervale might have thought her odd, even accused her of sloth, but no one, ever, had accused her of stupidity. Until now. Until him.

She spun to say...what? Her shoulders tensed. She would not give him cause to laugh at her a second time.

Fire drummed in her chest. Afraid of him? Hardly! Fury was fatal to fear. How dare he treat her like a silly girl who couldn't take care of herself? He knew nothing of what she'd overcome. So, she'd gotten into a few scrapes. She hadn't *asked* him to save her life. Twice.

Jarad burst through the trees, arms laden with broken branches.

Lyssanne fled from the firelight, hiding her burning eyes and cheeks in shadow to avoid questions.

"I'll stand watch," Sir Brennus said, as Reina trotted into view. "The rest of you should get some sleep. It will take time to complete disposal of the creature's body. Besides, I shall be on my way before sunrise." He addressed his words to Jarad and Reina, as if Lyssanne's presence were inconsequential. "Wherever you plan to journey next, avoid the road. News flies faster than the wind in these parts. I would caution you to stay clear of towns for a time."

"We'll travel west, then," Reina said, "through the wood to the Lyryan border."

"That," said Sir Brennus, "should be safe enough."

Lyssanne spread her blanket beneath a tree, her anger draining away with the last of her energy. She sighed. The forest, again. She could never go home, and now she dared not return to Westerfield. Once more, events and forces beyond her control decided her fate.

She closed her eyes, feeling as insignificant as the knight considered her. Those thoughts and more malevolent shadows chased her into restless slumber.

The following evening, Noire's wings assaulted the air over northern Cloistervale with unnecessary force. He was tired, he was irritable, and he was in no mood to deal with the witch.

After being up half the night—what with that unnatural creature and such—he'd slept all of an hour-and-a-half, thanks to Venefica's incessant summoning. She wanted a report? Fine. He'd tell her what he knew, then seek his solitude.

Even the trees seemed to sense his ire, for when he plunged into the mountainside forest, branches snapped out of his way faster than usual.

Noire shot through the open window of the bedchamber Venefica had assigned to his use, then sailed into the corridor. Broken statues littered the floor, here and there a portrait hung askew, and splintered tables lined the walls.

Near the landing of the once-grand staircase, Venefica's ancient maidservant stooped, scooping up shards of shattered statuary. She straightened and brandished her brush-broom at him. "You'll be food for your feathered kin if you aren't careful, Prince of Ravens."

Oh, the old hag would like that. Noire squawked and flew at Magda, just to make her duck. She should count herself fortunate he had such a talon-hold on his temper, else she might have found herself missing a pair of eyes.

Still, her warning gave him pause. Signs of Venefica's fury littered every room he'd passed. He hovered near the stairs, listening. A haunting sound drifted from the upper floors. Music? He arched his wings and propelled himself upward.

He found her once again in the music room, the same eerie melody as before emanating from the dusty pianoforte in the center of the chamber.

As he alighted atop the piano, his feathers twitched. He knew that tune, a mournful waltz once favored in the Navvarish court. How had this Lastarran-born woman learned it? The melody's dark beauty held him transfixed. He forgot everything, his caution, the events in Westerfield, the lateness of the hour.

Sudden, spiky tingles ran along his skin, as if the quills of his every feather were driving into his flesh. He snapped his gaze to the red glow seeping through the dirty windowpanes.

Sunset! He had been a fool to lose track of time.

As fire and ice warred for possession of his innards, he clamped his beak tight to keep from uttering a sound. His talons shortened and softened into fleshy toes. Feathers all over his body drove themselves inward, leaving behind pale skin. His wing joints contorted. The bones remolded themselves into long arms. His vision wavered, then cleared, less sharp than before. He blinked, feeling half blind for the few seconds it always took to adjust to the change.

Far worse than the shadow transformation Venefica's botched spell had forced upon him, this metamorphosis left his body solid and capable of feeling—everything. His arms ached from prolonged flight, as had his wings. Though he'd endured this change at every sunset and sunrise for more years than he cared to count, he would never grow accustomed to it. Worse still, he'd just shifted in another's presence.

He sat atop the piano, sweating, his legs dangling, hands on knees. Before Venefica could glance up, he straightened, adopting a casual pose. He had his pride, after all.

At length, she ended her song, acknowledging his presence with a look.

"My lady." He inclined his head. "Such a melody should grace the halls of a palace. A *Navvarish* palace."

"The great Brennus approves of my music?" Venefica said. "I *must* celebrate."

"I've not heard that waltz since childhood," he said, "but for whom do you play it?" He snatched up the portrait miniature in front of her, catching a fleeting glimpse of a golden-haired man of perhaps sixteen winters with startling silver eyes, before she jerked it from his hand.

"For myself." She placed the portrait facedown with a slow deliberation that didn't deceive him. "I often play when angry. And why do you think I had need to play tonight, pet?"

"Were you so impatient to see me?" he said with a half smile.

The sorceress glared at him.

"It isn't as if I can whisk myself here on a puff of wind the instant you wish." He slid from the piano and strode to a corner. He ran a finger along the dust-laden bones of a harp. "Flying over miles of forest takes time." He turned to her. "And even I require sleep."

Venefica waved that away. "A minor inconvenience. Your delay was probably wise. It gave my rage time to cool. Had you arrived *instantly*, as you say, you would doubtless now be nothing but a caw echoing through my chambers, and no longer of use to me."

"If my absence hasn't caused your…distress," he said, "what then could have driven you to such desperate straits as to make music?"

"You dare address me in that flippant tone after you've slain one of my creations?"

The smirk melted from his lips, leaving his expression as flat as his voice. "That creature in Westerfield, you sent it?"

"Hardly." She stood and paced the length of the room. "I abandoned that failed experiment years ago in the land of its birth. The stupid beast has searched for me ever since, but that is far from the point." She spun to face him. "The perfect opportunity arose, and you spoiled it! Even Diornian sensed what my bidding would be should it happen upon an enemy of mine."

His brows drew together at a sudden thought. "How did you know I killed this…Diornian? It was night. You claimed you can see through my eyes only when I take the form of the raven. Or was that a lie?"

"Do you think you are my only spy?" she said. "The Shadow Mist played a part in the beast's creation. Through it, I've been tracking Diornian's movements. When I realized it had smelled my curse on that girl, well, I could hardly resist the show."

"You used the water mirror?"

She nodded. "No one, ever, has survived an encounter with Diornian. Its stare alone causes such fear, it stops the heart."

"How is it, then, that Lyssanne didn't perish, as the innkeeper did?"

"Her eyes—the entire time Diornian's gaze was upon the girl, her eyes moved about in rapid, random patterns. Not once did she focus on the creature's stare."

"A symptom of fear?" Brennus asked, recalling similar behavior in Lyssanne's eyes when she'd stood near him in his true form.

"I think it rather a side effect of her poor vision. Ironic, that her limited sight should save her from a lethal gaze." She leveled her own deadly stare on him, eyes flashing with black fire.

Brennus fought the urge to step back.

"Imagine my surprise when, instead of letting Diornian feast on my enemy, my best agent saves her from the beast!"

"I saved the lives of the inn's patrons," he said, "including my own. Your pet beast didn't limit its appetite to the girl. She would have perished, despite my actions, if not for the unicorn." Folding his arms, he leaned against the wall. "Besides, I took certain oaths as a knight."

"What of your oath to me?"

"I have not broken it," he said through his teeth. "And I would remind you, Lady, you made an oath to me as well."

"I've told you, I will fulfill our bargain when I regain my full power. The girl—"

"Yes, yes. The girl is still too near Cloistervale."

"Mock me if you wish, knight, but should that girl discover the strength dormant within her, she will be a danger to us both."

Hard to believe, that. Still, besides wanting free of it, what did he know of magic?

Venefica walked to the dirty window and stood as if peering at the landscape. "Twice," she murmured. "Twice now, that unicorn has saved Lyssanne's life." At her chill words, ice crackled on the windowpane. "That nag prevented you destroying the girl when you first showed yourself to her. Now this." She spun and flung out a hand. The string-less harp beside him exploded, its fragments bursting into flame in midair then raining down as ash.

Brennus blinked the sting of charred wood from his eyes. Good thing he hadn't told her about the amphisbaena.

"You were wise to hide your true form while my enemy was in Cloistervale," she said. "Your appearing only at night would have raised suspicions that could have ruined my plans, but your role in this game has changed. No longer will gathering information suffice." She stepped close and prodded his chest with a blood-red nail. "I want that girl destroyed!"

"You wish me to slay her?"

"I prefer to do that myself," she said. "At your hand, her death would be too swift."

His shoulders relaxed. Though, why should he care how the girl perished?

"You will eliminate the obstacles that prevent her demise." Venefica said, kicking the harp's ashes. "I will be thwarted no longer!"

"I won't kill the boy, if that is your meaning," he said. "I am no coward to raise a hand against a child, and to slay a unicorn…" He barely suppressed a shudder. "That would bring upon my head a curse not even you, in all your fabled power, could lift."

"Fabled? You doubt my power?" Her eyes flashed as wind beat against the windows.

"I've seen precious little of what you promised in these two some years."

Deceptive softness overtook her voice. "Then, why do you stay?"

"Believe me, I've asked myself that question often enough."

"Because, I am your last chance, the only hope you have left."

"And a poor chance at that," he mumbled.

"Shall I show you, *pet?*" Darkness pooled around her midsection. Her hair tore loose of its pins and flew in all directions, as if the screaming wind had come inside with them.

"Don't threaten me, witch," he said through gritted teeth. "You need me."

Her hair settled back around her shoulders, and the howling wind subsided, but that thick darkness remained. "Perhaps. For now... perhaps we need each other."

10

THE WEAPONS OF OUR WARFARE

Reina's soft whinny broke through the pain-induced haze shrouding Lyssanne's mind. She blinked to ward off the sting of sunlight glaring greenish through the thatch of leaves and branches close overhead. Was it morning? Afternoon?

How many days had she lain beneath this shelter Jarad had constructed? Wispy memories flitted through her mind—a half-day's hasty ride from Westerfield, sudden pain leaving her draped like a sack of flour over Reina's back, the unicorn calling upon all the magic she possessed to keep Lyssanne's limp body from slipping to the ground.

Reina whinnied again, a single word, "Danger."

Lyssanne tensed. The searchers must be near. Blood pounded in her ears, intensifying the already unbearable pressure within her skull. She struggled to slow her racing heart. If she lay still, they wouldn't see her. Thank the King, Sir Brennus had described this method of concealment to Jarad. In her current state, she would have found no other escape.

Sudden nausea burned her throat. Jarad and Reina were...no, they would be safe. If they'd followed the plan, Jarad had shimmied up a tree at Reina's first whiff of humans, and the unicorn insisted her magic could render her all but invisible to the untrained eye.

Branches popped, and heavy footfalls crunched through dry leaves. Lyssanne's skull had become a drum, vibrating with each sound, amplifying the slightest snap of twig into a sharp hammer-blow. Lightning bolts of pain stabbed at her temples and streaked across her brow. She held her breath until the worst of the pain subsided. She mustn't so much as whimper.

At last, the heavy footsteps faded into the distance. Lyssanne lay unmoving until Reina's "all clear" brought to her ears the sounds of falling leaves and the thump of Jarad's feet hitting the ground. She exhaled a gust that stirred the roof of her hiding place. They were safe.

Noire shifted into shadow just beyond the sun-dappled clearing in which Lyssanne's party had stopped to rest. He'd wearied of sitting in branches, forever flicking bugs from his feathers. At least this transformation was painless…with the exception of the ill-fated day Venefica had cast the spell that should have ended his curse. Such was the price of magic.

Even the name he used while in this form was evidence of sorcery's stain.

"I shall call you Noire," Venefica had said when they'd first met. "It suits you better."

Doubtless, she'd thought it a cruel jest, this reminder that only in darkness could he take his true form. Ah, but nothing could be crueler than the transformation each dawn had forced upon his body since his ninth year. Still, thinking of himself by that name during daylight hours helped him maintain focus on his true quest while in the guise of the raven.

The obstacle to that quest's fulfillment sat in a pool of sunlight, tucking her copper-streaked hair behind one shoulder. Lyssanne crossed her legs beneath her skirts and rested her chin in cupped hands. Doubtless, had she known she was being observed, she would never adopt so unladylike a pose. Even when Jarad was near, she maintained a constant air of quiet dignity.

"What's amiss, child?" Reina asked.

"I'm just weary," Lyssanne murmured, her eyes shadowed with evidence of the recent toll her curse had taken, an ongoing affliction as devastating as the havoc shapeshifting had wrought upon Noire's life.

Ironic, the one person in all the Seven Lands who might have understood him was the person he was sworn to destroy.

"I've seen you tire often enough," Reina said, "but this..." She shook her mane. "You've hardly spoken in two days, and the sun has gone out in your eyes."

It was true. Noire leaned forward. How could he have failed to notice—until now, when it was all but gone—that her strange Light had always shone in her eyes? Not even when the curse was at its worst, or when her people had betrayed her, had she looked this forlorn.

"I'm sinking, Reina." Lyssanne's words dropped into the silence, heavy as millstones. "I dare not say this with Jarad present, but I, I must talk to someone. Else, I fear he will see."

"See what?"

She rubbed at the scar Reina's horn had left on her upper arm. "'Tis as if I'm back in the mud by Merchant's Bridge, clawing for solid ground. Only this time, the darkness is closing over my head." She covered her face then let her hands fall. "I can't breathe and I—Much as it shames me, I feel like letting go." She turned away, sniffling. "Oh, Reina, I almost *long* to let go."

"Dear child, what has changed? You never lose hope, no matter the circumstance."

Lyssanne leaned against Reina's side. "I'm so tired." Breath whooshed out between her lips. "And weary of *being* forever tired... and always afraid."

"Afraid of what, child?"

"Everything—that we won't find enough to eat, that some calamity will befall Jarad because he followed me, that I'll fall from your back when we travel." She drew in a slow breath. "But mostly, afraid they were right."

"Who?"

"The Council, my friends, even some in Westerfield. They think I'm—that there's something wrong in me, here." She covered her heart with both hands. "If they are right, then I truly have disappointed the King, and that is my worst fear of all."

She shivered, despite the heat of high summer. Even Noire, in this parody of a body, could almost have sweated. Yet there, in the direct gaze of the sun's burning eye, Lyssanne rubbed her hands up and down her arms, trembling.

"They weren't right, you know," Reina said.

Lyssanne shook her head. "Wh-what if the chief councilman's words were true? Perhaps I should have tried harder. There must have been something more I—"

"Tried harder?" Reina said, snorting. "Never have I seen anyone push themselves as you do. Even now, you can hardly stand, yet you insist upon preparing meals and washing and such. Why, were you to make any more effort, you'd have to be part horse."

"But the King is surely vexed with me," said Lyssanne. "The serpent in the wood, that monster at the inn...why would they single me out, if not because I've displeased Him?"

Reina craned her equine neck, her multifaceted azure eyes flashing a stern glance at Lyssanne. "The King of All Lands does not punish His children that way. He would never send deadly creatures to harm you."

Lyssanne hung her head. "I know, but if I've fallen out of favor..." She sighed. "I've opened the door to those things by failing Him." Her head snapped up, a hand flying to her mouth. "'Tis true! What they said the night they banished me—That I'd opened the door to that...that mist." Tears poured from her eyes. "I put them all in danger."

"Do not forget, child," Reina said, "there are other forces at work. Forces that have no love for those who honor the King." Her gaze

146

drifted toward the trees. "The King has protected you. There is a reason for that as well."

"I cannot imagine why."

"He still has need of you."

Lyssanne let out a sound as bitter as stinkweed. Reina's head whipped back around, and Lyssanne lifted her hands in surrender.

"I know, I know. The King has given us each a purpose. Only, I can't fathom what mine could be now. Once, I thought I knew, but…" She swiped at her eyes. "What purpose could I serve, l-like this?" Her voice grew strangled. "For you, I am a burden to carry. And Jarad…No child should have to look after his teacher."

"You are not a burden to me," Reina said. "You are a calling. The King orchestrated our meeting for my good as much as for yours. You have given *me* purpose. As for Jarad—Well, you give him something he's never had, a cause, someone to think on besides himself. A family."

"I do believe the King arranged our meeting, as He led Jarad to me," Lyssanne said. "How often He has preserved my life, but why go to such lengths? Once, I was guardian of a sacred trust, and through the children, I was useful." Her sigh trembled through the air. "What am I now, that He should let me live?"

"You are Lyssanne, His creation."

"Oh, yes, breathing air and using up resources best left to those who still make a difference." A tiny whimper escaped her throat, and she pressed a fist to her mouth for a moment. "What use can there be in a life that does nothing but suffer pain and consume the efforts of others?"

Noire stared. Perhaps the girl was not as strong as Venefica feared.

"Oh, child, don't you know?" Reina said, her voice nearly as strained as Lyssanne's. "As long as you can love even one other soul, as long as you have mind and heart enough to pray, your life has purpose."

"A lovely thought, if only…" Lyssanne's eyes closed, her chest heaving a silent sigh. Though her tears had ceased, tiny gems sparkled at the ends of her lashes.

Reina turned to face the dove who pecked at the ground several paces away, seeming to take in their every word. The unicorn's soft whinny drew the dove's eye. The little pest bent her head—nodding? In a sudden unfurling of wings, the dove took to the air, sailing in the opposite direction from Noire's hiding place.

"'Tis all I ever wanted," Lyssanne whispered, "a home, a purposeful life. Is it reaching too high—wishing to belong, to be useful?"

Noire slipped deeper into the shadows. Whatever his mission, 'twas unseemly to intrude on such private pain. Had Venefica been nearer, her Shadow Mist would have filled the clearing.

Reina's soft words arrested his thoughts...and his exit.

"The King doesn't create trades, Lyssanne. He creates people."

A current of heated air stirred the platter-sized leaves overhead, casting a wing-like shadow across Reina's mane. Lyssanne's entire body tensed. Ridiculous reaction. Two weeks should have been sufficient time to banish thoughts of the horrid monster's attack at the inn.

Reina's ears twitched. She raised her head and sniffed. "Let us stop here for a rest."

"But it isn't yet noon," Jarad said.

Lyssanne looked up into an unbroken tent of deepest green. "How can you tell?"

"The angle of the sun slanting through the trees."

"Then, perhaps we should go on," Lyssanne said. "I have strength enough."

"No." Steel undergirded the softness of Reina's voice. "It is time."

They stopped to share a meal of cold roast rabbit and berries, then Jarad pointed out a rather unusual plant. Lyssanne bent close to examine its velvety, blue leaves. Cupped to form an inverted bell, they shimmered iridescent in the gloom.

The faint glitter brightened to a sudden glow, and a geyser of green and white sparks shot from the center of the plant, pushing its leaves outward. Lyssanne yelped and jumped back.

A tiny pop overhead sent sparks raining to the ground. Atop the geyser of light, sat an emerald-clad faerie with spiky, black hair.

Jarad exclaimed something unintelligible, all but concealing the sound of a second pop. Then, a familiar voice spoke from above, wrenching Lyssanne's gaze from the geyser.

"Must you forever indulge in theatrics, Jada?" said the faerie Olivia, floating down from the trees. She poked her wand at her spiky-haired companion.

"Cut it out!" said Jada. "That tickles."

Lyssanne's breath hitched. It had been Jada's acerbic voice she'd heard just before meeting Olivia in the ring of flowers behind her cottage.

"That's—They're...flying!" Jarad said.

"Of course we're flying," Jada said. "We're faeries. Though, actually, we are *floating*."

Jarad began murmuring again.

"Hush, Jarad," Reina said, seeming unsurprised at the faeries' sudden appearance. "Come, let us search out more berries. I believe your supply is running low." She nudged him through the bundle slung over his shoulder. "Lyssanne will be quite safe in their company."

He followed her into the trees, still muttering about faeries and myths.

Olivia made formal introductions then asked Lyssanne to sit with her in the thick grass. Once they three were settled, she sighed. "You are losing your way, daughter of the King."

"I know," Lyssanne said, flushing at this lofty manner of address. "Autumn is soon upon us, and I have no notion how to find the nearest town. Can you help us?"

"You mistake me," Olivia said. "I speak of a concern far more important than the direction of your travels. You are losing your way within."

Lyssanne raised a brow. "Within?"

"How can you direct the power that resides in your spirit if you flounder in the dark?" Olivia said. "The youngest of faeries learn this before all else. Your mind must be centered. The smallest spark, without clarity of purpose, will wreak havoc."

"What has such to do with me?" Lyssanne asked. "I am no faerie."

Jada snorted.

"Unless you rediscover your center," said Olivia, "like that spark, the fire within you will either burn to no effect or cause great damage."

"You speak of sorcery," Lyssanne whispered. She rose; her gaze fixed on the faeries. "Since Reina holds affection for you, I ask your forgiveness if what I must say seems uncivil." She took a long breath, her face heating. "The *Kingsword* forbids sorcery, and if you practice such, I wish nothing further to do with you."

Olivia's leaf-green wings fluttered, and she floated up to Lyssanne's eye level. "You are wise to test us so," she said. "Always test the spirit of those who seek to influence you."

Jada whisked up beside her. "Olivia wasn't talking about magic, though," she said, "but of a gift from the King. What men call a faerie's magic is His power at work through us, not our own." She drew so near, Lyssanne could see tiny points of light dancing across her face. "The gift He has given you is far more powerful than that."

A nervous laugh escaped Lyssanne's throat. "You are mistaken. I have nothing of the sort. Such gifts would be wasted on me." She sighed. "His others certainly were."

"And you have the right to judge the choices of the King?" Jada said. "Will you dare tell *Him* His time and blessings are a waste?"

Heat draining from her face, Lyssanne shook her head. She'd meant nothing of the kind.

"Jada, that is enough," Olivia said.

"I intend no disrespect, Captain, but the time for coddling is past."

"Captain?" Lyssanne asked.

Olivia waved the question away. "My rank in the Royal Elfin Army."

"FAE division, of course," said Jada.

150

"Fay?"

"*F. A. E.* Faeries Against Evil," said Jada, as if that explained everything.

"We serve the King of All Lands, as you do," Olivia said. "The FAE are one small branch of His vast army."

"You are akin to angels, then?" Lyssanne asked.

"Nothing quite so grand," Olivia said, chuckling. "Angels go before the throne of the King and battle in the spirit realm. Faeries receive messages from Him and battle other so-called magical creatures. Mostly, we fight mortals who gain dark power from the Thief of Souls."

Lyssanne shivered. "Surely you don't think that I would ever—"

"No, dear child of the King," Olivia said, "quite the contrary. We have come to help you prepare for battle, and to fight beside you if necessary."

"Now, I know you are mistaken," Lyssanne said, laughing. "I am the last person you would wish beside you in a battle."

"The queen was right," Jada said. "Her spirit's wet as mud. You can't ignite that." She turned, waving her wand in Lyssanne's face. "Dry up, girl. Where's the fiery resolve that has kept you alive?"

"I'm sorry," Lyssanne said. "I am not what you think. I've never been like that."

"Humph. You learned to read when no one thought you could. Where is that spark now?"

"That's different. Mr. DeLivre and my mother—"

"Sure, they believed in you, but *you* had the fire to do the thing," Jada said. "Don't give me that look. Many still believe in you—Reina, the kid, our queen—though I can't fathom why."

"Jada!" Olivia said.

"Well, the King never gave up on her, so she has no right to give up on Him."

"I would never—"

"Giving up on yourself is the same thing, saying what He created wasn't good enough."

Heat bubbled up from Lyssanne's middle. Why must she forever

151

fight to prove herself? This faerie was no different from the people in Cloistervale. "I am not giving up!" she said. "You have no idea what effort is required of me just to rise each day. If I'd given up, I'd be dead!"

"Ha!" Jada said. "There it is. There's that fire!"

Lyssanne drew a deep breath to calm her voice. "Forgive me." She ducked her head. "The fault is not yours. How could immortal beings possibly understand what it is like to suffer prolonged illness or the kind of pain that saps the strength and steals the ability to truly live?"

"And poof," said Jada, "there it goes."

"I'm certain you mean well," Lyssanne said. "'Tis just, the King, I— I've failed Him."

"No," Olivia said, "you will only fail Him if you refuse His call, refuse to try."

Tears stung the corners of Lyssanne's eyes. "What must I do?"

"Acknowledge and use the gift He has placed inside you," Olivia said. "'Tis a powerful weapon, and you must learn to wield it."

"What weapon could I possibly possess? I haven't the strength to lift a sword, the sight to aim an arrow, or the nerve to wield a dagger."

"The ability to command Light is a weapon stronger than any blade, surer than any arrow. You've been granted the authority to command Light Himself."

"*Himself?*"

"Light is the very essence and nature of the King of All Lands," Olivia said.

"If that is true, how can you say I must command Him?" Lyssanne shivered. "I dare not even think it!"

"Not as a superior to a subordinate," Olivia said. "It is His power you may command. In placing a measure of it within you, He has chosen to shine through you."

"Yet, beware," said Jada. "This weapon can warm or burn, sustain life or consume it, destroy, create, reveal, all the things natural light can do, only to a greater degree. This Light operates in the realms of the spirit as well as the natural."

"But how do I—"

"Shh," Olivia hissed, glancing over her shoulder as a distant caw pierced the forest. "Leave questions for later. We have given you quite enough to think on. Here."

With a sizzle of sparks, a scroll unfurled from empty air.

"Study these passages in the *Kingsword*," Olivia said, handing Lyssanne the scroll. "They will help you understand the aspect of His nature that is Light."

Lyssanne held the parchment as if it might crumble. Rows of large, neat script covered it.

"Captain," Jada said, her voice full of warning.

"I know." Olivia placed a hand on Lyssanne's shoulder. "We must go. Be always on your guard, for the wings of darkness hover ever near."

With a pop and shower of sparks, the faeries vanished.

Brennus clenched and unclenched his fists, as his shadowy fingers took on solid form. Sunset, at last. He slipped from behind a plateris trunk just in time to intercept Jarad's blundering rush toward the tree line.

"C'mon, Lady Lyssanne!" the boy called over his shoulder. "The town's just through those trees, but if we don't hurry, they might close the gates."

"I just need…a moment," she said, stopping with hands on knees several paces behind.

Sighing, Jarad faced forward as if to continue walking. His gaze alighted on Brennus, and he straightened, the frown melting from his face. "Sir Brennus? Here? Brilliant!" He stepped forward, pointing through the trees. "Did you come from that town? We're headed there and—"

"Straight into a manhunt," Brennus said. "One that hunts you."

Jarad stared. "Us? Because of Westerfield? But we can't stay in the forest forever."

"Jarad, what...?" Lyssanne stumbled to a halt next to the boy. "Sir Brennus?"

He inclined his head, schooling his expression and voice to neutral civility as the unicorn trotted up to Lyssanne's side. "I advise a change in course, lest you risk imprisonment or worse."

Jarad slumped against the tree that had been Brennus' hiding place. "Camping, again."

"There is a small stream to the east," Brennus said. "Its banks are smooth enough for a campsite, and the tree cover will shelter you from view of the town." This would afford him the perfect opportunity to complete his odious mission.

As Brennus led the way to the small clearing, Jarad and Reina peppered him with questions, for which he'd prepared plausible responses, but Lyssanne remained silent. When she stumbled over a root, he caught her arm to steady her.

"You've gone pale," he said. "Have you contracted a fever?"

Shaking her head, she sank onto the pebble-strewn ground near the stream.

He crouched beside her, unable to resist this chance to discover what she might know of her curse. "What causes this lack of strength which so often plagues you?"

"I am not certain how to explain it," she said, squinting toward Jarad and Reina, who'd stopped farther downstream to drink and refill the water-skins. "I barely understand it myself."

"At times, you seem perfectly healthy," he said, "but with the least exertion, you fade."

She glanced about as if his scrutiny unsettled her, then her expression shifted. Leaning toward the stream, she gathered up a handful of pebbles. "Imagine, every day we are each given a measure of strength," she said. "Not strength of character or of muscle, but the energy to sustain life and perform all the tasks set before us."

Brennus murmured his understanding.

"Now, imagine these stones represent that measure of strength." She piled all the stones into a heap between them. "Let us say, this is the energy given most people—you, Jarad, others. The strength of one stone is required to keep the heart beating and breath flowing, one stone to rise from bed, one to dress, another to prepare food, one to eat it. You see?"

"Yes," he said. "And when that strength is used, you remove a stone?"

"Just so." She smiled. "Will you try an experiment with me?"

He consented.

"Then, if you please, close your eyes." He complied, and after a moment, she said. "Now, open them and tell me what you see."

"Nothing," he said, raising a brow at her. "That is, all is as it was."

"Is it? Let us say you've prepared and eaten a meal." She opened her hand, revealing two stones she'd hidden. "You have so many stones, you don't notice when two are used up."

She beckoned him to lean forward and showed him a spot on her side of the pile, from which she'd removed the stones she held.

"The height of the pile isn't diminished from the loss, but..." She arranged four stones into a square, with a fifth atop them. "Let us say this is the measure of strength with which I awaken." She removed the topmost stone and one other. "Now, I've prepared and eaten a meal."

"I take your meaning," he said. "The shape of your pile is greatly altered, and only the strength to sustain life and perform two other tasks remains. This for the entire day?"

"Yes," she said, "and if I fail to rest, I must borrow strength from tomorrow. Then, I may be unable to rise for several days thereafter."

"Why is it, your store of strength is so paltry compared with others'?"

"I, I am not certain," she said. "It wasn't always thus. I became quite ill early last year and have not been myself since."

He stared. Could she truly still have no knowledge of Venefica's power...or her own?

Lyssanne piled the kindling and small limbs Sir Brennus had gathered onto a smooth spot of ground well away from the stream—and the night bugs it attracted. She squinted at the rough pyramid she'd constructed. Would it hold the larger wood the knight had gone to collect?

She pulled her cloak tighter about her and sank onto the soft grass. Who would imagine a simple stream and patch of smooth ground could seem a luxury? Still, with fatigue leeching the heat from her, what she most needed was a bed and a couple weeks to spend in it. Since her illness had struck, that had been the only thing capable of restoring any semblance of energy.

Now, if she could just get the fire going, she might stop shivering. If only the faeries had spoken true, and she did possess a gift that could warm the coldest night. She shook her head at the notion, but a sudden thought struck. For once, she was alone. She would ask the King.

"If I do have such a gift, and it is your good purpose that I should use it," she whispered, "please grant me to know this. Show me, that I may never question a treasure you've given."

Continuing in silent converse with the King, she made several attempts at the fire. The wood refused to spark. Perhaps she should wait for Jarad's return. Surely he could get it going. Tossing the flint aside, she begged the King's pardon for her distraction and thanked Him for her companions—especially Sir Brennus, who seemed to appear just when they needed his aid.

Sudden warmth pulsed at the center of her being then wrapped its way outward, through and around her body. Such love for the King filled her, it mattered not what gifts she might possess or where she must go. He was with her. Nothing else could compare.

The warmth grew so intense she might soon catch fire. 'Twas no wonder the King was often called the Great Light of the world. This love must light the very air around her. Surely anyone who looked on her would see it. She smiled, her first true smile in an age.

Then, a flash lit up her closed lids.

Her eyes flew open, and she stared. A tiny flame danced on the kindling that had resisted the flint, and her hands...they glowed. Not with reflected firelight, but with some inner radiance that faded even as she watched. She glanced around. Had she somehow struck the kindling while in prayer? No, the flint lay several paces away from either her or the wood.

The faeries were right! This must be the sign she'd longed for, but why would the King use His great power for so mundane a task? The very thought seemed a sacrilege. Still, perhaps He'd known this small demonstration wouldn't frighten her.

"Thank you," she whispered. She stood on unsteady legs, in need of water and even more tired than before. She cared not. The joy of the King's gift spilled over into a laugh.

A twig snapped, and the laugh shrank back into the pit of her stomach.

"Witch!" Sir Brennus lunged from the shadows, tall, solid as the trees from whence he'd emerged. Ringing metal rent the air as he drew his sword.

Lyssanne shook her head. "What...where?"

Sir Brennus advanced toward her, firelight sparkling off the edge of his blade. He held the sword between them as if to guard against an impending blow. "What sorcery is this?"

"What? I..." She stepped back, spreading her arms.

"Do not think to use your witch tricks against me." The tip of his blade stopped inches from her chin. "You'd be dead before you have the chance."

"Me?" she whispered, her remaining strength draining away. "I'm not a witch."

"I saw what you did. Do not attempt to deceive me."

"What—what did I do?"

"The fire."

"That w-wasn't magic. It was just..." She longed to retreat, but her legs were about as steady as unbaked loaves. What could she tell him? She hadn't done magic. She *couldn't* have.

Her stomach plummeted to her feet, and air whooshed in her ears. To prevent falling, she dropped to her knees, then stared up at him, cold droplets beading on her upper lip and cheeks.

"Oh, you hide it well, behind that mask of helplessness." He let out a bitter laugh. "You nearly had me fooled, but I know intentional magic when I see it. No flint sparked that fire. It came from your hands, from somewhere inside you."

"It wasn't me," she said. How could she explain what the King had just done for her? She hadn't the strength to tell him everything, but he couldn't possibly understand otherwise.

He gave her no chance to try. "Where is the unicorn you have enspelled?"

"She...I didn't...She's grazing." Her breaths were coming in shallow puffs. She lifted a hand to indicate the direction Reina had gone. "But I've not enspelled her."

He stepped closer, his shadow blocking most of the firelight. "Better for her if you have. If she has forsaken her pure heart to willingly aid a sorceress, she too must be destroyed."

"De-destroyed?"

"The only fate sorcery deserves." His voice whipped at her ears. "And the boy? With what magic did you compel him to join you? Or does he seek to learn your sorcerous ways?"

"Hunting." She leaned on one arm, too weak to remain upright. "He's still hunting." All at once, the pain returned, bursting through her skull. "D-don't harm them. Please..."

His sword flashed. Her arm gave way, and she sank into darkness.

11

THE SHAMAN OF THE WOOD

a cool, wet softness slid across Lyssanne's brow, easing the tightness in her burning throat a bit. She sighed, only a trickle of air squeezing out. Why was breathing so difficult?

Voices drifted toward her from afar.

"We traveled too long today. It was too much for her."

So soft, those lilting tones, Lyssanne wished the sound would never cease.

"This is more than mere travel fatigue," said a smooth, deep voice. "She is most pale."

"True enough. The child is unwell."

The cloth ceased mopping Lyssanne's brow, lying heavy over her nose and one eye, and the man's cultured voice grew harsh. "She claimed she contracted no fever since last I saw you."

"What ails her is no fever," said his soft-spoken companion.

Reina. Recognition seeped into Lyssanne's sluggish mind. The speaker was Reina.

"Nor will any suffer from it but she," Reina said. "Do not look so disbelieving, young knight. Did you not witness Jarad in perfect health?"

The cloth resumed its progress across Lyssanne's face. "What is this, then?"

"I...have my suspicions."

"Will you say no more?"

"No," said Reina. "I haven't voiced them even to her."

Who was that man? When Lyssanne tried to identify his familiar voice, agony erupted in her head. She lay in silence for indeterminate moments. Her mind, groggy from the pressure besieging her skull, floated in and out of awareness—until a sudden shout, too familiar to be mistaken, roused her to full wakefulness.

"Reina!" Jarad cried, panting as if from a run. Grass crunched, and the ground vibrated beneath Lyssanne's legs. "Is she awake yet?"

A movement stirred the hem of Lyssanne's gown, and something thudded beside her knee. She eased her eyes open to slits and peered at Jarad. If only she could wipe the worry from his voice. He knelt near her toes, one hand upon a lump on the ground.

Then, the moist cloth left Lyssanne's brow. Her eyes traced the hand that held it, up the arm to which it was attached, and found Sir Brennus staring at her, his expression most solemn.

All at once, memory flooded her mind. The hazy languor of a moment ago fled on the heels of her racing heart. Sir Brennus, formidable knight, slayer of the monster at the inn. Sir Brennus, who wanted to kill her, perhaps wanted to kill them all.

"Reina?" she whispered, barely squeezing the word through the tiny tube of her throat.

"Yes, child. I am here."

"Run."

"Run? Whatever for, child?"

Lyssanne parted her lips to tell them what the knight had said, but her throat constricted. All she could do was fix her eyes on Sir Brennus and pray her gaze alone could hold him there long enough for the others to flee.

"Sir Brennus?" Jarad said. "What'd you do? Why is Lady Lyssanne afraid of you?"

Sir Brennus said nothing, his gaze locked with hers.

"Go! Please," Lyssanne whispered. She had to make them see they were in danger. Could they not hear it in her voice? A sob froze in her throat. Tears formed at the corners of her eyes. All the while, she couldn't look away from *his* face.

"I am not going to hurt them," the knight said, his eyes boring into hers. "Or you."

Truth rang through his words, and Lyssanne's shoulders loosened. Yet, memory drummed in her ears louder than the pain hammering against her brain. *Witch...destroyed...the only fate sorcery deserves.*

His large hand crept toward her face, and she flinched.

"I give you my word," he said, the harshness of his tone contradicting the gentleness with which he brushed the hair from her eyes. "I will bring no harm to you, any of you, this night. Nor shall I allow any other to do so."

"But you said..." Lyssanne had to pause for breath, even after so few words.

"I am well aware of what I said." He handed his cloth to Jarad. "However, once given, my word will not be broken. Any knight who does otherwise is no knight at all."

The fervor in his voice left little doubt. 'Twas no empty assurance Sir Brennus had spouted. Besides, the King hadn't shown Lyssanne such wonders only to abandon her now.

Still, she had to move, to sit up, anything but remain lying here with the knight looming above her. She tried to rise, but managed only to lift her head. Mistake, that. The world swam, and her head sank, heavy as two sacks of flour.

Sir Brennus laid a hand on her shoulder. "Rest."

"I brought you some water, Lady Lyssanne," Jarad said, his voice tense as a bowstring. "Maybe you'll feel better if you have some?" He looked to Sir Brennus, his next words more timid than any she'd heard him utter. "Could you, um, help her up? Or...or hold this, so I can?"

Before Lyssanne could protest, Sir Brennus lifted her into a sitting position and leaned her against him. Thanking him, Jarad held the water-skin to her lips. What could she do but drink? Once she'd had her fill, the knight lowered her back to the grass.

She must have fallen asleep mere moments afterward, for when next she aroused, deepest night shrouded their camp. Someone had draped a blanket over her. Soft snores wafted from a few feet away; and, across the campfire, Sir Brennus and Reina spoke in hushed voices.

"My word stands, Shining One," Sir Brennus said. "I'll not harm even a sorceress while she is ill and helpless, but how can you consort with her?"

"Fear not to keep company with her, knight," said Reina. "There is more magic at work in you than in her."

"You dare accuse me! I am no sorcerer."

"Precisely."

Silence stretched out like unfurling wings.

"I know what I saw," he said, at last.

"You saw what others cannot," said Reina. "'Tis a precious boon, that gift of sight. You must open your heart to recognize what it is you see."

Again, silence claimed him. Then he spoke, his tone unreadable. "What was it?"

"What you saw was…a mere reflection."

"No, she lit that fire without flint or coals. There was no glass, steel, or water near enough to reflect anything."

"Not that kind of reflection," Reina said. "It is she who is the mirror, reflecting a power far greater than mere magic, far greater than us all."

"What power?"

"Her King."

Magic. Would he never be free of it? Noire had begun to despair of the possibility.

Aiming his beak at the sun, he shot upward, beating the sky with the full fury of that thought. When the air thinned, he flipped into a sharp dive, plummeting toward the treetops. He pulled up so close; his talons tore loose a shower of leaves.

He soared over Cloistervale, his stunt having calmed his emotions and cleared his head. Mostly. He had a mission, and no shock, no magical creature, *nothing,* would prevent him from seeing it through.

The landscape below reflected his mood, bearing little resemblance to the village he'd flown over when first spying upon Lyssanne. The Shadow Mist covered almost every acre of ground, in places no more than wispy vapor, solid as cloth in others. Damaged buildings blemished many streets, testifying of violence, and once-verdant fields stood fallow.

The people trudged about, ragged and careworn, like peasants elsewhere. How had he failed to notice that Cloistervale's inhabitants had never before appeared thus?

Perhaps for the same reason he'd permitted Lyssanne to deceive him. Her intentional wielding of magic and conversation with Reina about faeries had almost cost him everything.

Clamping his beak so tight his jaw ached, Noire sailed toward the Lucent Mountains. At a shout from below, he dipped his head to peer beneath a wing. A fight had broken out. Fitting.

He angled upward to skim the mountainside, his talons raking the treetops. How could he allow Lyssanne's soft voice and quiet ways to deceive him? Oh, he'd been a fool, convincing himself the magic surrounding her resulted from forces beyond her knowledge or control.

Venefica must never know.

He plunged into the thicket, then through the open window of his chamber to rest his wings and await sunset. Once in his true form, he sought Venefica out.

He slipped without sound through her chamber doorway, his lips curving in anticipation of catching her off guard. Instead, the sudden, violent rattling of an ornate cask in one corner startled an exclamation from him. "What in the Seven Lands is that?"

Venefica drew a sharp breath, turning from her tall, gilded mirror. "An ally."

He strode to the cask, hands clasped behind his back. The vessel stood a foot tall and half that in diameter. Carved runes, painted in red and black, covered its stone surface.

"Do not venture too near," Venefica said. "It would be unwise to disturb the oni. I have not yet sufficient power to command them fully."

What menace could lurk in so small a vessel? Still, he stepped back. "If this poses such danger, why keep it here?"

"To test them, of course. As my power grows, I shall be able to transport them whither I will and compel them to attack whom I wish, all with a mere thought." She walked over and patted the domed lid of the cask as one might pat the head of a dog. "Already I have strength enough to send one oni as far as Cloistervale. Though, until I have full rein on its actions, I dare not. I didn't bring them here to feed on my village."

"Your village?" He smirked. "Those peasants don't even know you exist."

"All in good time. I must let them ripen before I pluck them up for my service. Soon, they will beg me to rule them." She returned to the mirror and resumed brushing her hair. "And you? Why have you returned? I didn't summon you, and the girl still lives."

"There has been a development which may make this task you desire more difficult."

"Difficult?" She huffed. "What of your vaunted stealth? Are you a warrior or a mere watcher?"

He narrowed his eyes. Well, he'd taken *her* by surprise. "And what of the faeries?"

She spun back to face him, eyes flashing. "Faeries?"

"I overheard the girl spouting some drivel to the unicorn about learning to wield a weapon," he said. "Apparently, she had a visitation from two faeries who spoke of this."

Venefica's voice all but growled. "When?"

He shrugged. "She mentioned it yestermorn, but I can't be certain when she saw them."

"The most crucial information concerning the girl in weeks," Venefica snapped, "and you learn of it secondhand?"

"The stretch of forest through which they've been traveling is thick with plateris trees," he said. "I've been forced to fly above the canopy and lose sight of them on occasion."

"Faeries," Venefica said, stalking away from him. "One more thing to stand in my way!"

He smirked. "Yes, well, surely you don't expect me to go up against that kind of power."

"No," she said. "They must not detect my hand in these matters. Even if they suspect I've returned to Lastarra, they mustn't learn of your true allegiance, lest they use you to gain information. As it is, I do not think them aware of the full extent of my power." She fixed him with a glittering gaze. "We must discover what they know."

"How do you propose we do that?"

"Make some excuse to encounter the girl. Gain her trust. Give the faeries no cause to suspect you, but find out what they have told her, and what she can do with that power of hers."

"Easy enough," he said. "Though it will take time. I must return to that border town to retrieve the stallion you bewitched for me." He folded his arms. "We must find another way to converse. As Lyssanne's distance from Cloistervale grows, so does the time it takes me to fly back here. Soon, relocating them will grow near impossible."

After a long silence, Venefica bade him follow her to the tower. She scooped one of her odd powders into a cloth packet and handed it to him. "This will enable you to speak with me through any pool or puddle," she said. "Drop a pinch of it into the water while in your human form. I shall be able to see and hear you. The powder will have no ill effect, so fear not to use it, even in your only source of drinking water."

He glared at the packet. More magic.

~

The sun was again sinking by the time Noire made his way back toward Lyssanne's camp. The girl was a distraction and, for that alone, should be eliminated. Still, he must remember his role had reverted to that of spy, not assassin. Not yet.

At least the crack he'd allowed to form in his heart's armor had sealed, harder and stronger than ever. Venefica's promise might not be worth much, but it was all he had. His family's survival—nay, the fate of an entire people—hinged on this quest to break his curse.

He alighted in a thick patch of wood a safe distance from the stream where Lyssanne had rested since his attack. Once darkness fell and he had shifted, he trudged through the underbrush to inform the girl and her friends of the road he'd *discovered.*

"It leads out of the forest?" Jarad said. "That will make travel easier for Lady Lyssanne."

"That would be most welcome," Lyssanne said. Her more sedate manner curbed some of Jarad's exuberance.

"We should set out at once," Brennus said. "Traveling by night, we will avoid notice."

Reina nodded, eyeing him for long moments.

Later that night, Brennus dismounted to hack a path through a tangle of vines. As he swung back into the saddle, Lyssanne and Reina stopped alongside him.

"Why do you travel with us?" Lyssanne asked with uncharacteristic abruptness.

He shrugged. He'd prepared for this. "My destination lies in this general direction."

"Yes, but," she hesitated as if choosing her words. "'Tis obvious what you think of me." She looked away. "Why slow your journey to keep pace with us?"

Oh, she was astute. He must tread cautiously. "As a knight," he said, "I can't leave a woman to journey alone when she is ill and has only a boy as escort." He thought for a moment, then added a touch sure to appeal to her feminine sensibilities. "Besides, I feel somewhat responsible for your worsened state."

Lyssanne and Reina lagged behind, allowing him to again take the lead. When they reached the road, they found it deserted. About an hour into their journey along the packed dirt path, Brennus slowed, having pulled well ahead of the others. He turned to await them.

Moonlight spilled down upon Lyssanne as she rode into view, rendering the lantern Jarad held beside her unnecessary. She resembled a faerie queen in some legend, sitting atop a unicorn, her pale skin shining, hair flying loose behind her, a dove perched on one shoulder.

Brennus shook himself and whipped back around. She was a sorceress, like Venefica, and not to be trusted or pitied. Clenching his jaw, he rode on without looking back.

Later, as they rounded a bend, the moon sank behind the trees. Jarad's lantern now proved a rather useful convenience. About a mile farther, something shone white in the lantern light. Brennus slowed as they approached, the brightness revealing itself as the snowy hair of a shriveled old man who stood between the road and a steep, shadowy embankment.

"What's such an old man doin' out here this late at night?" Jarad asked.

"Perhaps we should stop and see if he needs assistance," Lyssanne said.

"Unwise," said Brennus. "He could be a thief, a madman, or worse."

Rather than agreeing as he'd hoped, Reina stopped near the white-haired man, forcing Brennus to rein in and double back.

He positioned his stallion between Reina and the stranger. If there was to be trouble, he wanted no obstacle to hinder his battle. He kept his gaze trained on the man, until a swish and thud announced Lyssanne's dismount behind him. Gritting his teeth, he did likewise. Keeping one hand on his hilt, he approached the old man, who also held a blade.

The stranger stood with his sword stuck partway in the ground, leaning on it like a cane. He indeed appeared mad, bent as he was to one side, his tongue lolling out. Perhaps he was a vagabond; for, his wispy, matted hair and stringy goatee trailed over clothes that hung in baggy folds from his bony shoulders to sandaled feet.

Jarad's lantern banged against the handle of Lyssanne's cart, rousing the old man from his stupor. His eyes fell upon Brennus, and he struggled to free his sword from the turf. He pushed against the blade with a foot, heedless of the gouge he was cutting into his sandal. After one last yank, the blade swung free in a wide arc, straight toward Brennus.

Jumping back, Brennus raised his hands. "Easy, man." He spoke low, unwilling to startle the stranger into doing something rash. He preferred not to kill the old man if possible.

Lyssanne's skirts brushed his leg as she backed away from the stranger. "Perhaps you were right," she whispered, stirring the back of his sleeve. "We should be on our way."

The old man's gaze flashed to Lyssanne, and he lowered his sword with unsteady hands. "Nay, fair lady," he said. "We've not yet been introduced."

Brennus had no patience for civilities. "Who are you, peasant?"

"I'm no peasant!" The stranger shifted his weight, tottering on his severed sandal as he raised his sword hand in an old-fashioned salute. "Sir Fizzil, at your servi—*ee*!"

With his last word trailing off like the squealing of a pig, Sir Fizzil tripped backward, his sword flying from his flailing hand. He tumbled head over heels down the steep slope then hit a bump that sent him flying. At length, he landed and crashed up against a boulder.

"We must see if that poor man has come to harm," Lyssanne said. She began picking her way down the slope.

Sighing, Brennus followed. It would serve her right if she tumbled after the crazy old coot. Yet, to maintain his cover, he had no choice but go after her. He caught up with Lyssanne and gripped her elbow to guide her down the slope. They found Sir Fizzil bruised but not broken and, of all things, laughing. Together Brennus and Lyssanne helped him up.

"Sorry if I gave you a fright, fair lady," the old man said, patting her arm. "A fellow can't be too cautious, traveling these woods alone at night."

"Why are you traveling alone?" she asked.

"I have no companions."

"Obviously," Brennus couldn't help saying. Lyssanne shot him a look he was sure she'd once used on her students. He ignored it. "Where are you headed, old man?"

"I'm off to see a shaman. The Shaman of the Wood."

Lyssanne stiffened as Brennus eyed the old man. Did he mean the mystic the addled peddler in Westerfield had claimed as mentor?

"His home's at the edge of the wood," said Sir Fizzil, "a few days' journey along yon road. Mind giving me a hand up this hill?"

They did so, and Lyssanne went so far as to offer the old man to share their camp and travel with them. They were, after all, going the same direction.

"Just follow the smoke," said Sir Fizzil, his voice dreamy.

Mad? Most certainly.

Jarad and Reina agreed to Lyssanne's suggestion, so Sir Fizzil joined them, further slowing their journey. As before, Brennus traveled ahead during daylight and rejoined them at night. On occasion, he permitted Jarad to spot him at a distance, weaving among dark trees in shadow form. For once, Venefica's magic served his needs, enabling his insubstantial body to sit atop his stallion and preventing the animal from shying in his presence.

The night air had grown cold. Lyssanne pulled on her cloak and settled closer to the fire, weary after another day's traveling in company with Sir Brennus and the rather odd Sir Fizzil. A few paces away, the younger of the two knights leaned toward the firelight to inspect a flaw in his harness. She shivered, the air not the only source of her chill.

At least her head pain hadn't lingered past the night Sir Brennus had threatened her life. Most of her fear of him had also faded, as he'd since remained civil, if distant. Still, his mere nearness set her heart to racing, and not in a good way.

"A cup of flyl would sure do us some good," Jarad said, settling beside her.

"As it happens," she said, "I have the makings for a small pot of flyl."

"You jest!"

She shook her head. "One piquantine fruit hadn't yet ripened when I left the village, so I brought it along, and I have several honcin sticks."

"Think the fruit's still good?"

"Oh, yes, piquantines last many months. But, Jarad, I don't think I'm up to the task of brewing flyl. I haven't the strength to grind honcin or stand over a boiling pot."

"I'll do it!" Jarad bounced to his feet. "Just tell me how. You make the best flyl. I know you could teach me."

Once Jarad had squeezed all the juice from the piquantine, Lyssanne took over the task of slicing it and scraping the pulp from its tough but pliant hull. When Jarad began grinding the honcin, a harrumph from Sir Brennus drew her gaze.

"Why not use your unique...talents?" he said. "Instead, you persuade the boy to do woman's work."

The sound of Jarad's grinding ceased, as a lump formed in Lyssanne's throat. Heat rose from her tightening chest, up her neck, into her cheeks.

"She didn't persuade me anything," Jarad said. "What makes this woman's work anyway? I wanted flyl, so why shouldn't I make it?"

"Jarad," Lyssanne said, forcing a level tone, "don't be uncivil."

"Me? But—"

"Add this to your pot," she said, handing him the hull containing the loosened pulp. "Once the honcin is ground as fine as you can make it, stir it in with slow strokes."

Fortunately, the flyl was soon brewed, preventing more questions for which Lyssanne had no answers. The warm, fruity beverage soothed the churning within her, and its energizing properties did boost her stamina, if only a little.

"Mm," Jarad said, a grin breaking out across his face. "Almost as good as yours!"

Sir Fizzil gulped down his first cup without waiting for it to cool. "Careful, fair lady," he said. "You'll have gnomes and faeries and, I daresay, even a dragon or two swarmin' this camp. He-he! Even they've never had anything so good!" He stood and danced an awkward little jig around the campfire, before suddenly sinking to the ground and letting out a loud snore.

Sir Brennus sipped at his cup, but only after the others had all but emptied theirs. Perhaps he thought it poisoned, or some witch's potion. In the end, he pronounced it rather tasty.

Once the flyl pot was drained and the trappings of cookery put away, Sir Brennus called Jarad over for a lesson in combat. A few days before, Jarad had asked the knight to teach him to defend himself and others. The incident in Westerfield had shaken him, and he'd vowed to be prepared should they ever again meet with trouble.

"Had you a knife," Sir Brennus said, "I could teach you hand-to-hand fighting. In close-range combat, your arrows will not serve."

"Oh," Jarad said, his voice thick. "I had a hunting knife, a pretty good one, but I broke it on that monster's cocoon."

"I have this," Lyssanne said, handing him the dagger she'd used to slice the piquantine. As much as she loathed the idea of Jarad fighting, it might someday prove necessary. Besides, every boy dreamt of learning combat from a knight. How could she deny Jarad this opportunity?

"This will do for practice," Sir Brennus said, "and it may prove useful in combat if you have nothing else, but a kitchen knife is no match for a proper weapon."

Lyssanne curled up on her blanket and watched a little more of Jarad's boyhood fade.

Lyssanne and her friends passed the following week in much the same manner as the previous one, at times leaving the road to avoid a nearby village and camping just within the tree-line at night. Jarad continued his lessons with Sir Brennus, Sir Fizzil piping up with occasional suggestions. Though, most of his advice was little more than confused rambling.

However addled the old knight might be, his constant squeals of "follow the smoke" proved quite sane. Late one afternoon, Jarad spotted a plume of smoke rising above the trees and, as they neared, the top of the stone tower from which it wafted.

"That's him!" Sir Fizzil said. "Shaman of the Wood. Follow the smoke, he-he!"

Indeed, without Sir Fizzil's smoke to follow, the tower would have proven all but invisible against the greying sky. Storm clouds rolled in as the sun began to set.

When night fell, they stopped as usual to await Sir Brennus. He, too, had seen the tower and investigated. It stood at the edge of the forest, he reported, several miles through the woods in the opposite direction of the road. They agreed to escort Sir Fizzil thither, lest he lose his way. Lyssanne prayed they journeyed not into a danger worse than the impending storm.

Sir Brennus broke through the trees just ahead of Lyssanne and Reina. He drew to a halt and wheeled his mount to the north. Reina turned alongside him. The tower loomed ahead.

Even in the darkness of clouded moonlight, the ruin cast its shadow over them. Though Lyssanne had read of such fortresses in tales and histories, the height of the stone pile before her stole her breath. She craned her neck, nearly toppling backward in the attempt to behold its roof.

Jarad whistled, stepping between Reina and the stallion. "Was that part of a castle?"

"More likely a guard tower for a small fortress," said Sir Brennus. "Remnants of the curtain wall are still affixed to its side." He pointed to the jagged outline of the otherwise cylindrical structure. "And notice the arrow slits spiraling at intervals up the tower."

Sir Fizzil hobbled past, heading toward the single door set into the mottled gray stone.

"Wait, old man," Sir Brennus said, dismounting.

"Perhaps you should walk from here as well, Lyssanne," Reina said. "The ground appears quite uneven. I wouldn't wish to throw you."

Lyssanne dismounted and picked her way toward the tower, her feet molding to the waves and holes beneath them. The toe of her right shoe slammed against a hard, unyielding lump, and she stumbled. Her hands shot out to break her fall, one scraping against a protrusion. Inches from her nose, lay a jagged block of stone smeared with green stains.

She rose, brushed off her skirts, and glanced about. Overgrown foundation stones and shards of wall jutted from the grass at odd angles, like a trail of broken teeth leading to the tower.

Jarad stopped beside her, half carrying their cart over the uneven ground. They made their way slowly forward, Jarad warning her of hidden stones or furrows.

Sir Brennus had outstripped the older knight's awkward stride to reach the door first. He knocked with the hilt of his sword. No response.

"Perhaps he's out back," Sir Fizzil said, Then he shuffled off around the tower before anyone could stop him.

"Crazy old man," Sir Brennus said, hastening after him.

Lyssanne and Jarad followed.

Just as they reached Sir Fizzil, a figure emerged from behind a garden wall, hooded and holding a staff across his body as if ready for a fight. "Begone!" he shouted.

"Show yourself," Sir Brennus ordered, one hand on his sword hilt. "We mean no harm."

The hooded man flicked his staff side to side, and both ends blazed up, their flames casting his face further in shadow. "Begone or face your doom!" He twirled the flaming staff in a dizzying display, then swung it toward Sir Brennus, who dodged it with expert grace.

"King of All Lands, preserve us!" Lyssanne cried, as steel hissed beside her.

Sir Brennus lunged forward. His sword clashed with the middle of the fiery staff, and both men held still.

The stranger's hood turned toward Lyssanne. "You serve the King, miss?"

"Y-yes," she said.

"And these ruffians accompany you?" he asked, his voice strained.

"Ruffians?" said Sir Fizzil. "We're knights o' the Seven Lands, 'cept the squire here." He pointed to Jarad. "You the shaman? Sure y'are. We followed the smoke."

"If you honor the King, you are no enemy of mine," the man said. He took a step away from Sir Brennus. "Forgive the theatrics. Let us dispense with them, shall we?"

He backed toward the wall then tipped his staff to plunge one end into a bucket. A loud hiss and plume of steam arose. He did likewise with the other end of the staff before taking a step forward and extending a hand toward Sir Brennus.

"The name's Fescue, but yes, some persist in calling me Shaman of the Wood."

"Keep your distance, sorcerer," Sir Brennus said, stepping in front of Lyssanne.

"I am no wizard, Sir Knight," the stranger said, throwing back his hood to reveal waves of silver and onyx hair. "This was merely the work of powders and air, not unlike what fuels a torch. The title your elder friend affords me springs from the curse of unwarranted notoriety."

"I know a thing or two about curses," said Sir Brennus, lowering his sword.

"Yes, well," the stranger said, as if at a loss for how to respond. He turned to Lyssanne. "You startled me, riding up so late, but servants of the King are most welcome here."

"Sir," Lyssanne said, her voice still tremulous, "did you say your name is Fescue?"

"Indeed, Seanan Fescue at your service, Mistress…?"

"Lyssanne," she said. "I think we may have a mutual acquaintance."

"That is possible. As a former Steward of the King, I've traveled most of the Seven Lands at one time or other. Whence does this acquaintance hail?"

"His current residence is Cloistervale, in northern Lastarra," she said.

"Ah, wouldn't be Gierre DeLivre you speak of, perchance?"

"You jest!" Jarad said. He glanced at Lyssanne. "*Our* Mr. DeLivre?"

"We know him well," she said, breathless. "How are you acquainted with him?"

"Met him in Lyrya many years ago," Mr. Fescue said. "I believe he was serving at court, scribe or clerk to Lyrya's king. Good man, Gierre."

"Yes," Lyssanne said, her heart swelling. If this man was a friend to Mr. DeLivre, she could be safe here. "He has been like family to me. I miss him terribly."

"Lyssanne…" he murmured. "That's why your name sounded familiar. He wrote of you, I think. Said you were his most prized student, the granddaughter he'd never had. Taught you Lyryan, did he?"

She nodded. "He wrote about me?"

"We keep in touch. How is my old friend?"

"Quite well when last I saw him."

Mr. Fescue smiled then spun in a circle, surveying the group as thunder rumbled overhead. "You are all welcome to dine and rest. I treat the sick, so I have beds aplenty if you wish to shelter here for the night." He turned back to Lyssanne. "You and your elderly friend look ready to collapse where you stand. Do allow me the honor of assisting you." .

Despite Lyssanne's trepidations, she could have wept at the thought of sleeping in a bed. "Thank you, sir."

"Well then, by all that is good, let us not stand out here tempting the rain. Come, take your ease inside." He swept a hand toward the tower. "After you."

As Lyssanne picked her way around the tower's base, Sir Brennus strode up beside her. "You'd be foolish to trust this man, any of you," he murmured.

"Perhaps," Lyssanne said, "but I do trust the King, and I'm past tired."

Fat, cold droplets began pelting her from above, fast turning into a hard onslaught.

"Pardon, Mr. Fescue," she said over her shoulder, "have you shelter for our horses?"

He glanced toward Sir Brennus's stallion and Reina, who'd again hidden her true nature. "I have an old gray gelding stabled out back of the tower. Afraid it's little more than a shed, but there should be room enough for your steeds."

As Sir Brennus strode toward his stallion, Reina trotted in the direction Fescue indicated.

"Intelligent mare, that one," Mr. Fescue said. "Now, let's get indoors."

WISPS OF DARKNESS AND LIGHT

*W*hile Sir Fizzil regaled Mr. Fescue with tales of an old battle wound that refused to heal, Lyssanne glanced about the circular chamber. The grasshopper she'd once found at the bottom of her stone cistern must have felt akin to this. The lofty ceiling gave the small room a more expansive ambiance and doubtless supported a stack of single chambers, similar to this one.

Shivering, she stepped nearer the flames flickering within the arched stone fireplace. Lamps and candles warmed the edges of the rounded interior, setting the few, tidy furnishings aglow. The flickering dimness soothed her weary eyes, and she suppressed a yawn.

As she turned to warm her back, an open book on a table beneath the window caught her eye. She strode over to it and peered at its ornate pages.

Mr. Fescue paused in the midst of dragging a chair toward the hearth. "Do you read, mistress?"

"Oh, yes," she said. "Is this your work?"

"Indeed, the writing and the illustrations, that is. The words are those of another." He showed her a tattered, yellowed volume open to the same passage of text. "How did you guess?"

"I recognized your handwriting." She went to her cart, which Jarad had parked beside the door, and withdrew the book Mr. DeLivre had given her the day she left Cloistervale.

"My word!" Mr. Fescue said. "Ha, or rather, the King's. I never thought to clap eyes upon this again. Quite a thick volume to copy, that." He laughed. "How did you come by it?"

Lyssanne told him.

"She taught me to read, too," said Jarad. "So, when her eyes are weary, I can take over."

"Well, I'm blessed!" Mr. Fescue said. "I gave you a way 'round the limits of sight? And you, passing on the King's words to this young fellow, turning a weapon of the enemy to good purpose—That'll put a wasp in the old Thief's whiskers."

He shuffled off but soon returned to hang a kettle over the fire.

"Sit, warm yourselves while I heat up a pot of soup," he said, his smooth voice comforting, almost musical. "Won't take long."

Sir Brennus strode into the tower. "Tell me, old man," he said, his tone souring the harmonious atmosphere, "are you acquainted with a talisman peddler in Westerfield?"

All eyes turned to Brennus, Lyssanne's shoulders jolting as if his appearance startled her. Brennus locked his gaze on the stranger, lest he make any sudden moves. A sorcerer in close proximity to a kettle and fire was nothing to trifle with.

'Westerfield, you say?" Fescue straightened, his eyes wary.

"A squat, bedraggled man, selling trinkets and charms," said Brennus.

"You met him too?" Jarad asked. "The man with the animal claws and stuff?"

"I daresay anyone who enters the market square is afforded that pleasure, willingly or not." Brennus returned his sharp gaze to the supposed shaman. "You say you are no sorcerer, but this peddler's boasting of you would indicate otherwise. He claimed you as mentor."

"That much is true," said Fescue. "He was once my student, a gifted dreamer in the King's service. Alas, he let greed and arrogance consume him. Now he's a bit mad and preys on the superstitions of others, always longing for a restoration of the gift he squandered."

"A dreamer?" Lyssanne asked.

"A young man chosen to receive messages from the King during slumber. I taught him as best I could how to use his gift, to write down his visions at first waking, so they could be passed on as the King directed." Fescue chuckled. "He tended to speak and write most often in riddles."

"Yeah," Jarad said. "I didn't understand half of what he said. Something about shadows and birds that bark and stone trees or, hang on." He dug the rolled parchment from Lyssanne's cart. "He gave us this."

Fescue unfurled the parchment, frowned over it, then passed it back to Jarad. "I see he hasn't lost his talent entirely." He turned to stir his kettle. "Perhaps there is yet hope for him."

"But what does it mean?" Jarad asked, dropping the parchment into the cart.

"His description sounds akin to a legendary creature I once heard of in Lyrya."

"Is it a bird?" Jarad asked. "A dog? The riddle said something about a lion, too."

"A bird, I believe, of grand proportions, with the head of a dog, the tail of a peacock, and the claws of a lion."

Brennus frowned. Despite his extensive research into every legend surrounding magic, even he was hard-pressed to picture such a creature.

"It is said to symbolize the union betwixt land and sky," Fescue said, scratching his chin. "Like a bridge, or messenger between the King and His creation. Though, we need no bridge, save our own loyalty, between us and the King."

"Do you think such a creature could exist?" Lyssanne asked.

"No idea, but one never can tell. Stranger things there are in the King's domain than can be conceived in the heart of man. His arts aren't limited by our knowledge." Fescue chuckled. "But if my old student had a vision of it, I'd say it must exist—or something very like it. One thing's certain, the King has a message for you, and some creature carries it."

"If this man abandoned the King," Lyssanne said, "how can I trust his words?"

"A wise question, my dear," said Fescue. "The King oft uses unlikely messengers. Still, I shall search out his words for confirmation. You should also seek guidance in the *Kingsword*."

"Where would I find such a creature?" Lyssanne asked.

"Legend claims, its lair can only be found if one has already visited it."

Jarad's groan elicited a smirk from Brennus. "Then, 'tis impossible!" the boy said.

"Not so." Fescue hefted the kettle from the fire with an iron rod. "If the King intends to speak through this creature, He'll show you the way." Grunting, he set the kettle atop a cloth on his scarred table. "But He won't make it easy."

"Why would the King hinder a path he wishes me to take?" Lyssanne asked.

"Oh, I don't mean to imply He'll hinder you, quite the contrary." Fescue waved them to the table. "Just don't expect the creature to fly into your lap and cry, 'Lo, were you looking for me?'" He laughed. "Course, based on what I've heard, if it did, it'd probably crush you. The King will light your path, but you must be watching for the flame."

Lyssanne sighed, taking a seat next to Jarad. "More journeys with no certain destination."

Fescue ladled out soup. Brennus declined. He would settle for less pleasant and, perchance, safer fare on the morrow. After dinner, they again fell to discussing the riddle.

"Where the sun lays its head," Jarad said. "That's west, right? I don't know about the snow and sea part, but what's west of here?"

"Gian Plain," said Fescue, "just beyond this tower."

"I wonder..." Lyssanne rose and rummaged through her cart. At length, she pulled out a crude map and spread it on the table. "Mr. DeLivre sketched this."

They all peered at it, except Sir Fizzil, who hummed to himself while twirling a feather.

"Here it is," Jarad said. "Gian Plain. And look, just beyond it, Lyrya."

"Mr. DeLivre's homeland," Lyssanne said. "He often spoke of the sea. Is Lyrya coastal?"

"A small strip of it borders the Noorzad Sea," said Brennus. "I've visited the shore with friends who reside in the realm."

"Hmm, the riddle mentioned a…what was it?" said Fescue. "A marble tree?"

"Granite," Lyssanne said.

"Ah, yes. I heard talk of such a thing, long ago, when I traveled in Lyrya. I think it, too, is a local legend of theirs. Might give you a place to start."

Further cause for Lyssanne to leave Lastarra. Perhaps fortune at last smiled on Brennus.

"This rain's set in," said Fescue. "Autumn storms can last days. Why not ride out the weather here? Meantime, I'll look into this mystery a bit further. Before you retire for the night, though, tell me, did my old student say anything else?"

Lyssanne glanced around as if hesitant. Her gaze passed over Sir Fizzil, slumped and snoring, to rest on Brennus. Drawing breath, she turned to Fescue. "He said I must beware the shadows that take fog as form." She then described the Mist she'd seen in Cloistervale. "Could it be this, he spoke of?"

Brennus tensed.

"I'm not certain," said Fescue. "Did he say what this fog is?"

"He said it is shadow and spirit, that it both creates and feeds on dark emotions."

"I shall research this as thoroughly as my library allows," Fescue said. "Meanwhile, the tower and gardens are yours to explore."

"Your library?" Lyssanne said.

"When I traveled the realms sharing the King's joyous tidings, I collected old books and scrolls on dark magics," he said. "The best way to counteract an enemy is to understand him. Perhaps your answer lies in one of those." Fescue rose and strode to an alcove containing a winding, stone stair. "Mistress Lyssanne, you are welcome to the guest chamber on the first landing." He swung to face Brennus. "If you'll assist me, Sir Knight, I've cots for you and Sir Fizzil beneath the stair. I trust a pallet will suffice for you, young Jarad?"

Nodding, Jarad rushed to help Brennus and Fescue with the bedding.

Once Sir Fizzil was settled, Lyssanne started for the alcove, but Brennus caught her arm. "I shall bid you farewell. My quest is not yet complete, and I must be on my way."

"You're leaving? In this storm?"

"At dawn." In truth, he'd depart long before that to secure his mount elsewhere, but she mustn't know this. "I've spoken with Reina. She believes it is wise that you rest here. I'm certain she will see to your protection."

"Then, I bid you safe journey," Lyssanne said.

Two days later, Lyssanne lounged upon a woven chair in Mr. Fescue's lush gardens. Shelter and bed rest had restored her to a new vigor rivaling his rain-freshened flowers and herbs. Still, after attempting to peruse the tiny, handwritten scrawls and faded texts in his dim library, she'd left research into the matter of shadows to him.

As if summoned by her thoughts, Mr. Fescue burst from the tower. "I've found it!"

Lyssanne set her *Kingsword* atop a garden table and rose. "The creature or the shadows?"

"The latter," he said. "'Tis a tale best told in sunlight. I'll fetch another chair."

"I shall find Jarad," she said. "I'd prefer he hear everything you've discovered."

In moments, all were assembled. Even Reina and Serena peeked over the garden wall.

Mr. Fescue opened a dusty, yellowed volume that looked as if it might crumble. "Shadow and spirit, that was the key," he said. "I spent all that time looking up spells that bring on darkness, or fog, or whatnot—and there are hundreds. Humph, the spirit part finally led me to it." He flipped pages with care. "Here we are...a spiritual parasite." He looked up. "The book calls it Shadow Mist. I'm almost certain this is what my old student described to you."

"But what is it?" Lyssanne asked.

He patted the book. "According to this, 'tis a melding of spiritual and physical darkness." Peering at the page, he began to read. "The spiritual element influences minds and hearts to evil thought and emotion. The shadow blinds the victim to its presence and intent. While the Mist fuels the darkness in men, that darkness feeds the Mist. As a result of every feeding, the power of the Mist's keeper grows." He closed the book and leaned back against the slats of his chair.

Lyssanne shivered. "The Mist's keeper?"

"The sorcerer who commands it," he said. "One who has given himself over completely to Darkness, but who is deceived. No human can control the spirit of the Mist. It allows you to think so to fulfill its own ends. In truth, the Thief of Souls is in control."

"Like the spirits who left the King's service to join the Thief's rebellion?" Lyssanne said.

"I daresay, it is precisely that," said Mr. Fescue. "You have a formidable enemy."

"But why? To my knowledge, I've never even met a sorcerer."

"That, only you can discover. But know this, your foe's influence is spreading rapidly."

Lyssanne leaned forward, her eyes widening. "You've seen this... Shadow Mist, too?"

"No, I've seen what I suspect to be its work, and I've received disturbing reports from your region of Lastarra." He sighed. "Lyssanne, this Mist isn't normally visible to the human eye. Since you can see it, you doubtless pose a threat to its keeper, if only in the sorcerer's mind. Perhaps my student's warning and riddle are the King's way of advising you to leave Lastarra."

"I know not where to go."

"Seek out the creature." He stood and picked up his book. "Perhaps Lyrya holds answers for you."

Noire edged from beneath the bush where he'd sat frozen, listening to Fescue describe Venefica's favored weapon to her sworn enemy. Well, Lyssanne had been warned. Be it on her head if she chose to disregard that counsel.

He lurked outside the garden wall until well after nightfall, grateful he had the means to speak with Venefica from a distance. Once the tower's lights winked out, he vaulted over the low stone barrier and approached the pool in the midst of the gardens. Clouds obscured the moon, so he wouldn't easily be seen, even should the unicorn chance to look.

Brennus knelt at the water's edge and pulled the packet Venefica had given him from his waist pouch. He stared at the glassy water then sprinkled a pinch of the powder over its surface and tucked the packet away, watching, waiting.

Within moments, the entire pool had gone a murky black. Venefica's face appeared in its midst. She had, as he'd suspected, witnessed Fescue's revelation. Her ranting lasted quite some time. Doubtless, Magda had spent much of that evening cleaning up broken household items.

"My enemy learns of my power, yet you fail to do likewise, discovering nothing of the FAE?" The water bubbled. "Now, you've allowed her to seek shelter with a former Steward of the King and can no longer show yourself? I begin to question your usefulness." She sneered. "If I did not know you so well, I might question your loyalty instead."

"Would you have me further expose myself to suspicion?" He

shook his head. "Lyssanne is wary of me, with reason. Should the faeries reappear, I'll not miss them again."

"See that you don't. You stand to lose much if you fail me." Across her image, she waved an ebony feather, *his* feather. "Watch."

The water blackened again. Had Venefica severed their connection? Then, the darkness parted, revealing an aerial view of Cloistervale. Ah, Shadow Mist—the blackness was a solid blanket of it covering the village.

In a field to the north, a fire raged. Boarded windows and burned-out buildings marred the once tidy rows of homes and shops. His vantage focused in on the moonlit square, where a brawl raged. The image shifted to a youth and his friends taking hammers to someone's wagon.

As if he'd been yanked upward, the scene fell away at dizzying speed. Half of Lastarra stretched out before him—the Cloister Valley, the River Esten, and several towns beyond. Cloistervale was little more than a black smudge north of the forest.

Wisps of Mist stretched to the villages just beyond Merchant's Bridge, and a dusting of the fog covered a town nestled in the curve of the woods bordering Gian Plain.

"Westerfield?" he asked, uncertain Venefica could still hear him.

She reappeared, sweeping away the landscape with the feather. "Indeed. You and Diornian gave me entrance into that town. Marvelous, is it not?"

"Your power has grown much since last I saw you."

"Certainly. And the people of my village have begun to cry out for my rule. Though, they do not yet realize it is me they long for. They begin to think with fondness of times past, when the lord and lady of the land could solve their ancestors' cares. They vent their displeasure with that council in spectacular ways. An uprising is eminent. Soon, they will serve me gladly." Her eyes lost their dreamy glaze and snapped to his face with stiletto sharpness. "As should you."

He swept her a bow, closing his eyes, lest she recognize in them the mockery of the gesture. "My lady." He straightened. "One question, that I may be certain of your wishes—"

"They have not changed," she said. "Remain hidden until the girl leaves the safety of that tower. The old man may be a further danger to our secrecy. I know neither his abilities nor what further information he possesses. Once the girl departs, ensure she leaves Lastarra forever, by any means necessary."

"And the FAE?"

"If your failure to ferret out what the faeries know continues, you'll simply have to kill Lyssanne yourself. Already, she knows too much. One way or another, I *will* be rid of her."

Lyssanne plucked a summerstar and held the yellow blossom to her nose. Its sweet scent conjured images of those hearty, five-petal flowers growing wild along the slope of Rowan Hill and watered her ache for home into full bloom.

Two faint pops chopped her remembrances short at their roots. She looked up, dropping her flower. Olivia and Jada hovered near her chair.

"The King has granted us permission to instruct you in the use of your gift," Olivia said.

Jada floated over and peered at Lyssanne. "That is, if you've accepted it."

"I thought I'd seen proof of your claims," Lyssanne said, "but it almost cost my life. The King started a fire, using light from within me. At least, I thought it was He. How can I know—"

"The knight acted out of fear," Olivia said. "The King stayed his hand. Now, watch."

As if drawing in the air, she swept her wand downward, forming a shimmering silver line. She repeated the motion twice more, starting from the same point, then connected the three lines at their base. The figure solidified into a triangular, glass prism.

"Like natural light," Olivia said, "the King's power can be refracted, divided into many directions or colors." She shot a beam of light into the floating pyramid. A rainbow spread out on all sides. "Angle the prism just so, and you can direct the light or produce a particular color."

She turned the pyramid, and a shaft of green light speared the ground at an oblique angle.

"You are the prism, Lyssanne," she said. "Your faith, the hand that turns it. Depending on the aim of your faith, you can direct the King's Light to fulfill any goal aligned with His word."

She turned the glass, allowing the light to wash the ground in multiple hues.

"And the colors? They are the varied manifestations of His Light—healing, sustenance for life, restoration, a shield of protection, a beacon to guide your path, and yes,"—she angled the pyramid again—"even a powerful weapon in times of warfare."

A thin ray of blinding light stabbed a leaf, sizzling, then both prism and light vanished. She handed Lyssanne the leaf. The beam had burned a hole through it.

"His Light is always within you," Olivia said, "but you must release your faith in order to direct its purpose and function."

"How?"

"Learn the King's wishes," Olivia said, "then aim your faith accordingly. Ah, just in time." She beckoned past Lyssanne's shoulder. "Come closer, young Jarad."

"Sorry," Jarad said, limping across the garden. "I didn't mean to disturb you. I'll just—"

"Nonsense," said Olivia. "Let me see that knee."

Olivia sketched a rapid pattern with her wand, and a wooden block pushed its way into being, as if through a membrane, then thudded to the ground.

"Prop your foot on this. It'll remain solid for a few hours, not that you'll need it that long," said Olivia. "Mm, as I thought, swollen and growing more so."

"What happened?" Lyssanne asked, leaning closer to inspect Jarad's knee.

"I'm fine, really," he said.

"He stepped in a rabbit warren," said Jada. "Ha! A hunter injured by his prey."

"The ground gave way under my foot," he said. "Guess one of their tunnels ran just beneath the surface. Caught two of 'em in my snare, though. Mr. Fescue'll like that."

"I daresay he will," Lyssanne said. "You need to prop that leg up. I shall dampen a cloth in the garden pool. The cold should reduce the swelling."

"Not so hasty," Olivia said. "Jarad, remain where you are. Lyssanne, what do you believe the King's wishes to be for this boy?"

Lyssanne shrugged. "I dare not attempt to guess His thoughts."

"Recall what He has said of those thoughts, of His care for His creations."

"Well…" she said, "'tis written, it is not His wish that the least of His creatures should suffer. When He called everything into being, it was perfect and whole."

"Then, if it is your belief the King would wish *this* creature whole,"—Olivia took Lyssanne's hand and placed it onto Jarad's knee —"ask it and let His Light do its work."

"Y-you speak of healing?"

"I do."

Many were the tales of the medicine-less healings the King had wrought when He'd walked the Seven Lands. Doubtless, He still sent such boons to His subjects from His Shining Land, but to think of such healing as one of the colors within the Light He'd placed inside her…'twas a notion as foreign as the tribal languages of Zyungland.

What might the King's power do if it did flow through her like light through a prism? Would it burn? Even if she could withstand such an outpouring of His divine nature, how could He use her, a broken vessel, to carry healing to anyone?

Lyssanne fidgeted beneath the faeries' weighty attention. With her fingertips brushing Jarad's knee, she silently petitioned the King to heal it of all injury. She tensed. At any moment, glorious warmth would fill her, as it had the night the King lit the fire. Any moment…

Was she wording her request amiss? She focused all her will on the

King's desire to restore those who were hurting, and repeated her petition many different ways. Why was she feeling nothing? She cracked her eyelids open. No glow shone upon her hands. She closed them again and reached within the deepest realms of her spirit, aching for the King's warm presence.

At length, she grew lightheaded, her legs too weak to support her. She sank to the ground, careful not to exert pressure on Jarad's knee. For long moments, she sat there praying, one hand raised to his knee above her head, feeling nothing but the folly of her own efforts. Finally, she wiped moisture from her brow and opened her eyes.

She had failed. That seemed all she was capable of doing anymore, disappointing someone—the Council, the faeries, perhaps even the King.

"I'm sorry," she said to Jarad then turned to Olivia. "I did something wrong or—"

"You're trying too hard," Jada said, arms folded, wand sparking aimless sizzles.

"This isn't about effort or struggle," Olivia said. "It is a matter of surrender."

"You said this Light is a weapon I must wield," Lyssanne said. "Surrender is giving up."

"When surrendering to an enemy," said Olivia. "This is surrender to a loved one. Such absolute trust grants the King the power and authority to act through you. Only then can you take control over your enemy."

"He does all the work," said Jada. "Your task is to let Him so suffuse you with His Light, it spills out to those you wish to aid."

"The lantern isn't the source of its glow," Olivia said. "It allows the flame to shine through its surface."

"What if I cannot learn to do this?" Lyssanne asked. "To at once surrender and take control? What will become of me? And what of Jarad's knee?"

"You will learn. Have patience with yourself," Olivia said. "The King does. Besides, you've used your gift several times already, though unawares."

"No, I, I couldn't have."

"You did," said Jada, "in Cloistervale and on this journey. The King doesn't need your consent or even your knowledge for His power to shine through you, only your faith."

"However," Olivia said, "if you learn to wield your gift, you can direct His strength where it is most needed." She rested a tiny hand on Lyssanne's shoulder. "Be not swayed by what you see or feel in the natural world. Whatever your senses perceive, believe the King has done the thing you've asked. Then, His Light can shine forth to accomplish it."

"Should I try again?" Lyssanne asked.

"Not today," Olivia said. "Let Jarad tend his knee in the natural way. Try again only if you feel the King's hand tugging at your heart."

"Will you return tomorrow?" Lyssanne asked. "I so wish to learn, to please the King. I have many questions." She averted her eyes. "Many fears."

"What fears?" the faeries asked as one.

"There is a darkness following me." She shivered. "Mr. Fescue, a servant of the King, warned me of an enemy who wields it. I don't understand. Has the foe of us all, the Thief of Souls, singled me out for some purpose? Is that why so many dangers have befallen us?"

The faeries exchanged glances. Olivia held up a hand as if to prevent Jada from speaking. "We shall discuss all this when next we meet," she said. "You've grown too pale and will be no help to any creature if fatigue renders you ill." She grasped Lyssanne's hand in both of hers. "Make use of this refuge while you may. The instant our duties permit, we shall return to you."

Noire spread his wings and let the bracing air lift him high. Autumn had knocked, and the land was cracking open the door. He glided in lazy spirals, allowing the air currents to carry him where they would.

Lyssanne would sleep a few hours yet, if not most of the morning. His own rest had been minimal, dawn bringing it to an abrupt end, along with his nightly stay in his natural body. Perhaps, if ever his curse was broken, he could sleep an entire night through.

If only he could ensure that Lyssanne would cross Gian Plain into Lyrya as Fescue advised, he might at last be rid of her and this detestable bargain. Though, the open spaces would afford no place to camouflage himself in shadow, and—for now, at least—wherever she journeyed, he must follow.

At present, she seemed intent on planting herself in Fescue's garden like one of the flowers. The faeries were certainly no help, insisting that she remain in the safety of the tower.

He shook off the memory and settled in a tree with a decent vantage of the door and gardens. Reina stood nearby, dozing. Moments later, Lyssanne emerged, and Reina's head jerked up, eyes alert.

Lyssanne paused to exchange greetings with the unicorn and assure her nothing was amiss. "I wish to find a quiet place to pray. A walk in the wood seems just the thing."

"Understandable," Reina said, "with Sir Fizzil's endless chatter. Still, don't wander far."

Noire took to the air. He dared not lose sight of Lyssanne. She had performed magic once before when she thought herself alone. She'd been praying that time, as well. He flowed into the shadows some distance ahead of her and waited.

She walked between the trees, her damp hair swaying in heavy, shining falls down her back. For the first time in months, the ever-present circles under her eyes were barely visible. She strolled toward his hiding place, graceful and fragile as a fawn.

"Thank you for this," she whispered, resting a hand against a trunk. "For its beauty and the shelter it brings. For Mr. Fescue's hospitality and kindness, I ask that you bless him." Sighing, she closed her eyes. "I thank you for Jarad and Reina. Few gifts could be as precious to me as their friendship. I pray you grant dear Sir Fizzil what healing he seeks."

She wandered deeper into the wood then glanced up, as a beam of sunlight pierced the canopy of leaves. The ghost of a smile danced across her lips. Her eyes shone as if she'd received an embrace from a beloved friend. Then, the light shifted and the spell was broken. Moving forward, much too near the place where he stood, she continued her monologue. He backed away, but at her next words, his legs forgot how to move.

"And I thank you for Sir Brennus," she whispered, "for shielding me throughout our journey with him. Though I confess I do not understand him, he is your creation, and his valiant actions have saved us from much calamity. For that and for his own sake, I ask—if it be an endeavor in keeping with your good purpose—please bless his quest."

What?

He must have spoken aloud. For, Lyssanne flinched, nearly coming out of her shoes. Her expression mirrored his own shock at her words…and she was looking right at him. Her hand flew to her mouth in concert with the further widening of her eyes.

He should slip away before she had a chance to scream or to swoon as she had the last time he'd frightened her. She just stood there, staring at him as if she were as frozen by his presence as he had been by her prayer.

She had seen him, *truly* seen him. Not just some vague image in the distance. This time, she was too close to mistake his shadowy form for a normal human body.

She need not recognize him, though.

Lyssanne could identify an acquaintance by utterance alone, but in this form, his voice was not his own. If he kept it gruff, closer to the caw of the raven, even she wouldn't know him.

This was a gift, a chance to rid himself of the girl without violating his knightly oaths. "You are not safe here," he said, growling the words.

She drew in a sharp breath. "Wh-who are you?"

"One who knows there is no longer a place for you in Lastarra."

She shuddered, a delicate flower trembling in a sudden rush of cold wind. He was that wind. He'd swept through the forest of her life, heedless of the tiny flower that had the misfortune of standing in his path. With enough force, one vicious blast of that wind could destroy the flower, shaking loose her glorious petals and leaving her in shreds.

Yet, this little orchid was stronger than he'd thought. Rather than fleeing—now or at his past threats—she had the strength and wisdom to bend beneath the force of the wind. Some would see this as weakness, but he was no fool. As long as she could bend, she would not break.

He must be fiercer, colder, truly give her reason to uproot from her home soil and flee.

He moved so close to her, he could have felt her breath if he could have felt anything at all. Steeling himself for what he must do, he filled his voice with all the menace of every foe he could call to mind and delivered his blast with bitter force.

"If you wish to live, leave Lastarra and never return. Should your feet again tread the ground of this land; the shadows will come for you!"

He roared and rushed...right through her.

Pain ripped at his very center, an almost welcome alternative to the nothingness of shadow. Without slowing, he blasted through his little flower and through the wood at such speed, by the time she turned around to see where he'd gone, he was out in the sunlight, high above her, a raven once more.

Of course, she didn't look up. To her mind, no doubt, he'd vanished. She shivered, ran her hands along her body as if to ensure she was uninjured, then hastened from the woods.

She had courage, he had to admit, and a surprising strength of spirit. Oh, he'd seen her more frightened than she had perhaps ever been, but never did she fall into hysterics or give way to blind panic. Though physically weakened, she'd born all her trials with dignity.

A sudden, sharp pain stung the skin beneath his tail feathers, sending him reeling beak over talon. He righted himself and came face-to-face with two green lights the size of fireflies. *Faeries!* Sparks flew from their wands, singeing his feathers. He snapped his beak at them then shot upward. He leveled out high above the tower and soared over the plain to await Lyssanne's next move.

What kind of sorceress could garner the protection of a unicorn and faeries? In all the time he'd watched her, she'd perform deliberate magic only once. Perhaps there was yet hope for her. If she renounced the ways of sorcery…But no, he couldn't allow himself to start down that path. His walls must remain impenetrable. Her future, her fate, was not his concern.

13

BEYOND THE SHADOWS

*L*yssanne's heart skittered in a fair imitation of hummingbird wings as she hastened to the tower. Tingles raced along the nape of her neck, but she dared not look back. That man, that *shadow*, might still be there, watching. She wanted the tower's solid walls around her...now.

"Heavens!" Reina said as Lyssanne brushed past her and bolted inside.

She slammed the door then leaned against it, running a hand along its surface above the knob. There must be a latch or crossbar. Finding none, she spun on her heel, eyes raking the rough wood and stone walls for something, anything, she could use to bar the entrance. At the creak of floorboards, she spun back around to find Mr. Fescue striding across the room.

"Where do you keep the crossbar?" she asked on a rush of breath.

"Never needed such precautions out here." He dropped whatever he was carrying onto a chair and turned to her. "What's amiss? You look as washed out as a marsh flower after a rain."

"Where is Jarad?" she asked.

"Out back, beyond the garden. He wanted to take a look at the plain, in case you should head for Lyrya." His stare seemed to burn right through her heart. "What happened?"

"Do—do you think you could find him?"

"Sure, but I'm certain he'll return soon. If there's anything you need done, I could—"

She shook her head. "There's something in the woods." She hugged her elbows. "Will you, please, will you find Jarad? I would go, but I, my vision is not…" She shook her head again, unable to make sense of her own words. "You would see him sooner."

He consented.

Lyssanne leaned against the wall beside the window and called to Reina, asking that she, too, keep an eye out for Jarad. Her breathing steadied only when Mr. Fescue returned with him.

"Lady Lyssanne," Jarad said, rushing to her side. "Are you…*huff*… are you ill again? Mr. Fescue said you…What's wrong?"

She struggled to rein in her disjointed thoughts. "How quickly can we be ready to leave?"

"Whenever you want, I guess," he said. "Everything's still in your cart, and my bundle's all tied up. I just have to grab my bow, but I thought you wanted to rest here a while longer."

"We must hurry, all of us," she said. "Mr. Fescue, could you and Sir Fizzil be ready within the hour? Jarad and I can help you gather what you need."

"Dear girl, I'm going nowhere, and I daresay Sir Fizzil has journeyed as far as he can for the near future. What's this all about?"

"Please, you must come with us. I fear we're all in danger, perhaps more so every moment we remain here."

His voice grew as ominous as when they'd first met. "What did you see in my woods?"

"A man, or…the shadow of a man. I don't know." She sank into a chair beneath the window. "It was as if shadow had taken on life, depth, and independent movement. He wasn't solid or natural—but all wispy, and his eyes…" She shivered. "Dark, empty…like burned-out coals…just floating there in that misty void that should have been a face."

196

"If this entity had no face," said Mr. Fescue, "how do you know it was a man?"

"His voice." She shuddered again. "It was a man's voice, but as unnatural as his eyes. More like a croak, and hollow as a pit, yet strangely...familiar." She shrugged. "His speech was at once cultured and rough, coarse but somehow refined. Dignified."

"How'd you see its eyes?" asked Jarad, "You can't even tell what color mine are."

"He was so close. Not at first, but then he...h-he passed...*through* me."

Jarad gasped, pulling up a chair beside her. "It went through your body?"

Lyssanne nodded.

"Tell me, child," Mr. Fescue said, seating himself, his voice low and serious. "What did you feel when this creature did so? Was it icy?"

"No."

"Are you certain? This is important. We could be dealing with one of the captive spirits who have forsaken their celestial purpose to serve the Thief of Souls."

"There was no chill," she said, "only a stirring of air, as if a lukewarm breeze passed through my skin." She cupped her elbows. "And a fleeting impression of heart-wrenching pain."

"It hurt you?" Jarad leaned forward, peering at her.

"Not physical pain," she said. "This was agony rooted so deep as to puncture the spirit." She closed her eyes, unable to shake the feeling she'd divulged the most private of confidences.

"Did the faeries chase him off?" Jarad asked. "Or turn him into a rat or something?"

"Faeries?" Lyssanne and Mr. Fescue said in unison.

"Yeah, they buzzed right past my ear and flew around the tower. Didn't you see them?"

"I did," Reina's voice whispered in Lyssanne's mind. "They didn't stop to converse."

"Did this, er, man threaten you?" asked Mr. Fescue. "You claimed we are all in peril."

She told them what the shadow man had said. "That mist spirit you spoke of—could they be one and the same?"

"I think not," said Fescue. "This creature sounds like it is, or was at one time, human. I shudder to imagine the curse which could create such a being."

Lyssanne nodded.

"One thing seems certain," said Mr. Fescue, "it is stalking you. I suspect the rest of us are safe enough. After all, it said *you* must leave Lastarra. It made no mention of anyone else."

"Even so," Lyssanne said, "I think we must leave."

"I daresay you should," said Fescue. "Whatever this creature is, you shouldn't risk angering it. I would gladly shelter you, but anything that can pass through a human body can doubtless penetrate these walls." He reached for her hand. "Before you decide, I feel compelled to pray for you. If you will permit me?"

"That would be most welcome," she said.

He began in the traditional manner, thanking the King for bringing Lyssanne this far in her journeys and asking for protection against this new threat. He stopped, mid-sentence, and mumbled words she couldn't understand. Then, his voice grew dreamy.

"Look to the past to save the future," he said. "Darkness..." Again, he mumbled for a moment. "Darkness will soon cover this land. If you stay, you will find no escape." He pressed her hand, then released it and leaned back.

Lyssanne blinked up at him, unsure what to make of his odd, yet somehow comforting, prayer. "What is this darkness you speak of?" she asked. "The mist? The man in the woods?"

"I speak only what I'm shown." He lifted a hand as if to forestall further questions. "I uttered every word as it was given me. This, I do know, a great battle is yet to come, and it involves you somehow. You must ready yourself."

"Me?" she asked. Why did such strange people continue to insist she must fight in some battle? "Wise counsel, surely, had your words been spoken to Sir Brennus, but—"

"No, milady, they are meant for you." He held her gaze. "If you feel

Lyrya is where the King is leading, you should go, straightaway." He stood and stared down at her. "Seek out the King's message, Lyssanne. If anyone can help you, it is He."

She rose as well. "I have a last boon to ask. May Jarad remain here until his knee heals?"

Jarad lurched to his feet. "I'm going with you."

"Do not be foolish," Lyssanne said. "You've difficulty just hobbling to the gardens. Once you are mended, I've no doubt you can find your way back to Cloistervale."

"I'm not leaving your side," Jarad said, arms folded. "I made a promise to the King."

"Take the grey gelding, young Jarad," said Mr. Fescue. "He's old but sturdy."

"We wouldn't think of depriving you of your horse," Lyssanne said. "We certainly haven't sufficient coins to—"

"I'd take no payment even if you had it," Mr. Fescue said. "Besides, you helped Sir Fizzil find his way here. He's more than compensated me for my services."

They filled the gelding's saddlebags with items from Lyssanne's cart, which she'd offered Mr. Fescue as partial payment. Their host helped Jarad cut thick tree limbs into poles, so the travelers could construct a shelter to guard against sun fever. As they bid Mr. Fescue and Sir Fizzil farewell, Lyssanne's thoughts turned to Lyrya. Perhaps the land that had birthed Mr. DeLivre might hold some kindness for her.

Gian Plain stretched out far and wide beneath Noire. A stream glistened in the sunlight, like a blue-white ribbon tossed onto the living carpet of green. Here and there, patches of brown mottled the emerald canvas, but overall, the grasslands had refused to accept the exodus of summer—as reluctant as Lyssanne seemed in accepting hers from Lastarra.

As she had countless times in the past week, she glanced eastward over her shoulder, almost unseating herself from Reina's back. A flower so deep-rooted wouldn't easily give way, even to the strongest of winds.

Noire circled the group, high above the dove who glided just over Lyssanne's head. Had that flying nuisance possessed his own capacity for thought, he might have suspected her of increased protectiveness. Foolish notion, even if she did demonstrate uncommon loyalty.

As heat beat down upon Noire's wings, Lyssanne's tedious progress slowed to a halt. She dismounted and withdrew provisions from the saddlebags, while Jarad drove three poles into the ground and tied cloaks and blankets to them. The travelers would doubtless rest beneath the cloth's shadow until sunset, as they had each day upon Gian Plain. Autumn might chill the nights, but the sun's direct gaze drained Lyssanne's strength, preventing travel past noon.

Noire landed behind a clump of tall weeds along the streambed to take his own rest. One good thing could be said for this agonizing crawl across the plain, it afforded him more sleep than he'd had in years. Before night fell, however, he must fly well away from Lyssanne's party. They mustn't spot him once he shifted, not even as a dark lump against the distant, moonlit sky.

Night's increasing chill had left him envious of their campfires, but Jarad's tracking skill grew by the day. Thus, before each dawn draped him in feathers, he fluffed the grass where he'd lain, leaving no trace of his presence, as if he had indeed become nothing more than shadow.

In a daze, Lyssanne unwrapped their midday meal while Jarad put the finishing touches on their shelter, chattering about the fresh game he'd hunt once they crossed the plain. Her thoughts drowned his words, boiling through her mind like ingredients in a stew. A creature of legend held a message for her from the King, and she could only find it if she'd already been to its lair. A fallen spirit, bound to shadow, served a sorcerer who wished her ill. And somehow, she must learn to direct the very power of the King.

One question bobbed to the surface over and over. Why?

At Jarad's sudden cry and the following thud, she spun around. One of his boots stuck out from beneath a fallen section of the shelter. Gathering up her skirts, she rushed to him. He sat sprawled, clutching his injured knee.

"Are you hurt?" she asked, helping him heave the shelter pole and canopy off his leg.

"My knee," he said, his voice laced with pain. "It gave way. I just need a minute."

She knelt on the dry grass and reached toward his leg. "Let me look at it."

He moved his hands aside to allow her fingers' gentle probing. How could she detect whether anything was broken through the cloth of his breeches, stretched tight over a knee swollen triple its proper size?

"D'you think," Jarad said, "the King would help me? I mean, I don't mind the pain so much, but it's slowing our travels. We need to get you to real shelter soon."

Dear Jarad, always thinking of others before himself. "I'm certain He would wish to do so," she said, Jarad's pain squeezing her heart. Given a choice, she would take it in his stead.

"Can you, um, ask Him for me?" Jarad said, for the first time in an age sounding like the boy he still was. "I don't know how to say it right."

"There is no wrong way," she said. "He loves you, as I do. You need only speak to Him as you would to me."

"Please."

"Very well, we shall ask together, but you must believe in His willingness to aid you."

"I do."

She nodded, closed her eyes, and prayed for this child who had left all, risked all, to come to her aid. He'd tried to be strong for both of them throughout everything they'd endured. His courage would rival the knights of legend. If ever anyone deserved aid, it was he.

Jarad gasped, and Lyssanne's eyes flew open. Had she pressed too hard against his knee? She moved her hand and stared. The swelling had diminished.

"It doesn't hurt anymore!" he said. "Could you step back? I wanna check something."

Lyssanne stood and backed away. Jarad climbed to his feet and tested his weight on the injured leg. He flexed it several times, laughing.

"He did it! He heard us." Jarad gave Lyssanne a swift hug. "Thank you."

"No," she said, her stomach aflutter. "Thank the King. I did nothing but seek His aid."

"Yeah," said Jarad, "but you really know how to talk to Him."

More dazed than before, Lyssanne returned to their supplies while Jarad righted the shelter. The King had mended in an instant what should have taken days or weeks to heal.

Two sudden pops almost caused her to drop the bread she'd just unwrapped.

"Why are you here?" Jarad snapped, glaring at the faeries.

"We've come to rejoice with you at Lyssanne's success," Olivia said.

"Success?" Lyssanne asked.

"With your gift, of course," said Jada. "You don't think the boy's knee fixed itself?"

"You show yourselves now, when we're safe?" said Jarad. "But when Lady Lyssanne was in danger, when that shadow man—"

"A creature to be pitied, for certain," Olivia said.

"*Pitied?*" said Jarad.

"If he doesn't rectify his path, it is likely to end in a fate that causes even the FAE to tremble. An eternity lost to the King."

"You're so worried over his fate," Jarad said, his voice rising, "what about Lady Lyssanne's? That shadow thing could've killed her! You just flew past like a couple of bumblebees." He drew a sudden breath then snatched his bow from the ground and aimed it at Olivia. "Maybe you're in league with him."

"Jarad, no!" Lyssanne cried.

Jada flashed to Olivia's side, her wand trained on Jarad. "Don't be so foolish as to attack the FAE, mortal boy."

"Easy, Jada," Olivia said. With the flat of her hand, she lowered her friend's wand. "Young Jarad is merely following his calling. His arrows can cause us no harm."

"But his words can bring *him* harm," said Jada. "Alienate us, and you rid yourselves of your best hope. Not even the King will force our aid upon those who don't want it."

"To answer your question, Jarad," Olivia said, "the FAE are forbidden to interfere in a mortal's life unless she gives us the authority to act. We are only put to flight by the King's words upon a mortal's lips."

"The King's words?" Lyssanne asked, as Jarad lowered his bow. "What do you mean?"

"He has given you many," said Jada. "Have you not been reading His book? Olivia gave you parts of it to study and—"

"Enough," Olivia said. "The fault is mine. I must be more diligent in her instruction. Lyssanne, in this war, you will face danger in many forms. As such, commanding the Light must become your first thought in every situation."

"I had no time to think of anything," Lyssanne said. "He was just there, and then—"

"That's because you surrendered to circumstance," Jada said, vanishing her wand. "You let what was happening in the natural world control your expectations, steal your power. You either take back the right to control your destiny in the name of the King,"—she gestured as if snapping a twig—"or give it over to the Thief of Souls. There is no neutral ground. This is war, and the Thief will take any advantage."

"The King, however," said Olivia, "is a gentleman. He and His servants will only intervene if you proclaim His right to do so."

"I do this by reciting the *Kingsword*?" Lyssanne asked.

"You needn't quote it verbatim," Olivia said. "Yet, the words you speak hold much power. If not in line with the King's will for all life, they relinquish that power to His enemy."

"The Council in Cloistervale claimed mere words can never harm or—"

"It is law," said Jada. "It'll hold true whether you believe it or not. You may think you can fly, but if you jump from a cliff, you *will* fall. Same goes for the law of words."

"Are you saying the Council lied to us?" Jarad asked.

"Not intentionally," Olivia said. "One of the Thief's greatest weapons is misleading followers of the King just enough to rob them of true power."

"Why should my words carry such power?" Lyssanne said. "I am but a peasant."

"That," said Jada, "is a place of high honor. Faeries are created to serve. Humans, whether peasant or noble-born, are created to reign."

"Still," Olivia said, "changing one's thought pattern is only possible with constant repetition. The King's book holds clues to His will for every circumstance. Learn them, recite them, and those words will fall from your lips whenever you need them."

"Oh, I suppose words can defeat shadows, too?" Jarad said with a half laugh.

"Yes," Olivia said. "Your knee is proof."

Warmth flooded Lyssanne as the truth struck home. She'd wielded the King's gift. She had been blind, far beyond the limitations of her natural sight. A broken vessel, she might be, but cracks in a lantern wouldn't prevent the flame's light from spilling forth.

"I begin to understand," she whispered. "Anyone could do as I did. 'Twas neither I, nor even the gift of Light, that accomplished it, but absolute trust in the King." She brushed away a tear. "Yet, He has chosen to demonstrate His power through me."

"Well spoken," said Olivia.

"I treasure your wisdom," Lyssanne said. "If you will indulge me, I have questions."

"Ask them. We shall answer what we are permitted."

Lyssanne told them of the Shadow Mist in Cloistervale and of Mr.

Fescue's warnings. Then, she repeated the question she'd posed when last they'd met. Who was her enemy?

"It is well that you see the shadows," Olivia said, "and recognize the truth of what they are, for such is the very nature of Light. But to succeed in the King's plan, you must learn to look beyond the shadows, to the truth that is the King's law."

"What is this truth?"

"The law of love, which is the core of all else. The King is Love, as He is Light."

"It was because of love, you succeeded this morning," Jada said. "You neither thought nor tried. You only loved and believed."

"Indeed," Olivia said. "Whatever the shadows might show you, whatever shape they take, remember this—Shadow is created when something attempts to block the light. There is no truth in darkness."

"Then...what of my enem—"

"No more lessons, this day," said Olivia. "You are weary from many surprises."

Lyssanne sighed. She didn't want lessons. She wanted answers.

"Never let fear reign," Olivia said. "You must give no power to the shadows, not in word, thought, or deed." With that warning fading into the air, she and Jada vanished.

Brennus rode through a patch of woodland just beyond the Lyryan border, heading toward Lyssanne's campsite. He flexed his shoulders, still stiff after flying back across Gian Plain to retrieve his mount, then traversing it again on horseback. Venefica owed him much.

A plume of smoke billowed above the treetops ahead. Brennus dismounted and led his horse nearer the camp. The stallion hung its head, following, meek as a gelding.

"What?" Brennus whispered. "Lost your bravado now that your master's no longer the size of a tasty snack?" He smirked. "I daresay you'll rethink snapping at ravens, henceforth."

He stepped into the clearing and stopped short. Despite the early hour, Lyssanne lay already abed.

Jarad glanced up from stirring the fire. "Sir Brennus?" The boy jumped to his feet, his words hushed. "Where'd you come from?"

"I had business in the area and happened upon your trail," he said, infusing his practiced lines with nonchalance. "It takes no seasoned tracker to detect your passage."

Jarad held a finger to his lips, grasping Brennus by the arm as if to lead him farther from the campfire. "Lady Lyssanne's ill," he whispered, looking over his shoulder to where she lay.

The threadbare cloak she often wore covered her to the chin. Her face was turned away, her cheek resting upon a rolled blanket. Reina lay between Lyssanne and the fire, partially blocking her from view.

"Her ailment has returned?"

The boy nodded, the firelight revealing his haggard features. "I've never seen it this bad."

"She sleeps?"

"If only." Jarad shook his head. "She can't rest, but she can't rise either."

"Perhaps she should lie closer to the fire. The unicorn blocks all the warmth."

"No, Reina's shielding her from the light. It hurts, y'know, too much light…and noise."

"How long has she been thus?"

"Five days."

"Five—*days*?"

"It started nearly a fortnight ago, but kept getting worse. We stopped here five days ago, and she's hardly stirred since."

"Has she run short on some remedy needed to combat this… illness?" Jarad would expect such a question. "There is a town a half-day's ride north of here. Perhaps you should—"

Jarad shook his head again. "Nothing can be done. She just has to wait until it stops." He folded his arms and looked back toward Lyssanne. "Except…"

"What?"

"Well, Mistress Evlia, our healer, sometimes massaged Lady Lyssanne's head. You know, like they do to calm horses or dogs? I think it maybe helped a little." He sighed, slumping. "I thought about trying it, but I fear to hurt her. She can't even bear to brush her hair right now."

Brennus had to see for himself how the girl fared. The curse Venefica had cast was strong, but to not rise once in five days, despite the discomfort of hard ground?

Reina lifted her head at his approach, piercing him with her fathomless eyes. Her gaze weighed upon him even as he turned his back on her to crouch beside Venefica's enemy.

"Lyssanne?"

She turned her head then opened her eyes with equal slowness, as if her lids bore the weight of serving platters. He stiffened.

Her face shone pale as the unicorn. And her eyes! What he saw there chilled him. Those sapphire depths, forever filled with the sparkle of hope or fire of determination, had become twin, dull pools of pain. He'd known torture victims with eyes less haunted.

"Sir Brennus?" she whispered, her weak voice barely audible. She lifted her head and shoulders with obvious effort.

Slipping to his knees, he placed a hand behind her shoulder to help her sit up. She swayed. He caught her against his shoulder and held her there, her body limp as a soggy blanket.

"Sorry," she whispered, "so dizzy."

Jarad brought her a cup of water. Cradling her in one arm, Brennus held the cup for her. Once she'd drunk her fill, he shifted her body to free her left arm, which had become pinned between them. As he lifted her arm, her hand dangled, limp, from the wrist.

Brennus settled onto the ground and slid her blanket roll into his lap, then eased her head atop it. She lay facing away from him, her long hair spilling into her eyes. He brushed it aside. She shifted as if to rise from his lap, but he forestalled her with a firm grasp of her shoulder.

"Rest," he said, a quiet yet unmistakable command. "Jarad spoke of a method your healer once used to ease your pain. With your permission, I shall try it."

"You're...a knight," she said. "Healer's craft is...beneath you."

"It is my right to decide what is beneath me," he said, already moving his fingers lightly over her hair and temples. "I've seen the pain in your eyes. Perhaps I may ease it, if only a bit."

What had prompted this odd compulsion to offer her aid? Perhaps his return to Lyrya had reawakened his training in knighthood at the knee of his oldest friend's sire. Though he and Duncan had oft made jest of the old man's serious nature, they'd taken his lessons as law. If a knight couldn't fight a lady's battle for her, he was oath-bound to provide whatever assistance he may. Well, if ever a maiden had been distressed, it was this one. Inconvenient, chivalry.

Another strand of hair fell to Lyssanne's brow. As he tucked it behind her ear, her pulse jumped beneath the skin at her temple. She stiffened and gasped.

"What was that?" he asked.

"You felt it?" she whispered, a mere breath on the wind.

"Yes."

"Don't know."

It struck again, and her eyes clenched. A hard ridge ran beneath his fingertips where the twitch had occurred.

"The pain increases? Here?"

She nodded, a motion imperceptible except to his fingertips resting against her head.

His gentle explorations revealed ridges running in intricate patterns all along the surface of her scalp. At times, pulses ran through them. Never had he known such small vessels to swell and harden thus. Each time one of the ridges jumped, she stiffened or gasped. Not in all his watching, had he been aware of this aspect of the curse.

Jarad hovered nearby until Brennus commanded him to sleep, pledging he would keep watch. No lad of Jarad's age should have dark circles ringing his eyes. Besides, riding for so many nights in succession had left Brennus wakeful at odd hours.

Perhaps this would afford Brennus the chance to discover the information Venefica sought…and the answers to a few questions of his own. Why, for instance, did Lyssanne not call upon her magic to aid her? Perhaps a sorceress couldn't counter spells directed at herself. He could not, alas, voice such theories.

As he continued his delicate massage, the muscles of Lyssanne's shoulders and back loosened, until she lay in a boneless heap. When he began to knead her brow, she turned toward him. He traced a pattern up to her hairline and found the area swollen and spongy. She groaned.

"Forgive me," he whispered, reducing his fingers' pressure to a feather's brush.

A ridge rose along her brow, and a twitch ran across it. Lyssanne's lids tightened, and her jaw clenched. A sudden impulse seized Brennus to press that ridge away, as one might smooth out a wrinkle in parchment. As he did so, she let out a long breath, tension ebbing from her brow.

Her breathing evened out, and her entire body relaxed into his arms. He stared down into her face, so open and vulnerable. She sighed, and her eyes drifted open. She gazed up at him with a look of such surrender, his chest constricted. For that stolen bit of time, she trusted him.

She turned away again, and he began kneading the steely chords of her neck muscles. His fingers stretched along the sides of her throat, a slim column they could span with room to spare.

The opportunity could not be more perfect. If he rid Venefica of her enemy, she could have no further excuse to delay fulfilling their bargain. He could make it swift. Already in such pain, Lyssanne would never feel a thing. He'd be granting her a mercy, ending her curse.

As if sensing her vulnerability, she looked up at him, fear again shadowing her eyes.

He couldn't do it. She wasn't his enemy, though his oath to Venefica had set him as hers. He longed to see trust again in her eyes, that look of surrender on her face. Was such not, after all, his current mission?

"You're safe," he whispered. "I shall see that you come to no harm."

She only blinked up at him.

"I give you my word."

With a soundless sigh, she allowed her eyes to drift shut—the fear fading from them as if expelled along with her breath. Could his mere word hold such sway over her?

He cradled her thus throughout the night. He'd offered to keep watch; he may as well make himself useful. The trust and gratitude in Lyssanne's eyes each time she opened them had no bearing on his actions. None whatsoever.

Bursts of increased pain continued to drive sleep from Lyssanne every time it dared approach. Despite this, she uttered no complaint. Far into the night, she began to shiver.

He draped his mantle over her, to no avail. "Have you more blankets?" he asked.

"Not cold," she whispered. "Just tired."

At length, she dozed in fitful intervals. Brennus stared into the distant woods, reflecting on the series of events that had led them each to this moment. All this time, he'd lamented his fate at the hands of a generational curse, but his woes were nothing to hers. How could anyone, especially one so small, so fragile, withstand that kind of pain?

She whimpered in her sleep, drawing his eye. He ran a knuckle along her pale cheek, barely touching her, lest he disturb what rest she'd found. His breath hitched, and he drew back as if from a nest of vipers.

No!

With careful haste, he eased Lyssanne and her makeshift pillow to the ground, then sprang to his feet. He could almost hear a fissure creaking open in his carefully constructed walls. Through that hairline crack, lay a path he could not, dared not, tread. Time to move on, before that path beckoned further. Besides, dawn couldn't be far off.

As Brennus circled the camp, Jarad stirred, then rose with admirable stealth to join him. In silence, they walked to the opposite side of the camp from Lyssanne's resting place.

"I shall ride to Edgemond and arrange a room for Lyssanne at an inn," Brennus said in hushed tones. At what point during the long night had he decided upon this course? Regardless, he would see it through. "She mustn't remain in the wild. Her illness will worsen. However, she lacks the strength to travel. She would be incapable of keeping her seat even on Reina's back."

"What can we do?" Jarad looked at him as if his world's fate rested in Brennus's hands.

"I shall return once I've made provision at the inn. She can ride with me." They reached his stallion, and Brennus took up the reins. "Until my return, do not leave her unattended longer than absolutely necessary."

Jarad's effusive gratitude prompted an odd churning in Brennus's stomach. He mounted his steed with all haste, wheeled about, and thundered through the woods.

14

AVERY HALL

*S*ir Brennus returned after sunset, as Jarad had predicted. He offered scant greetings before lifting Lyssanne into his arms and carrying her past Jarad's gelding to his stallion. Necessary though such attentions were, she hid flaming cheeks against the folds of his tunic.

"I cannot mount with you in my arms," he said. "Can you sit for a moment unaided?"

"I shall try," she whispered.

He set her atop the saddle, her feet dangling to one side. With a speed and grace she could only envy, he swung up behind her. She clutched the saddle horn with what strength she possessed until he grasped her waist and adjusted her to fit more securely before him.

He took up the reins and motioned for Jarad and Reina to follow. Lyssanne struggled to hold herself upright. Weakness, the heaviness of her head, and her fuzzy awareness made the task all but impossible.

"Rest against me," he said. "It may prevent our travels from jarring you overmuch."

"I thank you for your kindness, sir," she said, "but I shouldn't wish to impose."

"Nonsense," he said, with uncharacteristic gentleness. "Your pallor rivals Reina's. How could I watch a lady wage such a battle, when I am equipped to assist?" He sighed, pressing a hand to her shoulder. "Lyssanne, allow me to aid you."

She hadn't the energy to protest. They rode thus for several hours, the circle of his arms holding her steady. As the night deepened, her entire body grew lax. Had she gone daft? As if this were the safest place in the Seven Lands, she rested helpless in the arms of a man she barely knew. A man of vast strength and skill—a man who had twice threatened her life.

Yet, serenity engulfed her, a safety she hadn't thought ever to find after her banishment.

She must have surrendered to slumber soon thereafter, for she woke with a start, choking on shadows.

"Easy. You'll unseat us both," Sir Brennus said. "What's amiss?"

"Dreams," she whispered, unable to stop trembling.

He tightened his arms about her. "Unpleasant ones, I daresay."

"Yes." After slumbering free of such night terrors ever since she'd met Mr. Fescue, she'd dared hope she'd left them behind in the western forests of Lastarra. Alas, they had found her.

Sir Brennus transferred the reins into his right hand and brushed back her hair with his left. "You've nothing to fear here," he said. "You're safe."

But who will keep me safe from you?

"I will," he said.

She stiffened. She'd spoken her thoughts aloud?

His next words chilled her despite their gentleness. "There exists no other who can."

She shuddered. Sir Brennus pulled his mantle around them both.

His solicitous manner continued when they reached the inn. He dismounted and lifted her from the saddle. Instead of releasing her as she expected, he carried her into the building, up the stairs, and to the room the innkeeper showed them. After Jarad pulled back the blankets, Sir Brennus settled her upon the bed, holding her a moment longer than necessary.

"Take your ease," he said, staring into her eyes. "I must see to business."

He arranged the blankets over her and motioned Jarad to follow him to the door.

"I shall return in two days to see how she fares," Sir Brennus said in hushed tones. "I've left instructions with the innkeeper to deliver meals for you both here. Should you lack sufficient coin to cover the costs, I shall make good the difference. I advise you not to leave Lyssanne unattended. One cannot be certain what sort of ruffians might be lingering about."

~

When Lyssanne awoke the next morning, she nearly wept. The pain was gone, at last. She spent the greater part of that day and the next in bed, recovering what strength she could. The severity and length of this latest attack had left her fuzzy-minded and weak-limbed.

She and Jarad had just finished their evening meal, when a knock sounded. Sir Brennus stood in the doorway. "I've concluded my business and shall soon depart Edgemond."

"We, too, must leave on the morrow," she said. Their bag of coins was all but spent.

"Jarad tells me you've recovered enough to ride," Sir Brennus said, "but I think it imprudent to venture far without proper shelter. I have friends residing less than a day's journey from here and am certain they would afford you temporary lodging. Duncan Avery is lord of this region and would also know of any employment to be found in the area."

At his insistence, they set out within the hour, to take advantage of nighttime's diminished activity along the road. Lyssanne found deferring to his wishes less taxing than trying to determine whether this was the best course to take. Surely there could be no harm in sheltering in the home of his friends.

Midnight had come and gone when they rounded a bend, and the trees fell away, revealing a spot of gleaming white on the horizon. As they drew nearer, the whiteness resolved into a roughly triangular structure projecting above the landscape, then into a multilevel fortification, the likes of which Lyssanne had only imagined.

A high wall, flanked by rounded towers, with square turrets at intervals along its sides, stretched wider and wider as they approached. Flickering lights, which Lyssanne assumed to be sentry torches, were spaced along its top. Behind the wall, the roofs of taller structures rose like white spikes in the moonlight. Sir Brennus slowed his stallion, and Reina followed suit.

Then, a second row of torches came into view. Lyssanne leaned forward, straining her eyes to determine whether soldiers held the flames at the wall's base or they were pole lights stuck into the ground. As she rode forward, the fresh scent of water washed over her. Only then did the truth become clear. The wall wasn't as high as she'd thought. A third of it, along with that lower row of torches, was actually a reflection in a dark moat surrounding the outer defenses of the castle.

Remaining a half-stride behind Sir Brennus, Reina and Jarad's mount clopped onto the planks of a bridge spanning the moat. Though the boards were wide enough to support wagons or several armed knights riding abreast, Lyssanne was grateful Reina kept to the middle.

Sir Brennus pulled to a halt and hailed the inhabitants of the castle.

"Who goes there?" a man shouted from atop the barbican.

"Brennus Xavier. I have business with your lord, Duncan."

The gatekeeper vanished from the crenelated battlement. Shouts echoed behind the imposing curtain wall. Lyssanne sat frozen, eyeing the black depths of the water sloshing beneath the bridge. Sir Brennus claimed these people were his friends, but minutes stretched on with no sound in reply to his request, save the lapping of the moat.

Lyssanne could just make out several figures atop the outer wall. Were those bows they held? Whatever devices they brandished appeared pointed in her party's direction.

A sudden groaning and clanking shook the ground. The

drawbridge descended, its planks falling into place with a deafening bang. The portcullis then creaked upward.

Sir Brennus spurred his mount forward. Holding Reina's mane, Lyssanne rode beside Jarad in his wake. She looked up as they passed beneath the still-rising iron grate. Spikes along its bottom warned of what could befall those who lost favor with its handlers.

They emerged from beneath the gatehouse into an outer court teeming with armed men. Sir Brennus halted midway across the packed dirt. Before him, stood a stocky man in fine armor.

"Well, well. The Raven Prince returns at last," the man said, his accent akin to Mr. DeLivre's, yet his Starransi was flawless. "I was beginning to think you dead." He laughed. "Come, my friend! Oh, but 'tis good to see you!"

"And you, Duncan," said Sir Brennus, dismounting. He embraced the shorter man, as a groom led his stallion away. "Expecting trouble?" he asked, releasing his friend and glancing around the be-knighted courtyard.

"Not especially, why do you...? Oh!" The man laughed, a hearty sound that bounced off the stone walls enclosing them. "Just a bit of nighttime training for the newer recruits. What they teach these lads when they squire these days, I have to wonder! I told them, you can't expect a battle to await the convenience of daylight."

"Duncan, you sound remarkably like your sire," said Sir Brennus.

"Quick, draw your sword," his friend said, a hand flying to his chest. "Save me from my fate!" He laughed again, scratching his beard. "But the old man did know his business." He clapped Sir Brennus on the back and led him away, sparing but a glance for Lyssanne and Jarad. "Steward!" he shouted. "Prepare the forest chamber for our noble guest and instruct the cook that we're to hold a feast in his honor."

"At once, Lord Avery," a man shouted.

Unsure what was expected of her, Lyssanne remained on Reina's back. Since she'd not been introduced, she dared not ask if she should follow.

Another groom scurried up to Jarad. "You can take yer mare and gelding to the lower stable. A maid'll show ya the servants' quarters."

Jarad dismounted and asked Lyssanne to hand him her cloak. When she moved to dismount, he rested a hand on her skirt and whispered, "Not yet. Give me a moment."

Reina bobbed her head as if in agreement with that odd request. Mystified, Lyssanne waited as Jarad ran after Sir Brennus and his friend.

"Lord Avery!"

The two men halted, and Lord Avery turned.

"Forgive my impertinence, milord," Jarad said, "but where shall I take my lady's things?"

"Your lady?"

"Yes, milord. Lady Lyssanne." Jared gestured with his cloak-draped arm.

Cold sweat beaded on Lyssanne's brow. Calling her a lady in jest was one thing, but to pass her as such to a real nobleman? That could get one killed, or at least imprisoned.

"And, please pardon my boldness," Jarad said, "but might I request an end stall for the lady's mare? She's a bit of a solitary creature."

Lord Avery studied Lyssanne and Reina for a moment then strode back toward them. "Brennus, you cur. You didn't introduce your lady!" When he reached Lyssanne, he grasped her hand, bowing over it. "I beg your forgiveness, Milady Lyssanne. I fear I mistook you for a servant. My only excuse is the excitement of seeing an old friend." A grin broke out across his merry, round face. "Still, I've been gravely remiss as your host. I shall do all in my power to remedy the offense. Please, allow me to assist you." He held her hand as if to help her dismount.

Blushing, she accepted. "Truly, my lord, there's been no offense. I am not really—"

"At her best at present," Jarad said in a rush. "Lady Lyssanne's too wise to undertake a harsh journey in finery."

"Indeed," said Lord Avery. "Still, I should have noticed at once. For, no servant would travel upon so fine a steed as this." He turned and ordered an attendant to prepare a lady's chambers and take Lyssanne's belongings thither. He commanded his groom to lead Reina away, but Jarad insisted on doing so himself.

"You are bold for a lad."

"It would be best to heed the boy on that matter, at least," Sir Brennus said, remaining where Lord Avery had left him. "This particular mare is not fond of strangers."

"As you will," said Lord Avery, waving the matter, and Jarad, away. "Welcome to Avery Hall, Lady Lyssanne." He looped her arm through his and led her toward the inner wall and onward to the courtyard within.

How could she reveal the truth of her identity, now, with preparations being made for her in the style of a noblewoman, not to mention her separation from Jarad? To contradict Jarad's words would doubtless mean a terrible fate for him, and perhaps even worse for herself.

Sir Brennus had resumed his aloof manner, his solicitous treatment of her vanishing. Would he keep his silence or dispute Jarad's claims?

Might a castle this size have a dungeon? If so, what were the chances of surviving it?

Dungeon or no, the sight that greeted Lyssanne as she entered the inner court stole her breath. Ahead, stood a building at least thrice as long as Cloistervale's meeting hall and as high as Mr. Fescue's tower. Three rounded turrets graced the center of the manor, the tallest in the middle. Each end of the building was also rounded, though an even height with its wings. Off to one side, stood a narrow building with a conical roof. The outer walls of both that and the manor house shone like new-fallen snow, even whiter than the protective, surrounding walls.

Lord Avery led Lyssanne up more than a score of white marble steps, streaked with silver. On closer inspection, the walls of the manor shone with the same brilliance. What untold wealth must be herein, that one could build an entire mansion of so costly a stone?

~

Brennus would never grow weary of the splendor of Duncan's home. The moment they breeched the entrance hall, Duncan proceeded toward the left-hand grand stairway. Recessed between the two staircases, the ornate double doors to the Great Hall stood sealed for the night.

"My steward will have informed my lady wife of your arrival," said Duncan. "She will greet us with some refreshment or other in my private study." He turned to Brennus, gesturing him forward. "You remember the way, I trust?"

"Certainly." Brennus took the lead up the curving stairs. Doubtless, Duncan wished to give Lyssanne ample opportunity to admire the finery of his twin flaring staircases, chandeliers, and other such ornaments. "How fares Lady MeMe?"

"Still the loveliest creature in the Seven Lands," Duncan said. "Though, I daresay I am the most fortunate of men to have her close second as my newest guest."

Brennus smirked. He could all but feel Lyssanne blushing behind him. Duncan's legend as a charmer was well earned. Lyssanne made no reply. She'd said precious little since their first sighting of Avery Hall. Well, the place should awe one such as she.

Then again, perhaps she feared making some backward comment that would give away her true station. This was how she repaid his kindness? Bad enough, she persisted in claiming no knowledge of sorcery when he'd caught her in the act, but to allow the boy to pass her off as a lady! Brennus would say nothing of it, yet. She would expose herself as a fraud soon enough.

They reached the second-level landing in moments. Brennus ate up the distance to Duncan's favored room. He was weary of travel and idle vigilance. A respite in a proper hall would do much to restore his spirits.

At the door, a servant garbed in the pale green livery of Avery Hall met them. Bowing, she informed Duncan that Lady Avery awaited them within.

Brennus pushed open the heavy, oak door and inhaled. Leather, smoke, and sandalwood—ah, a place where he could truly breathe. A generous fire and strategically placed lamps set the room's dark paneling aglow.

With a practiced grace Brennus had long admired, Lady MeMe rose to greet them. "Welcome," she said, offering an elegant curtsey and dazzling smile. "It has been too long since you honored us with your company."

"Agreed, fair lady," Brennus said, bowing over MeMe's hand. "But the honor is mine." On impulse, he embraced this woman who had become like a sister. She'd certainly done Duncan a service in marrying him.

"Had we known you were coming," she said, "we would have made all ready before you arrived." She flipped her long, auburn braid over one shoulder and pinned him with that saucy look which once had so vexed Duncan. Then her genteel manner slipped back into place. "I've ordered a feast, but it will take time to prepare. Tomorrow, we shall dine in the style befitting you. I'm afraid all I can offer tonight is lighter fare." She waved to indicate a sideboard, laden with warm tea, cheese, bread, and a selection of fruits.

"We dined in Edgemond," he said. "This will more than meet our needs."

She glanced at Lyssanne then tilted her chin at her husband. Duncan cleared his throat and made introductions.

Lyssanne curtseyed in her simple manner and said, with eyes downcast, "My lady."

"I am most pleased to share your company, Lady Lyssanne," MeMe said, gazing down at her guest with a raised brow. "The moment your chamber is ready, I shall conduct you thither personally. Until then, do make yourself comfortable."

"You are most kind. Thank you."

Brennus crossed his arms. *An odd way to show gratitude, lying to one's hosts.*

They passed the next hour nibbling on fruit and enjoying Duncan's fire. Brennus endured Duncan's good-natured teasing about their various past adventures, while the women smiled and nodded in the appropriate places. Ah, to be in civilized company again.

At length, Lyssanne turned to Lady MeMe and said, "If I might ask, where is Jarad to pass the night?"

"Your boy?" Duncan asked from across the room. "Not to worry, the stable lads will find him a bed. We've plenty to spare." With a wave, he dismissed the matter.

A knock sounded. At Duncan's command, a maid entered, carrying a silver tray, which bore a book. She strode to MeMe.

"Milady." She curtseyed and awaited MeMe's nod to continue. "I was unpacking the young lady's things while Lily changed the linens, and I found these books. I thought Her Ladyship might like some recreation while awaitin' her room?" She paused for breath. "I hope I done right, milady. I don't know nothin' about books, so I brought the smaller one."

"Most considerate, Emma," MeMe said. "I am certain my husband's ramblings bore our guest. Your forethought is a boon." She inclined her head toward Lyssanne.

Emma held the tray out and curtseyed. "Your book, my lady."

"A thick one, that," said Duncan. "And it's the smallest, you say? Impressive."

Brennus peered over Lyssanne's shoulder. "*Ar Popinpopii?*" He spoke the title of the collection of Navvarish legends in a tone as hard as his fists were clenched. "You read Navvarish?" The thought of her perpetrating another deception turned his very being to stone.

"Only a few words," she said. "This translation is in Lyryan."

"Where did you learn to read Lyryan?" Brennus lifted the book from her lap without warning and leafed through its pages. "I was under the impression your home lies as far from the Lyryan border as one can get in Lastarra." It was astounding Lyssanne could read at all. Cloistervale was so backward, women traipsed about with unbound hair like overage children.

"Our scribe, Mr. DeLivre, taught me," she said. "'Tis his native tongue. This was a childhood gift from him."

"How delightful!" said MeMe. "You must browse our library while here."

Lyssanne gasped. "A library? I would be honored. Thank you."

"Do you speak it as well?" Duncan asked.

"*Fii,*" she said, then continued in Lyryan. "Though, I fear my accent is quite terrible." She laughed. "I understand it more fluently."

"Duncan is half Lastarran, you know," MeMe said in Starransi.

"Raised on the border of two lands," Duncan said, "one can expect to be a man of both."

If that were true, Brennus was a man of every land but his own.

Moments later, Lady Avery escorted Lyssanne back down the corridor. Perhaps this would afford Lyssanne an opportunity to confess her true station. Lady Avery seemed kind and might understand Jarad's wish to protect Lyssanne, given her latest bout with illness. She could only hope her hostess would know how to set things right without endangering Jarad.

"Lyssanne..." Lady Avery said, interrupting her reverie.

"Yes, my lady?"

"I was just trying to place the origin of your unusual name, but alas, I'm at a loss."

"I believe I was named after my father, Lysander. Though, I'm not certain," she said. "If I might ask, yours is a rather unusual name as well, is it not?"

"In truth, my given name is Melanie Marie." Lady Avery laughed. "My younger brother couldn't pronounce it properly when he was small, and his version stuck."

Lyssanne followed her hostess up another flight of stairs, one hand gliding along the lace-like banister.

"This wing's tower holds my chambers and private solar," said Lady Avery. "The other wing boasts the library tower. The Great Hall is set between them. Once you know that, the manor's size is less daunting." The staircase narrowed and curved as they continued upward. "Your chambers are on the third level."

Even in the faint light of ensconced torches, the walls of the corridor shone bright against the dark hardwood flooring. At intervals between doorways, stood vases of various sizes, some on stands, others so large they sat upon the floor. On occasion, a sculpture stood sentry instead.

Near the end of the corridor, Lady MeMe stopped at a set of double doors with shining golden fittings. She flung them wide and ushered Lyssanne inside.

The first thing to catch Lyssanne's eye was the change in flooring. The chamber stretched out upon glossy tiles of marbled rose. She followed Lady Avery into a sitting room populated with a settee and several chairs, each cushioned in the loveliest shade of blue she'd ever beheld, a hue befitting the chamber of a king.

A writing desk stood in one corner. Sapphire vases stuffed with white flowers sat atop small tables made of the same pale, silvery wood. Oh, how Flora Whitfield would have longed to capture the sweet perfume of those blossoms for her candles and soaps! That, combined with the fresh-scrubbed scent wafting in from the corridors, bathed the room in an aroma of contentment.

Lyssanne followed Lady Avery to a door set in the left-hand wall of the chamber. As she neared it, she reached out to the wall, not marble as she'd thought. The lower half was paneled in the same silvery wood as the furniture. Above this, stretched a blue as pale as frosted lake water. Lyssanne traced the tiny silver flowers patterning the wall. The pale blue was silk!

Voices drew Lyssanne to the door through which her hostess had gone. A maid finished fluffing a pillow on the bed dominating the next room, then curtseyed to Lady Avery and moved toward the door. Lyssanne stepped aside to let her pass.

"I hope these rooms are to your liking," said Lady Avery. "Should you need anything, pull this bell chord. Our chief housekeeper, Madam Bedford, will ensure someone attends you. Your things have been placed in the wardrobe and trunk." She glanced about. "Ah, yes, and a warm bath has been prepared in the alcove."

Lyssanne's throat constricted. How was she to tell this generous lady her household had gone to such bother for a peasant? To receive such kindness from strangers, after the coldness she'd endured from her own people…

"Ah, you are weary from your travels," Lady Avery said. "I'll leave you to your rest."

"All this…'tis too much, too fine for me. You've gone to such pains, but I—"

Lady Avery laughed. "A few changed linens and heated water are no trouble, I assure you. Especially for a guest of our dear Brennus. Why, I'd begun to despair of his ever finding—"

A knock interrupted her. Lyssanne followed her into the sitting room. The maid who had fluffed the pillows stood in the corridor.

"I beg your pardon, milady," the maid said, "but Madam Bedford bade me inform you, His Highness has retired and is pleased with his accommodations. Prince Brennus sends his complements to Your Ladyship."

"Thank you, Lily."

Lyssanne stood frozen until Lily's footsteps faded. "*Prince* Brennus?" she whispered.

"You didn't know?" Lady Avery stared so long, Lyssanne dropped her gaze. "You *don't* know, do you?"

"Know what, my lady?"

"Come, let us sit a moment. And, call me MeMe." They settled into chairs comfortable enough to sleep in. "Brennus's tale is a long and sad one. In short, he is indeed a prince, the rightful crown prince of Navvar."

Lyssanne gasped. She ran a hand over the book of Navvarish legends she still held. "I thought a band of warlords ruled Navvar, the Blackthorne Brotherhood."

"Indeed. For many generations, Brennus's family has lived in exile. The Brotherhood deposed them long ago. It is Duncan's hope to someday see the Xavier throne restored."

Lyssanne could only shake her head like a simpleton.

"Surely you knew," said Lady MeMe. "'Tis obvious you've traveled with him for some time. Are you not the lady he wrote of to Duncan, the one for whom he's undertaken a quest?"

"Not I," Lyssanne said. "Though he has shown me great kindness."

"I am glad of it."

'Twas more inconceivable than ever, that kindness. He, a prince, had held her while plying healer's craft to ease her pain. He'd ridden with her, seen she had shelter, and twice had saved her life—the life of a peasant not even from his homeland.

Then, another thought struck her. "I do not wish to pry," she said, choosing her words with caution, "but why does your husband call Sir, er, *Prince* Brennus the raven prince? Lord Avery addressed him thus when we arrived and later referred to him as prince of carrion." She took a steadying breath. "It seems almost a cruel jest, as if Lord Avery mocks him for ruling over only common or base things."

"I see my husband's oldest friend has found a champion as fierce as he is."

Lyssanne shook her head. "I didn't mean to imply—"

"I'm pleased to see it," Lady MeMe said, resting a hand atop Lyssanne's. "Be assured, Duncan means no ill by his teasing. Though, I think it unkind to remind Brennus so often of..." She sprang to her feet. "Well, but I've said too much already. If I'd known he hadn't told you this much...No matter. Surely there is no harm done."

Lyssanne rose and followed her to the door.

"Rest well," said Lady MeMe. "If your bath has cooled, ring the bell. On the morrow, would you consent to join me in my solar for a late brunch?"

"I would be honored."

"Lily can show you the way. I'm happy you've joined us, Lyssanne. Good night."

Warm, lavender-scented water lapped at Lyssanne's chin, its subtle sloshing lulling her muscles into liquid languor. Soon, her cheeks grew as moist as the rest of her, from tears rather than the tub's contents.

The scent of her favorite flower conjured visions of Rowan Hill Cottage. Oh, she was out of her depth, here amid such opulence! Months of turbulent emotion rained into the water.

At last, silent tears ran dry, and her body floated on a river of semi-wakefulness, her mind churning in the shallows of a single thought. A prince. Brennus…a prince.

At length, wrapped in thick linen, Lyssanne left the shelter of the screened alcove. She stood for long moments as if lost. A clean chemise and plush bed awaited her.

She stared at the bed, a massive four-posted affair with mattresses piled so thick, a dainty three-legged stool had been provided to give one a boost. She ran her fingertips over the silken, royal blue coverlet. How could she dare sleep beneath such finery?

She hopped onto the cloud-soft confection and pulled the coverlet and matching curtains about her. Thus cocooned, she sank into the deepest sleep, perhaps, of her life.

15

REVELATION

*L*yssanne rose to answer a knock at her door then hesitated, smoothing a hand down the deep blue skirts of her feast-day gown. A bit wrinkled, but stain-free. Would it be fitting attire for such company as a lady and her attendants?

The maid Lily stood in the doorway. "I've come to escort you to Lady Avery's solar," she said, curtseying. "Oh, I would've come sooner had I known you required aid with your hair."

"There is no need to fret. I managed well enough."

"But you can't go like that!" Lily said.

Lyssanne raised a hand to her freshly washed hair. What could be amiss with it?

"Beggin' your pardon, milady, but only young girls wear their hair loose."

"Oh." Lyssanne's brows drew together.

"Not to worry, miss," Lily said, bustling into the room. "I'll fix it up for you." She beckoned Lyssanne into the bedchamber then gestured to the cushioned stool beneath a gilded vanity. "I s'pose, you not being from these parts, you might do things a bit different. Never heard of such, myself, but I never been outside of Averton."

Lily fashioned Lyssanne's hair into a simple braid and wound it around her head in a halo. As she worked, Lyssanne's visage in the looking glass took on a maturity and elegance she would never have attributed to herself.

"I know this is a far simpler style than befits a lady," Lily said, "but we haven't time for anything finer."

～

"How long will you favor us with your company?" Lady MeMe asked.

Lyssanne glanced around the elegant solar. "Jarad and I shall depart this afternoon."

"Oh, but you must remain for the feast honoring our mutual friend, at the least." Lady MeMe offered her a seat while servants set out dainty refreshments. "What is your destination? If you have a set time for reaching it, perhaps Duncan can suggest a swifter route."

Lyssanne's palms grew moist. "I have no particular destination in view, but—"

"Then, it is settled," Lady MeMe said. "I insist you stay the week. My husband's cousin and her party are set to leave on the morrow. They've delayed their departure to pay honor to Prince Brennus." She took Lyssanne's hand, a gesture so reminiscent of Aderyn, Lyssanne's throat constricted. "I would so appreciate your company once they've gone."

How could Lyssanne refuse? Yet, she must seek Reina's advice on the matter and determine how Jarad fared. Above all, she must tell them both what she'd learned. Jarad's manner had become far too relaxed with Prince Brennus as it was.

A servant admitted several women in fine silk and taffeta gowns.

"Ah, there you are," Lady MeMe said. "Lady Lyssanne, I present Duncan's cousin Countess Fynnette and her mother, Dowager Baroness of Harmon. You'll doubtless meet Fynnette's brother tonight. His barony lies in the south of Lyrya."

Lord Duncan's cousin took a seat opposite, eyeing Lyssanne. "What an adorably quaint gown," she said. "That antique style is just charming!"

Lyssanne traced the stitchery at her neckline, far higher than those of the other ladies.

"The color matches your eyes," Lady MeMe said. "And such intricate embroidery. Where did your seamstress study? Llytlesby? Etoilia?"

"Madam Sewell learned weaving and stitchery from her mother," Lyssanne said. "She's never left the village."

"This is the work of a village seamstress?" Countess Fynnette asked. "Why, those intricate flowers and vines stitched along the hem could rival the work of Lyrya's court embroiderers. Less costly, too, I daresay."

Lyssanne smiled. "Indeed. The stitchery was a gift, adornment for a friend's wedding."

"Astounding," the willowy dowager baroness said. "Your people must truly love you."

"Well," said Countess Fynette, "I, for one, am eager to see what finery she'll wear to the prince's feast. If this is her idea of a morning dress, it promises to be dazzling."

"Lyssanne, are you well," Lady MeMe asked. "You've gone pale."

"Might we speak a moment in private?" she asked.

They stepped outside, Lyssanne's heart lodging in her throat as she explained that this gown was her finest. Would wearing the same dress to dinner cause offense?

"Fear not," Lady MeMe said. "I shall have Lily alter one of my gowns for your use. Now, think nothing of it," she said, before Lyssanne could protest. "You've journeyed in the wilds for months; it is only right you have proper attire, for one night, at least."

Lyssanne tensed. "I've not spoken of my travels. How do you—?"

"Brennus mentioned something of it to Duncan. I shall send Lily to you when the gown is ready. She will help you dress, since no lady's maid accompanies you."

With every kindness shown her, Lyssanne sank deeper into the mire of Jarad's deception. Perhaps Reina could suggest a gracious way to extract them all from it.

~

Raised elfin faces peered back at Lyssanne from the shiny, rounded escutcheons securing the nose-high, brass handle to the door. She ran a forefinger over their sculpted, childlike features and pointed ears, then gripped the handle in both hands. Her fingers barely spanned its width. Had she the strength? These massive, twin slabs of oak barring her exit from the manor stood as tall as three men and nearly as wide. She stepped back and pulled.

The door swung inward with surprising ease, threatening to bowl her over. Calling forth every vestige of strength, she arrested its swing, pulled it behind her, and stepped outside.

The early afternoon sun glared off a solid sheet of white and silver marble—a trick of the eye, the sun's position and dark silver veins in the stone conspiring to mask the edges of the steps. The rush of open air from below dispelled the illusion, as Lyssanne paused atop the twenty-eight stairs she'd counted the night before to prevent future stumbling.

She cast surreptitious glances at the guards standing sentry on either side of the door. They stared straight ahead, statue-still in their pale green finery.

She turned back to the steps, her entire body braced to help her *see* their edges. Alas, no railings. Instead, rectangular shrubbery beds flanked the wide expanse of stone, containing a shoulder-high honor guard of evenly spaced, conical trees…well, shoulder-high to her.

Fighting the slight vertigo that always plagued her at a precipice of unknown depth, she stretched out her hands, as if to use the air for a banister, and let the toe of her shoe find her way.

At the bottom, she spun to admire Avery Hall's inner court. The emerald lawn sloped upward, forming the wide hill upon which the blue-roofed manor perched. The steps lay like a snowy carpet unrolled to welcome royal guests.

Like Prince Brennus. She must remember to address him properly when next they spoke. If they spoke. What could she say to him? She and Jarad should have departed hours ago, leaving behind these kind people who thought her something she was not—and the prince whose contradictory actions so confounded her.

However desperate her yearning to remain amidst the kindness and shelter she'd so long craved, she risked much in staying her journey for even another moment.

She rushed through the open inner gate and turned right, then paused. Had Lady MeMe said *left* instead? The high stables in which Reina was housed stood in the corner of the outer bailey nearest the sally port, but which way?

She turned to resume her hurried pace, but walked right into a wall...or had the wall run into her? She stumbled backward and found herself looking up at the tallest man she'd ever beheld, a man who would have dwarfed even Prince Brennus.

"Beggin' yer pardon, mistress," he said, bowing.

"Forgive me, sir. The fault is mine. My thoughts were elsewhere." She bobbed a small curtsey, in case he was one of the many knights who seemed to be everywhere.

"Name's Clark, mistress. No *sir* attached," he said, his voice deep as a well but brimming with merriment. He lifted a wide shoulder, and sunlight glinted off the sword he carried across one arm, the shimmer dazzling against his plain brown tunic and leather apron. "My only dealing with weapons, nowadays, is over a forge."

Lyssanne gasped. "You're a blacksmith?"

"That, I am." He touched his bald brow in a little salute.

"My father was a blacksmith."

"Sword smith or farrier? Or was he a general craftsman?"

"I confess, I know nothing of his trade. He died before I was born."

"A shame," he said. "The state of his forge might tell you much, though. Was it—?"

"I never saw his forge. It, too, was destroyed in the accident."

"Accident?"

"They say, my father died in an explosion. All that remained was a blackened lump of stone that once housed his fire. There wasn't even anything of him to bury."

Clark whistled through his teeth. "Powerful hot explosion, that. Puzzles me, what could cause such unnatural heat?"

"No one knows, or at least, they've never spoken of it."

He cleared his throat. "Well, you just out for a stroll or lookin' fer somethin' particular?"

"I'm in search of the high stables."

"That's a bit of a walk, but I'd be glad to show you the way. If you'll follow me, I'll just drop this blade at my forge. It's over by yon wall."

"I should be most grateful for the assistance," she said.

Moments later, as Clark deposited his burden, Lyssanne stood well away from the door to his forge, her breath catching in the heat even at this distance.

"I'll have that back in shape in no time," Clark said. "Now, to get you sorted out."

He led the way past people and animals engaged in such a flurry of activity, Lyssanne couldn't distinguish any of it. All was a swirl of color and sound. As they walked, he described the makeup of the castle's outer reaches.

"The outer bailey's a square," he said. "Each leg has its purpose. This section holds craftsmen's shops and work areas. The front-facing side's fer merchants' stalls, the gatehouse, and the armory. Along the right, are the garrison house, the lists, and the lower stables. The rear holds gardens and pens for the animals that serve the kitchens."

He stopped, gesturing to a red-roofed building in the rear corner. "There y'are, the high stables, home to Their Graces' finest horses. There's grooms aplenty to serve your needs."

"I thank you, Mr. Clark. It was truly an honor to make your acquaintance."

"Well, now," he said, his big voice sheepish. "Clark'll do. I'm a simple man with a simple name, Mistress, er..."

"Lady Lyssanne!" Jarad shouted, running from the stables. "I thought it was you."

"Yer pardon, my lady," Clark said, bowing. "I should've known you fer a lady, but with yer saying yer father was a blacksmith and all, I just s'posed..."

"You supposed rightly," she said. "I, too, am just a simple girl from a distant valley."

"I get the feeling," he said, "whatever ya be, simple has nothing to do with it." He chuckled. "Like the starlings nestin' by my house. Stop by my forge anytime. I'll show you a bit of what yer father may have done to pass the hours."

"It would be a delight. I've often wished I knew more of his life."

Clark offered one last half bow and lumbered off.

As Lyssanne strode toward the stables, Jarad fell into pace beside her. "That man's huge!" he whispered. "Think he needs an apprentice? I could be a blacksmith."

She laughed. "I have no doubt of it."

"And everybody here speaks Starransi, even the stable boys. Lyryan *and* Starransi!"

"Well, ours is the common language of trade throughout the Seven Lands."

"Yeah, but can you imagine anyone in Cloistervale knowin' two languages?" He paused. "We could stay here. One of the grooms says there's always work to be found. It's a nice place, too, don't you think?"

"That, it is," she said, her voice thick, "but we have much to discuss. First, let us find Reina and a bit of privacy."

Noire crouched on the crimson roof, immersed in Jarad's conversation with a stable boy.

"You any good with that bow?" the boy asked, passing Jarad a bucket of clean water. "Cuz if y'are, see, Lord Av'ry lets us hunt on his lands. Anything we want. 'Cept ravens." He shivered. "Shoot one, an' you're for the stocks. That's if ya just wound it. It's death to any man who kills one."

"Why? Is it like…a religion thing?"

"Nah, just the law. 'Specially when His Lordship's friend's in residence." He leaned close and spoke low. "They say he trains 'em as spies, y'know. Like, whatever one o' his birds overhears, he knows by nightfall. You came with him; is it true?"

"Sir Brennus?" Jarad asked. "No, that's silly. I've never even seen him with a raven. Lady Lyssanne would say that kind of superstition's only good for scaring people." Jarad glanced over his shoulder and dropped his bucket. "Lady Lyssanne!"

Noire's feathers ruffled. She'd emerged, and he hadn't seen her approach? He fought his feathers into submission. Distractions! He couldn't afford them, not even here.

Jarad disappeared with Lyssanne into the stables. After long moments, he emerged with her and Reina in tow, heading for the sally port. "Please," he was saying. "The stable hands all want me to join in the game."

"Very well," she said. "But remember what I've told you."

"I promise. I still think it's brilliant, though, us knowing...someone like him." Grinning, he dashed off, pell-mell, careening into one of the guards who held the gate open for Lyssanne.

Reina and Lyssanne wandered out into the meadow. When they halted, still within shouting distance of the castle, Noire circled high above. While Lyssanne spread her blanket upon the soft grass, he alighted in a convenient clump of tall wildflowers a safe distance away, just in time to catch her and Reina mid-conversation.

"Perhaps," Reina said, stretching out next to Lyssanne, "he simply feels more comfortable in the role of ordinary knight. If that's the only life he's known, he may not even think of himself otherwise." She paused as Lyssanne's dove landed on a corner of the blanket.

Perchance, denied the sport of raven-hunting, Duncan's men would find the dove an appealing target. A pleasant thought, that.

"If his family's in exile," Reina said, flicking her tail at a bee, "he can't have ever truly lived the life of a prince. Besides, his family may still have enemies."

She knew?

"Whatever his reasons for silence," Lyssanne said, "I can't un-hear what I was told. What do I say to him, Reina? Do I go on as if I have no knowledge of this?" She twirled a blade of grass. "The revelation wasn't of his choosing, but Lady MeMe may have told him of it."

Noire's stomach tightened. Duncan had mentioned nothing of this. Oh, he'd known the risk in bringing her here, but he hadn't expected her to discover anything so soon. Ice rushed through his veins. What else had MeMe told her?

Lyssanne sighed and let the grass fall from her fingers like a discarded thought. She stared off into the distance then gasped. "I allowed him to…to tend me when I was ill."

"I daresay, you had not the presence of mind to prevent him," Reina said. "Had you known, his station would have made no difference."

"Yes, but," Lyssanne buried her face in her hands. "Of all things, he massaged my head!" She looked up, flushed. "How can I dare speak to him again? He's a prince!"

"Who's a prince?" The voice sizzled through the empty air an instant before its owner materialized over Lyssanne's right shoulder.

Lyssanne jumped up and spun to face the spiky-haired faerie. "Please, Jada, could you give some warning before you do that?"

"What?" the faerie said, arms splayed. "I sent air ahead. It always pops or sizzles a little fanfare. You just need to be more watchful. So, who's this prince you're in such a bother about?"

Lyssanne released her death-grip on her pendant and exhaled. "Sir Brennus. He's…but I'm not certain who knows of this. Perhaps I shouldn't—"

"Oh, feathers, we know who he is." Jada waved the matter away. "Why should that vex you? He's only a human prince. You spoke well enough with the exalted queen of the FAE, and that wasn't even your first time in the presence of royalty. Why, Princess Tria—"

"Jada." With warning in her voice, the faerie Olivia resolved into view.

"Princess?" Lyssanne said. "What princess?"

"Well, you didn't actually meet her," Jada said. "Not face to face." She shot a glance at Olivia. "Anyway, we should cut the chatter and get on with your lessons."

"Now may not be the time, after all," Olivia said, peering at Lyssanne. "You look drained. I suspect there is more to that than the unexpected origins of a knight you barely know."

"She's been unwell, of late," said Reina. "More so than I've ever seen her."

The unicorn detailed the nature of Lyssanne's recent battle against pain. How much did the faeries, or even Reina, know of its true cause?

"Yes, the King said you'd had a rough time of it," Olivia said, fluttering down to rest a hand atop Lyssanne's shoulder. "I thought some practice in directing His Light might cheer you, but I see your heart and mind are elsewhere. Understandable."

Lyssanne shook her head. "I can do this. You've come all this way, and I do wish to learn." She squared her shoulders. "I shall think only on what you tell me."

"No," Olivia said. "You must first build up your strength."

"Lyssanne has been invited to remain a guest of the border lord," Reina said. "What think you? I sensed nothing untrustworthy in the man, but my skills in such matters are limited."

Olivia turned to survey the walls of Avery Hall. "His lady honors the King," she said. "You should all be safe in his hall, at least for a time."

"That time may be shorter than you suppose," said Lyssanne. "They think me an equal."

"We are all equal in the eyes of the King," said Jada.

"Yes, but 'tis not so among men," said Lyssanne. "If they discover who I am—"

"Rest while you have the chance," Jada said. "Dangers far worse than discovery of your station lurk beyond those high walls."

Olivia jabbed the tip of her wand into Jada's side.

"Like the sorcerer responsible for that mist in Cloistervale?" In its tone, Lyssanne's question carried its own answer. She fixed the faeries with beseeching eyes. "Who is the enemy in Mr. Fescue's warning?"

The faeries fluttered there, gazes locked in silent battle.

"You know, don't you?" Lyssanne said. She sighed, perhaps as weary of asking this question as Noire was of hearing it. "Who have I wronged so terribly they wish me harm?"

"Now, Lyssanne," said Olivia, "we did not say any such thing."

"You've said nothing at all," Lyssanne snapped. She hung her head. "Forgive me, but 'tis obvious you hold answers. If I have brought danger upon us, I must know, so I may make amends. If such is possible."

"You are weary," Olivia said. "Fret not over such things."

"You say I carry the King's Light within me," Lyssanne said, "that it will guide my path, but how am I to walk that path if you keep me in the dark? In the past pair of fortnights, I've stumbled over enough surprises to make me question my own reason."

She sank onto her blanket and leaned forward, elbows on knees, feet curled to one side. Lifting her chin from her cupped hands, she looked up at the faeries with eyes far older than her nineteen years. Sitting there, bedecked in embroidery, with her neatly wound hair and soul-weary eyes, she more resembled the careworn widow of some lesser knight than the serene peasant maiden Noire had first spied upon in the village.

"When last we spoke," she said, "you warned that I must give no place to fear. Yet, I've discovered that the mist I alone can see is a tool of the Thief of Souls, that a sorcerer wishes me ill, and that I've been keeping company with a prince. How can I but dread what else lies in wait for me amid the shadows of secrecy?"

"She's right, Captain," Jada said without her usual fire. "Light reveals. If she is to truly embrace Light's gifts, she needs to know what the darkness is."

Olivia's eyes remained fixed on Lyssanne, her countenance grave. "It is time." She floated down to sit before Lyssanne, motioning Jada to join her. "It began just before your birth."

The tale that followed so ensnared Noire, he didn't even twitch when a fly crawled through his feathers.

The faerie spoke of a day when Lyssanne's mother ventured to the bottom of Rowan Hill, bearing refreshment to her husband at his forge. A stranger's appearance had interrupted their cheerful converse. The couple treated the woman with all deference, attired as she was in silks and velvet brocade. But they soon learned this lady of high birth was there for no noble purpose.

"The stranger had come to claim their unborn child," said Olivia. "She was all solicitude and generous condescension at first. Her reasons were simple; she had no children to carry on her family legacy and could provide what Lysander and his young wife could not. When they refused, the lady revealed her true nature.

"With a sudden burst of power that blasted apart one wall of Lysander's forge, the lady acknowledged herself as a sorceress, bent on the child's destruction."

Noire tensed. *Venefica.*

Olivia's words conjured vivid images of Lysander shielding his wife. "Run. Hide yourself and the babe," he'd whispered, nudging her toward the rowan grove. "I shall speak with the lady and settle this."

"He must have known this wouldn't end in peaceful resolution," said Olivia. "For, even as he ushered his wife away, heavy tools and unfinished metal hurtled toward him. Brianne ran, or rather waddled, as fast as a woman eight months with child could. Through the rowan grove and into the wood behind her cottage, she fled, intending to conceal her path back toward Cloistervale so she could rally the men of the village. She never got that far.

"Just as she entered the wood, a boom shook the ground. She turned back, gazing in horror upon the geyser of flame that had once been the seat of her husband's trade. So violent was the fire, flame rose above the trees."

"The accident," Lyssanne whispered.

"Yes," Olivia said. "Drowning in tears and fear, Brianne plunged deeper into the wood. Soon, sounds of pursuit shadowed her aimless flight. Winded and unable to go on, she stopped in a clearing and turned to face her attacker."

"What neither Brianne nor the sorceress knew," said Jada, "was that a young faerie of particular skill in the healing arts had been assigned to watch over your mother, to nurture her health and yours until your birth."

"So, this faerie," Lyssanne said, her voice hoarse, "she confronted the sorceress?"

"In a manner of speaking," Olivia said. "No warrior faerie she, Tria suddenly found herself the only defense between her charge and certain death."

"She may have been no fighter," Jada said, "but she took her mission as seriously as any battle. Volunteered for it, in fact, our queen's own daughter, and paid the highest price."

Lyssanne gasped and covered her mouth with a trembling hand.

"Yes, well…" Olivia cleared her throat. "The sorceress insisted she would have you. If Brianne resisted, she would share Lysander's fate. Brianne said you were a gift from the King, and what He had given, the sorceress had not the right to steal.

"Tria shot across the clearing like an arrow snapping free of its bow. The King's own words upon Brianne's lips had loosed her. So, when the sorceress flung forth her hand, hurling a bolt of darkness at Brianne—at *you*—it met Tria instead."

"She gave her life for love," Jada said. "Love of the King, love of your mother who so faithfully followed him." She turned away, blinking rapidly, and mumbled under her breath, "Love of the mortals you would one day save."

Noire's head twitched. Save? Ha! Lyssanne couldn't even save herself.

"What happened to the sorceress?" Lyssanne asked. "To my mother?"

"She fled," said Olivia. "The King's own power was released in that clearing, and I daresay it terrified her. Your mother was unharmed, for only a trickle of the dark magic reached her. It left you with physical limitations, but wasn't strong enough to take your life."

"My sight," Lyssanne said.

"Yes. That wasn't the only change left behind. Where Tria fell, a ring of white blossomed, a living testimony forged of sacrifice. The faerie ring you've twice discovered is, for you, a sanctuary. For, it testifies of the King's action on your behalf."

"Like in the *Kingsword*," Lyssanne whispered. "'They overcame by His sacrifice and the word of their testimony.'"

"Exactly," Jada said. "No enemy can reach you within Tria's ring—or even see you once you're inside. For, none can touch or take from you what the King has done."

Lyssanne sat in silence, myriad emotions flitting across her face. "The sorceress..." she said. "If she wanted a child to inherit her legacy, why did she try to kill me?"

"Your death was always her goal," Olivia said. "If possible, without revealing her power. Once the ruse she perpetrated on your parents failed, I doubt she intended to let any of you live."

"She made that much obvious in her words to Brianne," said Jada, her fists clenched at her hips. "If Brianne had consented to give you up, you'd have died, never having been born."

"Mother told me none of this," Lyssanne said.

"Perhaps our queen advised against it," Olivia said, glancing at Reina and the dove. "She visited your mother just after the attack. What they spoke of, no one knows. This much is certain; Brianne feared the sorceress would return. Perhaps she thought you'd be safer if she kept silent."

"'The Shadow Mist,'" Lyssanne whispered, eyes widening. "She's the one, that sorceress, the Keeper of the Mist."

"She is."

Olivia's words rippled through the emotion-thickened air like boulders through water. Lyssanne shuddered with the impact. Their distant vibration reached even Noire, in the sharp tingles that stabbed his length from beak to tail feathers.

Venefica had heard...everything.

"I feel like one lost in a wood," Lyssanne said. "I've pressed through branches, stumbled over underbrush, only to find I'm back where I began." She shook her head. "'Tis the same old question I must ask. Why?" She speared Olivia with a steely look. "Why did she wish me harm? Why does she still?"

Jada inhaled as if to speak, but Olivia grasped her by the arm.

"It is forbidden," she said, low and ominous.

Jada paled, nodding.

Olivia released her and turned back to Lyssanne. "Some things, you must discover for yourself," she said, her wings lifting her into the air. "Nor do we know all. This, though, I can tell you. Trust in what the King puts before you. When He has fully prepared you, He will lead you to the answers you seek."

The faeries departed, leaving stillness in their wake. As the afternoon waned, Lyssanne and Reina lingered in the meadow. They spoke little, and then only to rehash what they'd already discussed. Noire remained among his weeds, in case any further insight should strike them.

The full story of Venefica's first attempt to destroy Lyssanne spawned musings of his own. To think, a sorceress who seemed so confident of her own power had feared an unborn child! Lyssanne must have shown potential for great power, indeed, to prompt Venefica's fear and a faerie princess's self-sacrifice.

Another realization struck him. In the earliest days of his service to her, Venefica had only suspected Lyssanne as the child she'd attacked years before, the one she'd called Light-Wielder. Not until she'd witnessed that Light through his eyes, had she been certain.

And she dared question Noire's usefulness? Nearly every bit of progress she'd made toward regaining her power, she owed to him.

By the time Lyssanne left the meadow, the sun was fading. Noire shook off the stiffness of the afternoon's indolence in favor of frantic flight. He must reach the Hall before light vanished from the horizon.

Towers and walls blurred beneath him as he pointed his beak toward the library turret. That window would be open even at this time of day. He alighted on the sill then hopped to the carpet-strewn floor an instant before shifting.

The library's hourglass revealed that he had scant time to dress for dinner. Arriving late to a feast held in his honor would be bad form.

At least the evening's activities, unnecessary though they were, would afford him an excuse to delay speaking with Venefica. He wanted his full wits about him for that conversation.

~

Lyssanne quickened her pace, all but jogging through the corridors. She hadn't intended to remain so long out of doors or return this late.

A hundred thoughts raced through her mind. Her father had been murdered. He and a faerie—not just any faerie, but the daughter of their queen—had died to save her. A powerful sorceress had wanted her dead, likely still did. And the most difficult to bear—her mother, with whom she'd believed she had no secrets, had withheld those truths. Doubtless, she'd had reason, but that couldn't lessen the pain.

What would have changed, had Lyssanne known? The truth of the Shadow Mist, and the sorceress responsible for it, might have helped her sway the Council. Would they have sent her away, knowing such a person wished to kill her?

What was done couldn't be altered, as Reina had pointed out. "Only you can choose how to use the light you've been given, the Light of your gift and the light of this information."

Lyssanne's skirts threatened to trip her as she raced up the grand staircase. She couldn't risk insulting her hosts. Oh, what if she were already late? She turned a corner and nearly collided with a tall figure.

Her breath hitched. *Prince Brennus!*

The corridor lurched, and her stomach fell into her feet. She wasn't ready for this! Her intention to plan her next words to him had gotten lost in Olivia's tale. She must say something. She couldn't just stand there, fish-faced.

"Your Highness." She dropped into as deep a curtsey as she dared. It would not do to fall over in front of a prince.

He merely nodded and continued walking. Just as he passed her, he stopped. The top of her head prickled from his gaze. The warmth of his hand enveloped hers, and he lifted it. Belatedly, she realized he meant to lift her from her curtsey.

"These corridors can be quite drafty," he murmured. "The dining hall is warmer, but perhaps you should don your cloak or a shawl."

"I am not cold," she whispered.

"Don't be foolish," he said, still holding her hand. "You're shivering."

"I, 'tis just..." Her face heated. "Forgive me, Your Highness. I did not know!"

"Know what?"

"That you were...*who* you were."

He dropped her hand. "You knew what I wished you to know." His voice was steel wrapped in black silk.

"But I, I spoke to you so familiarly. And Jarad—he all but scolded you. Surely you must know, had we been aware...Still, it was not our place."

He waved a dismissive hand. "I have matters to see to."

She stepped back to allow him passage. The wide corridor seemed suddenly too small for the two of them. She leaned against the wall to collect her scattered thoughts. The emotions of the past pair of days collided in a dizzying melee.

The feast! She pushed herself off the wall and rushed toward the corridor that led to her chambers—in the opposite direction Prince Brennus had gone.

PERCEPTION

*B*rennus stood amidst the swirl of silken gowns, brocaded tunics, and festive, idle chatter filling the receiving chamber off Duncan's great hall. From the free-flowing, sparkling wines and juices, to the jewel-encrusted hilts of daggers and gem-laden tiaras glowing in the soft lamplight, everything in the room scintillated with opulence.

He was no exception. To honor the trouble Duncan's household had undertaken, he'd unearthed his best court attire from the valuables he kept locked in Duncan's towers. He shrugged to ensure his knee-length, ornamental cape remained fastened to the gold raven's-head broaches at his shoulders. The motion shifted his ancestral sword, and it brushed the leg of the man nearest, jabbing one of the metallic wings beneath the sword's guard into Brennus's hip.

Grimacing, Brennus shifted the weapon. If he were to wear this bejeweled, ceremonial scabbard any more often, he must have it fitted with a leather backing like the one his battle sheath provided between the cross-guard's wings and his body. "I beg your pardon," he said, turning to the man his blade had jostled. He blinked in the glare of the man's tunic—a garish ensemble the exact shade of the orange fruit on Duncan's sideboard, covered in gaudy, gold embellishments.

Busy expounding on some exaggerated adventure, the man paid Brennus no heed.

"I daresay there's more adventure in Sir Fenard's flirtations than in his feats as a knight," the captain of the Avery guard murmured in Brennus's ear. "Hard to believe he's Duncan's kin."

"Indeed," Brennus said, though his thoughts had shifted elsewhere.

The object of those musings entered the room, saving Brennus from further inane chatter. Indeed, Lyssanne's appearance arrested all conversation—along with his breath.

Her hair, arranged in an intricate cloud of braids, beads, and ribbons, glowed beneath the soft light. Ribbons and spirals of hair cascaded over her left shoulder. A common affectation designed to give calculating ladies an air of guilelessness. With her averted eyes and youthful features, however, Lyssanne radiated a shy innocence no prickly flower of the court could feign.

Again, Brennus had to shake off images of a faerie princess in some tale. How many other knights in that chamber felt a stirring of protective instinct? Most, he would wager.

The golden insets and trim adorning Lyssanne's silken, jewel green gown set the copper in her hair aflame, completing the fey illusion. The gown, one of MeMe's, no doubt, flowed about Lyssanne as if designed for her.

She glanced his way and gasped. Doubtless, as in awe of his finery as of his station.

He favored her with a nod as the room's hush swelled into a surf of whispers.

What drew all eyes to Lyssanne? Certainly not uncommon beauty. Compared with such cultivated roses as Sir Fenard's sister, Countess Fynnette, she was a wildflower springing from the underbrush. Ah, but Lyssanne was a mystery begging to be solved. Despite devoting a year-and-a-half to watching her, even he felt as if he were seeing her for the first time.

Lyssanne stood frozen, a flightless sparrow facing a brace of trained falcons. MeMe rushed forward, the consummate hostess, allowing not a moment to stretch into awkwardness. She introduced Lyssanne to those nearest, then ushered her past Brennus toward a group of ladies, pausing only long enough to exchange the proper courtesies.

How had he never noticed the grace with which Lyssanne carried herself? Silks and ribbons had transformed her delicacy and fine features, for which he'd thought her weak and insignificant, into the marks of a gentle lady's elegance. He shook his head. She was a peasant—an outcast, homeless peasant—enemy of his oath-sworn lady, and a sorceress.

She laughed at something one of the ladies said, interacting smoothly with those of a rank no inhabitant of her village would likely ever encounter. Ah, but the mask of her easy manner couldn't conceal from Brennus the tense lift of her shoulders or the increased darting of her eyes.

Lyssanne wouldn't look at him, though she faced his direction. His jaw clenched, and his stomach tightened as it had in the corridor. At least his parentage was the only information MeMe had disclosed. He must make certain that remained the case.

A sudden impact against his midsection and a high-pitched squeal of "Uncle Bren!" drove all other thought from his mind.

"Noel?" he muttered. How had Duncan's daughter managed to enter without his notice?

The child flung her arms around his waist and laughed. "Madam Stingeford said Papa had a guest, but I didn't know it was you!"

"And you," Brennus said. "How you've grown in the past three years!" He swept her up and twirled with her, as he'd done countless times since her infancy, then settled her upon her feet. "Soon, I shan't be able to do that."

"I'm pleased you noticed, Uncle, uh, I mean, Your Highness," Noel said, shooting a look over her shoulder. Her grin shrank to a dignified smile.

A pinch-faced woman, swathed from hair to toes in severe grey, scowled back. Ah, Noel's nurse, Madam Stingeford.

Noel backed away a pace to offer Brennus a curtsey, her eyes still sparkling. "This winter will be my tenth, you know." She glanced at the other guests awaiting the announcement of dinner. Lifting a brow, she leaned close and said in a stage whisper, "Papa didn't introduce me."

She coughed into her hand, casting her eyes toward her father as if to mask the gesture as a hint. But that cough held a rasp no subtle lady's ploy would produce.

Feigning a grave air, Duncan sauntered over to present his daughter, Lady Noel Avery, to the room at large. Then, he introduced Lyssanne as the friend and guest of Brennus.

"I am honored to make your acquaintance, My Lady Noel," Lyssanne said, offering Noel as deep a curtsey as she had MeMe the night before, though not so deep as the one she'd offered Brennus in the hallway a scant two hours past.

Noel beamed, maintaining her courtly air barely long enough to return the courtesy. With eyes a-twinkle, she edged closer to Lyssanne and said under her breath, "Uncle Bren is the bravest knight in the Seven Lands, except for my Papa. Would you not say?"

"I know little of such things," Lyssanne said, "but I have witnessed his courage, yes."

"Have you met Lady Shelly?"

"I do not believe I've had the pleasure," Lyssanne said.

"She's in the corner behind you," Noel whispered. "Her brother is Papa's captain." She again flitted to a new subject. "Is Uncle Bren guarding you on your journeys?"

"Not precisely," Lyssanne said, flushing. "Though, your, um… uncle?…has come to my rescue a time or two."

"I knew it!" Noel clapped her hands. "I knew you could help me. I told Lady Shelly's daughter he was the bravest. If you meet her, you could tell her I'm right."

"Careful with your flattery, daughter," said Duncan, "else Brennus will need to ply his sword to fit his head through my door!"

Amid the good-natured chuckles of those nearest, Noel again spoke to Lyssanne in that conspiratorial way of little girls. "He's not really my uncle," she said, "just Papa's dearest friend. I'm the only one who's permitted to call him that, you know. Papa doesn't even call him Bren."

"A position of high honor, to be sure," Lyssanne said.

"He taught me to ride, too." Noel swiveled back to him. "You must see me ride Honeybee, I—" Coughs seized her again, and she doubled over, struggling for breath.

"You'll not be riding tonight, Noel," MeMe said. "Nor until you are well. It's off to bed with you, and no protesting your medicine."

Just then, the herald entered, announcing dinner. MeMe ushered Noel off in the care of her nurse. Brennus followed them to the door to bid Noel a pleasant night.

Once the child was out of earshot, he said, "She's radiating more warmth than is normal. I thought the healers claimed she would outgrow that malady."

"It's been a difficult year," MeMe said. "She's battled this fever off and on for a month."

As guests filed into the great hall through a doorway farther along the wall, MeMe rested her elegant hand atop Brennus's arm. Together, they wove through the crowd to stand behind Duncan and Lyssanne.

When all others had left the receiving chamber, the herald cleared his throat and addressed the lesser knights and ladies assembled in the hall. "Our noble host, Duncan, Lord Avery. And presenting Lyssanne, Lady of Rowanhill." He ran the two words together as though Rowan Hill were a great hall or titled holding. "Her Grace, MeMe, Lady Avery, escorted by our guest of honor, His Highness, Sir Brennus Xavier, Prince of Ravenshold."

Brennus led MeMe down the center of a hall ablaze with color. In conspicuous absence, though, was any hue resembling scarlet. He rounded the head table and passed behind Lyssanne's chair to seat his hostess.

Just then, Lyssanne whispered to Duncan, "I thought he was Prince of Navvar."

"He is, by birth," Duncan said, "but does not hold the office. By rights, he should be addressed as His Royal Highness, but cannot be introduced as such while another rules the land."

As Brennus settled in the chair at Duncan's right hand, Jarad took up a protective stance behind Lyssanne's chair, having made it plain he considered himself her personal servant. A wise move, and his only means of remaining close to her. He might admire Brennus, but trusted even him only so far with her welfare. Wise, indeed.

The easy smiles and light conversation between Lyssanne and MeMe set Brennus's teeth on edge. With a word, he could expose Lyssanne for the fraud she was, but doing so would endanger the boy as well.

With Lyrya's severe penalties for perpetrating a deception upon one's host, especially a lord, and Duncan's strict adherence to the law, Jarad could lose his tongue or end up locked away. Brennus had no wish to land him even in Duncan's relatively civilized dungeon. If, however, he ever thought Lyssanne meant his friends harm, he would put a swift end to this. Until then, he would watch—as usual.

"I must say, Your Highness," said Sir Fenard, seated to his right, "you have excellent taste. Though, I suppose that is to be expected."

Brennus sighed. If he must endure this nuisance throughout dinner, he may as well respond as propriety demanded. "To what do I owe the compliment?"

"Your lady, of course," said Sir Fenard. "Where is this Rowanhill? No manor in Lyrya bears the name. Lastarra, perhaps?"

"It is in Lastarra, yes."

"A fine hall, I daresay. I should exert myself to visit. Perchance, has your lady a sister?"

"She isn't my lady," Brennus said between his teeth.

"No? She arrived with you, did she not? I just assumed." He popped a fig into his mouth with almost feminine delicacy. "Then, you won't mind if I...acquaint myself with the fair lady?"

Brennus went cold, recalling rumors of Sir Fenard leaving the ladies he wooed with crushed emotions and shattered reputations. "I doubt, sir," he said, "that you are of the sort to invite the lady's attentions." He set down his forkful of herbed mutton, no longer interested. "Your...sophistication...is of an entirely different class from hers."

"She can hardly object to my acquaintance," said Fenard. "Why, so fine a lady must have a taste as superb as your own."

Precisely what Brennus was counting on, her taste. Though, why should he care? Perhaps whatever was left of his chivalry simply didn't wish to see heartbreak added to her sufferings.

"How goes your quest?" Duncan asked, putting the matter to rest. "I'd hoped your presence here meant you'd found what you seek, but...Are you any closer to your goal?"

"At times, I despair of ever reaching it," Brennus said. "Lady Effie persists in altering the terms of my service." He smirked, taking secret pleasure in calling Venefica by the name she detested.

"A fickle liege lady can be a trial. Some would say a trial not worth enduring."

"You've no idea, friend. I begin to wonder if she ever intends to call an end to it."

So, Duncan assume Brennus still pursued the vain notion of a noble quest, to end his curse in the manner proscribed. Good. What Duncan would think of his consorting with a sorceress instead...Well, he'd never have to know.

The evening progressed as such occasions always did, with inane chatter, gossip, and favor mongering. Brennus exhaled as, at last, Duncan led the occupants of the high table back into the drawing room, where they would partake of sumptuous desserts, while servants cleared supper dishes and rearranged the hall for the remainder of the festivities.

A few servants attended the gathering, Jarad insinuating himself among them. He stood ready behind Lyssanne's chair, making certain he alone handed her whatever refreshment she took. Brennus wouldn't have been surprised had the boy insisted on tasting her food.

"What talents have you, Lady Lyssanne?" Duncan asked, seating himself in the chair with the best view of all his guests. "Do you play the harp? Sing?"

Lyssanne shook her head, flushed.

"Ah, perhaps you prefer the pianoforte? Fynnette has entertained us for the past fortnight, but I thought, as our newest guest, you should have first choice to grace us with your gifts. The hired musicians have only just arrived, you see, and must prepare."

"Thank you for the honor, milord," Lyssanne said, "but I shall defer to your cousin. She would know best the songs you enjoy and is doubtless more skilled than I in the musical arts."

She covered it well with her eloquent words, but pretty speech couldn't hide her agitation from Brennus. Here, was where her deception would fall apart. What could she have learned of the arts expected from a noble lady as entertainment in a manor hall?

"Surely the lady is too modest," Sir Fenard said, slapping Duncan on the shoulder as he rounded his chair. "My sister's talents notwithstanding, we're fair drowning in every form of art Lyrya can boast." He skirted around Jarad then executed a bow, a blatant excuse to lean closer to Lyssanne. "I, for one," he murmured, "would prefer to discover what Lastarra has to offer."

Lyssanne darted a wide-eyed glance at Jarad, then toward Brennus.

Brennus pinned her with his gaze, a silent reminder. Neither of them could save her from the jaws of this deception, a monster of her own making. "Perhaps," he said, "the lady would favor us with a tale. She is, after all, so fond of telling stories."

Lyssanne flinched.

"We're no gaggle of children at some peasant fair, flocking to the voice of a tale-spinner," a man said.

"On the contrary," Duncan said. "A storyteller's gift would be most welcome. It's long since a decent bard graced my hall. What wonder will you weave for us, Lady Lyssanne?"

"What tales I know," said Lyssanne, folding and unfolding her hands, "I share with children. Surely those are too familiar to interest this fine company."

"Doubtless the tales of Navvar are not so familiar," Brennus said in a sudden flash of inspiration. "So little is heard from that region. You might share a story from *Ar Popinpopii*."

Lyssanne stared at him, her eyes wide. Had he indeed caught her in another lie? Was her ability to read a foreign tongue a mere pretense to gain favor, as he'd suspected?

"Never have I heard any of their legends," MeMe said. "Have you, Duncan?"

"Long ago, when Brennus and I were boys, but I've forgotten most of his grandmother's stories. Remind me, won't you, Lady Lyssanne?"

Perhaps emboldened by their encouragement, she began the tale of the Great Faerie War, shattering yet another of Brennus's perceptions of her.

She spoke of a time long passed, when there awoke a terrible uprising among the faeries. An enemy of all life persuaded some of the winged warriors to rebel against their ruling house and the benevolent human kings they protected. Before the end, one third of the faeries were deceived. Ultimately defeated, they were banished to the Land of Lightless Fire.

Lyssanne recited the long but lyrical tale as if translating word for word from the original Navvarish. The warm, expressive way she told it drew even Brennus into the legend.

As her voice rose and fell, weaving the images of betrayal, love, and intense battle, the knights and ladies left their fine desserts untouched. Even the servants abandoned their duties to listen, but only Brennus paid this any heed.

Lyssanne ended her story, sharing in the bittersweet triumph of the fabled faerie court. She'd survived the test. The room erupted in pleased chatter, but Prince Brennus, whose gaze had weighed upon her throughout her tale, rose without a word and strode to the fireplace.

"Lastarran cider all around!" Lord Duncan said to his chief servant.

"Let us toast Lady Lyssanne and the gifts of my wife's homeland with the fruits of their orchards!"

"Here, here!" said Sir Fenard, leaning on the arm of the settee facing Lyssanne.

"Yer lady's tale was right innerestin'," said the maid Jarad was assisting to fill glasses at a sideboard behind Lyssanne's chair. "I could listen to 'er fer hours."

"Yeah," Jarad said. "That one's even better than those I've read about King Aleric."

"You can read?" the maid squealed, and conversations nearest them ceased.

"Lady Lyssanne taught me," Jarad said in a near whisper.

"You taught your servant to read?" Countess Fynnette asked. "What in the Seven Lands for? Do you teach all your servants, or just this one?"

"Jarad isn't my servant," Lyssanne said, her entire body revolting at the assumption. "He's a friend." By rights, she should be serving refreshment alongside him.

"Milady honors me too highly," Jarad said, nudging her arm as he handed her a glass.

Lyssanne glanced at the prince, his gaze again prickling her skin. He seemed at perfect ease, leaning against the mantelpiece, arms crossed over his deep blue velvet doublet, one foot propped on the hearthstone. Would this be the moment he revealed her secret?

His continued silence frightened her almost more than the condemning words she expected him to utter at any moment.

"I can understand employing a lettered servant," grated the deep voice of a portly man seated across from Lord Duncan. "If it's a highly trusted steward or the head of your household."

Lyssanne nearly spilled her cider at the man's abrupt words, reminding her she and Prince Brennus weren't the chamber's sole inhabitants.

"Still," the gentleman said, "any other servant who can read is dangerous. Yes, dangerous to the peace and privacy of any decent house."

"But, sir," Lyssanne said, "should your people be denied the joys or knowledge found in books, simply because they were not born to noble parents?"

"Such modern ideas," Countess Fynnette's mother said with a hiss.

"You've obviously not been to court for some time, Mother," Sir Fenard said, laughing. "I've heard far more scandalous notions than that."

"You would," the dowager baroness said.

"Besides," Sir Fenard said, "I find ladies with modern ideas most...interesting."

Lord Duncan raised his glass. "To interesting ladies and their enchanting tales."

Just how *interesting* might Sir Fenard find Lyssanne after their dance? The guests hadn't long returned to the great hall when, with courtly grace rivaling anything she'd read in books, Lord Duncan's charming cousin asked for the favor of her company upon the dance floor.

As they approached the other dancers, the music turned from a simple folk ballad common throughout the Seven Lands to a fast, intricate reel. Ladies' skirts whirled by as Lyssanne tugged at the baron's arm. "Perhaps we should postpone. I do not know this dance."

"All the better!" Sir Fenard said. "Then, you'll learn it properly. I've astounded King Luteson's court with my mastery of this dance a dozen times."

Grasping her hands, he whirled her into the fray. He executed a complex set of steps and swung her first one way, then the other. Lyssanne nearly tripped over her hem trying to keep up.

"Just watch my feet," he yelled above the raucous music.

Even if she could have distinguished anything about his feet, all her attention was consumed with simply staying on hers.

As the music rose to a crescendo, Sir Fenard spun her faster and faster to match it. Breathless, her knees wobbly, Lyssanne feared she might twirl to pieces.

The sudden force of the next spin flung her damp palms free of the baron's. Reeling, she stumbled into the grasp of strong hands. Those hands twirled her, in one seamless motion steadying her and making the move appear part of the dance. The twist ended with the hands' owner behind her, Lyssanne encircled in his arms.

Sir Fenard continued to dance, seeming unaware he'd lost hold of his partner.

Prince Brennus's voice, behind and above Lyssanne, called his attention to the fact. "With your permission," He said, his tone far from a request.

"Oh...but of course." The baron bowed, a hand outstretched as if graciously relinquishing her company. "Until later, fair lady." He backed away, bowed again, then left the crowd.

Prince Brennus stepped from behind Lyssanne then gestured to the musicians. The music's tempo slowed to a soothing waltz as unfamiliar to her as the raucous tune had been.

He extended a hand. "Shall we?"

She stared at his strong fingers, longing for a seat and a glass of anything cool—or better still, a hole in which to hide. Instead, as courtesy demanded, she placed her hand in his. Besides, he'd just rescued her again, albeit from no greater danger than that of falling on her face.

"I do not know the steps," she said, perchance finding a way to bow out. "I wouldn't wish to embarrass you as I surely did Sir Fenard."

"Very little embarrasses the baron." He moved closer. "The steps are simple," he murmured. "Fear not, I shall guide you. Place your free hand at my shoulder."

"Is such a posture proper?" she asked, glancing about.

"For this waltz," said Prince Brennus, "it is perfectly suitable."

She complied, though she must look foolish, one arm extended as if reaching for the ceiling. Her fingertips barely brushed his shoulder. Before having occasion to take his measure with touch, she'd sensed his great height as a mere notion. Everyone was tall to her eyes.

"Here," he said, a chuckle lightening his low voice. "Perhaps this will serve." He covered her hand with his and moved it down to the middle of his upper arm. "Better?"

She nodded, her cheeks aflame.

"Good. Now, all you need do is move when I do. Mirror my steps."

How could she do thus when she knew not which way he would move next? Her limbs grew taut as Jarad's bowstring. Prince Brennus took a step forward and to her right. She stepped back a moment too late. He retracted his boot just in time to prevent crushing her toes.

He whispered the direction of his next step before executing it, and continued likewise until she fell into a rhythm with him. "Relax," he whispered. "The dance will come easier."

No longer focused on their feet, futile as that had been, Lyssanne found herself staring at the medallion hanging from the ornamental chain he wore across his shoulders. Gold trimmed the brilliant blue, shield-shaped emblem and slashed it diagonally in two. The lower left corner boasted a smaller version of the golden, encircled birds that made up part of his chain. A bit of fancy scrollwork in the upper right corner resembled the letter *n*.

At length, she closed her eyes and let the music and Prince Brennus's whispered directions carry her along. Now, in much the same way she could detect changes in her surroundings in the dark of night, the slight shifting of his muscles beneath her hand and the pressure of his nearness alerted her to his intent even before he whispered it. Tension melted from her limbs, and she flowed through the dance, for the first time in her life feeling graceful.

Her entire body relaxed; and, as during their ride to Edgemond, she sank into a sense of safety in the prince's company.

The joy of the dance swept her away until, at last, the musicians paused. As Prince Brennus escorted her to a chair, she drew a silent breath. She'd taken two turns with him!

While the prince escorted Lady MeMe onto the floor, Sir Fenard's voice drifted to Lyssanne's hearing from behind a nearby pillar. "Why does he wear the elf-heads of House Avery in his chain of office?" he asked. "Surely a man of his station hasn't sworn fealty to a border holding, even one as vast as yours?"

"That's a sign of alliance, not fealty," Lord Duncan said. "I saved his life once in battle, so he wears my signet in equal measure with his own house crest. Told him it wasn't necessary, seeing as he's done the same for me countless times, but he has this strict code about repaying debts. Loyalty and honor go bone-deep in that man."

"So, the other links in the chain, the ravens in flight surrounded by circles—?"

"Crowns," Lord Duncan said. "They, along with the x-shaped links that connect the crests, represent House Xavier. When the crest was first designed, it was said to represent the royal house's duty to protect the land from all dangers. Scavengers, you know. The raven is held to the crown at wingtips, beak, and talon to signify a king's obligation to restrain threats in any form, by word or weapon. Later, the raven came to symbolize the family."

"And his medallion?"

"That, cousin, hasn't been seen in public for two hundred years."

Lyssanne inched as near the pillar as discretion allowed.

"It bears the crest of Navvar under the rule of the Royal House of Xavier," Lord Duncan said. "The final reigning king in the Xavier line was last to wear the medallion and chain…without the Avery links, of course. Legend has it, when he was deposed, the chain shattered at his feet. In her haste to flee, his queen gathered up the shards then passed them down to her heirs. Brennus had it re-forged a few years back, the Avery links replacing those lost."

"This is the first time he's worn it?" asked Sir Fenard. "Dangerous thing to do, is it not?"

"Well, nobody here is bound to inform the Blackthorne Brotherhood of it." Lord Duncan laughed. "If there were Blackthorne agents hereabouts, I daresay he'd make certain they saw it."

"He does mean to reclaim the throne, then?" asked a third man.

Lyssanne turned in her chair. The captain of the Avery forces stood just beyond the pillar.

Lord Duncan emerged and clapped him on the shoulder. "Not tonight, Captain Gunther. Not tonight." Laughing, he strode off to claim a dance with his wife.

Lyssanne rose and sought out a fresh cup of iced berry punch to sooth her dry throat. She skirted a group of ladies near a sideboard laden with tankards of chilled juices.

"He is handsome, certainly," Countess Fynnette's high voice twittered.

"Yes, all that dark hair and serious countenance," said a smoky-voiced woman.

"But dangerous, or so I've heard," a lady in pale rose silk whispered.

"Think you?"

"Lady Lyssanne travels with him," Countess Fynnette said. "She'd know if 'tis true."

Male laughter drifted to them from a few paces away. Prince Brennus stood with several other gentlemen, his head thrown back in mirth.

"Lyssanne, what say you?" Countess Fynnette asked. "Is Prince Brennus dangerous?"

"Yes," she whispered, his deep laugh echoing in her ears. "Yes, I daresay he is."

An hour later, Lyssanne sat enjoying the spectacle of nobles flitting about like butterflies bobbing upon the wind, when a splash of orange detached itself from the rest. Sir Fenard strode across the room toward her as if marching to a quest. Intending to seek another dance? In the midst of a bare expanse of floor, he stopped short and, with an abrupt turn, changed course.

Cloth rustled behind Lyssanne. She glanced over her shoulder. Prince Brennus stood within arm's reach of her chair, staring in the direction Sir Fenard had gone.

For the rest of the evening, wherever Lyssanne went, the prince stood nearby. The music continued long into the night, but Lord Duncan's cousin didn't ask her to dance again.

17

REFRACTION

*J*ust after sunset the following evening, Brennus was still shaking the thoughts of the raven from his mind, when Duncan burst into his chamber. Brennus greeted his friend with a grin, determined to relish every extended moment autumn's lengthening nights afforded him in his true form. Ah, how a man could come to long for the dark of winter.

The request Duncan conveyed from MeMe, however, set his teeth on edge. Conduct Lyssanne on a tour of the castle's upper reaches? Him?

"She says Lyssanne's been quiet all day," Duncan said. "You know how fussy MeMe is about pleasing guests. She thinks a tour will cheer and occupy Lyssanne, especially since my cousins just departed."

None too soon for Brennus's liking, but he held his tongue.

Duncan turned to face him, his eyes flat as gravestones. "Truth is, Noel's taken a bad turn. MeMe and I wish to sit with her this evening after the healer's done, but MeMe won't rest—and neither shall I—if she thinks something's amiss with a guest."

Brennus grimaced at the thought of playing nursemaid to Lyssanne's moods. Still, this would afford him the chance to learn of her plans. He'd welcome any information that might offset Venefica's fury over Lyssanne's latest discoveries.

He followed Duncan to meet the ladies outside the little white shrine in the inner bailey. MeMe bade Lyssanne farewell then tugged Duncan into the shrine.

"What would you most like to see?" Brennus asked, turning toward the manor.

"I do not wish to impose," Lyssanne said, lowering her shawl from her hair. "I'm certain you have more entertaining things to do than conduct me about the manor."

His gaze darted to her averted face. Perceptive, and not what he'd expected. "It is MeMe's wish," he said at last, "that you enjoy the splendor of her home."

They walked up the lush, sloping ground in strained silence.

"Have you seen the gardens?" he asked.

"Yes," she said, her eyes brightening. "Lady MeMe and I had tea there this afternoon."

"The Library?"

She nodded. "Never have I beheld a place of such wonder."

"Indeed. The view from its lofty windows is spectacular."

"I confess," she said, her gaze straying to the blue, conical roofs of the highest spires, "I had eyes only for what lay within."

He couldn't prevent smiling. "Then, there is another place of wonder I should show you." He waved her before him as the guards held the doors ajar for their passage.

They crossed the foyer to the alcove sheltering the double doors of the great hall. Two plainer doors stood facing each other across that alcove. One led to the antechamber in which they'd awaited dinner the previous evening. The other, Brennus opened.

He took a torch from the rack just inside the doorway and lit it from the flame ensconced upon the wall. "Follow close," he said. "The stair is sound but steep."

They ascended a succession of winding stone steps unbroken by door or landing. When the stairs gave way to a smooth ramp, Lyssanne asked its purpose.

"At one time, this tower offered the castle's best defensive position. The ramp prevented troops tripping as they ran to and from battle." He paused to ensure her footing. "The towers haven't been used in war for decades, with the outer walls all but impenetrable, but you can still see the arrow slits, carved through the stone this high above the manor's wings."

At length, the ramp opened into a crescent-shaped alcove and the balcony encircling it.

"Look down there," he said, gesturing to the opening in the alcove.

As she moved to the parapet, he set the torch in a wall bracket, where its flame wouldn't hamper their view. Her soft gasp drew him alongside her. A smile lit her face, her gaze fixed on the lights dotting the outer bailey.

"How beautiful! Like stars." Her eyes drifted upward, as if to determine whether what she saw below was a reflection of the sky. Leaning forward, she asked in a small voice, "What are they, the lights?"

What were they? Any fool could see...He uncurled his fist. She could *not* see. To her, the flames below doubtless did look like tiny pinpricks of light. His chest tightened. She'd been embarrassed to ask and admit her ignorance to one who'd so often met it with scorn.

"They are torches," he murmured, unwilling to break the spell the view had cast over her. "Sentry torches mostly, in brackets all along the outer and inner walls."

"Oh," she said, more breath than word. A little frown creased her brow. "But the lights do not all follow uniform rows. Some are clustered in the midst of the bailey."

"Those are pole lights, torches stuck into the ground near artisans' stalls," he said. "They brighten the area while the craftsmen pack up for the day."

"And the larger ones?" she asked, her voice still awestruck.

"Bonfires." He stepped behind her. "That one," he said, reaching around her shoulder to indicate a fire just below, "is near the saddler's stall, where the leather merchants cook dinner."

He rested his hands to either side of hers on the ledge, concealing her tiny body in the circle of his arms and the parapet. She stiffened, the chill of her skin seeping through his tunic. Thus, he remained where he stood, warming her as she relished this view she couldn't truly see. In it, she beheld beauty he'd forgotten to notice. What else might she see that others could not?

The Shadow Mist. He took a swift step back then crossed to the alcove. He must not forget who she was or what his mission required. "Come, the wind is increasing."

She obeyed, though she glanced back at the view. As he jerked the torch from its bracket, her fingertips brushed his arm. "Thank you," she said. "I shall remember this, always."

He nodded and strode toward the ramp.

"Is there a higher place still?" she asked.

He turned to find her gazing at the narrow stair that wound upward from the opposite side of the alcove. Hiding a smirk, he led her up to the castle's pinnacle; the prison chamber that once held highborn enemies of state and nobles who'd crossed the lords of Avery Hall.

"There is no view from here," he said. "Only a slit for ventilation near the roof."

He swung open the door, into which was cut a slot for the passing of food and a high, barred window. Torchlight flooded the small, round cell.

"You are fond of stories," Brennus said, as they stepped into the room. "This chamber would have many to tell. In fact, it was once used to teach. Though, I doubt its student was pleased with the lesson."

"What sort of lesson?"

"Long ago, a merchant fell victim to a band of highwaymen. Footsore and weary, he came upon the broken carriage of a Lyryan nobleman. The lord and his retainers had been slain, but the attackers had overlooked one trunk. Beneath a few fine garments, the merchant found the nobleman's signet ring. He donned the clothes and put the ring in his pocket, intending to sell it."

Brennus paused, gesturing Lyssanne toward the flat ledge built into one wall. She eyed the stone chamber pot still resting beneath it, then perched at the opposite end of the bench.

"After a day's journey," Brennus said, "the merchant reached Avery Hall. By the crest on his borrowed mantle, the inhabitants mistook him for the dead baron. Seeing he would be feasted and treated with dignity, he put on the dead man's ring and kept up the pretense. However, Lord Avery's son, a friend of the dead baron, whispered the truth to his father. Lord Avery led the merchant up here, saying only this highest chamber would befit a baron such as he."

Lyssanne's eyes widened, and she clasped her hands. Brennus forged on, relentless.

"To the merchant's shock, he found himself surrounded, not by silken tapestries, but bare stone. Just before bolting the door, Lord Avery assured him that his was a penalty befitting any nobleman who acted in war against this holding. The man protested he'd not done so. Deception, said Lord Avery, was the greatest form of betrayal. The merchant remained here until he died."

Lyssanne shot to her feet and glanced back at the ledge, perhaps picturing the merchant breathing his last upon it.

"The lords of Avery Hall do not take kindly to deception," Brennus whispered.

Lyssanne stood silent in the center of the room. She pivoted, as if imagining confinement in this tiny space. He stepped from the room, bringing the torch with him and allowing the door to swing inward. Let her feel the darkness for a moment, the danger of the game she played.

Gasping, she spun around, then rushed from the chamber, stumbling over her hem in her haste. "Might we go back now?" she asked, breathless and pale as Reina's mane.

"Certainly, my lady." He turned, hiding a mocking smile.

Lyssanne flexed her cramped fingers then dipped her quill into the ornate inkwell resting between her and Lady MeMe on the little table in Lord Duncan's study. By the time she detailed for Mr. DeLivre all that had happened since she'd left Cloistervale, she'd have enough material to fill one of his books.

"You're certain your courier won't mind the journey?" she asked her hostess. "It is quite far and out of the way."

Lady MeMe set another sealed missive atop the stack of letters and packages she intended to send to her family in Lastarra the next day. "He travels throughout the realm," she said. "Besides, I shall see to it he doesn't begrudge a few extra leagues."

Lyssanne rubbed her eyes then folded Mr. DeLivre's letter, together with a note for Aderyn, and addressed the lot. Smiling, she handed it to MeMe.

"I daresay you could do with another cup of this wondrous flyl," Lady MeMe said.

Lyssanne's lips twitched. "Not if I wish to sleep this night."

"Indeed," said Lord Duncan, raising his steaming cup to Lyssanne as if in salute. "Rather than dull the senses like wine or mead, it sharpens the wit and wakes the mind." He glanced at his wife and Prince Brennus. "Henceforth, it is flyl I shall serve honored guests on special occasions. With so fine a brew, Avery Hall will be the envy of the land!"

"It has proven a boon to me these past nights beside Noel's sickbed," Lady MeMe said. "What gives it such stimulating properties? That twig-like spice our cook had never beheld?"

"Honcin, yes," Lyssanne said. "I'm told it grows nowhere but the Cloister Valley."

"It was most kind of you to instruct our cook in flyl's brewing, and more so to delay your departure out of concern for Noel. I only regret I must leave you so oft unattended. Fevers are common among children, but the healer says Noel's is severe, and each dawn adds danger."

"I pray she recovers quickly," Lyssanne said. "Please do not concern yourself with me. Your home and grounds have afforded me a peace I've not known in months."

That was, during the day, at least. In the cool of the mornings,

Lyssanne found a divine serenity in strolling the lush ornamental gardens, with their musical fountains and white pathways. Afternoons, she spent visiting the blacksmith, wandering the meadow with Reina, or sitting with a book in the forest of knowledge that was the Avery library.

The inevitable fall of evening, however, brought her into company with Prince Brennus. They'd shared a tense cordiality at dinners in the hall or private dining room, after which they lounged with their hosts in Lord Duncan's study. The tale he'd told in the prison chamber still haunted her thoughts, and shadows stalked her dreams.

Such thoughts dredged up memories of the fog that menaced Cloistervale. Did it still? Was the sorceress who'd murdered Lyssanne's father yet plaguing the village, despite Lyssanne's departure? Or did the Shadow Mist's presence there even have anything to do with the sorceress's desire to see her dead?

At least her concern for Jarad seemed, for the moment, unnecessary.

Lord Duncan's steward knocked and entered. "The boy Jarad to see His Highness, as requested."

A lump of ice dropped into Lyssanne's stomach as Jarad made his bows and the steward left the room. Why had the prince summoned him?

"Word has reached me from some of Duncan's men," said Prince Brennus, "that you won a game of throwing-knives against the stable lads."

"I did," Jarad said, his voice light enough to lift his feet from the floor. "You should've seen it! Uh, I mean...Yes, Your Highness, 'tis true."

Chuckling, Prince Brennus rose and tousled Jarad's hair. "I would indeed like to see that. Duncan has a target in this very room. Perhaps you would show me your skill?"

"That would be...Oh, but I don't have a knife. I used Mr. Thane's for the game."

"Duncan, have you the key to my chest?" Prince Brennus asked.

He produced the key, and the prince pulled a plain, leather-

265

covered chest from beneath a table. He withdrew from it a bundle half the length of his forearm.

"Try this." He unwrapped the object and handed it to Jarad.

"A real fighting dagger!" Jarad said. "With a raven's head pommel, just like your sword."

"It belonged to my uncle," Prince Brennus said. "Let us see if that old knife can still fly."

The men and Jarad took turns trying to skewer the eye of a round target, Prince Brennus occasionally advising Jarad on how to make best use of the weighty dagger.

Once they'd ceased their game, Lord Duncan said, "Impressive, young man."

"Anyone with that much skill should have a dagger to call his own," said the prince. "The one you hold is a good fit for your hand. Consider it yours."

Lord Duncan swung to face Prince Brennus.

"But I couldn't," Jarad said, his gaze riveted to the dagger. "It's too fine, and a family weapon, besides."

"I have others," the prince said. "I assure you, I'll not miss it."

Lyssanne stared at him. He favored Jarad, he'd made that plain. Still, such a gift was never offered lightly.

"You'll need daily practice to accustom yourself to the balance of the blade," Prince Brennus said. "I am certain, though, it will prove useful. As I've said, you can't always rely on your bow to safeguard yourself or your companions."

"Why is it, a boy of your skill has no dagger?" Lord Duncan asked. "Had you known Brennus longer, I might suspect his guidance in your handiwork. Who trained you, lad?"

"No one, milord," Jarad said. "I never threw a knife like that until Mr. Thane and the boys asked me to join them."

"Nonsense," said Lord Duncan. "No one has that kind of aim without practice."

"Begging your pardon, milord," Jarad said, bowing. "It isn't all that different from throwing rocks into honeymunk holes. I used to scare them out so Madam Colby could harvest their honey. You have to stand well away from their trees," he said. "They come out mad, spittin' stingspray. If that stuff gets you just right, you could lose an eye, or end up all scarred from burns like Wally Redman. So, you learn to hit 'em just right, from as far away as possible."

"Come, Lyssanne," Lady MeMe said. "Let us leave the men to their practice."

Lyssanne followed her into the corridor, where they parted. MeMe adjourned to her daughter's sickroom, Lyssanne to her chamber, praying the shadows would keep to its corners.

Brennus sat in the shadows of the sickroom, a tiny, windowless chamber adjacent to the herbal. He stretched his shadowy limbs, unfeeling even after his hours spent recounting anecdotes of Noel's early childhood at her request. It was unseemly—a beautiful, vibrant child confined in this dark place. He clenched fists of smoke and ground teeth that would not grind.

Despite every remedy the healer had tried, Noel's fever raged. Now, the infection threatened her mind, heart, and other delicate functions. She had but days, perhaps hours.

"I like Uncle Bren's new trick," Noel whispered to MeMe.

"I'm certain," MeMe said, taking her hand. "But you must speak of it to no one else."

"I know."

At a knock, MeMe straightened. "That will be Lady Lyssanne. You remember Uncle Bren's friend? She's agreed to tell you a story while your papa and I speak with Healer Laud."

Brennus stiffened. Rather than slip from the room as he'd intended, he must remain, appearing to lounge in the chair, to make certain Lyssanne's presence caused Noel no harm.

At the door, MeMe paused, nodding a farewell to him.

Lyssanne entered and perched on a stool at Noel's bedside, her eyes only for the child. Noel responded to her honeyed tones like a man reaching for water in the Navvarish Desert.

Brennus lost the thread of the tale Lyssanne shared to his own musings. Once, he'd thought of her as a common sparrow watching over her chicks. He'd not been far wrong, but she wasn't so common, after all. Her plain feathers hid colors he'd not then seen.

"The King of All Lands?" Noel said, arresting his attention. "The one Mama sometimes talks with?"

"Indeed, the very same," Lyssanne said.

"Papa made her a special place to talk to him, ya know," Noel said, her voice faint. "Mama told him she didn't need it, but he said, if the lords and ladies of Lyrya have shrines to talk to their statues, his wife should have somewhere to talk to her invisible King."

MeMe worshiped the same deity as Lyssanne? Brennus had relegated the notion of this invisible King to the imaginings of half-crazed hermits and Lyssanne's backward village. Sure, Duncan had mentioned erecting the little building in the inner bailey for MeMe's religious pursuits, but they'd never discussed the nature of her beliefs.

"That was very kind of him," Lyssanne said. "Does he talk to the King as well?"

"No. Papa thinks the King is just a story."

"Ah. Do you know the King's story?"

"The Tale of the Dawning?" Noel whispered. "Yeah. 'Tis sad."

Lyssanne leaned closer. "Why do you say that?"

"'Cause the King died," Noel said. "He left his castle to go save the people, even though they'd let his papa's enemy take over. But they didn't want him. They killed him." A cough cut short her words. When she could again speak, her voice grew demanding. "Why didn't the King's papa destroy them all for that?"

"Well," Lyssanne said, "they didn't recognize the King."

"But he told them who he was. They didn't believe him."

"No." Lyssanne sighed. "But that wasn't the end of the tale. Since the King loved the people enough to die for them, He could save them. Then, His Father gave Him life again."

"He's still alive? He really can hear Mama when she talks to him?"

"Oh, yes," Lyssanne said. "He can hear you, as well."

"Is His castle really as wondrous as they say? So far away in the Shining Land."

"More so than we can imagine, but the King isn't far from us. He is the very Love and Light that shine in our hearts. He watches over us, as He did long ago."

"Is that why I'm sick?" Noel asked, her breath beginning to wheeze. "Do you think…He wants me to die, so I can go live with Him there?"

Lyssanne covered her mouth with her hand, her eyes misty in the candle glow.

"If that's what He wants," Noel said, "I wouldn't mind so much. 'Tis just, I love Mama and Papa so. I think they would be too sad if I go."

"Oh, Noel." Lyssanne's voice broke on the child's name. "The King did not make you ill. That, I know. He is Light, while illness is darkness. It steals from you—joy, strength, and sometimes, it steals life. Such darkness comes from the King's old enemy, the Thief of Souls."

"He steals other things, too?" Noel asked.

"Yes, and he lies, like any thief. He tries to make us afraid."

Nodding, Noel reached for Lyssanne's hand. "He scares me."

"He has frightened me a fair bit as well," Lyssanne said, clasping the child's fingers, "but the King is much stronger than the darkness."

"He can make me better?"

Brennus parted his lips to put an end to this game Lyssanne played. He wouldn't permit her to give Noel false hopes, but her words forestalled him.

"For the King, nothing is impossible, but we oft prevent Him doing what we most wish."

Lyssanne rose and took an unlit candle from a tray on the side table.

"A candle can banish shadows, but only if you put a match to it." She touched the wick to the flame of the lamp near the door then brought the candle back to Noel's bedside table. "In the same way, you must spark your faith, so the King's Light can banish the sickness."

"I want the King to light me up," Noel whispered, "to scare away the dark fever. I believe Him, just like Mama, just like you." She coughed, a wet, strangled sound. "Will He?"

"I pray He will," Lyssanne said.

Noel sighed and closed her eyes. As if Lyssanne's words had worked a magic of their own, she drifted into sleep, her breathing ragged. Lyssanne kissed Noel's brow, tears glistening in her eyes and running in twin, sparkling lines down her cheeks.

Why did she weep so for a child she hardly knew?

Lyssanne whispered a prayer, then opened her eyes and peered at Noel's midsection as if seeing something besides the thin coverlet. She stared with the intense concentration she'd once fixed upon the Shadow Mist. Brennus leaned forward, searching out whatever she saw.

Lyssanne's eyes narrowed, her jawline firmed, and her shoulders stiffened to a high, hard line. She spoke, her voice holding a tone of authority she'd never used in Brennus's hearing.

"Fever, illness, Thief's foul darkness, you have no place here. This innocent child belongs to the King of All Lands. In His name, I command you to flee before His Light. In His name, I command that Light to flood Noel's body." Her voice softened, tears splashing onto the coverlet. "As she loves and is loved, let the Love and Light of her King wash her to new life."

Brennus barely suppressed an exclamation as Lyssanne began to shine. She laid her hands upon Noel's abdomen; glassy, multihued light shimmering just beneath them. The colors coalesced as if refracted through a lens, forming a smaller, brighter pool of green, so pure and pale it was nearly white. It lingered for some moments, then the center of its brightness moved up to Noel's chest. As if pulled by the light, Lyssanne's hands moved with it.

Brennus blinked. What in the Seven Lands? In the light's center, an almost solid darkness took shape. It resembled some sickly, dark-green, horned thing one might find in a bog. The next instant, the darkness recoiled and vanished.

Then, the light seeped deep into Noel and faded.

Lyssanne looked up, her pupils retaining their normal size, as if she'd not even beheld that light. "Let it be so, oh King," she whispered, sinking onto her stool with a sigh.

Brennus drew a silent breath. Sweat began to bead on Noel's brow!

Just then, the healer and Noel's parents returned.

"The fever has broken," the healer said, resting a hand on Noel's cheek. "Her body is cooling rapidly, and her breathing is steadier. The illness seems to drain from her as I watch." He looked up at Duncan, doffing his washtub hat to mop his brow. "Never have I seen the like. This child was on the point of death, yet 'tis as if she's had three days' recovery in the past hour."

Had Lyssanne's Light driven out the illness? What magic could do such?

Venefica wielded her skills to destroy and gained vigor from the deeds. Lyssanne had only ever used her power to heal or to warm and, apparently, did so at the expense of her own strength. For, she was growing paler before Brennus's eyes.

"Brennus," Duncan said, his voice thick. "Did you hear that? My little princess is...she's not leaving us." He reached for MeMe, who smiled through fresh tears.

Brennus sank farther into the shadows, struggling to mask the hollow croak of his voice. "It is the best tiding I've heard in years, my friend." He glanced back at Lyssanne.

She stared in his direction, her eyes wide pools of sapphire in a face white as marble.

"Perhaps Mr. Laud would send for a maid to escort Lady Lyssanne to her chambers?" he said. "You will want time alone with Noel, and I believe the lady is in need of rest."

The healer gasped. "Why, she looks quite faint! Come, miss, I have smelling salts in my bag in the herbal." He pulled Lyssanne to her feet and ushered her from the room.

Brennus would permit Lyssanne time to regain her strength, but he wanted answers; and come sunset, he would have them.

18

REFLECTION

*L*yssanne struggled to prevent her limbs shaking as Lily helped her drape a thick dressing gown over her chemise. "You're certain this is proper?" she whispered.

"Proper enough, milady," Lily murmured. "You'd not want to keep him waiting."

"No." Lyssanne stared at her bedchamber's closed door. He'd been in that sickroom, had seen what she'd done. Had he come to make her leave or...or worse?

She drew breath and, as if trudging through syrup, walked into the sitting room.

Prince Brennus turned to face her. "Lyssanne—"

"Good eve to you, Your Highness," she said, struggling to keep her voice steady.

As she curtseyed, her knees betrayed her, folding like soggy parchment. She flung out a hand to brace against the impact. Arms caught her around the middle before her knees could hit the rose marble tile. Prince Brennus held her there, peering into her face.

"I, I just need a moment," she said.

"You're ill." Keeping an arm around her waist, he guided her to the settee, then lifted her and stretched her out upon its cushions. "Is it the ailment that plagued you in the forest?"

"No," Lyssanne said. "It…is a small thing. It will pass."

"Oh, my lady!" Lily said, rushing over to a sideboard. A splash followed her words, then she hurried to the settee with a glass and pitcher in hand. "I fetched some water."

"Good," Prince Brennus said, passing the glass to Lyssanne. "I shall see to the lady's needs. Leave the pitcher on the end table. I'll ring if you are required."

"Very well, Your Highness," Lily said, bowing as she backed into the corridor.

Lyssanne sipped at the water, grateful for the excuse not to look at him or to speak.

"Does this happen," he said, "this weakness, every time?"

"I'm not certain what you mean," Lyssanne said.

"I speak of your use of…unnatural abilities." A sharp edge laced his voice. "Is that so great an exertion, it causes you to collapse? Or is this the price for altering nature?"

Lyssanne stiffened. "What happened with Noel was…wasn't magic."

Shivers overtook her. What would they do to her? She'd heard tales of the horrors that befell people suspected of witchcraft in lands where magic was forbidden.

Prince Brennus stood and crossed the room. To call Lord Duncan's guards? Were they awaiting summons outside her door?

Instead, he returned with the woven coverlet that had decorated her window seat. He draped it over her and knelt beside the settee. "Lyssanne," he murmured, tucking the blanket about her shoulders, "I have not come to accuse you."

She stared at him, unsure what to say, what to believe.

"You're safe. No harm will befall you here. What you've done…"

"I'm not a witch," she whispered.

"I know."

"You…?"

"At least, I know there was no evil in what you did." He shook his head, his raven hair feathering out in a dark cloud. "I spoke with Reina. Just this past hour."

"Reina?" Lyssanne's heart pounded in her temples. Dared she allow herself to hope?

"I had to know, Lyssanne." Emotion thickened his voice. "What I saw was…" He shook his head again.

"What did you see?" The lump in her throat strangled her words.

"Light," he said, "and…something else." He took a long breath. "You spoke—prayed, I suppose—and, as if you'd become a lamp, you shone from within. Then, the light seemed to outgrow your body. It spilled forth from your hands, yet it wasn't *from* your hands. I know not how to explain it."

He rose and paced the length of the room.

"It spread over Noel like a blanket. Then, in it, just beneath your hands, was this pool of…darkness." He spun to face her. "It had form, yet was shapeless. At once a faceless creature and an inanimate mass." He pulled an armchair around and sat, his knees brushing the settee.

Lyssanne could only stare, stunned.

"What was it?" he asked. "That darkness?"

She shrugged. "Perhaps, 'twas some manifestation of the illness plaguing Noel's body."

"You saw it not, then?"

"No, neither it nor the light you speak of, but I, I felt it." A sudden thought seized her heart. "You don't think, surely you don't think I conjured it?"

He laughed. "No, the darkness fled before your words, your Light."

Sighing, she leaned her head against the settee's winged back.

"Reina agrees it was the illness I saw fleeing," he said. "She claims few could have seen it as I did. I was certain you would have."

"Did she say why you saw it thus?" Was this akin to Lyssanne's ability to see the Shadow Mist? Might he, if it were near, be able to perceive it as well?

"She says it was because I've been permitted to see your Light. The disease was entirely encompassed in it, and Light reveals the truth behind shadow."

"Oh."

"It makes an odd sense, I suppose," he said. "Reina claims I have some kind of gift." He made a sound deep in his throat. His next words tumbled out as if breaking free of a fist. "She's spoken of it before, this…discernment…that lets me witness what she calls the King's Light. Says Light's the only power worth pursuing, because it isn't granted for its wielder, but for the aid of others. She insists I've seen the truth of this in you and claims my *gift*, too, has a purpose beyond its own ends."

"Do you believe her?" Lyssanne asked.

"I'm not certain what to believe, but I know this, magic always has a price." He paused. "I asked Reina about that, as well."

"About magic?"

"That, and your fatigue after what you did. I asked what toll it might require of you."

"You were concerned? For me?"

"I needed answers," he said. "You weren't available to provide them."

Lyssanne's voice flattened. "Did she satisfy your *curiosity*?"

"In part, though her explanation more befits superstitious tales."

"What, may I ask, did she say?"

"She insists your fabled King would lay no such price upon you for using a gift he granted. However, his enemy despises such gifts and those who wield them. You'd used your power to heal, so this enemy, this"—he chuckled—"Thief of Souls, attacked your health."

Lyssanne offered a silent prayer of thanks for an answer she had long sought.

"Whatever the case," Prince Brennus said, "what you did can't have been magic."

"Why?" she asked. "You were so certain, before."

"You received no benefit from it. Had you done this for wealth, acclaim, or even for gratitude, you would have taken credit when the healer pronounced Noel recovered. I daresay you thought no one was present to witness what you did."

She nodded and buried her fingers in the coverlet, recalling the

275

shock of his hoarse voice rising like an ill wind from the corner of the sickroom. "Has Noel awakened?"

"Moments after you left," he said. "She asked for you, seemed surprised by your absence. She wasted no time in telling MeMe your fabled King had chased away the, er, evil sickness."

Lyssanne had to smile at that. "How is she feeling?"

"Her fever was gone within the hour. After another, her cough had ceased. She's been moved back into her chambers, but ordered to rest. The healer will take no chances on a relapse."

"There won't be a relapse," she said. "What the King of All Lands makes whole is truly whole. That isn't to say she will never catch a chill or some other malady."

"MeMe seems of the same opinion. Still, she'll follow the healer's advice."

"Are they—does she know...?"

"What really happened?" He leaned closer. "Yes."

Clutching the blanket, she took a deep breath, but her throat locked around her words.

"Duncan asked," Prince Brennus said, refilling her water glass. "He wanted to know if Noel was right, if you had indeed spoken to the same King who holds his wife's devotion."

"And the rest?" Lyssanne made herself ask. "Do they know what you saw?"

"MeMe wasn't interested in the particulars, but Duncan had questions. He took me aside, and I told him everything. He is Noel's father. He deserves to know what befalls his child."

Lyssanne nodded, tensing for his next words. Lord Duncan must think her a sorceress.

"Duncan might have attributed the entire business to a stroke of good fortune," Prince Brennus said, "but he couldn't deny the evidence of his eyes, nor of mine. After we'd spoken, he went to MeMe and Noel and asked, sounding more like a nervous squire than the lord of his own hall, how he might introduce himself to this King you so adore—and offer his fealty."

Lyssanne gasped. "Fealty? Lady MeMe must be overjoyed!"

"I left them, then," he said. "I had questions of my own. You'd just sent word that you wouldn't join us for dinner, so I sought Reina out instead."

"They aren't angry?" She had to be certain. "They don't think me a, a sorceress?"

"Angry? Hardly." He leaned back in his chair. "MeMe has decided you should stay here. For as long as you wish." He took the empty glass from her numbed fingers. "Duncan agrees."

Warmth swelled in her chest for an instant, then deflated into a hard kernel and dropped into the pit of her stomach. "They think me something I am not."

She looked away, unable to face him in this, the conversation they'd so often skirted since their arrival. Would this destroy the fragile peace so newly forged between them?

"Fear not," he said, his tone flat as Gian Plain. "I shall say nothing of your true station."

"You haven't told them? Still?" She cleared her throat and blinked away moisture. "I am grateful, for I know it cost you." She could no longer hold back her tears. "But if I stay, they must know the truth. I despise deceiving them."

"Why is it you weep?" He asked, his words soft as the handkerchief he held out to her.

"I am just so frightened." In the face of his candor, she could hold nothing back. "I know I must tell them, but what will become of us when I do?"

"After what you did for Noel, they would care not if they discovered you to be a thief."

"It isn't so much for myself that I fear, but for Jarad."

"Ah," he said. "I will not say such concerns are unfounded. However—"

"We shall leave," she said, latching onto the only possible course. "If you will allow me this night to rest, Jarad and I will set out at first light."

"Autumn is upon us and winter not far behind." He crooked a finger beneath her chin, forcing her to face him. "In the farmland and villages beyond this hall, you will find no shelter but that for which you must pay, and you haven't the coin to last a week." He rested a hand atop hers. "The nights already grow chill, Lyssanne, you would not survive."

"Jarad could," she said. "I'll send him to another town. He can start a new life, be safe."

"He won't leave your side."

"No," she whispered then raised beseeching eyes to meet his. "What must I do?" She shivered again. "Only tell me, and I shall do it."

He rose and walked to the window where he stood for an age, head bowed, thumbs looped in his belt. At length, he said, "Do not put your fate in my hands."

"Forgive me," she said. "I shouldn't trouble you so with my concerns. I, I thank you for your silence. I shan't ask it of you any longer." She swung her feet over the side of the settee to stand. "I must ask you to excuse me. For, I need to gather my things. On the morrow I shall—"

"Rest,' he said, spinning to face her. "On the morrow, you will rest."

"But—"

"I shall speak with Duncan on Jarad's behalf," he said, striding to the door, "but only after you recover your strength. Truth and choices will wait a few days more."

The next morning, Lady MeMe paid Lyssanne a visit. They spoke of Noel's returned vigor and of the goodness of the King.

"Duncan wishes to reward you for what you've done," Lady MeMe said.

"I did nothing but pray," Lyssanne said. "As anyone might."

"If that were so, Noel would have long since recovered." MeMe clasped Lyssanne's hands. "You have a rare connection to the King, or some understanding of His ways others lack."

Lyssanne shook her head.

"Whatever the case, we wish you to accept our hospitality, at least through the winter. Brennus told us, my friend, that you fight your own battles with health." She chuckled. "Why, last night, he fair frightened the head of our staff into seeing to your every need. He insists you must have rest, and I agree. Oh, Lyssanne, I do hope you will consider it."

"There is something I must tell you," Lyssanne said. "Once I have, you may wish to rescind your offer."

"Nonsense. What could be so grave?"

"I wanted to tell you from the first." Lyssanne closed her eyes. "'Twas the need to protect a child in my care that prevented me. As a mother, you will understand, I trust."

"A child—Jarad? Is he in some sort of trouble? Is that why you've left Lastarra?"

"Please, may I have your word to help me protect him, once I've told you everything? I know I have no right to ask, but Jarad is dear to me as a brother."

"Of course, you have it. I don't know what this involves, but I shall do what I can to see him safe. He has conducted himself admirably while here."

"I fear Jarad has deceived your husband…from the moment we arrived. And I failed to prevent him or call an end to it."

"In what way?" MeMe asked.

"He introduced me as a lady." The truth flooded out in a rush. "I am no daughter of a noble house, but of a blacksmith."

Lady MeMe laughed. "Is that all?"

Lyssanne's lips parted, but closed without sound.

"Lyssanne, I've suspected almost since we met," MeMe said. "I became certain the first time we had brunch together."

"My clothes?" Lyssanne asked.

"No. You could have been in disguise, fleeing an undesirable marriage or tyrannical relative, or hiding your station in case of bandits. It was your manner that alerted me."

Lyssanne flushed. Had she been so uncouth?

"There is no false modesty in you," Lady MeMe said, "and your face reveals your every emotion. I learned early how to play the detestable games of court and how to recognize the players. You, my friend, are not one of them. Since Brennus said nothing, I thought no harm could come of it. Besides, your company is refreshing."

"Will Jarad be in danger when your husband learns the truth? Misguided as his actions were, he only did so believing I would be safer if everyone thought me a lady."

"He wasn't far wrong," MeMe said. "In some places, a title might be your only protection." She sighed. "I can't speak for Duncan. He enforces all law here, his own and that of the crown, but you did us a kindness we can never repay. Duncan will honor that."

A late autumn breeze rippled Venefica's image in the secluded pool beside which Brennus knelt. Crushing her powder packet in his fist, he glanced about, but only the family and exclusive guests were permitted in MeMe's walled gardens. His privacy was assured.

"Do you not think me beautiful?" Venefica asked.

He smirked. "Any man with eyes would." That beauty, after all, had overthrown even his loathing of magic. Her lustrous hair, regal grace, and tall, confident bearing had painted a portrait of how life could be once his curse was removed.

Now, she wanted him to make her his queen?

"I am nobly born," she said, "and know how to rule."

Her arguments held merit, but the thought of spending a lifetime with her...

"You hesitate," she said. "Had I done so when I found you, near death, on that road—"

"It was no altruism that moved you to save me."

"Perhaps," she said. "My father taught me never to discard anything that might be turned to my use. You are fortunate I saw the man within the raven. And forget not, *you* sought *me* out."

He inclined his head. "True."

Still, 'twas plain what she sought. Power. An entire kingdom under the dominion of the Shadow Mist—she would be unstoppable.

With his hereditary right to rule Navvar, their union would grant her the irreversible authority to inflict her dark magic upon his subjects.

They, like the people of Cloistervale, would sink into black despair, rage, and self-neglect—violence erupting daily in the streets, villagers and livestock falling ill from poorly tended foodstuffs or disease.

What Venefica did to Cloistervale, or even to the kingdom of Lastarra, was no concern to Brennus. Those fools in that backwater village had brought this upon their own heads, their Council continuing to blame Lyssanne's *slothful ways*, as control slipped from their grasp. But Navvar was *his* land. He hadn't fought so long to free it from tyranny only to enslave it through marriage to her. Still, he couldn't tell her that. Yet.

"Well," Venefica said, stilling his thoughts. "Is not my proposition to your taste?"

"That wasn't part of our bargain."

"I speak of a new bargain," she said. "You will need powerful allies to reclaim your kingdom. I will soon have that power. Make me your queen, and I shall ensure your victory."

He schooled his face to an expressionless mask. "I shall think on it."

"Very well. For now, remain where you are. Inform me of the slightest change."

"As you will."

Venefica's image faded, and light returned to the pool. Brennus's reflection stared back at him unchanged, though he hardly recognized the man within. He rose, feeling as if he'd just fought a battle in a rainstorm, soiled and weary. He needed privacy of a different sort. The tower.

Why was Venefica so certain he would require her aid to reclaim his throne? Could his suspicions be true, that she was somehow betraying him? The shadow transformation she'd wrought upon him was, as the hermit had said, a curse all its own.

His purposeful strides faltered. Had she *known* she couldn't restore him when she'd attempted that spell? Would she be capable of lifting his curse, even once her power was secure?

He swept into the manor, grabbed a torch, and mounted the winding stair to the tower. Then, he froze. Only three torches had stood inside the doorway. Where was the fourth?

When he reached the battlement, a lighted torch already waited in the wall bracket. He nearly dropped the one in his hand when he espied the figure standing at the parapet. "What are you doing here?" he snapped.

Lyssanne turned, hugging her old cloak tighter about her.

His jaw clenched as he looked into her wide eyes. Here! Must she, of all people, be here in *his* place, when all he wished was privacy to ponder options for his future?

"I am sorry," she murmured. "You said I might come here if I wished. I'll go."

"No need. This part of the castle is open to all." He certainly couldn't tell her his reasons for wishing the tower to himself. "Still, should you not be resting? After so recent a bout with your...ailment, you shouldn't chance catching a chill. This wind can be fierce."

"This place is so peaceful," she said. "I came here to pray."

"An odd place for prayer, a battlement."

He extinguished his torch then stepped to the railing, casting a surreptitious glance down at her. For once, her eyes were free of circles. Fear hadn't shadowed her countenance in weeks. Duncan's hospitality had doubtless saved her life.

Brennus rested his forearms on the parapet, his sleeve brushing her cloak. She didn't pull away. Her decreased wariness and occasional laughter in his presence pleased him more than it should. The honesty they'd shared after Noel's recovery had opened the door to things best left buried, for both their sakes.

"I feel close to the King, so high up here," she said. "The lights below call Him to mind."

"Why?"

"They make me think of His gifts, His goodness, shining through the darkest times."

Brennus forced his jaw apart to stop his teeth grinding. That *gift* had brought Venefica's wrath down upon her. "How can you love a king who would give you so much pain?" he said, straightening. "I've witnessed your ailment. That is no gift of joy."

"Illness doesn't come from the King of All Lands."

"He has not ended it."

"He lessened it," she said. "'Twas far worse, before."

"You've served Him most of your life, I suspect," he said, an accusation.

She nodded.

"Then, how could this king of yours allow his faithful one to be cast from her home?" She gasped, but he plunged ahead. "Don't try to deny it, Lyssanne. You are in exile."

"Did Jarad—?"

"The boy said nothing, but I am no fool."

She turned away. "It was the will of the Council that I leave, not—"

"Again, not this king's doing? Then, answer me this," he said, thumping a hand onto the railing next to hers, crowding her space. "Your Council, they serve Him, as well?"

"Of...course."

"Whose good was he seeing to when he let them banish you?" For months, this question had burned within him. "By what capricious whim does he choose between his servants?"

"He'd do nothing so cruel." She looked up at Brennus, so earnest he wanted to shake her. "The King gives us the freedom to follow His path or not. If our choices harm ourselves or others, well...we can only seek His guidance in remedying that." She touched his hand; a feather's brush, there and gone. "We are but His servants, Highness. Far from perfect, we cannot boast His virtues. We imitate His goodness as best we can."

"What, then, has He done to aid you?" Brennus asked, softening his tone. She was not the cause of his bitterness. "I've seen no evidence of His protection or gifts. You travel in poverty and have yet to find a home, unless it is here. And that is a gift from Duncan, not this king."

"He sent me help along my journey, friends to save me from

danger. He sent Jarad, saw that we had food to eat." Lyssanne stepped away and looked out over the castle yards. Her face flushing, she whispered, "He sent you, and I am thankful."

Brennus expelled a huff.

She swung back around, one brow raised. "Is it your role in my survival you question, or my gratitude?" She flushed again, as if surprised she'd spoken thus.

"Your king had no part in…" Brennus clamped his jaw shut.

"He did," she whispered. "You've been a refuge and shield to me, yet I sense the storm within you permits no shelter." She rested a hand atop his and held it. "What tortures you so?"

Brennus stood frozen. Oh, he was tempted to end this charade, to tell her…everything.

"Can you not trust me, as I have trusted you?" she asked, her eyes misting. "The King's Light is strong enough to banish whatever haunts you."

He wanted her to know him, truly know him. But, if she learned what he was, what he'd done…He shook his head. "You would flee to the farthest reaches of the realm if I spoke of it."

Her fingers flexed, squeezing his hand for an instant. "I do not fear your shadows."

"You should," he said, staring into her serene eyes. Fear was the least of her dangers. His unmasking would force Venefica's hand, *his* hand. Then, life would end…for one of them.

~

"It isn't in this one either," said Jarad. Groaning, he shoved another book of legends across the polished table, nearly toppling a tower of tomes.

Lyssanne sighed. The creature Mr. Fescue described wasn't to be found in the collection of children's tales she'd perused. The Avery library had again yielded nothing but sore backs and aching eyes. "How many more are there?" she asked.

"Three, from that wall of shelves."

"Do you have the time to search them now?"

Jarad stood, stretched his arms above his head, and walked to the giant hourglass in its gilded stand. "I can do a few more before I report to Captain Gunther."

"Jarad, you needn't stay. I can—"

"No, Lady Lyssanne," he said, strolling back to her. "I don't have any duties until after dinner. I've been granted the honor of nighttime training with Prince Brennus." He laughed. "Besides, you'd miss all the silly ways I say the names of the creatures I do find."

"Well," she said, "there is one other volume with text I can read. Let's be about it, so we can sooner savor our dinner." She smiled. "You enjoy training with the squires, don't you?"

"Yeah, even more than you're enjoying the new wardrobe Lady MeMe made you accept, I'd wager." He flipped another book open. "I thought Prince Brennus was jesting when he insisted they let me train." He deepened his voice, imitating the prince. "As his lady's sole companion, the boy has need of such skills."

Laughing, Lyssanne resumed her quest for the key to the talisman peddler's riddle. With all she'd learned of mists and sorceresses, and her own past, she ached to discover what message the King had hidden for her.

Besides scouring every book of legend or myth, collection of tales, and bestiary for the creature, she and Jarad had already searched tomes on the topography of the Seven Lands for any reference to the granite tree mentioned in the riddle.

"Will you share stories with the castle children again tomorrow?" Jarad asked, flipping pages in another book. "Captain Gunther's niece was pestering me to find out."

"Yes, but in the Hall this week. The weather has grown too chill for the gardens."

"Thought so," Jarad said. "The servant's children have been everywhere, asking anybody they see for extra work they might do. Trying to earn their story time, I suspect."

Lyssanne laughed. "I daresay Lady Noel had no notion what she was beginning when she rushed up to me in the gardens that afternoon and requested the favor of a tale."

"Showing off her new friend to Captain Gunther's niece, I heard," Jarad said. "Shocked everyone, though, when you invited the servants' children to listen and made it a weekly affair."

"Well, the King's love is for everyone," Lyssanne said, "and so are my stories. Besides, it affords me one small way to repay the kindness Noel's parents have shown us."

Lyssanne flipped to the next tale in her book. 'Twas as if she'd stepped into its pages and borrowed the life of one of its characters, with the Averys' continued treatment of her as a lady.. Despite its beginnings, this role she played seemed a gift from the King. What other life would afford her the freedom to rest in luxury when head pain or weakness assaulted her body?

Jarad yawned. "Think Lord Duncan will meet us in the shrine for Kingsday, tomorrow?"

"I hope so," Lyssanne said. "I'm sure Lady MeMe can persuade him."

"Here it is!" Jarad shouted, startling her. "The creature, it's here!"

She sprang to her feet and rounded the table.

He tapped a tiny drawing in the upper right corner of the page. "See, head of a dog, wings of a peacock, claws of a lion." His finger trailed down to the text beneath. "It says this *simurgh* is a creature of ancient origins and great wisdom. It can purify water and air, and symbolizes the union between earth and sky. The rest is in Lyryan."

Lyssanne took the book and squinted at the text. "Its feathers are said to shine like new copper coins and…ah. Several tales of the simurgh's lair mention mountains and the sea."

Just then, someone knocked at the open doorway.

"Pardon, my lady," said a maid. "Might you spare Master Jarad a bit early? The squires are to serve at dinner. Some of His Lordship's officers just returned from the far-flung villages."

"Of course," Lyssanne said. "Jarad, don't forget to eat a hearty meal yourself before the bustle begins. We've had a long day, and you ate little."

"I will," he said, "but searching books doesn't make me hungry like training does."

"I thought every activity made you hungry."

Laughing, Jarad gathered his things and followed the maid from the library.

Lyssanne walked to the window to give her eyes a rest. The snows had begun again, not yet heavy enough to blanket the ground. Still, she'd be forced to forego her customary visits with the blacksmith and Reina on the morrow. Would the knights continue to train outdoors? If so, Jarad would need warmer clothes.

An image of Prince Brennus training in the moonlit lists with select warriors filled her mind. Twice, she and Lady MeMe had witnessed friendly, after-dinner duels of swords between the prince and Lord Duncan. In fact, Lyssanne only ever encountered the prince at evening.

Ah, but those evenings were turning an uneasy friendship into a source of joy. Warmth stole over her at the memory of the prince's humorous fireside stories about Lord Duncan and Lady MeMe, his descriptions of foreign lands, and their discussions of books and other interests.

A sudden prickle at the back of her neck pierced her peaceful thoughts. She spun around, half expecting to find the prince watching her. As with the other times this sensation had assailed her in the library, none but the eerie eyes of portraits stared back at her.

Still, she hastened back into the pool of lamplight, casting a wary glance at the shadowed corners of the room. Foolish as it was, darkened recesses had unnerved her since she'd been accosted in Mr. Fescue's wood. Perhaps it was time to end this day's search, after all.

Light. It was everywhere Brennus looked. From the roaring flames in the great hall's man-high fireplaces, to the tiny candles in the center of each tray of food and drink circulating among the guests, to the bonfires and torches burning throughout the castle grounds and surrounding villages—the night blazed with it. As if every star had left the heavens and come to rest here in honor of the occasion, Avery Hall's annual Celebration of Lights was in full flare.

"On this, the shortest day of the year," Duncan said, opening the festivities, "we gather to set the night aglow. Candles adorn every window, bonfires light the snow-covered squares, and peasants and nobles alike laugh and dance to show we've overcome the long dark of winter."

"Here, here!" cheered several guests, glasses raised.

"Each of the Seven Lands has its version of the festivities," Duncan said. "Ships sail the canals of Aquatonia, catapulting flaming balls into the air. Nobles of Opali parade with gilded lanterns in hand, flame glinting off multihued gems encrusting every garment. Even the earthy tribesmen of Zyungland are rumored to dance about, waving rush torches to the beat of ceremonial drums, and chanting riddles only they can comprehend."

Amid rising laughter, Navvar filled Brennus's thoughts. Did its people still celebrate?

"Here in Lyrya, music fuels the festivities," Duncan said, and his minstrels played a little fanfare. "Ah, but Lastarra, with its fireworks that rival any jewel or flame, holds claim to originating the celebration. Some say it once held religious significance."

A movement across the room caught Brennus's eye, a nod from the one light in the hall capable of arresting his attention—Lyssanne.

She wore a gown of blue so rich it would have done credit to the Royal House of Xavier. It shimmered when she moved, like water in the azure Pools of Aquatia. A paler, gauzy fabric flowed from her shoulders and draped from the clinging sleeves at her wrists.

A tiny chain of finely wrought gold girded her waist. Brennus suppressed a gasp. The medallion clasping it at its center bore the Avery elf-head crest. This symbolized as great a loyalty and affection between Lyssanne and House Avery as did his chain of office. Lyssanne's only other adornment was her perpetual blue and gold star-shaped pendant.

The green she'd worn to his feast had served her loveliness well, but this ensemble fair stilled his breath. She belonged in Xavier blue.

Lyssanne had transformed Avery Hall into a place of light—and not just on this occasion. The wall torches and colored paper lanterns surrounding Duncan's guests paled in comparison to her gift. Though no judge of such things, Brennus was certain she'd grown stronger in its use.

The household children flocked to her, glowing with reflected Light, as had those in Cloistervale. MeMe had shone with that luminescence since Noel's escape from death. Even Duncan shimmered at times. And Lily, who had asked to serve as Lyssanne's lady's maid, bustled past Brennus with the effervescence of sparkling wine. Did their reflected glow and heightened cheer have anything to do with belief in her invisible King?

Lyssanne's glow shone without effect over the man who now sidled up to her. Sir Fenard and his sister had arrived ten days prior, both expressing delight to find her still in residence—Sir Fenard, a bit too delighted.

His freedom to stroll the halls with her during the day, while Brennus was trapped in his feathers, inflicted Brennus's skull with a semblance of the pain her curse caused hers.

He set his empty cup on a sideboard. If only the cook's steamy flyl could banish the ice settling in his stomach at the sight of that cad again fawning over her.

The baron kept his distance when Brennus was present, but took every opportunity to insinuate himself into Lyssanne's days. He sat with her in the conservatory, comparing her to the greenhouse flowers; lounged with her by the library fires, reading her poetry or trying to impress her with his travels. He'd even lurked about when the children gathered to hear her stories.

Lyssanne favored the baron often enough with her smiles, but ensured any time in his company was properly chaperoned, a precaution she seemed not to find necessary with Brennus.

He flicked a speck of lint from his black velvet sleeve, straightened the blue sash that cut a diagonal swath across his linen shirt, then approached the group forming around Lyssanne.

"You're saying it was a simple victor's feast?" Sir Fenard asked, leaning close to Lyssanne despite the lull in music.

"Not simple," she said, "but a celebration of victory, yes."

Tonight, it was adults of highest rank she enchanted with her tale. Several of Lyrya's brightest stars gathered round to hear her version of their feast's origins. She outshone them all.

Brennus stepped forward, just behind Lyssanne, as she concluded her tale.

"From that time on," she said, "every ruler vowed to keep the day sacred each year, so none should forget how the King of All overcame the darkness the Thief of Souls once poured out upon the Seven Lands."

Brennus rested a hand on Lyssanne's shoulder. She turned, her eyes widening.

"Would you honor me with a dance, my lady?"

She offered her hand, her eyes reflecting the flames of half the candles in the hall. At Brennus's wave, the musicians began a slow, sinuous melody, and he and Lyssanne centered the room. She closed her eyes in learned surrender to his lead.

Truth was stranger than tales, for shadow again slithered across the land. No celebratory light would flare in Lastarra's northern skies tonight. Cloistervale had fallen. And in this story, there was no hero-King to overcome the darkness. Only a prince who had helped reawaken it.

19

_____

ORDERS

Spring, year 1123 After the Dawning

*J*arad stared at Lyssanne across the library table. "It's nothing but an adventure tale? Someone made it up?" He uttered a sound akin to a disgruntled pig. "Is the rest fiction, too?"

"I think not. All this means is—"

"They lied to us," he said. "Both of them." Leaning forward, he snatched her hand from atop the parchment she'd just unrolled. "What if it wasn't the King who sent us this message? What if the Thief of Souls did it to put you in more danger, to get you to leave this place?"

"Jarad, I truly don't believe—"

"Yeah, but think about it. You're safe here." He released her hand. "They all like you. If we go looking for a stone tree that doesn't exist, just so we can find a creature that can't possibly have been born...For what? A message some crazy peddler says the King has for you?"

"I know it sounds foolish, mad even," she said, "but I just know we must do this. Besides, you liked Mr. Fescue."

"Yeah, he's brilliant." Jarad sighed. "Sorry, I know I'm just a kid, but…"

"You're happy here," she said. "As am I. You've found a new life. A useful life. Jarad, you repay the kindness we've been granted tenfold every day, while I…" She shook her head. "The King didn't bring me safely this far just to live idle on their generosity. I'm certain He has something more for me to do. Even the faeries hint that this is the path I should follow."

"It's just, you almost died before and…" He turned away. "You're all the family I have."

"Oh, Jarad." She resisted the impulse to skirt the table and hug him. Squires didn't go about hugging their teachers, after all. "It frightens me as well, to ask this of you, to set out into unknown dangers again. I can hardly bear it." She closed her eyes. "If I thought I could manage on my own, or that you would heed me, I would bid you stay behind."

"I'd follow you," he said.

"I know." She inhaled the scents of new spring wafting through the open windows. "Perhaps if I tell you everything Lord Duncan said, matters won't seem so grave. And Jarad?" She waited until he faced her. "Never discount your feelings or ideas because of your youth. You have a keen mind and astonishing wisdom. They've served us well, and I cherish your opinions."

"So, uh," he said. "H-how did he know we were looking for it? People don't just sit around talking about granite trees."

"No." Lyssanne laughed. "Lady MeMe asked whether I was looking for something particular in the library or merely furthering your studies. When I told her I sought the answer to a riddle, she said she adores mysteries. I shared with her only the last few lines."

"Seek out the King's message where the sun lays its head in snow and sea," Jarad quoted. "For you and all, one hope remains. Seek it beyond the granite tree."

"Yes." Lyssanne glanced at the parchment beneath her hand.

"Had she heard of it? The granite tree?"

"No, but that evening, she asked Lord Duncan if he had."

"And he said it's a myth." Jarad folded his arms.

"An old legend. The tree was fabled to bring travelers ill fortune when they attempted to cross the Lyrynn Mountains. Something about taking the easy path." She shrugged. "He suggested we search legends for descriptions of landforms akin to those leading to lost treasure."

"So, it *is* just nonsense."

"Perhaps," she said, "but remember, many would say the King of All Lands is a fable."

"All this time," Jarad said, "we've been looking in legend books for that simurgh thing, and we should've been looking for the tree? We have to search 'em all again?"

"Not all. Lord Duncan says the tale became part of Lyrya's history. It influenced early exploration of the realm. So, we can eliminate stories from other lands and recent collections."

"Exploration? I think I saw some travel tales over by the histories and maps." He jumped to his feet and strode to a crammed set of shelves. "Here they are. I didn't look in these before."

Lyssanne rose to join him as he rolled the ingenious wheel-bottomed ladder into place. He climbed several rungs then began passing dusty volumes down to her. One little book proved unyielding. It gave way at last, dislodging another. Leaning backward, Jarad caught the extra book an instant before it could bash him on the head.

He glared at it. "Just a book of noble houses. I wonder if Prince Brennus is in here."

Lyssanne took the book and read its cover. "No, this lists only the prominent families of Lastarra. Still, perhaps some of our newfound friends or their ancestors are included."

"Like Lady MeMe?" he said, climbing back down.

Nodding, she set the books on the table and sifted through each. Besides the volume on noble families, she could read only one. Finding no mention of the granite tree there, she opened *Hereditary Houses, Heraldry, and History*. Was MeMe's ancestral home far from Cloistervale?

For each family, the book listed a brief history, house crest, and description of holdings. Lyssanne turned to the index, searching the *c* listings for MeMe's maiden name, Cintilla.

"Hmm, *ca...ce*," she whispered, flipping pages, "*co*...too far...*cl*." A word a few lines down the page arrested her attention. It couldn't be. "Cloistervale?"

She turned to the page indicated. There it was, Cloistervale, listed as the village allotted to a noble family. This must be the history of the Noble Oppressors, of whom the village elders often spoke. Intrigued, she flipped back to the beginning of the entry, then gasped.

"Did you find it?" Jarad asked.

She explained what she'd discovered, then began to read aloud. "Since the days when the first warrior king established the High Houses, several noble families have become extinct or fallen into disgrace—being lowered in rank or losing title and lands altogether. Of all the High Houses of Lastarra, only one has ever suffered both, the family Mortifer."

"Mortifer," Jarad said, "I wonder if that's what the mountain's named for. You know, Mount Mortiferra? The one that's supposed to be haunted?"

"I suppose 'tis likely," she said, then read on. "After committing an unrecorded offense during the third king's reign, Lord Mortifer was stripped of his dukedom and lush lands near the capitol. His family was relegated to a northern valley ringed on all sides by mountains, forests, and river. His eldest daughter declared the region bleak and remote as a cloister. The village which grew up there to serve the manor was thenceforth named Cloistervale."

Lyssanne skimmed lists of subsequent lords until she again found an anecdote.

"Before the royal courts of King Staren IV, representatives from Cloistervale accused the family Mortifer of cruelty, neglect of their subjects' most basic needs, and sorcery. Receiving no aid from their elderly king, the villagers took matters into their own hands. After fleeing the valley, servants of the Mortifer household reported that none of the family survived. The king's investigators recovered the bodies of the lord and lady. However, their young son was never found. House Mortifer was no more."

Lyssanne stared out the window, one fact eclipsing all else. The family had been accused of sorcery. "The keeper of the Shadow Mist," she whispered. Was she that boy's descendant?

"Sorry?" Jarad said. "What was that?"

"Mere idle musings."

As Jarad continued his search for the tree, Lyssanne renewed her quest for Lady MeMe's family history. Though she located the Cintilla entry straightaway, she stared at it, unseeing.

"I found it!" Jarad shouted. "Er, maybe. This book's in Lyryan, I think. There's a picture of a tree that looks like part of a mountain. Could be granite."

Lyssanne reached for the book. With the aid of several more lamps and considerable eyestrain, she deciphered the text. "You are brilliant!" she said. "According to this, the granite tree is an ill omen for those who try to cross the Lyrynn Mountains through Stupasce."

"Stew pots?" Jarad asked.

"Stupasce," Lyssanne said, laughing. "It means fool's pass."

"Oh."

"Many a traveler never returned once having seen the granite tree," she read. "Those who lived to speak of it lost their wits, rambling of haunted music and creatures so fearsome, the travelers never again smiled or slept a peaceful night. Many said the pass was a trap to ensnare those who would seek an easy path rather than make the wiser journey."

"So, we need to find out if that's a real place, that Stew, Stu...that pass," Jarad said. "If it is, I suppose we'll at least know where to start."

"Yes." How would she make such a journey, over mountains and through whatever lay between them and Avery Hall?

"Oh, Look at the sun!" Jarad said. "I was to meet the squires in the armory."

Lyssanne sighed. "Do you never rest?"

"I'm having too much fun to rest." He sprang to his feet and bounded out the door.

Lyssanne soon followed, her mind full of legendary mountain passes and slain sorcerers.

~

Venefica's summons screamed through Noire's mind as he slipped along the library wall like so much mortar. A few inches more, and sunlight stretched arms into wings. He shook them for the simple pleasure of renewed sensation.

Had Jarad not sat facing the little nook between two shelves in which Noire had hidden, he would have exited an age ago. Ah, but a raven sliding from within a wall would have raised a clamor. Perhaps that would have been preferable. It might have prevented Lyssanne's newest discovery, or his witnessing of it.

He took to the air to search the castle for a shadowed place in which to speak with Duncan and announce his departure. The trick would be coaxing Duncan to follow him there.

~

Strolling toward the stables to meet Reina, Lyssanne searched the bustling outer bailey for signs of Jarad. He could be any number of places; training with blade or bow, tending a knight's steed, running to and fro with messages. They'd spent precious little time together in the two days since Prince Brennus had departed on some urgent matter.

The prince's absence left the castle somehow diminished. His quiet intensity had filled those walls, and not even the renewed bustle of knights and squires in training could replace it.

As Lyssanne waved to the guards stationed at the sally port near the stables, Clark's voice boomed from the other side of the gate, requesting entrance. She changed course to greet him.

"Ah, Little Starling!" Clark said, as the guards shoved the gate closed behind him. "My Carol's just been scolding me for not having you join us for a meal."

A sudden bang and shout cut off Lyssanne's intended reply. Clark whirled around, giving her a clear view of several large men forcing the gate back open. Clark lunged forward, but before he could reach the gate, it swung wide, tossing the guards to the ground.

The intruders rushed through en masse, bristling with weapons. At the forefront, strode a bulky, odd-shaped man with something large strapped to his back. Lyssanne caught a glimpse of brown, pale pink, and a sickly green, before a hand clamped onto her arm and spun her around.

Something whistled past her cheek, slicing the air inches from her skin.

"Come on!" Jarad shouted, pulling her across the outer bailey.

As armed men ran past them toward the intruders, Jarad slowed, his head swiveling to and fro. Fighting had broken out, blocking their route to the stable.

"This way!" Jarad ran toward the front of the castle, pulling her after him.

She hitched up her skirts, improperly exposed ankles her least concern. Jarad skidded to a halt then overturned a craftsman's table and ushered her behind it. The instant they were shielded, he unslung his bow from his shoulder and reached for an arrow.

Scuffling footsteps, grunts, and the clang of steel filled the air. Jarad crouched beside Lyssanne, peeping around his end of their improvised shield, an arrow at the ready.

"It isn't dead!" a man shouted near their hiding place.

"Use your sword!" another yelled. "That'll finish him."

"That creature just keeps coming," Jarad whispered.

"What creature?" Lyssanne asked.

"The vomit-green man-thing with the big pink shell on its back," he said. "The one that tried to skewer you with his knife when they broke in. Looks like a human hermit crab." He peeked out again. "How many daggers is he carrying? And where does he keep 'em all?"

It was a testament to everything they'd endured that Jarad was astounded not at the horror of such a creature, but at the number of its weapons. At least the table spared Lyssanne the sight.

As if in response to her thought, a thud rocked their shield.

"Stay down," Jarad whispered. "He's coming this way." He peered around the table long enough to loose an arrow, then ducked back in to nock another. "Creature looks like a pincushion. Knives and arrows stickin' out all over him." He leaned out and shot again.

"Jarad," she whispered, "Let the soldiers—"

"They're busy with those other intruders, and that thing's getting closer," he said.

Another thud, this time too near where Jarad's head had just been. He changed tactics, aiming from above the table instead of to the side.

"Be careful," Lyssanne whispered.

Jarad loosed another arrow. Just as he lowered his head, something whizzed through the air above him and clanged behind Lyssanne. She twisted around. A leaf-shaped blade as long as her hand lay at her feet. Each of its barbed edges looked sharp as Prince Brennus's sword.

A thwack near her ear forced her attention back around.

Jarad dropped his bow and fumbled with his belt pouch. "I'm out," he said. "Hold this." He handed her a narrow leather sheath, then hefted the dagger it had housed.

"I know you're back there, missy," shouted a voice akin to stones grinding together. "Yer little shelter won't save ya."

Jarad leaned out and threw with such force, his body nearly overturned the table.

A clicking sound filled the air just beyond their hiding place.

"I don't believe it," Jarad said. "He's laughing. Every arrow I own is sticking out of that creature, and I just hit him dead in the chest with the prince's dagger. He didn't even flinch." Jarad gasped and lunged toward Lyssanne. "Look out!"

As he pushed her to the ground, a mighty crash assailed her ears.

"Outa the way, whelp," the creature's grating voice roared, closer.

Jarad's weight suddenly lifted from Lyssanne's side, and he flew across the yard. A flash of pink and brown blocked him from view. Then, a deafening clang reverberated above her head.

"Aim for the shell!" Clark yelled, his boat-sized shoe landing near Lyssanne's nose.

The man-crab reeled away from her. She sat up just as Clark's shoe kicked up dirt and he swung his massive hammer at the creature. It struck the spiky pink shell with a clang that resonated through Lyssanne's skull. A splintering sound and an inhuman shriek rent the air. The creature stumbled, spun around, and tipped over onto its back like an overbalanced turtle.

Their attacker lay gasping inches from Lyssanne's feet, his stringy grey hair splayed in all directions. Lyssanne pulled her legs beneath her and shifted up onto her knees.

Clark squatted on the other side of the knife-thrower. "What are you called, creature?"

"Bob."

"Bob?" Lyssanne and Clark said in unison, their gazes locking as Jarad joined them.

"What business have you at Avery Hall...Bob?" Clark asked.

The creature turned its head toward Lyssanne and pinned her with its large, dead-black eyes. "You'll wish...it'd been me...killed ya." Its mouth spread in a gruesome grin.

Clark jerked the creature's head back to face him. "You speak to me, creature." Even Lyssanne flinched at his fierceness. "Now, answer me. Why are you here?"

"On...orders."

"Whose?"

"She...promised me...gold."

"Who? For what?"

"Sh-Shadow...Kee-Keeper." The creature's right arm jerked, he gasped, then he stilled.

Clark levered himself up but swayed before he could stand. Clutching at his left side, he wobbled then slipped back to the ground.

"Clark, you're bleeding!" Jarad shouted.

Lyssanne rushed to Clark's side, skirting around the bloody blade that lay between the creature's green, crab-like pincers. She crouched and looked down at Clark's plate-sized hand and the stain spreading through his fingers.

"Ha, would ya look at that," he said, then gasped. "Got me, eh? H-had his revenge with his…final breath." Groaning, he toppled over.

"Help!" Lyssanne shouted to the knights dragging away fallen attackers, to the stablemen calming horses, to anyone who would hear. "Help, he's wounded!"

As she removed her cloak and folded it to press against Clark's wound, a knight ran toward them. He knelt, lifted Clark's hand aside, and shook his head. "I'm sorry, my lady."

"That bad?" Clark asked, his voice raspy.

"Afraid so," said the knight. "It's a gut wound. Deep." He looked up at Lyssanne. "I'll see to it Lord Avery gets word to his family." He rested a hand on Clark's shoulder. "You'll have your soldier's sendoff after all, friend." He stood and walked away.

Lyssanne pressed her cloak to Clark's side, tears falling onto her hands.

"S'why I gave up soldiering." Clark's weak chuckle ended as a liquid cough.

"I'm sorry," Lyssanne whispered, as blood soaked her cloak. "I'm so sorry."

A faerie's words from what seemed an age past buzzed through her mind. *You let what was happening in the natural world steal your power.*

No, not this time. "You haven't the right," she said under her breath. "Thief, Soul-deceiver, you've no right to steal this man from his family—all because of me. He's a gift to his kin, to this hall, to me. The King of All Lands gave him life, how dare you wrest it from him!"

Boldness welled up in her, a sense of right and authority she'd felt only once before.

"Light and Life of all," she whispered, "don't leave him now. Shine brighter within him."

Clark's ragged wheezes slowed. He was slipping away! Lyssanne wept harder. Above her sobs, rose a groan that could have issued from her own spirit.

"Might ya ease up a bit?" Clark murmured. "My side's afire already,"

Lyssanne's eyes flew open. Clark grinned up at her, pushing at her fingers.

"No, your wound!"

Even in his weakened state, Clark's strength overcame hers. The sodden cloak fell away, revealing the gash in his side—blackened and sealed as if it had been seared.

"You aren't, perchance, a seamstress?" he whispered. "Think I need a bit o' patching."

~

Brennus halted in the doorway of the parlor, his gaze fixed on Venefica. She stared into the fireplace, pulsing with power.

Within the flames, an image formed—a familiar woman, the mother of the twins with whom Lyssanne had shared a tale the day he'd stolen her rowan blossom for Venefica's curse. The woman turned, just as a man draped in Shadow Mist stepped behind her. Willem the carpenter grabbed a fistful of her hair, wrenched her head around, and snapped her neck.

The image followed a tendril of Mist slithering away from the woman's fallen body—right up to one of the twins, a girl Noel's age. She peered, wide-eyed, from behind a tree. Brennus went cold as the Mist snaked up her legs.

Shadows poured into Venefica. She flung back her head, her face exultant. "Another child," she whispered. "Such pure power." She straightened and stroked a thumb over the portrait miniature on the mantelpiece. "Ah, Vynasyr, if only you'd lived to see this. Our reign would have been magnificent."

"Vynasyr?"

Venefica spun, flinging out a hand. An unseen force crashed into Brennus's chest, slamming him against the corridor wall. Her gaze snapped to his. A seductive smile stretched her lips, and she released him. "You startled me, pet. I was just thinking of you."

Struggling for breath, he arched a brow toward the mantelpiece. "Me, indeed?"

She waved a dismissive hand toward the portrait miniature. "An echo of the past, to remind me of our future. He, like you, was robbed of his rightful rule."

"Yours appears secured," Brennus said, eyeing the gleaming wood, rugs beaten free of dust, and portraits hanging in new frames. "The manor bears little resemblance to the derelict shell into which you carried me two years ago. Though, Cloistervale hasn't fared so well."

She glided over to a sideboard. "After the overthrow of the Council," she said, pouring dark red liquid into a gleaming crystal goblet, "I delayed stepping in for a fortnight, permitting anarchy to flourish, so the alternative to my rule would be clear." She glanced up. "Wine?"

"Water." He dared drink nothing else in her presence. "Doubtless, your entrance and magnanimous offer of assistance were a performance worthy of the courts of Skriptaan."

"Indeed." She laughed. "They fair begged me to reclaim my family's title and aid them. Now, they live to serve my whims." She handed him a goblet. "The carpenter certainly has his uses." Deep purple velvet billowed around her as she sank into a chair. "Henceforth, not even the Light-Wielder will trouble me."

Brennus stared. "So certain? I rather expected the opposite after her recent discovery."

"I've sent someone to see to the matter."

He lowered his goblet, the water gone bitter on his tongue. "Who?"

"One of my many agents." She smoothed her skirts. "He should have arrived by now. I shall require you to return there once more, to discover whether his attack has succeeded."

"If that was your wish, why summon me thence?"

"I couldn't have you around to get in his way." She laughed. "Why, your honor would have compelled you to defend the place. I saved us both the trouble of your one, tiny weakness."

"*This* is why it was so urgent I attend you?" His mind screamed, but his voice only grew colder. "Six days I've flown without rest, so you could attack Avery Hall?"

"If my agent succeeds, you will thank me for it."

"There are those in that fortress I would not see harmed."

"All the more reason to ensure the girl's death," Venefica said. "She is a danger to anyone fool enough to aid her." A languid smile stretched her lips. "Should my agent fail, and those who so concern you still live, you may finish her by more subtle means, sparing them."

"Why waste the effort?" He forced his voice to an air of boredom. "We both, my lady, have matters of far greater importance before us. Your power is restored. Extend your reach." He expelled a breath and sliced a hand through the air. "I tire of this game. Forget that peasant."

"I *will* see her destroyed." She sat forward. "And anyone who stands in the way of it."

"To what purpose?" Turning from the sight of her, he strode to the window. "You have taken her home, her health, her very way of life. Her entire village is under your command, and soon, all of Lastarra with it. She is no threat to you."

"No threat? She is *the* threat!"

"How? So, she can light a fire. At your weakest, you could do so with a thought."

"Her mere presence thwarted every advance of the Shadow Mist. Imagine what she could do now, when she is learning to harness her power."

He laughed. "Her *power* is unpredictable. Unlike yours, it isn't hers to manipulate at a whim. If she stays away from Lastarra, you've nothing to fear of her."

"If!" A creak accompanied Venefica's hasty rise from her chair. "*If* she persists in her foolish quest, she will become more dangerous—to us both. Already, she knows too much."

"She knows nothing definitive. Not even your name." He spun to face her. "Had you not pursued her, she wouldn't even know you exist."

"Such matters are of no consequence." She glided toward him. "You swore an oath. One that is yet unfulfilled. Have you forgotten your own words?"

A cloud of Shadow Mist formed between Venefica's outstretched palms, and Brennus's voice echoed from its center. "In payment for this boon I ask," he'd said, so long ago, "I give my solemn knight's oath to assist you in reclaiming your birthright and power—whatever that may require. Else, let my boon, my honor, my life, be forfeit."

"*Whatever* that requires," she said. "Swear to it anew. You need a reminder of your duty, I think." She reached up and pressed her nails to the back of his neck. "And of the cost of failing it."

"My word is never broken." He lowered his voice. "I made no vow to kill innocents."

"Going soft, great Prince?" She trailed her nails around his upper arm. "I am disappointed. How is a man to rule if he is unwilling to eliminate his enemies?"

"To free my people, I will eliminate anyone who stands in my way, but she—"

"*She* stands in your way! For, while she lives, your curse will remain."

He glared at her.

"Still, you hesitate. Why? Honor, again? What of your land? Your lineage?"

"What care you for my family or my land?"

"Nothing," she said. "But you care. Time grows short, Prince. You feel it with each transformation. The magic bound in your blood begins to wreak its vengeance. Soon, you will be lost—your line, your land with you. I offer you a chance. Can your honor grant that? Can she?"

The goblet's stem snapped in his fist, glass shattering to the floor. He was a statue, cold granite, unseeing, unmoving. When he spoke, his voice was ice. "How do you wish it done?"

20

PASSAGE

"*S*tupasce?" Lord Duncan moved another piece on his game board. "Oh, *fii*, it's a real place. Though, why anyone would want to go there, I can't imagine."

Closing her *Kingsword*, Lyssanne glanced at him across the study. "Is it so dangerous?"

"Don't know about danger," he said, watching Lady MeMe's next move in their game of strategy. "Just a dead end. I'm not even sure it's a real pass. Could be just a chunk gouged out of the mountain by a dried up waterfall or landslide. Whatever the case, you can't go through it."

"Have many tried?"

"Oh, to be sure, but not in years." He paused to inspect the board, scratched his chin, and slapped the table, jiggling the game pieces. "Ha! Thought to outflank me? Not today, Lady Wife." He plunked his piece down with deliberate force then turned to Lyssanne. "I do a fair trade with the miners and rockhind herdsmen. They complain often enough that it would decrease their travel—and prices—if they could use the pass instead of the old spine-tree trail."

Lyssanne's heart fluttered. Was she, at last, to have a clear destination? In the pair of days since the intruders broke through the sally port, her urgency to depart had grown. "Is it nearby?"

"Depends what you consider near. I'd say, about the width of Gian Plain's broadest point."

How long had their trek across the plain taken? One week? Two? She'd lost much of the memory to the fog of pain.

"Ahah!" Lord Duncan said, thrusting a fist into the air. "So seals the game!"

Lady MeMe sighed. "Will I never conquer you?"

"Not in this, perhaps, but you conquered me long ago in all the ways that matter."

Lyssanne joined in their laughter.

"Why such an interest in Stupasce?" Lord Duncan asked.

"I…read about it in your library and wondered where it might be in relation to your hall."

"Is it not marked on one of your maps, Love?" MeMe asked.

"It is, indeed." He strode to his desk and peered into a nook filled with paper tubes.

He withdrew a tube nearly as tall as Lyssanne. Unrolled, the map covered the wide table where he and the prince had debated strategy on long winter evenings. Lyssanne joined him, smiling as she recalled their discussions of how the outcomes of historic battles might have differed, had an army taken an alternate route or made better use of the landscape.

"Here it is." Lord Duncan poked at a spot in the midst of a strip of squiggles. "Stupasce."

Lyssanne leaned close, her nose near his finger. A narrow slash of blank paper cut partway through the squiggles representing the Lyrynn Mountains. "What is this?" she asked, pointing to a sizable blank area running alongside the mountain chain.

"Open country," he said. "Some fields, but mostly unclaimed lands. The mountains are the only landmarks out there. Travelers use Stupasce as a guidepost."

"Sounds like a lonely place," Lady MeMe said, moving to stand beside them.

"Mm. It is."

"Might I borrow this?" Lyssanne asked. "I'd like to look at it in the light of your library. I know so little of your beautiful land, and this map is large enough that I believe I can read it."

"I shall have it delivered to the library first thing on the morrow," he said.

~

The following day, light flooded the Avery library through its two-story windows. The map of Lyrya glowed beneath those sunbeams and four lamps.

"So, we'd take this road out of Averton," Jarad said, tracing a route with his finger. "Then, pass through three towns before we get to the big farms, here." He looked up. "We can stay at inns until then. You won't have to sleep outside the first week of the journey, I think."

"Oh, Jarad," Lyssanne said, laughing. "I lived out of doors all summer."

"Yeah, and it almost killed you."

"The King will protect me. Fear not." She rested a hand on his arm for a heartbeat. "If He sets us a task, He will not leave us ill-equipped to accomplish it."

"I know." Jarad's voice took on more briskness. "After those towns, it's nothing but us and the mountains. Not sure how long that'll take, but I figure, if we head straight for them, we can ride alongside the mountains until we see the pass."

"That is a sound plan," she said. "We should set out at once. 'Tis best, for everyone."

"Did I tell you?" Jarad asked. "Captain Gunther finally got something out of that intruder they captured, the one who tried to run away during the fight."

"What did he say?"

"Said that crab-man hired him and a bunch of other thieves to distract whoever might be around, so he could go after his real target."

He looked at her for a long moment, then murmured, "He didn't know why that Bob creature wanted to kill you."

"All the more reason we should leave."

She pushed back thoughts of sorcerers, Mists, and long-ago accidents that weren't accidents. Whatever reason the Keeper of the Shadow Mist had for wanting her dead, it had endangered her friends. She mustn't remain and give the sorceress reason to attack them again.

"Think Prince Brennus will be back before we leave?" Jarad asked.

"Only if he returns by morning. I'd like to be on our way by then."

Jarad's sigh sliced at her heart. The prince had treated him with an almost fatherly consideration. For that alone, she would forever lift his name to the King with thanksgiving.

"That doesn't give us much time." Jarad rolled up the map. "We have to gather our gear, find supplies, tell Reina." He turned to face her. "Think she'll want to come?"

"I shall speak with her. She may wish to return to her forests. Why she's chosen to remain here all winter, confined to the stables with common horses, I can't fathom."

"She's protecting you," he said. "It's like, she thinks you're her foal or something."

They both laughed.

"We'll have more to carry this time, too," Jarad said, "with all your new gowns."

"I'm leaving those behind."

"Oh." He studied the map in its protective tube. "Lady MeMe won't like that. They won't fit anybody else, anyway."

Jarad's prediction proved true. After several valiant attempts to persuade Lyssanne to stay, Lady MeMe insisted she take the clothing and other conveniences she'd been given. "Brennus will be disappointed you've gone," she said.

Doubtless, his disappointment wouldn't match Lyssanne's, or

Jarad's. He'd likely be relieved. "Will you give him my farewell?" she asked. "And my thanks? For…everything."

"Of course."

"He is a good and noble man," Lyssanne said. "The Navvarish people would be fortunate should he seek to regain his throne."

"Yes," Lady MeMe said. "If only he'd accept the King's truth. Well, I'll see you shortly."

As MeMe departed, Lyssanne resumed her preparations. Oh, how she would miss those long winter evenings spent in his company. As she folded one gown after another, memories of their playful banter brought a smile to her lips.

An odd emptiness engulfed her at the thought of never again seeing him, but the urgency growing in her spirit would not be denied. It tightened her stomach, demanding she leave at once, lest something prevent her ever hearing the King's message. A chill shot through her, as though an angel of death had laid a hand on her shoulder.

"Everything's ready, miss," Lily said, breaking into Lyssanne's thoughts. "One of the men'll settle it all on the pack horse Lord Avery's sendin' with you."

"Thank you, Lily."

"If it's not overseppin', my lady," Lily said, "I'm wishin' you wouldn't be leavin'."

"I shall miss you, Lily. You've been a good friend." Lyssanne caught her up in a farewell hug, then turned to take a last, long look at the chambers she'd occupied for the past six months.

Lady MeMe met her in the entry hall. "Duncan and Jarad await us at the outer gates," she said. "I've had saddlebags packed with provisions. Though, your mare wouldn't let the stable hands saddle her. Your young Jarad says she'll sit still only for you."

"She is rather particular."

Lyssanne hid a smile as they walked down the marble steps. Reina's insistence that she would not be left behind for this journey still rang in her ears. And Serena? Well, Lyssanne's shoulder bore the marks of the dove's refusal to loose her talons at the mere suggestion.

"My offer of a carriage still stands," MeMe said, stopping to face her near the inner gate. "Lyssanne, I worry for you out there, with the pain you battle."

"I shall be safe enough. Besides, neither of us has ever driven a carriage, and I know not when, or if, I shall have occasion to return it."

"Well, should you again venture this way," MeMe said, embracing her, "Avery Hall will open to you."

Several members of the household staff greeted Lyssanne at the gatehouse. Lord Duncan's men filed past Jarad, giving him jovial slaps on the back.

"Lady Lyssanne!" a chorus of high-pitched voices shouted.

Noel led a swarm of castle children toward the gate. The offspring of knights and servants jostled each other, all trying to embrace Lyssanne at once.

"Don't go," Noel said.

Lyssanne returned her hug. "I must."

Noel pulled away and waved at the other children. "We have a gift for you."

A servant girl stepped forward and handed Lyssanne a stack of paper, tied with string.

"They're drawings," Noel said, "of your stories. We each chose the tale we liked best, and we signed the pictures so you'd know who drew them." She stepped closer and whispered, "I wrote some of their names for them. I'm teaching them to read like you did in your village."

"Thank you, all of you," Lyssanne said, fighting tears.

"I want to be a great lady like you," Noel said, "with servants who read and lots of conversations with the King."

"Enough farewells, daughter," Lord Duncan said.

After one last hug, Noel led the children away, every bit the lady directing her household.

"I have something for you as well," Duncan said. "You'll find it in the saddlebags." He held a hand out to her. "Safe journey to you both."

"I shall remember your kindness, always."

"It's our honor to know you. Now, I believe your escort is waiting."

"Escort?"

Clark stepped forward. "I'll see you as far as the road out of Averton."

Lyssanne draped a blanket over Reina's back, declining the saddle a stableman held out to her. Reina knelt, drawing gasps from the onlookers, and Lyssanne settled atop the blanket. Her breath hitched as they rode through the gatehouse and out of Avery Hall.

Along the empty road to the nearby village of Averton, Clark spoke of his recovery from the knife wound that should have claimed his life. He'd told anyone who would listen that the King of All Lands had heeded Lyssanne's plea on his behalf. He would not, however, share his certainty that she had been the instrument of that healing.

"Rumors can endanger one's life sure as any weapon," he said. "Good thing the knight who saw my wound is convinced it couldn't have been as deep as he thought." He glanced at her. "I tell ya, though, I'll never forget that warmth spreadin' from your hands all over my icy body."

Indeed, had tales of her part in Clark's recovery swept through the castle, she doubted even Lord Duncan or Prince Brennus would have been able to save her.

Silence fell between the travelers as they wove through the busy streets of Averton. Lyssanne glanced about at the crowded but tidy village, charming in its simple beauty. Flowers bloomed in little cottage yards, shop windows poured forth pleasant scents, and laughter filled the air. Everywhere, were signs of a prosperous, happy people.

"Eighteen years," Clark said as they left the town square. "Who'd have thought it?"

"Eighteen years since what?" Jarad asked.

"My last battle. I was once a foot soldier." Clark grinned. "Hard to fathom, I know. Gave it up to wed my Carol."

"Did you ever miss it?" Jarad asked.

"Not a day." Clark cleared his throat, turning to Lyssanne. "But, Little Starling, should you ever have need, and I'm at hand, I'd lift blade or hammer to aid you. I'd fight a hundred such creatures as the one gave me this." He patted his side.

"Let us hope the need never arises," she said.

"May the King grant it so." Clark halted at a crossroads. "That dirt track straight ahead will take you to Melodine. Lord Avery said you'd be headed that way."

"Yes. Clark I—"

He lifted a hand. "Here I must leave you. Farewell, Little Starling."

Before she could speak, he vanished into the crowded streets of Averton.

Noire's wings beat slower and slower, the weight of his oath pressing heavier with each field or village he passed. Yet, the chain of his loyalty to those up ahead jerked at his throat, pulling him onward. What would he find once he reached Avery Hall?

Whatever form Venefica's attack had taken, every man in Duncan's service would raise hands to defend Lyssanne's life, as would Duncan and MeMe. Noire's feathers shook with a new thought. What if Lyssanne had been with the children when Venefica's agent struck? Noel was too fiery for her own good, and Lyssanne couldn't defend herself, let alone protect the children.

Noire beat the air as if to torture it into revealing the fate of his friends.

And what of Lyssanne? He shook his feathers again to dislodge the question, but it clamped its talons around his mind and wouldn't release him.

Venefica wished him to kill her. It was as simple and complex as that.

If only Lyssanne hadn't persisted in searching out the answer to that mad riddle, she never would have stumbled upon the truth of Venefica's past. Even if she'd survived the assassination attempt, Avery Hall was no longer safe for her.

Indeed, no place could now shield her from Noire's oath. Venefica had sent one attack without his knowledge, what more might she do if he failed her?

Perhaps he could send Lyssanne away to Duncan's cousin. As vassal to Avery Hall, Sir Fenard must comply with Duncan's wishes. Even his marriage was subject to the approval or arrangement of his liege lord. To protect Lyssanne, Duncan would issue such a command.

Bile coated Noire's throat at the thought of her wed to such a man, but she would be safe.

The plan had merit. If Noire avoided setting eyes on Lyssanne once he reached Avery Hall, he could deceive Venefica into believing she'd departed before his return, and that he didn't know where she'd gone. Venefica would never find her.

All thoughts of his well-laid scheme fell to ash as he flew over Duncan's outer wall.

Lyssanne was gone.

Whether by death or departure, her absence pulled at him, an inexplicable but tangible void permeating the air.

Noire sped through the dying sunlight, slowing only as he spotted Duncan leaving the armory with his captain. He squawked a hasty greeting, flapping above Duncan's head.

"Ah, I see Brennus has returned!" Duncan said.

Noire hovered before him, uttered two croaks, then clicked his beak thrice—a signal of urgency they'd prearranged long ago when fighting for the king of Lyrya.

"I shall speak with you later, Gunther," Duncan said, leaving his captain at a run.

Noire flew ahead, toward his chamber's balcony. An instant after landing, he shifted. He'd paced a furrow in the thick Navvarish rug by the time Duncan joined him.

"She set out nigh a week after you left," Duncan said, interrupting his volley of questions. "She was whole and well, Brennus, not to worry." Duncan stared into his eyes. "We had a bit of trouble just before she left, but she was unharmed."

Brennus forced his remaining questions to wait, while Duncan detailed the attack.

"What's most puzzling and worrisome," Duncan said, "is that the monstrous abomination leading the assault was bent on Lyssanne's death. I assured her we've taken every precaution to prevent another breech, but she insisted she must leave." He shrugged. "So, I gave her provisions and a purse of coins for the journey. Nothing more I could do."

Brennus fair growled. "Where?"

"She gave no destination." Duncan scratched his chin. "She did express an odd interest in Stupasce. I'd shown her the place on a map and, next evening, she announced her intentions."

So, she'd gone in search of the granite tree? Brennus's jaw clenched. Did she value his counsel so little? He'd thought she'd accepted his urging, weeks ago, to make a permanent home at Avery Hall, where she'd be well tended when her ailment struck.

He'd thought she had come to trust him, to rely on his judgment. To care for him.

Obviously, he'd been mistaken.

He had tried to shield her from his oath, but she'd denied herself that protection. Very well, let her reap the consequences.

"Brennus?" Duncan stepped forward then faltered.

"I leave at dawn," Brennus said. "Pardon my incivility, friend, but I must rest."

With arms aching from flying the greatest distance in the shortest time since he'd first sprouted wings, Brennus rang for a hot bath. Though his every muscle cried out to spend days ensconced in a soft bed, he had to find her. Duty required it.

If he didn't, Venefica would. And that would be worse...for all of them.

The next morning, Noire left his horse in the stables. He no longer needed to deceive Lyssanne or her companions as to his mode of travel. They would never even know he was near.

Venefica's command had been clear. Lyssanne mustn't suspect

danger. He could afford her no chance to use her magic or summon her faerie friends. Nor must the unicorn interfere.

As he hurtled toward the Lyrynn mountains and the fulfillment of a bargain he never should have struck, he sifted possibilities. He must make it look like an accident. A swift, decisive accident.

She would simply cease to be...no pain, no fear, just a quick passage into nothingness. Then, they would both be free.

At last, he found them encamped near a narrow pass into the Lyrynn Mountains. In the waning sunlight, Lyssanne and Jarad rearranged supplies into small packs, discussing the trek they would undertake afoot on the morrow.

"I shall ennsure your steeds await you," Reina said. "Rocky ground is no place for us."

Noire sailed over Stupasce, searching for the means to carry out his vow. The pass would provide cover when night fell and he shifted. He settled among the pebbles to wait.

Moments later, in his true form, Brennus arranged his trap. He laid a branch fallen from a mountaintop tree across the path and wedged it beneath a pile of loose stones. The narrowness of the canyon would aid his purpose. Impossible to walk around, yet gray as the rock, the branch would make the perfect tripwire, bringing the stones down upon anyone who dislodged it.

The stones he'd chosen would bruise, but were neither large enough nor piled high enough to kill. One glimpse of Lyssanne had turned his honor to dust. His oath and its consequences could hang. He could not be the hand that caused her death.

Venefica needn't be aware of that, though. His plan would appear an attempt at fulfilling her commands, and would discourage Lyssanne from pursuing this foolish quest.

All was proceeding as he'd anticipated. The midmorning sun crested the peaks as Jarad entered the pass ahead of Lyssanne, pointing out hazards. Even should he notice the branch in time to warn her, she would trigger the trap. Her legs were too short, especially in skirts, to step clear of it.

The minor rockslide would bar their way, and Lyssanne would doubtless refuse to risk a greater landslide or worse calamity that might endanger Jarad's life. She would turn back, perhaps for Avery Hall. Then, Brennus could put his earlier plan into play, sending her to safety.

Noire alighted on a ledge overlooking his trap. As Lyssanne and Jarad neared, cold lanced up his spine. Venefica was watching.

Jarad stepped over the branch but, seeming lost in thought, said nothing of it.

Seconds later, shuffling her feet as she often did to feel for unevenness in the ground, Lyssanne reached the spot. The toe of one shoe caught beneath the branch. She pitched forward, arms flailing, as a low rumble shook the mountainside.

The chill increased along Noire's back, and the ledge beneath him heaved in a violent lurch, propelling him into the air.

Venefica! She'd sent a burst of power through him to augment what he'd done! That power cracked open the mountainside.

Jarad spun around and looked up. His wordless yelp came seconds too late, as half the mountain slid toward him. He jumped back, fending off the wall of loose stones and dust that rained between him and Lyssanne.

In that instant, Lyssanne too looked up, but couldn't extricate her foot from the branch and small stones that had already fallen. Just as the larger rocks began their crushing descent, she cried something Noire couldn't make out, and Jarad loosed a scream of terror and loss that would have shattered the coldest of hearts.

21

THE PATH UNSEEN

*N*oire whipped the air into a vortex of feather and fury. He could do nothing but circle and croak. Nothing!

Lyssanne's indistinct cry and Jarad's scream nearly slammed him from the sky.

The next instant, a green haze coalesced from the air behind Lyssanne and resolved into a giant dog. The beast latched its teeth onto the back of her cloak and…vanished!

The mountainside fell, but Lyssanne was no longer beneath it.

Lyssanne closed her eyes and flung her arms up to shield her head from the falling dust and rubble. The world was breaking apart above her! Something snagged at her cloak, jerking her backward by the throat. She stumbled, her foot at last wresting free of the debris.

The ground heaved then gave way. Her stomach lurched as if she were spinning, and air whipped at her face. The next instant, her feet slammed into a floor that hadn't been there seconds before, jarring her spine. She flailed for balance, stones and dirt no longer pelting her.

The violent tremors stopped, but an ominous rumbling continued behind her.

Her eyes flew open. Darkness filled her vision. Gasping, she swept out a hand, but could discern no motion, no deepening of shadow where her hand should be...nothing. Her throat constricted, but a thought far worse than loss of sight crushed her heart in its frozen fist.

"Jarad!" she shouted. "Jarad, where are you? Are you hurt?"

Her voice rang hollow in the vast, black silence.

She had to find him. She stretched a hand toward the fallen rocks on her left, and met emptiness. Where was the mountainside? It had been within reach even before half of it had decided to bury them. Had the ground opened beneath her when the mountain had torn asunder?

"The King is our refuge, though all else gives way," she whispered, finishing the passage she'd shouted when the rocks first fell. "Jarad!"

She slid her foot forward, searching for whatever had pinned it. No debris met her toes. A guttural sound rumbled again behind her. Flinching, she ducked to ward off more falling rocks.

Then, hot breath puffed through her hair.

An animal! That rumble was its growl.

Lyssanne shuffled forward as swiftly as she dared. If she lost her footing, the beast would be upon her. Trusting her toes to detect any rubble in her path, she stretched one hand before her midsection, the other angled to shield her face.

As she moved ahead, the growls ceased.

Where was all the rubble? She halted mid-step, her questing feet finding only smooth ground. Even had she fallen into a hole, debris should have fallen with her.

The growl began anew, moist breath sliding down her nape.

She must keep moving, must find Jarad.

She brushed at moisture beading on her cheeks. The air had lost its crisp, mountain chill. Still, she shivered. The icy kernel of an idea had lodged in her heart.

What if...could she be...dead? Was this growling creature ushering her through the Great Dark to…what? Nothing she'd heard or read about the King's Shining Land had included this.

But where was Jarad? Where was the debris? And *where* was the light?

A sudden gust of air whooshed up her arm and struck her face, a stirring so vast it could only be coming from below. She skidded to a halt, flung her arms wide, and flexed her knees, as vertigo nearly sent her sprawling. Certain she stood at the edge of a precipice, she backed away a few paces…then froze again.

Something was behind her, something huge—and it wasn't the animal. In contrast to the maw ahead, the air at her back had thickened and grown warmer, as if trapped against a wall.

She reached behind her, intending to back against the wall and follow it with her palms, but instinct screamed that she mustn't touch it.

The great animal growled beside her, its breath hot against her left arm.

Flee, her mind shouted. But where, with some danger behind her, a vast openness before?

The air stirring from below seemed to whisper. *A light unto your path…*

"King of All…" She mouthed her words, lest she rouse the animal with true speech. "Direct my steps. I need your hand to guide me."

She blinked away unshed tears, and her vision shifted. A ribbon of brighter darkness stretched forth from her right foot, illuminating the ground a pace ahead as if she held a dim lantern shrouded in dark silk. She sidled along that indistinct path as she would a narrow ledge.

Noire flew in dizzying circles over Jarad and the mound of rock filling the pass. His keen eyes pierced every inch of the area, examining every pebble for a scrap of cloth, a discarded shoe, any sign of her. People simply didn't vanish before one's eyes.

Jarad broke free of his stupor and went mad with desperate action.

He shifted rock after rock, calling Lyssanne's name. Heedless of bruises and hands scraped raw and bloody, he dug through what he could lift and heaved at what he could not. His intent flashed in his eyes—he would dig her out of that heap if it killed him.

If he kept up such a pace, it likely would. At least he could do something besides fly about. Noire had no way to even utter what he knew. She was gone.

Just as Jarad reached up for another chunk of mountain, a flash lit the stone. He jerked his hand away from the leafy sparks sizzling at his fingertips.

The faerie Olivia stared down at the boy from atop the rock. She crossed her ankles and tapped her wand in a lazy rhythm across one knee. "She is not to be found here, young Jarad."

"The rocks fell...and she, she was...Help me!" Jarad shrieked.

"Hear me, Jarad," Olivia said, vanishing her wand to grasp his face in both hands. "She has been taken to the realm of the FAE."

Jarad blinked up at her.

"You must await her return." She slid her hands to his shoulders and gave them a gentle shake. "Jarad, travel farther along the pass, for 'tis there she will arrive. She will need you."

"She, she's alive?"

"Yes."

"When?" Jarad said, a mere rasp. "When will she return? Is she hurt?"

"The sun will not shine again before you see her face." Olivia released him and fluttered above the rubble. "Watch and wait." Another flash, and she vanished.

Lyssanne followed the vague path, each footfall surer than the last. Soon, she turned to walk it straight on. As she went, her surroundings gained definition. The animal's breath remained at her back.

At length, the deeper darkness to her left grew distinct, indicating the precipice she'd suspected. Shifting shades of gray played over the mass to her right, sharpening to reveal pointed spines peppering the wall.

A pinpoint of light punctured the gloom ahead. She froze. The light drew closer, growing in size and brightness. Then, rays of color shot forth from the light, illuminating the landscape. Even the precipice filled to bursting with hues so vivid she had to shield her eyes. Flowers?

Blinking, she turned from the gorge. The wall of spines resolved into the thorny, vine-covered base of an earthen terrace. She glanced back at the floating light and gasped. It had dimmed, sprouted wings, and taken on the form of a faerie.

The figure, a male, began to grow, soon exceeding Clark's height. His wings and tunic, a purple deep as dusk-painted forests, drank in the light. Hot breath fanned Lyssanne's hair as a hulking shape pushed past her. The faerie turned to pat the head of the beast—a great, green dog.

"Well done, Cusith," the faerie said, his voice deep and resonant as the creature's growl. He slapped the dog's flank, and it bounded off, vanishing mid-leap. The faerie turned to Lyssanne, his expression fierce. "You've passed the test," he said. "Barely."

"Test?" Lyssanne whispered.

"A trial of trust." He loomed close. "Does your trust truly rest in the King, or will you pay more heed to the counsel of your senses?" His tone grew icy. "Will you walk the path unknown, relying on His guidance—even if that guidance reveals nothing but the next step to be taken?"

"The darkness, the cliff...you were testing my *loyalty*?"

He nodded. "As yet, I am unconvinced."

Lyssanne clutched fistfuls of skirt and fought to keep her voice level. "Where is Jarad?" He could be hurt, and this faerie was toying with her?

"Already, you lose focus!" The faerie drew nearer, forcing her to step back. "This is no game. The path you've been called to walk is treacherous. If you turn aside, even by a single footfall, it could mean destruction—and not only for you."

She clutched at the pendant Aderyn had given her a lifetime ago. Its star-points bit into her palm. "His—his life isn't a game either."

The faerie tilted his head, as if listening to something she couldn't hear. "He lives."

"Thank the King," she whispered. "Wait…" She swung her gaze back to his face. "You speak of trust; how do I know I can trust you?"

"I am Alvar, a captain of the FAE."

"Like Olivia."

He laughed. "Olivia is assigned to protection detail. I, to offensive warfare. It is my task to vanquish the King's enemies. I do not wait for them to attack. I sweep them before me like dust." At his gesture, a whip-crack of air slashed past her, forcing her back another step. "You are at war. The Thief of Souls gives no quarter, and neither do I. It is time you join the battle."

"I'm no warrior."

"Are you afraid?"

Of him? "Yes."

"Do you place so high a trust in your enemy?"

"Of course not, but if you're in the King's army, you couldn't be—"

"I speak not of myself," he said. "In the war against the Thief of Souls, more than mere life is at stake. Fear is faith in the powers of darkness. If you expect the works of the enemy will come to pass, you can have no victory."

"But fear makes us cautious," she said, "restrains us from reckless action."

"Caution is born of the King's wisdom. Fear breeds doubt. That is death to faith."

"I…yes, I understand."

"See that you do. My queen has sacrificed too much, just to give you the chance to wield your gift as it was intended. Know this, I will not permit the enemy to use you to further harm her. Nor will I see your gift turned from the King's purpose. I'll see you destroyed myself first."

She shivered. "I wasn't even born when the queen's daughter—"

"My queen has lost far more than the Princess Tria for your sake, and recently. See that those sacrifices were not in vain. Else, you deal with me."

"Alvar."

Lyssanne spun. Jada hovered paces away, staring at the giant faerie as if he were a bug.

"Your charge got herself into trouble again, Jada," Alvar said.

"Who it was that got her into trouble isn't at issue, Captain. The question is, why's she here?"

"The voice of the King's word puts me to flight, as it does you."

"Yes, we heard her speak it, 'The King is our refuge.'" She fluttered around Lyssanne, partly shielding her. "She *is* our charge. Why was it you who snatched her from that trouble?"

"I was closer...or Cusith was."

"Where, exactly, are we?" Lyssanne asked. "And where is Jarad?"

"Where you left him, I expect," said Jada. "You've strayed into the realm of the faerie folk, and it is time you return to your young friend."

Jada turned to Alvar and spoke in a language Lyssanne had never heard. After a brief exchange, Alvar looked at Lyssanne, still babbling that odd tongue, as if expecting her to reply.

"I only speak Starransi and Lyryan," she said.

"Learn," he said, "if you wish to truly master your gift."

"Only the King can teach the language of the FAE," Jada said, "His language."

"Precisely," Alvar said. "Your natural skill in the tongues of men will not aid you here, but that is why you must learn. The Thief of Souls is a master of language as well, but cannot comprehend the tongue of the King."

"Then, how can I—"

"Time grows short," Jada said. "Take my hand, Lyssanne, you must return."

The instant she did so, the world spun and constricted into a swirl of color.

∾

Brennus leaned against the mountainside and, despite their agreement to keep watch in opposite directions, glanced at Jarad. The boy was exhausted. Jarad swiped at his eyes again, his bandaged hands glowing in the moonlight, but he refused to rest until Lyssanne returned. If the faerie had spoken true, she'd arrive before morning. Brennus would be there when she did.

"Reina!" Jarad said on a sudden gasp. "She must be frantic. We've been gone an age."

"She was," Brennus said, turning back to his vigil. "The instant I arrived at your camp, she all but skewered me, urging me toward the pass. Lyssanne's dove saw the landslide and told her somehow." He hid a smirk. His feigned shock had been a performance even Venefica would have admired. Then, he'd had to climb the rubble.

Precautions to keep up his cover would be for nothing, though, if Lyssanne's return waited until dawn. He swiped a tattered sleeve across his eyes, his scraped hand burning.

"If...*when* she gets back," Jarad said in a tremulous voice, "d-don't say anything about the faeries. I shouldn't have told you."

"You've done no wrong." Brennus kept his voice soft. "Your secret, and hers, is safe." His throat tightened at the memory of Jarad grasping him by the arm, begging him to find her.

"Maybe we went too far up the pass," Jarad said, his voice cracking. "What if she comes back and we aren't there. What if—"

"We will see her," Brennus said, his gaze fixed ahead. "With the moon glaring off the snowcaps, if anything moves in this pass, we'll know it."

A sudden, emerald flash lit the night. In its midst, stood Lyssanne and the spikey-haired faerie. Lyssanne seemed frozen, her face waxen as the mountaintops. Then, her knees buckled.

Swifter than flight, Brennus lunged forward and caught her against him. She flinched.

"Easy," he said. "I've got you."

"Let me help her," the faerie said, her tone sharp.

"No." Brennus stepped back, tightening his hold on Lyssanne.

"Lady Lyssanne!" Jarad cried. "Oh, thank you, King of All Lands, thank you!"

"Indeed," Brennus murmured. He shook himself. Perchance her King *had* saved her. What other power could snatch her from the very instant of death?

"You're…here?" Lyssanne whispered, peering up at him with watery eyes. "How?"

"That can wait." He sank to the ground, cradling her closer. "Are you harmed?"

She shook her head, but her hand fisted around a fold in his tunic, clinging to him as if to life itself. Then she began trembling.

"What have they done to you?" Brennus fair growled, squeezing her to him.

"Saved her life," the faerie said.

22

OF DOGS, DOVES, AND SNOW MEN

*J*arad's face leaned in, filling Lyssanne's vision. "What happened? Where were you?"

"Jarad," Lyssanne whispered, tears flooding her eyes. He *was* unharmed.

"Give her room," Prince Brennus said. "Questions can wait until she's recovered."

"But—"

"She is safe." The prince's voice cracked. "That's what matters."

"Jarad," Lyssanne murmured, "I thought you were…" She couldn't say it, even now. "I thought I'd lost you."

"Yeah," Jarad said, sniffling. "Me too."

Another hard tremor seized her. Why couldn't she stop shaking? The prince's arms seemed the only things holding her together.

Then, one of those arms loosened and left her.

"No!" She buried her face in his tunic, trembling harder, praying he wouldn't vanish as the dog had, as she had. Instead, he reached behind him to pull his mantle tight around them both. She looked up into his face, inches from hers. Her heart pounded, no longer from fear.

"Rest." His breath fanned the hair that had fallen across her nose. "I won't let go."

"The rocks," she whispered, staring into his eyes, so close she breathed his breath.

"It's over," he said. "Hours since."

"Hours?" she asked. What were they discussing? His scent—cedar, mint leaves, and intensity—filled her lungs, putting all thought to flight.

"What's wrong with her?" Jarad asked. "What happened to her in that place?"

"This will pass," Jada said. "She needs a moment to adjust. Time moves differently in the land of the faeries."

"How long…was I…?"

"Most of the day and half the night," Jarad said.

It had felt like mere moments. Oh, she had questions, but she could focus on nothing save Jarad and the prince. They were here. They were unharmed. They wouldn't leave her.

She closed her eyes, relaxing into Prince Brennus's hold. He settled her atop his crossed legs and brushed aside her hair, keeping both arms around her as if anticipating her need. His heart beat a steadying rhythm, coaxing hers to slow and match it.

The trembling in her limbs subsided. Safe, she was safe.

At length, Olivia popped into view. Lyssanne sat up. She must tell them what had befallen her, and her own questions wouldn't rest. Questions for the faeries and for the prince.

"Are you well?" Prince Brennus asked, keeping a steadying hand at her back.

"Yes." She cleared her throat as she slid to the ground beside him. "I am better now. Thank you, Your Highness, you—"

"Brennus," he said.

She stared at him.

"We are beyond formality," he said. "After all these months, after all we've seen…" He unfastened his mantle and draped it about her shoulders. "Call me Brennus."

"But you're…I'm—"

"I would have insisted sooner, but I knew it would cause you discomfort." He sighed. "You've not spoken my name since you discovered my title. Would you do me the honor now?"

"Yes," she said, her cheeks heating, "Brennus. How did you find us?"

"Duncan."

"We never said we were going to the mountains," Jarad said.

"He guessed your destination, and I...thought you might need assistance. These mountains can be treacherous."

Lyssanne nodded, took a deep breath, and told them of the FAE realm.

"I shall have words for Alvar," Olivia said, her tone ominous.

"Good," Jada said. "He didn't think much of mine."

"You didn't overstep yourself, I hope?"

"No, but I didn't know about his little *test*."

"That," said Olivia, "was ill-conceived. This was neither the time nor place."

"What he said about your queen," Lyssanne said. "What recent sacrifice has she made, and what has it to do with me?"

Olivia settled in front of her. "I have much to tell you, but we must speak in private."

"We have no secrets," Lyssanne said. "You may speak freely with my friends present."

"Jarad has proven his heart trustworthy, but—"

"As has His—Brennus," Lyssanne said. "I trust him."

"Very well." Olivia motioned, and Jada joined her on the ground before them. "This path is yours to walk. You alone can choose who walks it with you."

Olivia sketched intricate patterns in the air with her wand. A domed web of green light formed over them, settled, then vanished. The air and sound changed, as if they now sat indoors.

"All your life, our queen has watched over you from afar," Olivia said. "When you fell ill, she increased her vigilance. She went to you in disguise and has rarely left your side since."

"That isn't possible," Lyssanne said. "I was alone for months. I saw no sign of her."

"As I said, she was in disguise."

Silence unfurled over the entire group.

Jarad snapped his fingers. "Reina! Is Reina the queen of the faeries?"

Lyssanne's heart raced for an instant, then her shoulders slumped. "I only met Reina this summer past. That was weeks after we'd left Cloistervale."

"Yeah," Jarad said, "and people would've noticed a unicorn hanging around."

"Indeed," Olivia said. "Which is why our queen took on a form far smaller, more common. She was remarked upon, but attracted no suspicion from the townsfolk."

Small, commonplace...Lyssanne gasped. "Serena!"

"Yes," Olivia said. "You named her well. Doubtless, part of your mind recognized her from that long-ago night when Serena, Queen of the FAE, summoned a little girl into the wood."

Brennus's arm twitched at Lyssanne's side. She glanced at him, but he sat rigid.

"All this time, a dove," Lyssanne whispered. "Is that the sacrifice Captain Alvar meant?"

"No," Olivia said. "She has fallen under a spell of evil intent."

"Oh!" Lyssanne sprang to her feet. "We must go to her."

"There is no need for haste," Olivia said. "The spell was cast months ago. The day you left your home, she was trapped in her disguise by the same evil which besets Cloistervale."

"The Keeper of the Shadow Mist?" Lyssanne said, sinking back to the ground.

"Yes," Jada said. "That witch is getting stronger. Cloistervale is all but finished, and if she isn't stopped soon—"

Olivia lifted a hand, and Jada subsided.

"No wonder Captain Alvar was angry," Lyssanne said. "It *is* my fault."

"Lyssanne." Brennus rested a hand on her knee.

"No," she said. "If she hadn't been watching over me, she wouldn't have been in the village, near the sorceress." She stared at Olivia. "Why *was* Serena watching over me?"

"The King has many ways of protecting His people," Olivia said. "But be warned, Alvar's attitude is not uncommon. This shadow is growing across the land, and with Queen Serena confined, many of the FAE question our chances of defeating it."

"Whatever the cost," Lyssanne said, "we shall keep your queen safe."

"I can see where young Jarad learned of courage," Olivia said. "Now that we are assured you are well, other matters require our attendance...and yours."

"Yes," Lyssanne said. Now, more than ever, she must discover the King's message.

Olivia waved her wand, and the dome reappeared above them, only to dissolve. The sensation of enclosure vanished with it. They all rose.

"Before you depart, honorable faeries," Brennus said, slipping a hand beneath Lyssanne's elbow. "Might you assist us with the rubble blocking the path to Lyssanne's campsite?"

"I can't return to camp as yet," said Lyssanne.

"Of course you can," he said. "Your faerie friends can get you through the pass in time to rest for most of the night. On the morrow, we shall begin our return to Avery Hall."

She shook her head. "I must find the granite tree."

"Lyssanne..." His voice gentled. "You're exhausted. You were nearly killed today."

"Please, this is the path the King has set. I must follow His leading."

"Indeed," said Olivia. "We shall clear the pass, should you need it."

The faeries shrank to the size of sparks and whisked off.

"I see there is no dissuading you," Brennus said. "Let us move swiftly, then. Perchance we'll find a hollow or cave in which you can shelter overnight."

~

Dismissing another feeble excuse he might offer for what morning would bring, Brennus slowed again, matching Lyssanne's pace. Whatever may come, this night at least, he wouldn't leave her side.

After an hour's walk, she had already stumbled twice. She pushed herself onward with feigned cheer, but he wasn't fooled. Her eyes showed strain, and her mouth formed a tight line. Keeping her gaze fixed on the ground, she trudged beside him, leaving him and Jarad to keep watch for the elusive granite tree.

Without warning, Jarad halted. Focused on Lyssanne, Brennus plowed into the boy.

"Oof!" Jarad grunted, then spun to grasp Lyssanne's arm. "I think that's it!"

"What?"

"The granite tree." He pointed upward. "It looks like the picture in that book."

Jutting at an oblique angle from a ledge partway up the mountainside, a gnarled tree stood silhouetted against the circle of the full moon.

"Is it truly made of stone as the legend holds?" Lyssanne asked.

"Tell you in a moment," Jarad said, swinging his bundle down from his shoulder. He backed to the side of the pass opposite the tree, then took a running leap for the wall of stone. As he reached it, he thrust one foot up to connect with the mountainside. Momentum propelled his body upward. He grasped at the rock for a handhold then began to climb.

"Jarad, no!" Lyssanne said. "The rocks could fall again."

"I won't be long," he said then returned his attention to the mountain.

Brennus stood below him, in case he slipped. The boy was an expert climber, despite growing up near what amounted to forested hills compared with the Lyrynn Mountains. Soon, Jarad reached the ledge. With one hand cupping the narrow ridge, he reached up and backward to touch a lower branch of the tree. In moments, he scuttled back down the mountainside.

The instant his feet touched the ground, Lyssanne exhaled. "Jarad, if you ever—"

"That thing's rock, all right," Jarad said. "And I don't mean like wood that's older than Mr. DeLivre. It's like, part of the mountain broke off, and that's what was left."

"The granite tree," Lyssanne said. She looked up toward it, shading her eyes.

"What now?" Jarad asked. "He said to seek the message *beyond* the granite tree. There's snow aplenty up there, but no sea anywhere. How much farther will we have to go?"

Lyssanne shrugged. "All I know is, we must go past this place. The King will lead us."

At an unexpected bend in the pass, Brennus called a halt. Lyssanne and Jarad huddled close, shivering in the increased chill of night.

Jarad pointed down the short passage ahead, which ended in a cave. "Th-thank the King!"

Lyssanne nodded, wrapping Brennus's mantle tighter.

"I shall enter first," Brennus said, pushing ahead of Jarad. "Any manner of beast might make its home in these parts."

As he drew his sword, Jarad hefted his bow. Providing cover? The boy had learned much. He would make a fine squire, should anyone grant an orphaned peasant the opportunity.

Brennus eased forward on silent feet, listening for any telltale sound. The wall comprising the mouth of the cave stretched the breadth of the pass. No danger of ambush, then.

A sudden whoosh from above stopped him cold. Arching his back, he stared upward. Three cascades of snow slid from the rock atop the cave's mouth. *Not snow.* A trio of inhumanly tall, pallid figures dropped in front of him.

Moonlight flashed off long, slender objects in their hands. Brennus swung his sword forward to meet them, welcoming a clash of steel after the events of this accursed day.

Only empty air met his thrust.

The creatures backed away, brandishing not weapons but slender, silvery horns that shone translucent in the moonlight, as if sculpted from ice. A sound like no other filled the night, and Brennus's sword-arm began to jerk, then his legs. The spasms increased, growing rhythmic, fluid, a dance born of compulsion, and no exercise of his iron will could prevent his compliance.

Brennus concentrated every nerve, every sinew, every vestige of his not inconsequential strength, on controlling his wayward limbs. If only he could bring his blade to bear upon the source of that hypnotic music, all the more chilling for its crystalline, spirited beauty.

The creatures, too, Brennus might call beautiful, if not for the coercive power of their music. As if painted with the powdery drifts of deepest winter, their bodies flowed when they moved like waves of snow in a steady wind. Gossamer strands, glittering with the facets of falling flakes, hung from their elongated heads to brush tunics the shade of frosted pools.

"I can't...stop...wiggling!" Jarad cried.

Brennus dared not take his eyes from the sinister musicians to determine how Lyssanne fared. His efforts were consumed with fighting the weight of his sword. Its point dragged downward as if drawn by an invisible force, then the blade clattered to the ground. Grinding his teeth, he redoubled his struggle to reclaim mastery of his muscles.

Then, the music changed. Its high, smooth tones gave way to deep, haunting melancholy. Notes echoed off the mountains, mournful yet retaining a rhythmic swing.

Released at last from the bondage of the dance, Brennus's limbs grew leaden, as if the music's melancholy weighed upon them. He turned, keeping half his focus on the musicians, to assure himself of Lyssanne's welfare...and Jarad's.

She'd slumped against the mountainside, eyes closed, chest heaving. Jarad stood panting nearby, hands on knees, his bow and one arrow at his feet.

Brennus turned back to face the alabaster minstrels. Keeping his gaze fixed upon them, he eased into a crouch. He reached for his sword, and the music sped into a wild cacophony of trills and breathless quarter notes, thrusting the dance upon him anew.

A groan from Jarad proved the others fared no better than he. Brennus forced all his will into his hands, raising them through their unwilling movements to show he wouldn't try for the weapon again. Retreat was sometimes the only victory.

The music shifted to the lament of a moment before, and he expelled a breath. Still eyeing the musicians, he edged backward toward Lyssanne, snagging Jarad's arm as he passed. "Stay close," he whispered. "I cannot discern their intentions."

The musicians played on, their ice-blue eyes staring at nothing. Their song seeped into Brennus's soul. Was this wrenching sadness a window into the musicians' hearts, or was it his own? The haunting tones roused every disappointment or loss he'd faced, every futile effort he'd made in a lifetime of vain struggle.

"What shall we do?" Lyssanne whispered. "We can't go onward. Even if we could pass those…people, Stupasce is a dead end."

"We wait," Brennus said.

"This can't be," Lyssanne said, her voice low. "We've followed the riddle. We went beyond the granite tree."

"There's nothing here," said Jarad.

"Perhaps I've misunderstood the riddle."

A shudder passed through Lyssanne. Brennus's full attention snapped to her. She'd bent her head, eyes closed, hair spilling around her face.

"Seek out the bird whose bark is the soul of wisdom," she quoted, "that lion who has flown through every age. The copper wings that unite earth and sky carry words to set the Darkness ablaze. Seek out the King's message where the sun lays its head in snow and sea. For you and all, one hope remains. Seek it beyond the granite tree."

So oft had she recited the riddle in Duncan's library, even Brennus could have quoted it.

"Perhaps it isn't literal or…" Her voice fell. "Or I've already missed it."

Brennus stiffened. "Now is not the time for—"

"The head of a dog…" she said, tears glistening in her eyes. "What if the creature with the message was that green faerie dog?" She gasped and brought a fist to her mouth. "What if Captain Alvar's real test was to see if I'd recognize him?"

"How could you recognize someone you'd never met?" Brennus asked.

"From the riddle," she said.

"But it's supposed to be a bird," Jarad said, his voice flat as the low note emanating from the ice-horn of one of the minstrels.

"It could have been a reference to both of them, the faerie and his dog," Lyssanne said.

"Yeah, but neither of them had lion claws," Jarad said. "Did they?"

Lyssanne sighed. "I…don't think so."

"Besides, you said that faerie's wings were purple, not copper."

"This creature you seek matters not," Brennus said. "We must leave this place."

"But if I have missed it…" Lyssanne covered her face and sank to the ground.

"We came all this way for nothing," Jarad said. "Almost died, for nothing."

"I've failed again," Lyssanne whispered. "The King wanted to give me a message, and I can't even find the creature who carries it."

"Maybe that peddler *was* crazy." Jarad joined her on the ground. "Probably didn't even have a vision."

Lyssanne slumped, shivering in the growing chill. Her sapphire eyes dulled, as if everything for which she'd so long struggled had lain in her hands, only to dissolve as smoke through her fingers. It was like watching hope die, a feeling Brennus knew well.

His head snapped up. A spell! He should have seen it! This haunted melody held them just as enslaved as had the dance. The weight of its chains was crushing Lyssanne and Jarad.

Brennus wasn't immune, but dark thoughts and hopelessness had been his constant companions all his life. He was the last, the *only* hope for his people, bearing the burden of a quest that couldn't be fulfilled. He'd forced those feelings to fuel his resolve.

To Lyssanne's spirit, however, such would be death. Already, her skin had taken on the cast of a winter traveller preparing to die in the snow.

He crouched before her, cupping her chin in his hand. "Lyssanne," he said, filling his tone with command. "Look at me. Don't give in. You are the one person I know who never surrenders the fight. Let this not be the first time."

She blinked up at him.

"To relinquish the battle now, after all you've survived…" He bit his lip, drawing blood to distract himself from the music's pull. "Should you die in an accident or by the hand of an enemy, 'twould wound me, but to watch you die by this failing of the spirit—*that*, I can not, shall not permit." He clasped her hands in both of his. "We'll return to Avery Hall. You can make your home there or, failing that, I shall find a place for you. We—"

"No," she whispered. "You're right. The King never gave up on me." Her voice grew stronger. "I shan't give up on Him." She pushed herself up, but slipped back to the ground. Sighing, she closed her eyes. "The King's joy is my strength," she said. "His Light is my hope, my safekeeping." She drew in a deep breath. "Shine in this darkness. Light our path."

She flared—purer, whiter than the creatures whose music held their hearts in thrall.

The music ceased.

The minstrels froze, hands dripping, tunics soaked. Lyssanne's Light had melted their instruments of ice. They fell to their knees, hands outstretched. "Forgive us!"

"We beg your clemency!" said the one in the center, perhaps their leader. "We are no enemies of Light." He looked up at Lyssanne, his cerulean eyes beseeching. "We were only protecting what is ours to guard."

"What, a mere cave?" asked Brennus. "You enslave travelers who but seek shelter?"

As though Brennus's presence did not exist for him, the chief minstrel's eyes remained fixed on Lyssanne. "You may pass," he said. "The cave will lead you where you seek to go."

Still on their knees, all three creatures scooted to one side of the pass. Heads bowed, they gestured toward the cave.

She arose and stared down at the creatures as she might at wayward children. "How do I know some further trap doesn't await me?" she asked, her voice strong.

"Light favors you, protects you. We are no enemy of His or yours. We dare never provoke His displeasure."

Lyssanne nodded. She glanced at Jarad, then at Brennus, before turning toward the cave. She skirted around their discarded weapons with an uncharacteristic air of confidence.

"Lyssanne," Brennus said, "we know not what lurks in that cave."

"We need a torch," was her only reply.

"That which you need awaits within," the chief minstrel said. "Look to the cave mouth."

She strode forward as if on a quest. What could Brennus or Jarad do, but retrieve their weapons and follow? Brennus found a torch just inside the cave. He struck it to life with flint from his belt pouch. At the edge of its glow, a trough resolved from the gloom.

"Hold," Brennus said, sheathing his sword. Sweeping the torch before him, he walked to the near end of the trench then touched the flame to its surface. Fire sprang up within the trough, a line of light racing all along the cave's walls.

Jarad whistled. "No wonder they were guarding this place."

Heaps of shimmering treasure littered the chamber. Gold and silver caught the flicker of the flames. Gems of every hue sparkled around them.

"What were they? Those creatures?" Jarad asked.

"The fabled Snow Men of Lyrynn, I suspect," Brennus said. Another legend proven fact.

"This isn't all they guarded," Lyssanne said, moving past him toward the far end of the cave, toward an alcove half-concealed in darkness. "This is the way." She approached the stone stair just visible within, sparing not a glance at the wealth surrounding her.

"Then, take hold of my arm," Brennus said. "Jarad, stay close." He hefted his torch, and they ascended the winding stair into the belly of the mountain.

23

THE MESSENGER

ighting weariness, Lyssanne ascended the steep but smooth stairs alongside Brennus, his steadiness a comfort.

Such an unexpected gift, his arrival. He'd saved them all in front of that cave. 'Twas as if the voice of the King had spoken through his words, piercing the music's hold over her spirit.

"Are you in need of rest?" he asked.

Lyssanne sighed. She could have slept where she stood, but urgency had again seized her heart. "I thank you, but we must press on. The exit can't be much farther."

"Very well," he said, wrapping his arm about her waist, "but a fall here could be fatal."

They climbed until, at last, a stir of night air tickled a lock of hair across her brow, and dim light fell upon the stairs. She sniffed. Was that…salt?

A soft susurration of sound met her ears as she emerged onto a wide, flat expanse of rock. The night sky seemed to meet the mountaintop, bringing the stars near enough to touch.

She released the folds of Brennus's mantle and let it hang loose. How could it be so warm here? The salty scent intensified in the mild, moist air. And that sound! Like cloth sliding across a floor, it flowed toward them, then ebbed away—beautiful, lulling.

"Impossible," Brennus whispered.

"What?" Lyssanne asked.

"Wait here." With torch held high, he strode to the edge of the plateau.

Jarad joined him and gasped. "Is that…the ocean? Lady Lyssanne, you must see this!"

She hesitated, heeding Brennus's counsel. "Is it safe?"

The prince extended a hand behind him. She walked forward and took it. He brought her alongside him, his eyes remaining fixed on the view.

Water? Moonlight glinted off wave upon wave far below. Never had she dreamt so much water could occupy one place. Oh, she'd read of the great seas, and Mr. DeLivre had tried to describe them, but nothing had prepared her for this beauty, this vastness.

"Where's the snow?" Jarad asked. "It was all over the mountaintops. I can't even see the pass, and there's no ocean near the Lyrynn Mountains."

"The Ocean of Time knows no shore," said a smooth, musical voice. "You are neither in nor out of the Seven Lands."

Brennus tightened his hand around Lyssanne's. A warning? They turned; and, thrusting the torch before him, he stepped in front of her.

The mound of rock through which they'd emerged had vanished, leaving behind nothing but smooth plateau. Where the cave had been, stood a creature as tall as Lyssanne's cottage.

"Welcome, seekers of truth," the creature said in the firm, female voice that had so surprised them. "It is long since your kind found the Way to my domain."

Enormous wings furled around the creature's birdlike body, gleaming copper in the moonlight. She tilted her head, that of a dog, her large floppy ears and shiny black nose twitching. Catlike paws supported her weight. *The claws of a lion.*

"Who are you?" Brennus demanded. "What is this place?"

"Your mind brims over with questions, Prince of Navvar," said the creature, "but it was not for you I opened the Way. For a man with so many faces, you are frozen, changed by nothing, moved by nothing… or so you would have yourself believe."

Lyssanne could practically hear Brennus's teeth grinding.

The creature turned her great, canine head toward Lyssanne. "I am Seianelle, and this is my home. I am the one men call simurgh, the only one of my kind."

Lyssanne's heart skittered. The King's messenger, at last! She curtseyed.

"You need show me no such obeisance, dear one. I am a mere creation of the King, not of His family as are you."

"Mr. Fescue was right," Jarad whispered against Lyssanne's ear.

"Seanan Fescue?" Seianelle asked. "A wise human, if ever there was such."

Jarad gasped.

Seianelle laughed. "These canine ears aren't so large for nothing. Fear not, young one. Your curiosity is flattering. The King is a great artist, is He not? With such a sense of humor!"

"Then," Jarad said, "can you…can you fly?"

"You have not journeyed so far and braved dangers merely to ask of my abilities."

"No, my lady," Lyssanne said.

"Address me by name, for 'tis you who are higher in the King's service." Seianelle settled upon her haunches, her fanned tail spreading like an elaborate chair-back. "You found me, Hlyssaunna, because you seek the answer to no question."

"But Mr. Fescue said nobody could find your home unless they'd already been there," Jarad said. He turned to Lyssanne. "I've never been here. Have you?"

"Not even in dreams."

"Hlyssaunna has come not for self, but in obedience to the King's command—a place, such obedience, in which she has oft dwelt."

"Oh…" Jarad whispered.

Brennus stood rigid, a silent sentinel, as if ready to defend at the slightest provocation.

"Hear me, Hlyssaunna, Light's Grace," Seianelle said. "You are well named. For, like the Great Grace, which Light bestowed upon all men, you are a gift granted of the King of All Lands, undeserved, to your people." Her wings fluffed. "All who accept you, and accept whence you came, will be spared from disaster. Those who do not will suffer of their own choosing."

"Is that what the King wished you to tell me?" Lyssanne asked. "The meaning of my name, to remind me of His gift?"

"No. By your obedience to His call, I may speak for you the prophecy that shaped your past and destined your future. Heed me well. It can be spoken only once."

Lyssanne shivered. "I, I understand."

Seianelle nodded, her great head casting a shadow over them all, then began to recite.

> *"Child of Light*
> *Of Heaven born,*
> *Trapped within*
> *Her mortal form,*
> *Through Mist of doubt*
> *And Shadow rise,*
> *And bring release*
> *To a land that cries.*
> *One hidden gift*
> *To dispel the night,*
> *Destroy the Darkness*
> *And bring forth the Light.*
> *No common pow'r*
> *This strength she wields,*
> *When to the King*
> *Her weakness yields."*

Lyssanne stood frozen, uncertain what to say, what to think. She concentrated on committing Seianelle's words to memory.

"It is both prediction and call," Seianelle said. "It foretells the one with the ability to destroy the shadow which threatens the lands of men, and perhaps its master. More importantly, it is a call for the Child of Light to rise up and do so."

"Who is the—"

"That, Hlyssaunna, is your message. It alone I am commanded, I am permitted, to speak."

Lyssanne sighed, *more riddles*, but nodded.

Seianelle threw back her head and uttered the strangest birdsong Lyssanne had ever heard—between a trill, a growl, and a roar, yet somehow musical.

"While the Way is prepared for your return to the lands of men," she said, "this truth I will grant you, Prince. One shadow cannot guide you through another. To accept a mask over your eyes, expecting it will lead you out of darkness, is folly. Only Light can lead you home."

"I...thank you for your counsel, Wise One," Brennus said.

As he spoke, an echo of sound reached Lyssanne's ears from afar. It rose up, as if from the waters below or from within the cliff. The sound, the *music*, strengthened until it grew as loud as Lord Duncan's hired minstrels. Then, in the midst of a golden flash of flame that wasn't flame, stood the shining musicians who'd guarded the cave.

Lyssanne clutched Brennus's arm.

Like fluid marble, the creatures bowed, first to Seianelle, then to the humans.

"The Neigeans will play you a portal back to your companions," Seianelle said.

"Neigeans?" Lyssanne asked, her heart trembling.

"My guardians. They live in snow-covered regions wherever my gateway is found. They descend from their icy mountaintops only when travelers approach the Way." Seianelle rose to her full height. "You came to me on the last night they shall ever inhabit the mountains of Lyrynn. The Way of the Stupasce cave is no more."

The Neigeans lifted new instruments to their lips—these of a fiery golden metal flickering with life. Once again, their music created in Lyssanne the need to move. However, this was no enslavement of limb, but a bursting of uncontainable joy. Flames

343

swirled from the mouths of the horns and formed an upright ring, tall as Seianelle.

"Pass through the ring of song," Seianelle said. "Pass from my realm to yours." When none of them moved, she laughed. "Understandable. You have suffered much to reach me. Fear not, Hlyssaunna. The power of your King is at work in me, as in you."

"Thank you, Seianelle," Lyssanne said. "May the King's favor forever shine upon you." She stepped forward, but a hand upon her shoulder stopped her.

"Allow me." Brennus drew his sword and stepped through the circle of heatless fire.

~

Liquid air oozed over Brennus. He pushed through the center of the ring of flame as if through a taut membrane that was more presence than substance. One step stretched into a lifetime. His feet sank into the soft grass of Lyrya. Reina stood mere paces away. He'd taken but three strides, when Jarad's voice filled his ears.

"That's it? That's the message we've been waiting for all this time? A poem!"

As Brennus turned, Lyssanne emerged from a distortion of air no more distinct than a heat haze. "It wasn't a poem," she said, voice heavy from the lateness of a night bloated with tension. "It was a prophecy. The King has often given such predictions in rhyme."

"Lyssanne," Reina said, "come, sit. You are paler than my coat or Serena's feathers."

"Oh, Reina!" Lyssanne rushed forward and flung her arms about the unicorn's neck.

"What has happened, child?"

"I, I shall tell you, but first..." She turned and approached the dove nestled in the grass nearby. She curtseyed as low as she once had to Brennus. "Your Majesty."

The dove cooed.

"I'm sorry," Lyssanne whispered. "I've brought you such misery, such disaster."

Serena ruffled her feathers and shook her beak from side to side.

"We shall keep you safe, and…" Lyssanne rubbed a hand across her eyes. "If we can, find a way to undo this spell."

"Ah," Reina said, "you have discovered the truth."

"You knew?" Lyssanne spun to face her. "You knew and never told me?"

"'Twas Serena who called me to you," Reina said. "She commanded my silence."

Lyssanne sighed as if resigned to yet another secret kept from her by one she'd trusted.

And she had come to trust Brennus.

It was a testament to that trust or to the effects of the simurgh's and faeries' tidings, that not one of Brennus's companions inquired after the whereabouts of his horse.

While Lyssanne and Jarad recounted the day's events, Brennus cleared the ash from their previous campfire. He said little, except to greet the unicorn and, before setting off to find wood, pay formal homage to the be-feathered queen of faeries.

What did Serena know? What had she seen during their travels together, that interminable summer? He'd been careful to transform far from Reina's sight, but a bird could observe, concealed, where a unicorn could not.

Upon his return to camp, he kept his back to the dove, busying himself with the fire.

"Who do you think it's about?" Jarad asked. "Who's that *Child of Light?*"

Lyssanne leaned against Reina's side, folding and unfolding a corner of Brennus's mantle as if the answers lay hidden there. "Perhaps…Queen Serena? Faeries are heavenly creatures, in their way. The spell trapped her in the mortal form of a dove." She stared at the cloth. "But why did the King go to all that trouble to give *me* such a message, and in so cryptic a fashion?"

"Yeah," Jarad said. "Olivia already told us about her. I mean, of course the queen of faeries is somebody who could stop evil. So, why all the mystery?"

"Perhaps there is something He wishes me to do, some clue hidden in the verses." Lyssanne sighed. "Am I meant to somehow break the spell?"

"This is dark magic, Lyssanne," Reina said. "Likely, only its caster can lift it."

"Then, has she any hope?"

"There is always hope," Reina said.

"I'd thought," Lyssanne said, "the message would reveal the King's wishes for my destination and purpose." She rested her head against Reina's flank. "Or, failing that, what reason the sorceress had for wishing me harm."

"What if the prophecy's about you?" Jarad said. "All that Child of Light stuff. You know, the thing you do with light, like with those snow people?"

Lyssanne laughed, shaking her head. "I'm not trapped in my mortal form. My only form *is* mortal. Besides, I'm but the daughter of a blacksmith, not born of Heaven."

Brennus stiffened as Jarad walked over to the fire and tossed in a stick he'd bared of bark. So, this was the prophecy that prompted Venefica to target Lyssanne before her birth, before the Light-Wielder could pose a threat. Still, how could she have known of it? And why suspect Lyssanne as that child?

"What are your thoughts, Reina?" Lyssanne asked.

"The message was for you. Such tidings are meant only for the judgment of the hearer." She flicked her tail at a fly, sending it buzzing toward Brennus. "I was not among your party."

"What d'you think it means?" Jarad asked, glancing at Brennus.

"It all sounds like nonsense," Brennus said. The more Lyssanne learned of the hidden matters surrounding her life, the more danger found her.

"But you don't even believe in the King of All Lands, do you?" Jarad snapped.

"Jarad," Lyssanne said. "If you ask for an opinion, you must respect the answer."

"Sorry," Jarad said. "I think I'm just tired."

"We are all weary," Brennus said. "It is past time we take our rest."

"What did Seianelle mean," Jarad asked. "All that talk of shadows and masks?"

Brennus stared into the fire. The simurgh's words had played upon his mind since they'd stepped through the ring of flame. "More nonsense," he said then clapped the boy on the shoulder. "See to your blankets. I shall keep watch for what remains of the night." He strode to his pile of gear and retrieved a dagger and whetstone, needing something to occupy his hands, if not his thoughts.

"Perhaps Mr. Fescue has a book that could tell us another way to break the spell." Lyssanne walked around the fire to Brennus. "We could return to Avery Hall for a few days' rest, then journey back to his tower." She held his mantle out, half-folded.

"Keep it," he said. "The night is chill."

"I have blankets," she murmured, placing the cloth beside him. "You have only this."

As she passed him to lay out her bedding, he snapped his gaze to her face. She was in pain again. The curse, in its milder form, had seized hold of her sometime during the night. She'd said nothing of it, but he'd learned to read the signs.

After all she'd just endured, she should be crumbling or at least resting in the care of her companions, not pouring out her kindness upon him.

Within half an hour, the camp lay in deep repose. Throughout his patrols and aimless piddling, Brennus's gaze strayed to Lyssanne's curled form. At last, he ceased resisting and simply watched her sleep.

She thought him a hero, a knight of greatest honor. Her eyes had shone with the sentiment when she'd returned from the land of the FAE. For the first time in his life, he wished above all else—above even the removal of his curse—that he could be the man she thought him.

"You've given me reason," he whispered, "more than family allegiance, country, honor, or even love of my grandmother. However long this curse leaves me of life, I shall be that man."

And for however long that might be, he must live with the pain he'd caused her every day since he'd set eyes upon her. That was a penance far worse than any a sorcerer, warlord, or avenging faerie could devise.

~

The next day, Noire perched in the treetops, as Lyssanne's party searched for him. Two long years, he'd watched her thus, noting the multitude of changes life and Venefica wrought upon her. Through it all, she'd retained her character—loyal to friends, compassionate to those who harmed her, and above all, unfailing in her will to survive and serve her King. She saw light in places that had known only darkness. Including him.

"Do you think he is well?" Lyssanne asked. "He was more reticent than usual last night, and oh, he seemed so forlorn."

"He is strong, child," Reina said. "I am certain you've nothing to fear for his sake."

"Maybe he's scouting the land," Jarad said. "There's no sign of him in the woods."

"He left no word," Reina said. "Half the day is spent, I think his return unlikely."

How true, her words. He'd chosen his coarse in the night. He would watch Lyssanne only while she lingered here. When she departed, he wouldn't follow. He would fly away—to where, he cared not—but he wouldn't return to Venefica. Not ever.

His choice would forever end his own quest. His family's one hope died here. If only he could sever the bond his oath had forged with Venefica…To survive, Lyssanne would need greater aid than Reina or Jarad could provide, but he was more harm to her if he remained. He would not be Venefica's weapon again.

Throughout the afternoon, Lyssanne alternated searching and waiting for a man who would never come. He should leave now, but couldn't tear his gaze from the sight of her. He would remember every curve of her cheek, the way her eyes shone in the firelight, the wonder in her voice atop Duncan's tower, her delicacy and grace. She, alone, held what passed for his heart in her tiny hands.

"Come, child," Reina said, lowering herself so Lyssanne could mount. "Few hours remain of this day. We must move on, unless you wish to camp here another night and await your young prince."

"No," Lyssanne said, her voice thick. "He's gone, and he won't return." She stared at the mountains. "If he'd meant to do so, he would have made his intentions known…to one of us."

He'd hurt her, again. Whatever pain his leaving caused, 'twould be far worse if he stayed.

Farewell, Lyssanne. You will forever shine in my memory. The only true light I've known.

A sudden tingle ran beneath his feathers, a pain sharp as loss, cold as regret.

Something thumped on the ground just below him. He leaned forward, expecting a rabbit or fox. Instead, he found a small cask, covered in red and black runes.

Ice gripped his heart. The oni!

Venefica was strong enough to transport them, and she'd used him to do so! Acting as a conduit, their oath-bond had pulled the most fearsome of her minions into Lyssanne's presence.

But the creatures couldn't escape their vessel, lest external hands open the cask. Perchance no one would see it.

"Wait, Lady Lyssanne," Jarad said. "You've forgotten something."

No!

Lyssanne shaded her eyes. Jarad was pointing to a small, cylindrical shape beneath a tree.

He went to the object and lifted it in both hands. Lyssanne dismounted and joined him. How could she have overlooked something nearly the length of his torso? The object resembled a vase or urn, covered in red and black markings.

"What is it?" she asked.

"It isn't yours? A gift from Lady Avery or something?"

"I've never seen it, or its like," she said.

"Think it belongs to Prince Brennus?" he asked. "Maybe he dropped it or, or left it for us. He could've left a message inside." He stared at the object as if to read answers on its surface.

"If he wished to leave word, he would have simply spoken to us." Why though, after all they'd shared, leave without farewell? Had she somehow offended him? Had Jarad, perhaps with his impertinent questions?

Reina snorted and tossed her head, as Jarad gripped the top of the cask.

With a sudden, loud caw, a dark shape fluttered down from the treetops to circle them.

Talons of a nameless dread pierced Lyssanne's heart. "Jarad, I don't think you should—"

He popped the lid off the cask. It flew from his hands with such force, it knocked him off his feet. Two dark, silvery forms billowed out like plumes of smoke, then flew at Jarad.

Lyssanne hurled herself in front of him. Time slowed, as one of the creatures came for her. It halted within inches, a faceless mass of liquid pewter resembling a wispy, ragged cloak slung over a peg—a cloak with a frayed hem and gleaming claws that reached for her throat. Then, it was upon her.

The claws locked around her neck, piercing her skin and stifling her breath. She struggled to scream, to speak, even to whisper. The working of her throat only drove the claws deeper. She must call upon the faeries, give them authority to help her. She must call upon Light Himself to intervene. She must…she must…

A flutter and a raven's frantic call reached her fading senses. What was it she'd been thinking? Something she wanted? Needed? Perhaps she should try to wrest the pain from her throat, but she had not the will to move.

Her mind numbed. Where was she? Who was she? A part of her—identity, will—was suddenly ripped away. That severing, far worse than the piercing at her throat, tore a reflexive scream from her soul—a scream her body could not loose.

The ripping within her mind ceased, and she fell.

She lay on her back, her head slung to one side. A cask stood mere paces away. Something crashed behind her head, then flames leapt up, licking the sky. Heat buffeted her arms and neck, as the fire drew nearer. Still, she couldn't summon the will to move. She no longer cared even to scream. None of that was of importance. There was only the languor, the peaceful nothing, spreading through her.

A dark shape floated above her, stirring her hair. It spread out between her and the fire. A bird? Black wings beat against red flame, an omen of hovering death. Would she be swept away to meet it on those ebony feathers?

A sudden vibration shook the ground under her cheek. A blur of gold and white flashed beneath the bird's wings. Hooves?

Screeching, one of the silvery creatures returned to its cask. It was half in, half out, when that flash of gold—indeed a hoof—crashed down on the lid, crushing the creature and its vessel.

Feet ran to and fro in front of her face. A blanket snapped and waved, beating at the flames. At last, the fire dwindled, and the black shadow of the bird beat the air and flew upward.

Her eyes burned, but she could only stare ahead.

An equine face bent to nuzzle her, managing only to roll her head about. "Can you speak, child?" the unicorn asked.

She tried, but her efforts brought forth only unfeeling tears.

"Rest, child," the unicorn said. "We will help you. Serena will know what to do."

"She's gone," a boy's voice said. "That creature, the other one, it took Queen Serena. I tried to shoot it, but the arrow went right through." His hands shook her shoulder. "What did that thing do to Lady Lyssanne?"

Lyssanne? Yes, that was her name.

"I know not." The unicorn's voice sounded as heavy as Lyssanne's body. "She is trapped, somehow, within her mind. I'd thought Serena could call forth the FAE, but..."

A breeze fluttered Lyssanne's hair again. A dark bird landed in front of her.

"Go away, crow," the unicorn said, nudging the bird with her hoof. "There is no feast for you here. Nor will there be."

The bird croaked and pecked at the hoof, its feathers standing out in all directions. It hopped to one side, then settled and turned toward Lyssanne.

"Begone, I say." The unicorn swatted at the bird again.

It dodged her swipes, each time landing nearer Lyssanne's face, seeming to stare into her eyes. Finally, the unicorn just let it sit there.

Lyssanne remained immobile—with the boy, the unicorn, and that strange bird keeping vigil—until dusk began to darken the world.

A sudden hiss and the odor of acid filled the air. The raven leapt aside, away from the smoking heap that had been a cask. Sizzling, the vessel crumbled to ash.

Lyssanne blinked stinging smoke from her eyes. Blinked? She could move! Memory flooded back. She opened and closed her mouth a few times before she could whisper, "Reina?"

"Oh, child, thank the King!"

"Lady Lyssanne!" Jarad said. "You, you…"

"I know." She coughed, weakness stealing her breath. Jarad lifted her at the shoulders. "Wait," she whispered, fingers pressed to her injured throat. "Let me rest."

Before lowering her back to the ground, he handed her a water-skin.

"We must tell the faeries about Serena," Lyssanne said. "I, I couldn't save her."

Sunlight faded, mirroring her heart. The campfire cast a glow over Reina, the raven, and the trees behind them. A sudden, mighty twitch shook the raven, and…it began to change.

Its wings stretched like molasses candy, growing slimmer, paler. The raven threw back its head, and that, too, changed. Its entire body was growing into a misshapen…something. Within moments, it was over.

In the raven's place, sat Prince Brennus.

24

SERPENT'S TRUTH

*N*othing moved. Nothing made a sound. Lyssanne's heart didn't even beat in her ears. Then, Jarad's cry shattered the silence.

"Shapeshifter! Sorcerer!" He rushed around the campfire and hefted his bow.

Reina backed away from Brennus. Lyssanne levered herself up and managed to stand just as Jarad nocked an arrow, aiming it at Brennus's chest.

"Jarad, no!" Lyssanne took a few unsteady steps toward him. "Whatever we've just seen, whatever it means, *that* isn't the answer."

"He's a sorcerer!" Jarad said again, anger replacing the fear in his voice.

Brennus lifted his hands out to his sides, staring at Jarad. "I am no sorcerer." His soft words ended on a sigh heavy as a millstone. "What I am is far worse."

"We know what we saw," Jarad said. "You were a bird, a raven."

"Yes."

"A spell?" Lyssanne said. "It must have been a spell. Like Serena."

"Then, why's he human now?" Jarad asked, arrow and gaze still trained on Brennus. "How'd he break it?"

"Think, Jarad. He detests magic," she said. "One of those creatures must have—"

"It wasn't the creatures," said Brennus. "They do not possess the ability."

Jarad's bowstring creaked, and Lyssanne's heart took a pause.

As if in the presence of a ferocious animal, Brennus eased his elbows onto his knees then rested his head in his hands. "It is a spell, though, a curse."

"Who did this to you?" Lyssanne asked, taking a step toward him. "When? Surely not Seianelle, or those Neigeans?"

"The curse is generations old. Hereditary." He spoke in the flat tones of one resigned to the ice instruments' spell. "I was on a quest to free my family line of it. A quest that has failed."

"You said you're on a quest for some lady…Lady Effie," Jarad said. "Or was that a lie?"

"I am…was." Brennus looked up. "I shall tell you…everything…but, Jarad, either shoot me or lower that bow."

"Oh, you would like that," Jarad said.

"You'll only give your arms cramps if you remain thus." Brennus blew out a breath. "I will not harm you."

"That's what the two-headed snake told Lady Lyssanne. Just before it tried to choke her!"

"If such were my intention, I've had ample opportunity to do so."

"His words are truth," Lyssanne said. "How often have our lives rested in his hands? Let his past actions speak for him."

Jarad lowered his bow but kept it in hand, still eyeing the prince. "Tell us."

"As I said, the curse was cast upon the heirs of my house generations ago. Once the title passes to a man, or boy, he falls beneath its spell. By day, to take the form of a raven—by night alone, the man he truly is."

Lyssanne gasped. She took another step toward him, but Brennus lifted a hand, turning her way for the first time.

"No…" Jarad said. "No, we've seen you, she's spoken to you, during the day."

"Only at a distance," Brennus said, "in shadow."

"What does that have to do with—"

"It is an illusion." Brennus waved a hand. "But that's another tale altogether."

"What of your quest?" Lyssanne asked. "Why has it failed? Perhaps we can help."

A bitter syllable that might have been a laugh escaped Brennus's throat, and he stood. Jarad's bow snapped into position, trained on him.

"Just stretching my legs," Brennus said. "Here."

He unbuckled his sword belt and held it out. When Jarad made no move toward it, Brennus let it drop to the ground.

"The lady...her name, her true name, is Venefica." Brennus hung his head. "I sought her aid in breaking the curse. I'd come to understand that I couldn't succeed where my forefathers had failed. Not by their methods."

"How could this lady help?" Lyssanne asked. "Is she a faerie?"

He laughed, fully, this time. "Far from it." He rested his hands at his waist and turned away. "It is she who sent the oni."

"The what?" Jarad asked, his bow again dragging on the ground.

"The creatures from the cask. Soul-stealers, or so they are called. Nothing can truly steal a soul." He'd begun to babble, his words tumbling over one another. "The oni have the power to take one's identity, leave a person mindless. They steal the capacity for rational thought, rob their victim of the will to choose, to resist."

"And," whispered Lyssanne, "make you not care that they are doing so."

"Yes," He scrubbed a hand across his face then let it fall. "They leave the victim unaware he is even human." He spun to face her. "No one should suffer such a fate."

"You knew what they would do," Jarad said. "You knew and—"

"Tried to stop it," Lyssanne said. "It was you, flying over us. I heard you cry out. Then, with the fire...You tried to shield me."

"It was all I could do."

"But why?" Jarad said. "Why'd you bring them here? If you don't mean us harm?"

"I didn't bring them, though she used me to do so." His gaze burned into Lyssanne's. "She sent the cask by means of magic. Lady Venefica is a sorceress."

Lyssanne stiffened, the force of his next words slamming into her heart.

"Lady Venefica Mortifer, Keeper of the Shadow Mist. My liege lady."

Breath vanished from Lyssanne's lungs. The world fell in upon itself, constricting until it consisted of none but her and Brennus.

"I pledged myself to her service two years ago," Brennus said. "Since then, by day or night, you have scarcely been out of my sight."

"Me? You...you *watched* me?"

"Yes." He stepped closer. "It was part of the bargain, the oath I made to her in exchange for the lifting of my family curse. I was her spy, but no longer. Never again."

"No, you couldn't have." It was incomprehensible. This prince of knights who had so often saved her life couldn't be..."Sh-she attacked Cloistervale. You wouldn't—"

"I did," he said. "She can't see you from afar, save through my eyes or those of a creature ensnared in the Mist. I have served as her spy since just before your illness began...and I've done worse."

"Why?" Lyssanne whispered. "What has Cloistervale done to earn your loathing?"

"They are nothing to me."

"You swore to help her destroy them!"

"No, I vowed to help her avenge her family. I care nothing for her grudge against those peasants, nor did I care about her war with you. Then."

"What war?" This discussion was taking too many turns. Lyssanne vowed to have all the answers, here and now. She could unravel their meaning later. "Why would this Lady Effie, or Venefica, be at war with me? I've never even heard of her."

"She believes you are the one Seianelle's prophecy foretold."

"What? That's...impossible." Lyssanne struggled to maintain a hold on her splintering wits. "No one knows about that. Seianelle only told us yestereve."

"He is right," said a smooth voice from behind.

Lyssanne spun to find Olivia fluttering near the fire. "Oh, Olivia! Please forgive me. Serena...I couldn't save her. Those creatures—"

"Have taken her to the witch Venefica," Olivia said. "There was nothing you could do."

Lyssanne's hand flew to her mouth. The queen of faeries, in the hands of the sorceress who had killed her daughter, murdered Lyssanne's own father?

A sizzle drew Lyssanne's gaze toward Reina. Jada hovered above the unicorn's head.

"Let us not waste time on what we can't change," Jada said. "She knows where you are. You have to get moving."

"They are safe enough until morning, I think," Olivia said. "Venefica won't attack again." She glared at Brennus. "At least, she cannot use him to do so at night."

"You knew?" Lyssanne whispered. "About, about him?"

"About the curse, yes. I suspect the bargain he struck has forged a link to the sorceress, a foothold she can use when the darkness of his curse is in effect. As to the rest, we know what you know. Had I been aware of the depth of his treachery, well..."

"Yeah," Jada said. "That has to be dealt with, too. But first, there are things Lyssanne must know." She glanced at Olivia. "Things she should have known long ago." She darted toward Brennus and hovered nose-to-nose with him. "As much as I'd like to reduce you to a pile of charred feathers, here and now, you have information we need."

She jabbed a finger into his chest, green sparks sputtering, then dying, at her fingertips. Brennus leaned backward, breath hissing out between his teeth. The sparks sputtered twice more. Then, with every poke of her finger, they sizzled against his dark tunic.

"And," she said, sparks punctuating every word, "you...are going... to...give it."

Olivia cleared her throat.

With a grunt, Jada floated back to her captain's side, leaving Brennus's tunic front smoking. "You were saying, O?"

"Yes, well," Olivia said. "The man may be a traitor, but he spoke true a moment ago. You were not the first to hear the prophecy of the Light-Wielder. That vision was given long before your birth, revealed to a devout faerie. Somehow, the sorceress learned of it and bent her every effort to discovering who it foretold. She settled upon you."

"Why?" Lyssanne tensed. "It isn't about me. I'm no heaven-born being, trapped in a mortal body. She was mistaken." Sudden tears filled the corners of her eyes. "That? That's why she attacked my family? She was wrong! The Princess Tria, my father, they died for nothing!"

"She was not wrong."

"But, Olivia—"

"Lyssanne, the gifts of your fathers drew her eye upon you. First, because of the gift your mortal father bestowed upon you —your name."

"My...?"

"Caelestis," Jada said. "Your father's surname, in the old language, meant *of Heaven*."

"Once she'd singled your family out, Venefica went to your parents," Olivia said. "There, she sensed the gift the Father of us all had placed within you at the moment of your creation."

"Why didn't you tell me?"

"It was forbidden." Olivia sighed. "After the sorceress learned of the prophecy, we FAE and every member of the Royal Elfin Army were forbidden to speak of the vision. The King, alone, reserved the right to reveal it to you, in a way that could not be corrupted or overheard."

"That prophecy," Brennus said, "is why Venefica cast the curse on you."

Lyssanne turned to him. "What curse?"

"Wait," Jarad said. "Now you're saying this witch lady cast the curse? I thought it was generations ago."

"Not his curse," Jada said. "Lyssanne's."

"Your ailment," said Brennus, his gaze trained on Lyssanne. "It was a spell…or a potion. Actually, it was both."

Lyssanne shook her head. "I've never met a sorceress or drank a potion. I just…got sick."

"I was there, Lyssanne. I…watched her do it." He turned away, staring into the flames. "She wanted to hurt you, to weaken you, so you could no longer stop her. She said she was binding your gift, but that part didn't work."

"Stop her? How could I stop her? I saw the Mist, true, but could do nothing about it. I didn't even know what it was."

"You did thwart her. Your Light repels the Mist," he said. "I wondered, even then, if you realized you were doing it, using your gift."

She shook her head again, words deserting her.

"It's true, Lyssanne." He reached out a hand to her then dropped it. "I can see the Light when you…do whatever it is you do. That time with Noel, and…I watched you save Jarad from the Mist more than a year ago."

"Jarad?"

"Me?" Jarad said.

Brennus turned to him. "I saw the Mist attack you." He ran a hand through his raven hair. "It was drawn, I think, to your fears. The other boy was stuck in the tree, and you…Lyssanne freed you from it."

"The day I saved Gavan," Jarad said, sinking to the ground as if he'd been struck.

"What?" Lyssanne hastened to Jarad's side, but he kept speaking.

"That Shadow Mist stuff, it makes people sadder, scared, or mad, right?" He didn't wait for an answer. "Remember that day we came to visit? I'd started being angry all the time, and that day, you made me climb the tree, and well…" He spread his hands. "Everything got better after that. I wasn't so afraid anymore."

"You see, Lyssanne, the prince is right." Olivia rested a hand on her shoulder. "Your gift alone can stop the Shadow Mist and its Keeper.

You must return to Cloistervale and confront Venefica Mortifer before it is too late."

"I, I can't go back," Lyssanne said, focusing on the one certainty in this madness. "It is forbidden. I'm in exile."

"Every day that your friends live beneath her rule places them in greater peril of being lost to the King," Olivia said.

"Rule? The Council would never allow—"

"The Council is no more," Jada said. "As is public worship of the King."

"And without Queen Serena," Olivia said, "the restlessness of the FAE will grow worse."

"Can't *you* rescue her?" Brennus's voice was icy as a Neigean's. "You have an entire magical army at your disposal. Surely one witch is no match for the exalted power of the FAE."

"Do you not think we've tried?" Jada shouted. "We went straight there when Serena was taken." She brandished her wand at him. "That's why we weren't here to help Lyssanne, even though she gave us the authority. We, her appointed guardians!"

"Venefica was prepared for us," Olivia said. "She has set spells against nonhumans all over that mountain. We can't get near the place. No supernatural or magical creature can without her permission. Worse, she holds the queen in a cage of iron."

"Iron?" Lyssanne said.

"It is anathema to those born of the King's pure power," Reina said. "Unicorns, faeries."

"Captain…" Jada said.

"I feel it." Olivia waved her wand and began to shrink. "We must go. Rest tonight and make your preparations."

"You're leaving?" Lyssanne squeaked. "Now? But—"

"We shall find you again soon," Olivia said, "and will help in every way we can." She clasped Lyssanne's hands in miniature fingers. "Even in war, you are never alone."

The pressure of her fingertips lingered after she'd vanished.

Lyssanne stood for an age, staring into the space where Olivia had been. At length, she blinked stinging yet dry eyes and walked away from the campfire. She needed to think.

"Lady Lyssanne," Jarad called.

She held up a hand. It was all the explanation she could give.

"Let her be," Reina said.

She wandered toward the mountains. Well away from the pass, she sank to her knees and prayed. Short, simple, containing the essence of her entire being. "I need you."

She slipped from her knees and sat, legs folded to one side, staring at nothing, thinking of nothing and of everything. Night deepened, stars rose, and there she remained.

A shadow fell across the patch of moonlight in which Lyssanne sat.

"I've wounded you," Brennus said, "in so many ways. You did nothing to deserve it. You were no enemy of mine, sought no fight, harmed no one."

She pushed to her feet and turned to face him. "Please, you needn't—"

"I do not ask for your forgiveness, much as I wish it. I could never be worthy." He spread his hands. "I, who do not deserve the name of knight."

"Don't say such things." She cleared her throat. "You are a man of honor. How often have you saved my life? And, I daresay, those of countless others? Your word is ironclad and—"

"Oh yes, I keep my word. Look what that has done to you."

"So, you were her spy. 'Twas not you who did me harm. You say that is finished, and I do forgive you. I'm certain my heart shall soon follow my will in this."

He stepped closer. "Lyssanne…"

"It will all sort out, you'll see. Tomorrow, we'll start back for—"

He pressed his fingers to her lips. "Don't tell me your plans. If I don't know them, neither can Venefica."

"But you said you'll not spy for her again."

"Never. Not willingly, but she has ways even I do not know. And the Shadow Mist...She's kept it from me thus far, but if she suspects betrayal, she won't hesitate to use it. Then, not even my thoughts would escape her."

"I need your help," she whispered. "We aren't certain we know the way to—"

"If I go with you, she will find you." He looked toward the campsite. "Fly from me, Lyssanne. That is the greatest service I could do you, to never see you again." He turned back to her. "Only promise me you won't go near your homeland." He stared into her eyes, his voice breaking. "If you return, she will destroy you."

"Where could I go?" Hugging her arms, she paced away from him, then back again. "She found me even at Avery Hall."

"Because of me," he growled.

"She could find me anywhere. You said yourself, she has ways." Lyssanne hung her head. "Shall I never be safe again?"

Brennus moved without sound. He bent close, his brow nearly brushing hers. His breath stirred her hair as he placed a finger beneath her chin and lifted her face to his. "Had I the power, I'd slay her myself to free you. She'd see it in my eyes before I had the chance." He brushed a strand of hair from her cheek. "She may still be able to use my sight, but this I promise you. No harm will ever again befall you by my hand or my word."

Lyssanne dropped her gaze to his shoulder, her heart throbbing in her throat.

He laughed beneath his breath, a small, bitter sound. "Now, when you'd finally be safe in trusting me, for once, you cannot."

She parted her lips to protest, but he covered them.

"However much you might wish to, your face reveals your heart's truth."

"How can you know what I feel, when I do not? I meant it when I said I forgive you. 'Tis just"—she drew in a long breath—"I know not what you wish of me...or," she murmured, "what I should want of myself."

"Lyssanne."

She stepped back. "Forgive me, but you contradict your own words, Highness. Once, you told me I should trust no one, least of all you. That very night, you'd saved my life, yet you said I should fear you. Now, you admit betraying me ever since I've known you, and you wish me to trust you? What has changed?"

"Everything." He sliced the air with a hand. "My entire world is tossed on end, now, when it is too late." His head jerked toward the mountains. "When you vanished from that landslide, I thought I'd lost you." He cleared his throat. "Then, after we saw the simurgh, I realized the only way to save you *was* to lose you, to leave you. Now I, I don't know if even that will suffice."

Had he just made a declaration of love? Lyssanne couldn't contemplate that at present. Her emotions were too raw. She latched onto the one statement her mind could manage. "You saw the landslide? Were you a, a bird, watching it happen?"

"I saw it, watched it, I…" He crossed his arms. "I caused it."

"You…" She stared up at him, a nervous laugh bubbling forth. "You couldn't have. I tripped over a branch. Jarad said that dislodged some rocks and triggered it."

"A branch I put there, where I knew you wouldn't be able to see it." He rubbed the back of his neck. "The night before, I slipped past your camp and piled those rocks in the midst of the pass, wedging the branch beneath them for precisely that purpose."

"But Jarad might have—"

"I knew he would see the branch and step clear of it. You forget, Lyssanne, for months I watched the two of you traipse through all manner of terrain."

"You…set that up…for me? But if Cusith hadn't spirited me away, if all those rocks had fallen upon me, I might have…No, I *would* have been killed."

He merely stared at her.

"You…*tried*…to kill me?" Her hand flew to her mouth. She backed away, whispering, "Why?"

"Orders."

"Orders!" She breathed the word as if it were a poisonous fume. Unable to tear her eyes from his face, she continued backing away.

"I gave my word of honor."

"Your vow to that...Venefica," she said.

"I made that vow before I knew you."

"And you never break your word." It was a statement, flat as Seianelle's plateau.

"I never have, no." He sighed. "Nor has keeping my word ever come at so high a cost."

"What has it cost you?" The question was bitter acid. "Time, perhaps?"

"It has cost *you* everything," he said. "And cost me your trust. That is a price too high."

"My trust? We were friends. I thought that you, that you..."

"Cared for you?" He gripped the sides of his head then flung both hands toward her. "I did, I do care for you." His words rushed out like tree sprites fleeing a fire. "I hadn't intended to go through with it, but I was angry. You'd left Avery Hall, so I set the trap—not to kill you, to frighten you. But she—"

"No." Lifting her hands, Lyssanne at last freed her gaze from his. "No, I can't..."

She turned, but he caught her arm. His hand trembled, rigid muscles quivering in his forearm as if restraining his strength, barely. Lyssanne pulled free and fled on shaking legs.

She ran past the campsite, past Jarad rising to his feet and calling her name. She fled into the wood, heedless of the darkness or the tangled branches snatching at her hair and skirts. At last, her wobbling legs no longer able to hold her, she fell to her knees, shaking all over. Then, the tears came.

For an age, she huddled there, unable to breathe despite the great ragged gasps rocking her body. Each shudder further exhausted her, wave upon wave assaulting her even after the tears ran dry.

Weak from treading water in the bottomless river of pain and fear her heart had become, she lay on the ground. All strength and emotion had seeped into the soil with the last of her tears. Gradually, her mind recalled who and where she was and that, by some miracle of the King, she still lived.

How could her heart be lost to a man who had gone to such lengths to kill her? Lyssanne gasped. She *loved* him. Had for some time.

She hadn't allowed herself to admit it. For, how could he, a prince, love her in return? But this—that the man she loved could have, even for a moment, wanted her dead—'twas a pain worse even than the curse that had stolen her life.

After a time, another thought intruded. He didn't have to tell her what he'd done. She would never have known. If he'd wished to continue betraying her, he would have held his silence. Such honesty carried a measure of honor that, itself, was worthy of trust. Wasn't it?

At once, she knew what she must do. She rose, scrubbed at her face with the hem of her sleeve, and went to join the others.

Before anyone could speak, she outlined her plan. They would return to Avery Hall, all of them. Brennus would show them the way. If Venefica discovered their whereabouts, so be it. The castle had been defended against her once. This time, they would be prepared.

"I shan't remain there long," she said, then turned to Brennus. "Nor, I think, will I tell you where I shall venture thereafter. The rest, we shall sort out along the way."

As for her trusting Brennus, she would figure that out as well.

25

FEALTY

Fighting to ignore the increasing pain of Venefica's summons, Brennus sprinted toward Duncan's high stables. All the arrangements had been made. With a word, he could set either plan into motion. Now, all he had to do was persuade Lyssanne to change her mind.

Without breaking stride, he flung the stable door wide. "You can't do this," he said, his words plowing through the stench of hay and horse filling the dim enclosure.

Lyssanne turned from Reina's stall at the far end of the aisle. "Brennus? How did you—"

"Lily," he said. "I fair frightened your whereabouts from her when you left the hall." He fixed her with a stare that had withered many a trained soldier. He *would* make her see sense. "Faeries can fend for themselves, and those peasants brought this upon their own heads."

"You heard what Jada said." Lyssanne crossed the distance to him. "They can't help Serena, and my people—"

"They ceased being your people nearly a year ago."

"They are the only family I have left."

"Families do not betray their own."

She sighed and hung her head. "They can't fight her."

"Why you insist on protecting these people who hurt you so badly…"

He struggled to soften his voice. She, after all, was not the object of his ire.

"Whatever pain Venefica might cause you, whatever fear I might place in your heart, could never wound your spirit the way your *family* has. Lyssanne…" He grasped her shoulders. "I watched part of you die that day." Oh, how he longed to take her into his arms. "Every time they accused you of failing to try, giving up, or…of all things…sloth, another spark went out in your eyes."

"People say and do things they don't really mean," she said. "Even I didn't know it was a curse. Besides, I've forgiven them."

"They sentenced you to die! How can you forgive that?"

But then, she'd forgiven him.

"No, they sent me into exile."

"In your condition," he said between his teeth, "it is the same thing."

"They didn't realize—"

"They knew precisely what they were doing, Lyssanne." He waved toward Jarad, who had just passed them. "Even this boy was aware of it. That's why they enlisted the entire village in their decision, to assuage their guilt with shared blame. Oh yes, they knew." He hooked a finger beneath her chin and leaned down, inches from her face. "Even I knew."

"You…" She stared up at him, rubbing her arms, then took a step back. "Regardless, I must help them. As a knight, did you not vow to protect those who cannot fight for themselves? Surely, you understand."

"I vowed to defend the innocent, such as you. Those people were not defenseless, Lyssanne." He straightened. "They allowed her power to rule them."

"They didn't know. They couldn't see—"

"You did."

"Only because the King gave me sight."

"He gave them the sight as well." Brennus stared into her eyes. "He gave them you."

Sighing, she turned from him and hefted a bundle from a small stack near the door.

"Lyssanne."

"I understand," she said, her back to him. "You made promises to her. If I do this, it could interfere with having your family's curse broken. I...I don't wish to hurt you, but Aderyn and Mr. DeLivre, the children...and Serena—I *must* help them."

"My counsel is no enemy's ploy designed to thwart you." He rested a hand on each of her shoulders and turned her to face him. "What would be the penalty for violating your banishment? You might have to fight for your life before you ever reach Venefica."

"I have no choice." Her flat tone stabbed at his heart. "You said yourself, even she thinks I'm the one the prophecy foretold."

"I've spoken with Duncan," he said. "I'm still half surprised he didn't clap me in irons after learning everything I've done, but even now he is preparing troops to send to Cloistervale's aid. There is no need for you to go."

"You are sending soldiers?"

"Lastarra is MeMe's homeland as well, and her mother's tidings from court made it clear the realm's queen has fallen to the Mist."

"You speak of Queen Stella's uncharacteristic melancholy since Venefica's visit?"

"That and her all too swift agreement to reinstate Venefica's familial rule over the Cloister Valley." He scrubbed a hand across his chin. "So, Duncan's men will travel under cover of forests, lest Venefica should suspect attack or Queen Stella mistake an army marching through her land as an act of war."

"With what will you arm them?" Her voice held the ghost of a laugh. "What good are swords or arrows against magic?" She looked up at him with shadowed eyes. "What armor can shield them from the effects of the Shadow Mist?" She shook her head. "Your Highness, they can't even see it!" She averted her gaze again. "I can. I, alone. If there is a chance, however small, that I may stop it, I must try."

"You have an amazing gift, but you are no match for her." He huffed. "You can't heal evil." He gave her shoulders a gentle shake. "Venefica is ruthless. You cannot hope to negotiate with her. Even your eloquent words will hold no sway. She fears you more than she fears anything. Lyssanne, she will show you...no...mercy."

Lyssanne closed her eyes. "The King will protect me."

She pulled free of his hands and resumed her packing. As Jarad went to join her, Brennus strode across the stable to Reina.

"You could talk to her," he murmured. "Persuade her not to do this."

"And prevent her from following the King's path?" the unicorn said. "No."

"Is it His plan for her to walk to her own destruction?"

"He never sets us on a course without first seeing to our preparation for the journey."

"No? He just sends his faithful one down a path that can only lead to her death."

"If it does," said Reina, "she will have the truest victory."

"Death? You think she sees it that way?"

Reina pierced him with her sea-deep, blue gaze. "Yes."

"You're wrong, Shining One." He matched her unflinching stare. "I know Lyssanne, perhaps better than anyone. She doesn't wish to die. You'll never make me believe that. I've watched her fight for life too many times."

"True," Reina said. "She wishes to live and be of service as long as the King wills. Yet, if death should find her, she will go to the halls of her King with joy."

"What is my path, then?" he said. "To at last find my way free of darkness, only to stand by and watch as the one true light in this black world is destroyed?"

"Then, you've chosen to acknowledge the reality of the King?"

"That changes nothing!" he said, part growl. "Not for her."

"Meeting you was part of her preparation. You've given her strength and hope."

"Much good it has done her." He stared at his feet, fists digging into his hips. Then, his head snapped up with sudden purpose. "I could stop her."

"You could…"

The rest of Reina's thought hung heavy in the air behind him, as his strides ate up the distance to Lyssanne. "You are set on this?"

"Yes, Brennus," she said.

"Those people are nothing to me, but you have become… significant…in my life." He took her hand. "I cannot permit you to walk into her lair alone. You will be helpless against her traps. She'll know you're coming before you set foot on her mountain." He waited until Lyssanne's full gaze rested upon him. "I won't allow it."

A measure of fear crept into her eyes. "Brennus, please. You can't…"

Oh, yes, he could hold her here if he wished.

"I am going with you."

Her eyes flew wide, sparks dancing like tiny flames within sapphire. "You…?" She flung her arms around him as if on impulse, then pulled away, flushed.

~

Lyssanne settled into a chair facing the hearth, while Brennus paid the innkeeper then bolted the door to their private dining salon. 'Twas a wonder what coins could purchase. She stretched out her legs, thankful to be free of the carriage. As floorboards creaked behind her, she fingered the edges of her cowl. Was it safe?

"No need to hide our faces here," Brennus said, lifting his hood to reveal his eyes. "Clark and Jarad know the signal. I shall open the door to no other." He folded his cloak over one arm and indicated the adjacent chair. "Might I join you?"

Lyssanne tried for a lighthearted tone as she unfastened her cloak and let it fall over her chair back. "Certainly, sir."

"What's amiss?" he asked. "Something weighs upon your heart. I see it in your eyes."

Ah, he did know her well. "I mustn't speak of anything that may give power to darkness," she said, striving to guard her words as the faeries had counseled.

"The Mist hasn't reached this far," he said. "I would remove the shadows from your eyes, but how can I be of service if I know not the trouble?"

'Twas a moment of weakness, but she couldn't prevent uttering thoughts she'd struggled to banish. "It isn't the sorceress I fear, though I know I should. After everything I've endured, I almost feel numb to the prospect of meeting the cause of it all. 'Tis my own inadequacy I dread, to fail everyone, to waste the King's gift."

"Waste His gift? Lyssanne, you waste nothing."

"I've survived only by His grace and the aid of friends. What if my body should fail me? I must do this, but I…" She stood, unable to face him. "I fear I haven't the strength."

With a gentle but firm tug, he turned her to him. "Then, take mine." He placed her hand atop his wide shoulder and held it there. "Let my shoulders bear the weight of your burdens. Let me lift you, my legs bear you wherever you need go."

He slid from his chair onto one knee, his free hand resting at the hilt of his sword. For the first time, she was able to truly look into his eyes.

"Let my blade clear the obstacles from your path," he said, "my life be a shield to yours. If you must go into battle, let me be your armor."

She stared at him, as a complex rhythm rattled the chamber door. "You would openly set yourself against this one to whom you've vowed your life in service? I could not ask it of you."

"I have already broken that oath, every day since we left Stupasce."

"But…how?"

He rose, again looming over her. "I let you live."

Lyssanne picked at her meal, Brennus's fireside admission consuming her thoughts. She struggled to heed her companions' conversation. Brennus, too, had said little.

"Good thing our carriage has that starburst-shaped scratch on the door," Jarad said between mouthfuls. "Or I wouldn't be able to tell it from every other plain black coach in the carriage house. Why didn't Lord Avery loan us one with an insignia or at least house colors?"

"So we'll escape notice, I suspect," Clark said. "I must say, I'm rather enjoying all this stealth and strategy—playing the role of manservant, sneaking our noble folk past potential enemy spies. Still stunned Lord Avery chose me, though."

"Well," Jarad said, ducking his head, "after I told him you'd do anything to protect Lady Lyssanne, and since you'd kept how she saved you a secret even from him, he said your loyalty was unquestioned."

Clark's hearty chuckle made Lyssanne smile. He'd certainly accepted the involvement of magic in their adventure with admirable calm.

"How long must we travel concealed?" Jarad asked.

"Until we reach the forests south of Cloistervale," Brennus said. "Lyssanne will need all the rest we can afford her. Remember to keep the curtains drawn once we leave Lyrya. Should anyone ensnared in the Mist see either of us, Venefica will be instantly alerted."

"That reminds me, Highness," Clark said, "shall I meet you in your chamber at sun-up?"

"Earlier. I must don the falconer's hood before I transform, lest she discern my location."

"Then what?" Clark said with a snort. "Secure you atop the carriage with the baggage?"

"No, I'll ride in the driver's box with you. Should sunlight leave my body during our travels, I would transform anew into a shadow of myself. In that state, I'd pass through even the roof of the carriage, exposing Lyssanne to Venefica's sight."

A shock of memory trembled through Lyssanne. "You've watched me thus, before. In Noel's sickroom, were you...?"

"Yes."

"In the library, I felt your eyes, and..." A chill swept over her. "It was you? In...in the wood near Mr. Fescue's tower?"

He admitted to all of it, spinning her a harrowing tale of botched spells and betrayal.

Lyssanne shivered. He'd certainly been thorough in his role as spy. She set her spoon down and excused herself, wandering back to her seat before the fire.

As Clark and Jarad took their leave to check on the horses and ready their chambers, Brennus walked up to her. He held out a steaming mug. "Hot tea, my lady?"

"Thank you, Sir Knight." She smiled, hoping to banish heavy thoughts for them both.

"You've accepted my oath of fealty, then?"

His oath? Lyssanne gasped. Of course! His hand upon the hilt of his sword earlier, his subservient posture..."No," she said. "I shall accept your friendship."

He bowed. "That, you have for as long as I draw breath." He slumped into the chair beside hers. "I understand. One oath, I've already broken—"

"You mistake me," she said. "It is not your loyalty I question. It is your loyalty that prevents me." She reached out to cover his hand. "You honor me, but I would not bind you so."

"You are truly a lady, Lyssanne." He raised her hand to his lips, and bowed over it. "How, then, can I assure you of my intentions?"

"If you must pledge fealty to anyone," she said, "make your vow to the King of All Lands. He, alone, is worthy of such loyalty."

"Your King would not have a vow from one such as me."

"He would if you are sincere."

Brennus shook his head. "After all I've done, He would doubtless strike me down for presuming to approach Him. I am not fit to utter His name, let alone serve so great a King."

"None of us are, Brennus." Her heart ached for him, this man who had given his entire life to restore his family and help his people. "He is your King, whether you acknowledge him or no. He is just, but merciful, and forgives all who truly desire to serve Him. He loves you."

"How could He? How can you, for that matter? You should've petitioned Duncan for my arrest the moment we reached Avery Hall."

She shrugged. "You've explained your actions, and I believe you. Even what you did at Stupasce was meant only to frighten me. You could have harmed me many times, but—"

"Oh, I did harm you. I…Lyssanne, I gave Venefica the main ingredient for her potion. I made her curse on you possible." He scrubbed a hand across his face. "All those times you've suffered…If only I hadn't brought her that flower from your hair!"

"What flower?" She set her mug aside, no longer thirsty.

"The morning your curse struck, you told the children a tale. A little girl sat upon your lap and gave you a flower, a rowan blossom."

"Elaiza," she whispered.

"I should have left then, seeing what Venefica was. Anyone who can turn a child's innocent gift into a curse…" He shook his head. "She needed something for her potion, something that would target the spell to you." He sighed. "And I provided it."

Lyssanne forced herself to find voice. "That cannot be undone. What matters, for me, for us all, is what you do henceforth."

Brennus finished his circuit around the camp and settled by the fire to conclude his watch. A fortnight into their journey, and already the distance between villages had grown too great to span in a single day. He glanced up as Lyssanne joined him. "You should be resting."

She shrugged. "So much dozing in the carriage leaves me wakeful at odd hours."

A sudden pop startled them both. Faeries! Could they never be subtle?

"I've come to give you warning," Olivia said. "Some members of the FAE have broken faith with the King."

Lyssanne paled, staring at Olivia as if she'd never seen a faerie. "You're created to serve the King," she whispered. "Faeries wouldn't rebel against Him."

"I wish that were so," Olivia said. "It isn't yet a full-scale revolt, but if matters don't improve, and soon, we could have another faerie war on our hands."

"*Another* war?" said Brennus.

"The first occurred before the Dawning. I thought you knew this. Lyssanne shared a version of the tale at Avery Hall. Years of retelling have altered it a bit, but the essence remains."

Lyssanne turned to Brennus. "'Tis true? I thought the story a mere legend."

"I, too, had heard it as nothing more than a Navvarish children's tale."

"The FAE of old were once divided," Olivia said. "The Thief of Souls ensnared some who despised their lot, a standing between that of men and angels."

"Why?" Lyssanne asked. "That is a place of such high honor."

"They didn't see it thus. We Faeries had fought and died for the King, so why, they asked, should man, who often denied His very existence, be favored above all others? And why were angels granted access to the throne while faeries received only messages and assignments?"

"So, they tried to, what," Lyssanne asked, "overthrow the King?"

"What they thought to accomplish is unknown," said Olivia, "but the ramifications were disastrous and far-reaching. Now, with our queen imprisoned, some again believe the lie that the King's way is weaker and seek to ally with power. With the sorceress and her Mist in the mix, a revolt would be worse than the first war."

"Have many turned traitor?" Brennus asked. "To break fealty is an act worthy of death."

Olivia stared at him. "It is." She looked away. "We've lost fewer than a score, but the allegiance of many is in question. Most are set to await the outcome of this war with Venefica Mortifer."

A chilling thought struck Brennus. "Are the other nophel involved?"

"The who?" Lyssanne asked.

"None but those FAE who've recently fallen...yet," Olivia said.

"Though, other dark creatures roam the fringes of Cloistervale. Few citizens dare venture out at night."

Brennus's jaw clenched. Duncan's men facing a score of fallen faeries, as well as dark creatures and Shadow Mist? He didn't like their chances.

"So much rests on this," Lyssanne said. "Why? I understand their fear for Serena, but—"

"Venefica will move on to engulf other lands in hopeless darkness," Olivia said, "leaving many human spirits enslaved to the Thief of Souls. Our authority to act, our strength, will be greatly diminished. Then, Lyssanne, not even you could stop her."

Lyssanne shivered, despite the warmth of the night. Brennus draped his mantle around her and held her close. "Was that necessary?" he said, his gaze firing darts at Olivia. "She understands the importance of her task. She wouldn't be here, else."

"Yes, it was necessary," the FAE captain said. "Knowledge, as you well know, knight, is a warrior's greatest weapon."

"Olivia," Lyssanne said in a small voice, "what do you think she'll do to Serena?"

"That," Olivia said, "is a question for your princely friend. One Jada and I intended to pose when last we saw you."

"I once overheard Venefica telling her maidservant about a potion she wished to brew, which could increase her power tenfold," Brennus said. "The key ingredient is faerie wings."

Lyssanne paled further. "Is there any way to know if she has done this thing?"

"The potion can only be brewed at the dark of the moon, beneath a cloudless sky," Brennus said. "And the...ingredients, must be freshly severed."

Lyssanne closed her eyes, shuddering. He tightened his hold.

"We have perhaps a fortnight's grace, then," Olivia said.

Lyssanne stood on the terrace overlooking the garden of yet another inn. After passing an hour in prayer, she gave herself over to the King's leading as never before. Whatever cost His path required, she pledged obedience. She trembled, spent after this, her greatest act of surrender.

Wiping away the remnants of worshipful tears, she whispered the last of her prayer.

"I was right about you." Brennus's murmur flowed over her like a cloak of black silk.

She tensed. How long had he been there? So silent was his approach, she might have thought him a shadow. "R-right about what?"

"You are a sorceress."

She gripped the railing before her. "I assure you, I am not."

"But you must be," he said, his breath stirring the back of her hair. "Else, how is it, I have fallen beneath your spell?" He cupped her shoulder. "You've bewitched me, and I have not the will to object."

She laughed. "I think, sir, it is you who are the enchanter, seeking to ensorcel me with pretty words. But you forget, I am a storyteller. A weaver of tales will not be so easily ensnared."

"Would that I had such protection. I have no shield against the magic you wield."

"Truly," she said, facing him. "You must know by now, I have no magic."

"Lyssanne." Her name was a caress, foretelling his fingertips' feathered trail from her cheek to her throat. "Your every deed is magic. I see the light in you. You turn tragedy into hope, weakness into friendship, sorrow into resolve, betrayal into faith. You *are* light."

"Brennus—"

"Your courage shines like the sun."

"Courage?" She had to laugh at that.

"You shimmer with it, even now," he said. "I've watched battle-scarred knights endure less pain without half your strength, seasoned warriors flee when facing far better chances against an enemy. You are the soul of light, and I, a mere shadow in this darkened world."

"What light is in me," she said, longing to shatter the self-loathing in his voice, "is but a reflection of the King's goodness. Like the moon, without Him I'd be cold and devoid of life."

"Even stone may reflect light and heat," he said. "A shadow can only consume."

"I've seen light in you as well. Why, every shadow is evidence of light's presence."

~

Brennus stared into the empty hearth, his thoughts black as the feathers he'd just shed. One town yet to pass through, then they would reach Merchant's Bridge. The sound of Lyssanne's footfalls entering the room sent ice through his blood.

"Leave me," he said, keeping his back to her.

"Brennus? What's—?"

"Lyssanne, please." Her name was a cry for mercy, an agony to speak.

Her footsteps drew nearer.

"The Shadow Mist," he said, his voice hoarse. "It reached for me the moment we entered this inn. 'Tis drawn to my thoughts. If I fall to it, Venefica will sense your presence. And I surely shall fall."

"Oh, Brennus," she whispered. "I shan't leave you to such a fate. What so troubles you as to draw the Mist? Perhaps I may help."

"Help? I've failed my family. You can't undo that."

Her nearness spread warmth along his side. "Why are you so certain you've failed?"

"I am the last of my line," he said. "I shall do what I must to stop Venefica, but in so doing, I condemn my homeland to a tyrant's rule."

"Surely there's another way to break your curse. Is it even a certainty she could have done so? Darkness cannot undo darkness."

"There was only one other option," he said, the words bitter on his tongue. "An impossible option. The nonexistent *noble quest*."

He turned to her and gestured to a chair. If she wouldn't be persuaded to leave his side, he'd share with her the entire sordid tale.

"The last King Xavier was riddled with greed and vice. The disease of self-interest had long run in the veins of my family line, but he was consumed by it. This led him to provoke the sorcerer Blackthorne, though how, precisely, is lost to memory."

"Blackthorne," Lyssanne whispered. "Like the people who now rule Navvar?"

Brennus nodded. "Blackthorne was a warlord, merciless to any who crossed him. He stormed into the throne room and cast a curse upon the royal line, consigning us to take the fitting form of the carrion bird that represented our house, until the line should cease or one of its heirs fulfill a noble quest. He left a raven squawking upon the throne with the king's chain of office shattered on the floor at its feet. A sign, they say, the reign of Xavier was forever broken."

Lyssanne gazed at him, her eyes brimming with a compassion that seared his soul.

"Blackthorne's stipulations were clear," Brennus said. "The heir's quest must be a truly selfless act—a feat he believed no Xavier heir capable of performing. He was right. However honorable a quest may be, if undertaken to break the curse, it results in personal gain. 'Tis a circular riddle with no solution."

"But...you've done that," Lyssanne said. "You saved my life, several times. You had nothing to gain by rescuing me from those creatures."

"Yes I did," he said. "Reina would have skewered me if I'd let the amphisbaena strangle you. And Diornian, the monster in Westerfield?" he said. "I was protecting my honor as a knight, as much as Jarad or anyone else."

"Oh," she whispered. "How old were you when the curse struck?"

"Nine winters," he said. "Shortly after my birth, my father was slain. A farmer claimed to mistake him for a common crow. My uncle inherited the curse. When he died, it passed to me."

"You were just a boy," Lyssanne whispered, tears glittering in her eyes.

"There's more," he said. He may as well tell her all. "Once the curse strikes, we become unable to sire children." He sighed. "And no heir has lived to old age. I likely do not have long."

"Oh, Brennus," Lyssanne reached across the small dining table for his hand. "Put your trust in the King. Surely, He can provide the answer."

"I dare not presume to ask," he said. "I've aided the enemy of His chosen."

"You've also aided me," she said. "The King sent you to save me."

"How can you say such? It was Venefica who sent me."

"The King can guide even a tool of the enemy to bring about good."

"Would that I could see it as you do," he said, staring at their hands, "but you weren't privy to her intentions, or to mine."

"Brennus, I wouldn't have survived if you hadn't been there," she said, 'and I do not speak only of the times you battled creatures."

"I've caused you only fear and pain, Lyssanne. I mocked you, I threatened you—"

"You sheltered me, offered comfort," she said, "the benefit of your wisdom. You gave me strength, yours and...my own. You helped me find, within myself, that which I believed I could never possess."

Brennus's breathing grew difficult. A faint shimmer had settled around his hands as Lyssanne's words worked their magic within his heart. It wasn't what she'd said, but the depth of feeling in her voice. She cared for him.

"Have faith, Brennus," she pleaded, aglow with her gift. "The King will provide a way."

Almost, he could have wept.

Lyssanne sidled closer to the fire. Darkness lay so thick this near Cloistervale, she could taste its dank misery. The village was so bloated with the Shadow Mist, some of the foul fog had seeped into the forest. Thank the King, it couldn't long retain substance without a human host.

And Brennus remained free of its sway.

She hugged her knees, her icy fingers chilling her even through thick homespun skirts. Her gaze fell upon the trees to the north, toward Cloistervale. She sighed. At least they'd made it to this side of the river unharmed.

"Are you ill, Lady Lyssanne?" Jarad asked, settling beside her. "You've been pale since we crossed Merchant's Bridge. Was it the memories of last time?"

"I am well. How could I not feel safe with you and Brennus at my sides?"

He stared at her. "So safe you shivered the entire time we made the crossing?"

She nudged his arm with an elbow. "Not the sort of thing a gentleman should voice."

He snorted.

"You may be approaching a scant thirteen years," she said, "but I can no longer consider you a boy."

Jarad glanced about, doubtless eager for the others' return. Though, he would heed Brennus' orders that Lyssanne never be left alone. She offered silent thanks for that. When each moment could be the final step of one's journey, 'twas best to spend it with those most dear.

Much rustling and snapping of twigs preceded Clark's lumbering into their clearing.

"Since you're back," said Jarad, "I'm off to the river. If I don't wash out these clothes, you'll be able to use them as hammers in your forge."

"Indeed," Clark said, laughing, "that, I might. Only wait a bit. Prince Brennus is down there. I think it best you give the man some time alone with the King."

"The King?" Lyssanne asked, her breath grown shallow.

"He seeks an audience."

"At the river? How do you know?"

"I was lookin' for wood and came upon him patrolling the perimeter," Clark said. "Never seen him fidget like that. He asked how he might approach the King." Clark flopped onto the ground beside Jarad. "Said he felt...well, too rank to enter His presence. I suggested he wash."

"Wash?" Jarad asked.

"Yeah, well," Clark said, "he looked at me as if I'd gone mad. Told 'im the King'd take care of the stench for him, so he can make his pledge in peace."

Lyssanne turned away, a river flowing from her eyes.

∾

Beside the River Esten, Brennus dropped to one knee, prepared to make the greatest vow of his life, a vow more binding than any other...a binding that freed.

"King of all who live," he whispered. "I, most unworthy to be your vassal, beseech you. Take from me that part of my will which keeps me from you."

A sudden burst lit his closed eyelids. Blue-white heat seared him, burning painlessly through to the center of his soul. Drawn as if by unseen hands, he eased into the river. The ash of his former darkness floated away upon its chill waters.

∾

A half-hour later, still damp and silent, he stood in shadow just beyond the camp.

"Speak not of it, Jarad," Lyssanne was saying. "His business with the King is his alone."

Brennus stepped up beside her to reposition a fallen log on the fire. Heat licked at the blackened wood, as Light had eaten away at the weight petrifying his soul—that burden, too, now freely laid at the heart of the Flame, to be consumed in Light's embrace. He expelled a breath; so long it might have stirred the flags over Avery Hall.

"Are you well?" Lyssanne asked, her voice tremulous.

"Yes." He glanced her way. "Oh, yes, I am well." That final word crackled as if it, too, were aflame. Indeed, never had he known he could be so well.

26

SANCTUARY

*L*yssanne pulled the blanket over her eyes to block out the firelight, struggling to force her way into slumber. Weary as she was, her mind and emotions flitted about like birds before a storm. So much had happened...was yet to happen.

"Dear King," she whispered. "Give me strength. Let not my spirit grow faint."

The ghost of a sound vibrated the ground beneath her ear. It grew louder, pounding. Then a swish of leaves and crunch of twigs followed.

She peeked out from her blanket. Something shone white against the trees.

Brennus rose from his crouch by the campfire. "Shining One."

Lyssanne flung off the blanket. "Reina!" She rushed to the unicorn and embraced her about the neck. "How I've missed you!"

"Should you not be sleeping, child?" Reina said.

"I chase it, but slumber flies from me."

"Weighty thoughts, no doubt." Reina nuzzled her hair. "I see our night bird is keeping his vigilance. Ever the soldier."

"Were you successful?" Brennus asked.

"Yes and no. Many forest folk have fled the darkness that has seeped into these wild places. Those who remain have pledged to aid you. Though, I fear I shall be able to carry Lyssanne no nearer the village than the wood behind her cottage."

"Are you certain you can do that much?" he asked. "Already, your eyes show signs of pain. We cannot have you incapacitated, in case Lyssanne should need to flee."

"Very astute, but I am certain," Reina said. "I, too, see something new in your watcher's eyes, a light which never before shone there, like the star seldom found in black sapphire."

Lyssanne gazed up at him. If only she could see his eyes thus. Ah, but that light pulsed in his voice, in the air around him. His gaze weighed upon her, then he ducked his head.

"What's changed, children?" Reina asked.

"I've...pledged my sword, my service, my *life*, to the King of All Lands," he said.

"Then, you are free, at last," Reina swung her head about and whinnied, her horn glittering like faerie sparks. "Still, I smell the raven within you, but you are free of a curse far worse than man's magic can conjure. Knight of true honor, I salute you."

"It is you who honor me, Shining One," he said, offering a bow worthy of the highest courts. "I've done nothing deserving of such praise."

"To break the chains of darkness requires courage," she said. "I suspect you've broken other bonds as well. In severing the bargain you made with Venefica Mortifer, surely you've closed her eyes to your sight."

"Would that your words speak true," he whispered. "Still, we dare not take the risk. By day, I must continue shielding Lyssanne from my eyes and ears."

"A wise plan," Clark said, sitting up in his blankets. "I could carry you off and approach the village by some other route. The road, perhaps?"

"And leave Lyssanne vulnerable? No," Brennus said. "She may need you...and Jarad."

"You can't simply fly off someplace," Lyssanne said. "If the bond is still intact, Lady Mortifer will know you are near." She rubbed at the gooseflesh peppering her arms. "Tomorrow, while you rest beneath the hood, I shall just refrain from speech."

"Lyssanne…"

"It is the only way. Besides, I daresay I shall find conversation difficult, as it is."

~

Late the following afternoon, Lyssanne signaled for a halt. Reina had been sagging for some time, her head drooping in obvious discomfort. They all needed a brief repast. Clark handed out provisions, and Lyssanne ate to maintain strength, but tasted little.

Sizzles and sparks heralded the faeries' arrival. Reina set to whinnying, drawing Olivia and Jada to her side. The faeries hovered about her head, as if in wordless conference. How often had Reina spoken with Serena in like manner?

The faeries eyed the hooded raven then beckoned the group to follow them. Olivia led the little band onward, conversing with Clark and Reina in gestures impossible for Lyssanne's eyes to follow. Near dusk, they reached a point beyond which Reina could not venture.

Lyssanne dismounted and hugged her dear friend, perhaps for the last time.

Olivia took Lyssanne's hand and led her toward Cloistervale, leaving behind Clark and the raven he carried. She and Jada brandished their wands, creating a dome of silence around themselves, Lyssanne, and Jarad.

Olivia wasted no time on pleasantries. "You cannot go directly into the village," she said. "Dark creatures and humans under the influence of the Shadow Mist patrol the streets and wander the perimeter. They swarm even the outlying fields."

"Beware," said Jada, "Venefica has pressed a number of citizens into service, not all unwilling." She fluttered nearer. "However you might long to, you must trust none of them."

A shiver ran through Lyssanne. "What of Aderyn? Mr. DeLivre?"

"We know not where any one person's allegiance lies," Olivia said.

"I must know," Lyssanne said. "We're near my cottage. I recognize that gnarled tree." She moved toward the edge of the dome, uncertain she could pass through it. The green lines of the barrier shimmered into view then faded, returning sound to the forest around her.

"Captain," Jada said, "you can't let her—"

"She needs to see," Olivia said. "Lyssanne, don't leave the cover of trees."

Lyssanne tiptoed toward the edge of the wood. Trees thinned as she climbed the back of Rowan Hill. She peered around a large trunk and froze.

Overgrown grass feathered the rear lawn of her old cottage. Here and there, objects littered the ground. A faint light shone through the kitchen window.

'Twas passing strange, standing in the shadows, gazing upon the place she'd spent all but ten months of her life. The image of her cottage in her memories had seemed more real than this.

Aderyn's voice drifted through the open window. "You know it isn't safe to be out once dark falls."

"Had to make this delivery. For *her*," Madam Sewell said, her words raspy as if she'd aged a decade.

"You had to go there?" Aderyn's voice faltered. "Did you see Willem?"

"No, just the old woman." A chair scraped across the floor. "I dropped off the last gown I altered for her mistress, and she said the lady wanted me to find someone skilled enough to paint that wooden cask."

Paper rustled as Aderyn asked, "I'm to follow these drawings?"

"She said these symbols must be exact. Lady Mortifer wants it painted in three days."

"They know her?" Lyssanne whispered.

"Venefica rules openly now."

Lyssanne nearly cried out at that low murmur, but a hand covered her mouth.

"I didn't intend to startle you," Brennus whispered.

She nodded against his hand, and he removed it.

"You really must make a bit more noise when you approach people from behind."

"Hazard of the profession," he said.

They stood thus for some time, Lyssanne leaning against his solid warmth, listening to her friends speak of things which had been foreign to Cloistervale months before.

Her entire life had been little different, standing on the outside, looking in. However great her efforts to belong here, she never truly had. In this, she and Brennus were much alike. Only, Lyssanne hadn't chosen to live as a mere watcher among those she loved.

Behind her, Brennus stiffened. His arm wound around her waist, pulling her to him, while his fingers again covered her lips. He bent close and whispered, more sensation than sound, "Danger. Move." He clasped her hand and pulled her around, then started running.

Lyssanne had a fleeting glimpse of a hulking, dark shape and the glint of teeth. Then, all her concentration was required to simply remain upright as Brennus pulled her through the trees.

Snarls and high wheezes pursued them. Somewhere along their mindless flight, Jarad, Clark, and the faeries joined them.

"This way!" Olivia yelled.

Sudden hoof beats and a flash of white broke through the trees ahead. "There are two others," Reina said. "I dispatched a third."

A root leapt up to snag Lyssanne's toe, and she lurched. Brennus steadied her as she struggled to draw breath. Still panting, she stumbled onward beside him.

"She knows we're here!" Jarad shouted.

"I think not," Brennus said, matching his pace to Lyssanne's. "If she had, the forest would be swarming with her servants. But she'll know after this."

"Then, you must make your invasion now, before she can prepare," Jada said.

Blood hammered in Lyssanne's ears. No! She wasn't ready! She'd thought she had one more day to prepare. For what, though? How could one prepare to fight vapor and magic?

"Lyssanne is too weary from travel to cross the valley tonight," Brennus said, "let alone climb that mountain. She needs a safe place to rest."

"The faerie ring," Olivia said, buzzing just ahead. "We must get her within it, at once."

"But," Lyssanne said between gasps, "if she knows—"

"A warrior's no good in a fight if she collapses before reaching the battlefield," Jada said.

Reina, who'd been trotting ahead to Lyssanne's right, suddenly flung herself across their path, shouting, "Wait!"

Lyssanne and Brennus slid to a halt, just short of plowing into her.

"They're nearly upon us, Shining One!" Brennus said.

"Guard the rear, then. Something feels wrong here."

Reina backed up a step, forcing Lyssanne to do the same. The faeries shot sparks behind them, eliciting screeches from their pursuers. Reina bent her head and swept the leaves with her horn, then jumped aside. Something crashed to the ground where she'd stood.

"A net trap," Brennus said on a growl.

"Barbed, too, looks like," Clark said.

"How did you know to look for the trip-chord?" Brennus asked.

"I felt it in the air," Reina said. "That foul net is coated in poison. One prick of those barbs, and any human will die—unpleasantly."

Olivia gasped. "She knows about the sanctuary."

"Impossible," Jada whispered.

Brennus released Lyssanne to smack a fist into his palm. "Venefica heard you speak of it, months ago, when I watched you in Duncan's meadow. She's likely set traps all around the place, suspecting Lyssanne might someday return."

"Then," said Jada, "we shall have to spring them."

The faeries and Reina split off in separate directions to search out further snares. Brennus, Clark, and Jarad led Lyssanne around the poisoned net and took a stand well away from its dangers. The three men surrounded her, their backs to her and weapons drawn. Clark hefted his great blacksmith's hammer; so weighty even Brennus couldn't wield it.

Then, the creatures reached them.

Throughout the maelstrom of shrieks, blurs, grunts, slashes, and zings that followed, Lyssanne wielded the one weapon she possessed. She prayed.

Within moments, it was over, the ensuing silence almost painful to the ears. Lyssanne's three champions stood sweat-soaked, winded, and alive. None relaxed his stance.

The sliver of a moon rose higher, and still they waited. One by one, their mythic friends returned with reports of varying success. None had been harmed, however. When at last the circle of seven was complete, Lyssanne offered up silent gratitude.

They ventured on toward the site of Princess Tria's sacrifice, Brennus leading Lyssanne around the bodies of the slain creatures, more akin to misshapen mounds of muck than beasts.

At last, Olivia called a halt at the edge of a clearing. "Only Lyssanne, Reina, and we of the FAE may enter the sanctuary," she said. "I think it best the rest of you join the army of men which has encamped in the western foothills of the Lucent Mountains."

"Duncan has arrived, then?" Brennus asked.

"He and his troops traveled night and day, reaching the valley two days before you." Olivia said. "We've aided them in camouflaging their presence. As yet, I do not believe the sorceress is aware of their threat."

"Flowers!" Clark blurted. "Flowers are going to protect her?"

Lyssanne glanced about. They'd arrived. The ring of flowers that honored the saving of her unborn life would shelter her on perhaps her last night.

"Neither the Shadow Mist nor any other agent of darkness can enter here," Olivia said.

"One question, I have for you, Captain of the FAE," Brennus said, his voice harsh. "If this place is protected, why could Lyssanne not have stayed here from the first, and avoided this entire perilous journey?"

"You guard her interests well, knight," she said. "Our testimonies of the King's deeds are a sanctuary and renewal to our strength, but we cannot live within them. We must move on to the path the King has marked out for us. Lyssanne needed a true home and means of sustenance."

Brennus turned to Lyssanne. "I shall send Clark for you after sunset on the morrow. I once discovered an unused passage from the river to the old stone keep attached to Venefica's manor." He took her hand. "By that route, we should avoid most of her traps."

"I don't think I shall be able to sleep," she whispered.

"Is there anything you FAE can do?" Brennus asked. "The curse has been threatening to strike in full intensity for weeks. If she fails to rest—"

"Lyssanne," Olivia said, "if you wish, I shall grant you the King's gift of sweet sleep."

All at once, everyone was bidding Lyssanne farewell. Jarad gave her a tight but perfunctory hug. Clark clapped her on the shoulder, almost sending her sprawling. Reina nuzzled her hair before stepping through the ring. Brennus simply stared down at her, his intensity rendering her immobile.

The others seemed to sense Lyssanne needed a moment with Brennus, for they ranged themselves in a semicircle facing the wood, claiming to watch for threats.

Lyssanne looked up at him, that looming shadow of safety in the faint moonlight, and reached for his hand. Tears stung her eyes. She couldn't bear it. When she next saw him, he must lead her to almost certain death. They had no more time.

"Brennus, I…" Her voice broke. What could she say? I love you? She wouldn't burden his heart more than it already was, not when she was unlikely to survive the next pair of days.

"Shh." He cupped her cheek. "Let Olivia help you sleep. I…" He inhaled. "I shall meet you and Clark by the river." He leaned down and rested his brow against hers. She clung to his hand, and he clung back. Then, he released her and slipped into the night.

∿

Brennus concealed himself amid the shadows. As long as he remained in sight, Lyssanne wouldn't tear herself away and get to safety.

She glanced back then stepped over the flowers. A wall of brilliant light shot up from the circle. Brennus blinked to regain focus. Lyssanne was gone. The faeries passed through the cylindrical blue shimmer, then it, too, vanished. Only the ring of blossoms remained, empty.

27

STONE'S CRY

*A*s the hood of dusk fell across the face of Cloistervale, Brennus shook free of the cloth that had shrouded his raven eyes. He scanned the trees, his battle plan fully formed.

Jada met him just outside Duncan's camp. "There's something different about you," she said, "less repulsive. Not much, but somewhat."

Brennus shrugged. "I bathed two evenings past." He grinned. "When I swore fealty to your King."

"So, you're not made of stone after all," she said. "Good. I won't have to waste time deciding whether to fight at your side or use you as pillow stuffing. Now, let us do this thing."

"Once we reach Venefica," he said, "she'll likely loose her minions on the village, using the people's suffering to weaken Lyssanne's resolve. 'Tis best you and Duncan strike first, engage her forces and rob her of that one weapon."

"A wise strategy," she said, opening the dome of silence surrounding the camp to allow him entrance. "We FAE shall provide aerial support, but be warned. None shall see us, save Lord Avery and other followers of the King who accept the unexplainable."

He nodded. "Let us hope Duncan has prepared the troops for the host of unnatural things they're soon to witness."

Glancing up from the crude model of Cloistervale he'd constructed of rocks, leaves, and sword-drawn lines in the dirt, Brennus addressed the officers assembled in Duncan's war tent. "Command your men to beware dark thoughts," he said. "Regret, guilt, rage—such is the fuel and fodder of the Shadow Mist. This is an enemy all the deadlier because it is unseen. Still, forget not your advantage. The Mist has power only if you allow its tendrils to take root."

"Why will you not command us, Sire?" asked the captain of archers.

"My fight is against the one who controls the enemy forces." Brennus eyed the rising sliver of moon. "And it is time I be about it."

The men's voices rose in chorus, offering him a traditional battle wish for strength of arm and courage of heart.

He echoed this, adding, "May the King's hand be our might, His power guard our backs."

"For Lastarra and Lyrya!" a knight shouted, fist raised.

Duncan bellowed, "For Lady Lyssanne!"

Brennus's shout rose above them all, "For the King of All Lands!"

At that, every fist or sword was thrust into the air. For, many had followed Duncan in pledging fealty to the King.

Far into the night, Lyssanne and Clark met Brennus at an ancient, fallen tree beside the river. Lyssanne leaned against its petrified bark.

"The hidden passage is clear," Brennus said. "Lyssanne, you must rest." He lifted her onto the trunk. "The shadow of pain darkens your eyes. The curse again whispers its presence?"

She nodded, taking the water-skin he offered. "Is Jarad safe?"

"He wished to warn your friend Aderyn and the scribe of the

impending battle. Said he'd stay the night at your cottage and assemble the village children there at dawn. Olivia vowed to send a contingent of FAE warriors to protect them."

"Brennus," she said, her voice tentative, "there is one thing I must ask of you."

"Speak it," he said, "and it is yours."

"I-if..." She took a long breath. "Should I not return...please, may I have your promise to keep Jarad safe?"

"It is done," he said. "I've made provisions with Duncan. Whatever should befall either of us, Jarad is assured a place at Avery Hall for as long as he wishes it."

"You did that," she whispered, "without my having to ask?" She flung her arms, water-skin and all, around him. "Thank you."

She tried to pull away, but Brennus held her fast.

"One thing you've never asked, *would* never ask," he whispered, "yet it, too, is yours. So little I've found worthy of faith in this sham of a life, but, Lyssanne..." He stroked her hair. "I believe in you."

Brennus hacked through one last tangle of branches, revealing the lip of the stone basin from whence the river flowed. He beckoned the others into the cave concealed beneath it. Clark had to stoop almost double to navigate the narrow passage.

Near the tunnel's end, Brennus halted, sword raised. "Ready yourselves," he whispered.

They emerged in a servant's hall near the kitchens. All was silence. Brennus doused his torch and propped it against the panel concealing the passage. On soundless feet, he led the way toward the entry hall and main stairway. Still, nothing stirred.

Stone busts, vases, and gargoyles cast eerie shadows in the flickering dimness. Beside him, Lyssanne's soft footfalls whispered along the dark hardwood.

Then, an inhuman cry shattered the stillness. "The power of the King is at hand!"

Brennus spun, finding nothing but the hideous visage of a gargoyle staring at him.

"The daughter of the King of Light has come!" screamed another voice. This, from a statue near Lyssanne.

"That noise'll wake the house," Clark hissed.

All along the corridor, statues, gargoyles, and even busts sprang to sudden life.

"Get behind me!" Brennus shouted to Lyssanne.

He swung his sword at the nearest stone adversary. The blade clanged against the statue, the jolt numbing his arm. He spun his hilt in his hand to use its raven's-head pommel as a cudgel. With a leap and a mighty kick, he sent the statue crashing into a wall, where it shattered.

Before he could savor his victory, two more stone figures rushed him. "Beware!" he shouted, staring into the darkness swirling in the marble eyes of his nearest foe. "She's animated them with the Shadow Mist."

While Brennus kicked, spun, and pummeled, Clark's hammer rang out, making short work of sinister statuary.

Another spin left Brennus facing Lyssanne, and he nearly let a bewigged bust brain him. A gargoyle held her pinned to the wall. Stone claws pressed so hard to her throat, her face was purpling. Her lips moved, and a sudden, brilliant flash flung the gargoyle backward. It lay lifeless on the floor; its eyes empty of Mist.

By instinct alone, Brennus swung his arm up and back, smashing away the bust just before it could bash in his head. Then, he whirled to fend off another gargoyle. He'd dispatched two more by the time silence shocked him from his battle haze.

Shards of stone and shattered crockery littered the floor. It was over. For the moment.

Brennus bent to catch his breath, his thoughts racing to all the places Venefica might be lurking. At this predawn hour, her chambers would have been his first guess. The Mist-ensorcelled statues, however, left no doubt she was awake—and aware of their presence.

"You!" an all too familiar voice screeched from the shadows.

Magda. The crone shuffled forward at surprising speed.

"I always knew you for a bad egg!" she shouted. "You'll wish she'd left you to die when she finds out, crow!" She lunged for Brennus, brandishing…a broom handle?

Before Brennus could react, Clark caught the crone around the throat, his beefy forearm forcing her chin toward the ceiling.

"Where is she?" Brennus demanded. When Magda only stared, he pressed his sword's tip to her midsection. "Tell me, crone, and I'll spare your wretched life."

Magda's eyes bulged, and a rasp escaped her lips. "Tower."

"You know the place?" Clark asked.

"Yes," Brennus growled. Venefica had retreated to her site of greatest power to cast her spells. This did not bode well.

Clark nodded then smacked a fist atop Magda's head. She slumped, unconscious.

"Clark!" Lyssanne cried.

"She'll live," the blacksmith said. "Though, she may wish she hadn't."

Footfalls pounded overhead, drawing Brennus's eye to the ceiling.

"Which way?" Clark asked.

"Back down the corridor," Brennus said. "In the old keep."

"Go," Clark said. "I'll hold off whoever's coming."

"We don't know—"

"Go, man! Get our lady where she needs to be. I'll catch you up when it's done."

Lyssanne rushed to Clark and hugged him around the middle. "Be careful."

"And you, Little Starling," he said. "May the King's own hand be your shield." He turned and bounded up the grand stairs.

"Come," Brennus said. "It is time." He took Lyssanne's hand and led her back through the rubble toward the door to the old keep.

Fighting for breath, Lyssanne halted before an iron-studded, arched door. They'd climbed more stairs than Mr. Fescue's tower could boast. The pounding of her blood intensified the pain growing in her head.

Brennus squeezed her hand. She squeezed back, closed her eyes, then nodded once. A tooth-tingling creak met her ears, as he eased open the door.

She opened her eyes. In the center of a round, stone room stood a tall, slim figure. A fall of ebony hair, blacker than the Thief's heart, cascaded down the back of the shimmering burgundy gown draping the woman before them. Chills broke out over Lyssanne's skin, and she clutched at her homespun skirt.

Lady Venefica Mortifer turned to face them. "Ah, my prince returns," she said. "Bearing gifts, I see. You should have informed me you were coming, Brennus. I would have been better prepared to receive you."

"But it is so seldom that I can surprise you," he said, his tone flippant.

"Yes, I would ask how you managed it, but"—Venefica waved a hand, and the door banged behind them, the sound drawing Lyssanne's eye—"I fear your timing won't permit me. A shame, really."

A croak was the only answer.

Lyssanne swung back around. Brennus was gone! In a weak ray of dawn spilling through the slit window, flapped the raven.

Alone! She was alone. Lyssanne's blood pooled into her feet. She'd known she would face death in this tower, but had imagined Brennus beside her, through it all. His transformation hadn't even left her his sword—not that she had knowledge of its use.

The raven took to the air, his wing-beats stirring Lyssanne's hair as he flapped toward the shadowed stone walls.

"Clever of you, pet, luring such a prize my way." Venefica stepped forward, her words spinning out like spider silk. "Gaining her trust, even daring to feign betrayal of your oath."

Lyssanne retreated. Air constricted at her back, warning her the door was near. A cold that wasn't cold clawed at her skin, a sensation she'd only ever felt in the presence of the Mist. It intensified as the sorceress inched closer.

"Why, your skills in the art of deception are greater than I realized," Venefica said. "You will make an excellent consort."

A shrill caw echoed from the opposite side of the room.

Venefica turned her full stare upon Lyssanne. "Do you know who I am, peasant?"

Lyssanne swallowed, praying her voice wouldn't falter. "Lady Mortifer," she said. The custom of a lifetime compelled her to offer a minute curtsey.

"You must show more deference in the presence of your betters, girl."

Invisible hands pressed down upon Lyssanne's shoulders. Her knees buckled, but she pushed back—and did not fall.

"Do you know why you've come?" the sorceress asked, shedding her languid manner.

"To...save...Cloistervale," Lyssanne said, straining to remain upright.

"No," said Venefica. "You've come because your *hero* wearies of his charade and your tedious company. He wishes me to finish what began before your pathetic birth."

Lyssanne shook her head. "You're wrong."

Suddenly, the pressure left Lyssanne's shoulders, and she staggered.

"Still, you believe him?" Venefica's frosty laughter filled the chamber. "He should join a band of Skriptaanese players." She drew closer and, with a sharp fingernail, flicked the skin beneath Lyssanne's chin. "You thought he cared for you? How naive. You aren't the heroine of some tale. One such as you could inspire nothing but contempt in a prince. You were merely the means to achieve his goals."

Lyssanne backed against the door, then shuffled to one side. A wave of cold and darkness bled from the burgundy of Venefica's gown, then it reached for her!

"Don't listen to her," a hollow voice croaked from the shadows.

"Brennus?" Lyssanne whispered, barely dodging the Mist.

She glanced toward his voice, but he was nothing save a motion at the edges of the chamber. He'd flown into darkness, choosing the body of shadow to give himself voice.

She shivered in recollection—him, wearing that form in Fescue's wood, lunging through her body. She'd felt his pain as her own. Somehow, the memory gave her strength.

The Mist drew nearer. Lyssanne sidled along the wall, struggling to ignore Venefica as she spewed forth reason upon reason to suspect Brennus's betrayal. At last, she could bear no more. "You lie," she said. "His loyalty is—"

"To me!" Venefica said.

It wasn't true. It couldn't be. Brennus had given his vow to the King of All Lands.

How can you be certain? Whispered a lethal thought. *No one was there to hear him make such a vow.*

Like a wave upon the simurgh's black sea, the Mist lunged for Lyssanne. She leapt aside, just in time. Then, a fist of air slammed into her, pinning her to the wall.

With a loud caw, Brennus, again a raven, flew at Venefica from the shadows. His mad flight slammed to a sudden halt, as if he'd smashed into a solid wall of air that sent him reeling. Ebony feathers rained like black snow upon the stones below.

"No!" Lyssanne screamed. "Brennus!"

Then, the Mist enveloped her. Though it did not, could not, touch her, it encased her in a curtain of impenetrable darkness. She could see nothing, hear nothing but Venefica's taunts.

"The King...is my...freedom!" she whispered, as she had in the gargoyle's grip.

"Your tricks may repel the Mist," Venefica said, "but not she who controls it!" Her voice changed to a purr, as pressure increased against Lyssanne's limbs. "Where is your King now?"

"He will never abandon me," Lyssanne said.

The mist recoiled.

"Perhaps." Venefica resumed her lazy tone. "But you have failed Him. He gave you charge over children, and you left them to me.

Now, their tears feed my power!" She laughed again. "They will grow only to serve me all their days—those who survive that long."

The Mist boiled and closed in again.

"But I forget," Venefica said. "You've been *ill*..." She drew out the word. "You let a little pain interfere with your duty to them. You abandoned them, and thus, your King."

No, it was a trick. The Thief of Souls knew Lyssanne's weakness and was feeding it to Venefica. "The King loves me," she said, "just as I am. He..."

Her next words died unformed. Images flashed against the blackness, like moving paintings, only more lifelike than any canvas could portray. They depicted scene after scene of the children suffering in every way conceivable and in some she could never have imagined.

Those horrors soon gave way to scenes of death—little Gavan lying pale and still in his mother's arms.

Tears poured down Lyssanne's cheeks.

Then, scenes blurred by as if indicating the rapid passage of time. Lyssanne gasped. A teenage girl, who could only be Elaiza, knelt at Venefica's feet, scrubbing the floor. The image sped forward, Elaiza's eyes, dull and devoid of hope, filling Lyssanne's view.

A chunk of ice dropped into the pit of Lyssanne's stomach. This was the future of those she loved—and she was powerless to prevent it.

The pressure in her temples threatened to burst forth like horns from her skin. She struggled to move, to press her hands against the sides of her head and ease the pain, but her arms remained pinned to the wall.

Where was Brennus? Was he injured? Unconscious? Worse?

A rustle reached her ears, then a rattling, as of metal against stone.

"Quiet, Faerie Queen," Venefica said. "Not even you can escape a cage of iron. I should think, by now, the pain of its touch would have taught you the folly of trying."

"Serena?" Lyssanne whispered. "Wh-where...?"

The rustling and rattling intensified. Then the dove loosed a chilling cry of such bottomless desperation, it's utterance pulled fresh tears from Lyssanne's eyes. Never should any being have cause to make such a noise.

"Fool of a creature!" Venefica shouted. "Your struggles are as useless as a faerie without wings—which, you will soon be. As useless as your precious Light-Wielder."

The wall of darkness closed in on Lyssanne, filling the space that should have contained air. As if she'd returned to the monster's cocoon in Westerfield, she fought to breathe, to think.

Venefica's laughter faded, the purr returning to her silken voice. "Why resist? You are no use to the children, to my village, to your so-called King—to anyone. They all, even your princely hero, see the truth of it."

The pain in Lyssanne's head pressed outward with as much force as the darkness pressing inward. Between the two, she'd surely be crushed.

"Lyssanne!" Brennus's pain-laden cry pierced her shroud of agony.

"No need for continued pretense, pet," Venefica crooned. "The time of secrecy is at an end. *She* is at an end. Now, you can stand openly at my side."

No! Pain prevented Lyssanne's voicing even that feeble protest.

Above Cloistervale, Olivia froze mid-flight, wand poised to strike the traitorous faerie who commanded Venefica's inhuman forces. A sound had reached into her spirit, squeezing her heart. If urgency had a voice, if need were a note to be sung, it would be that sound. Serena! She was alive, and Lyssanne was in danger of losing all.

Olivia's wand shot forth sparks impotent as her fury. Her target had escaped.

She pivoted, surveying her forces. The nophel attacked human and FAE warrior alike. Dark creatures slashed and maimed villagers and soldiers. Worse, several of Duncan Avery's men had fallen to the Shadow Mist. Some surrendered to hopelessness, dropping their weapons, only to be cut down within moments. Others flew into mad rages, attacking friend as well as foe.

In the brief lull that surrounded her, Olivia glanced toward Mount Mortiferra. Darkness poured from the tower like uncorked wine, coating the mountainside.

"Lyssanne is losing ground," she said, sensing Jada's nearness. "She's smothered in shadow. If something doesn't change, and soon, the Light in her will be snuffed out, along with her life and any hope for Cloistervale or the Seven Lands."

"Then," Jada said, "we must change something."

THE MOUTHS OF BABES

*L*yssanne squeezed her eyes shut against the images upon the Mist and the pain. The horrid scenes only grew clearer behind her eyelids. Why hadn't the King's Light freed her?

"This is pointless." Brennus's hollow, shadow's voice brought her eyes flying wide again. "The Mist can't touch Lyssanne, never could. It is folly to waste your efforts, when she has only grown stronger in the Light."

"Your concern for my time and strength is touching, dear prince," Venefica said. "Revenge is a delicacy. A dish so long in the making must be savored."

"I know well how such a dish can tempt the appetite," he said, "but if you aren't careful, this one may burn your tongue."

"You grow tiresome, *pet*," the sorceress snapped.

"You can't hold back the Light, my lady. Believe me, I've tried."

"Silence!"

"Let me—" The thread of Brennus's words was snipped, mid-sentence.

"What have you done to him?" Lyssanne cried.

"Oh yes, fear for him," Venefica drawled, as shards of cold pierced

Lyssanne's skin. "Protect this messenger of your own torment, who delivered my power even into your dreams."

"The nightmares?" Lyssanne whispered. "You caused them?"

"Indeed, and he was the bridge that brought the shadows into your slumber."

"No, I had those dreams even in Cloistervale."

"When I was near enough to reach into your mind."

Fresh shivers shot up Lyssanne's spine. During her journey, the nightmares had always occurred when Brennus was encamped with them. And at Avery Hall, she'd slept free of them only after his mysterious departure.

"That no longer matters," she said. "Brennus! Brennus, are you—"

Venefica's chill laughter drowned her words. "Only my voice can penetrate the Mist now. You waste your breath, both of you."

Brennus was trying to speak to her? Lyssanne fought to free herself from the wall. What horror had the sorceress visited upon him? Again, she screamed his name.

"He is unharmed, for now," Venefica said. "Though, I fear this once useful vessel of my power has suffered a breech in his stony exterior and must be discarded. I shall see to him once I've wrung the last possible vestige of suffering from you."

Venefica's words wrapped Lyssanne's mind in a tightening noose. She mustn't surrender to fear. Brennus was right, the Mist couldn't touch her if she held onto the King's Light. Oh, but it tugged at the door to her soul, molding to her a hair's-breadth from her skin.

"Every flame must go out, eventually," Venefica said. "Yours should never have burned. I'm surprised the faeries didn't extinguish you, themselves, after you led their princess to her death. Soon, countless others will join her."

A new image formed on the Mist, so near it seemed Lyssanne stood within it. A delicate faerie, clothed in shimmering petals of white, turned toward her, silvery hair sweeping her shoulders. Lyssanne's vantage widened, revealing a woman, great with child. A soundless bolt of darkness streaked toward the woman, but the faerie intercepted it. She dropped like a stone. Just as her pearlescent wing touched the ground, a ring of white shimmered into existence around her.

"Because of you," Venefica said, "the dead faerie's mother, their queen, is forever my prisoner."

Serena appeared upon the mist in her true form, her iridescent wings missing. She grimaced, struggling against the iron bonds chaining her to a wall of stone.

"All this," Venefica said, "the faeries suffered for their fabled Light-Wielder? Lives lost, power wasted, for some mad faerie's hallucination! For *you*, who have betrayed your King."

"I would never betray the King of All Lands."

"No?" Venefica said. "Does His book not say, one who betrays His children betrays Him? You are a leech, girl, consuming the efforts of others with your sloth."

Lyssanne gasped. "It was you!" She leaned her throbbing head against the stone. "You convinced the council I'd broken the law against sloth."

"I?" Venefica laughed. "They saw the evidence of it for themselves. Their obsession with useful toil did that. And you permitted it."

Lyssanne was transported, via the Mist, to the day of her greatest sorrow.

"You scarcely resisted when they accused you," Venefica said, "allowing my Mist full reign in that village. If you truly are your King's chosen, you've failed Him utterly."

Lyssanne squeezed her eyes shut again, desperate to block out Venefica's voice, but there was no escape.

"Because of you," Venefica said, "the boy Jarad no longer has a home. And no one will accept a nameless peasant for any position much above that of a slave."

Jarad blurred into view, older, unshaven, and dressed in tatters. He appeared to be begging for bread in the streets of Westerfield. Rough hands gripped his arms from behind, and soldiers dragged him away.

"This is…a lie." Lyssanne forced breath out through her

constricted throat. "He has a home. He can go to..." She stopped herself just in time. "To a place far from you." She glared in the direction of Venefica's voice. "The King protects him."

With a sudden jolt, she pulled her left fist free of the wall.

"He cannot protect the dead!" Venefica shrieked.

Lyssanne's stomach lurched as unseen bonds jerked her upward, stone scraping her back, the ground falling away beneath her feet.

The mist rose with her, then erupted in images of malformed beasts swarming her cottage, the children inside screaming her name.

"No, don't!" Lyssanne cried.

"Those villagers you claim to love were safely under my control," Venefica said. "Now, not only do they dare resist, but you bring foreigners to die with them."

Flash after flash seared Lyssanne's eyes—Lord Duncan's knights torn apart by grotesque beasts or, enshrouded in Shadow Mist, turning their swords upon one another...Green fangs tearing away Mr. Whiskin's sleeve...Two lizard-men stretching Mr. Cutler between their jaws, fighting like dogs over a strip of bacon...

"The faerie seer should have named you Wielder of Death," Venefica said. "Even the unicorn has lost her immortality at your hands. To carry you, she gave up a measure of her purity and can never return to her former life."

In a forest, brown and withered, stood Reina, her coat and horn dull, her head drooping.

"No!" Lyssanne said through fresh tears. "That can only happen it she...if...she—"

"Takes a life," Venefica said. "As she did two nights past, when she slew my mud-beast."

Those *creatures* chasing them in the wood! Lyssanne's stomach boiled, as a storm of lightning bolts struck at random all along her scalp.

"Even in your mother's womb, you brought only death and sorrow."

Lyssanne's cottage appeared as if viewed from the edge of Broone's field. The image was so clear, she struggled to reach for it. At the bottom of the hill, a strong, lean man stepped to the open doorway of a forge. A white-hot flash burst from its fire, and the forge exploded. The man's screams, her father's screams, reverberated through Lyssanne's skull.

"You see, peasant," Venefica said, "all whom you love or who seek to aid you come to ruin. I should have done them all a service and slain you as a child."

"You tried," Lyssanne whispered.

"Only once!"

Venefica's fury punched Lyssanne's stomach, forcing all her breath out on a single puff.

"I was careless, not remaining to finish the task," she said, "but I was certain I'd destroyed your *gift* along with your sight. For, how could the half-blind bring light to anyone? A mistake I shan't make this time."

Lyssanne wheezed, shallow gasps insufficient to replace the air Venefica's power had driven from her lungs.

"For all you've cost me," Venefica said, "wasted years, wealth, *my betrothed*—you, Light-Wielder, will feed the darkness of the Shadow Mist with your pain!"

The pressure behind Lyssanne's brow built and bulged as if forming a lump beneath her hairline. Agony surged outward and inward at once, hot nausea filling her throat. Often, she'd thought her head pain could grow no worse and still be survived—Oh, how wrong she'd been.

She hung there, too spent even to weep. Tears required energy to spill. Were she not plastered to the wall, she would have fallen into a boneless heap upon the flagstones. Her neck went limp, her head too heavy to hold upright.

She lost the will to try.

∿

"What's Lyssanne's greatest source of strength?" Olivia shouted to Jada, then spun midair to fire a stream of power at a faerie she'd once called friend. "Aside from the King, Himself, what brings her most joy?"

"Queen Serena would know," Jada yelled between blasts of lethal faerie sparks. "She's been with her longest."

"She can't tell us!" Olivia swooped low over the rooftops, sending a dark creature flying before it could sink its teeth into the baker. The arc of her dive brought her level with Jada again. "We need someone who knows Lyssanne well."

"The boy!" Jada shouted. "He's been Lyssanne's student for years."

"Jarad?" Olivia said, over screams of men, clangs of metal, and booms of magic.

Jada shot upward and flipped backward to avoid a jet of acid breath. Mid-flip, she slammed a wall of light into the flying abomination attacking her. "Yeah," she said. "He's rather clever for a human child. He should know."

Three more sulfurbirds swarmed toward Jada. Olivia swung around to pick one off, but a blast hit her from behind, cartwheeling her forward. Mid-spin, she caught sight of Captain Alvar incinerating a nophel, saving her life.

"Alvar!" she shouted, scanning the air for foes. "You have temporary command of my forces. I'm needed elsewhere!"

He saluted, then turned back into the fray.

Olivia sped toward Lyssanne's old cottage, her gaze sweeping the allies of Light battling dark creatures in the forests, fields, and streets below. Her lips twitched as she passed the scribe's shop. Through his second floor window, Gierre DeLivre flung heavy books onto the heads of the witch's monsters. Several villagers snatched up the fallen volumes and bludgeoned the creatures.

Others brandished farm tools and anything else at hand, but the villagers weren't warriors. The Shadow Mist clouded their judgment and slowed their reactions, even if they hadn't yielded to its sway.

Lord Avery's men fared little better. Though he, at least, resisted the dulling power of the Shadow Mist. He reminded his troops, loud and often, for what and for whom they were fighting.

"Let me through!" Olivia bellowed to a FAE sentry she'd stationed outside the cottage. The protective barrier shimmered for an instant, and she shot past it to a window, pushing the shutters inward without slowing. She had no time to waste on doors.

Jarad sat upon a chair in a room stuffed to bursting with children.

"To the storage cupboard, boy," Olivia ordered. "War counsel. Now!"

Jarad leapt up and hurtled over three sprawled children. Olivia closed the cupboard door and sealed them in with silence. Jarad's face shone grave in the leaf-green light from her wand.

"Your lady's in trouble," Olivia said. "She's fading." Her eyes bored into his, willing him to hold the answer. "You've been closer to her than perhaps anyone, witness to good times and foul. What most fuels her gift?"

He closed his eyes, as if sifting through memory. It did not take him long.

"Children," he said. "When children are filled with love or joy, it's as if she has energy again." He ran a hand through his hair. "It was that way here...before she got sick. Then, last winter at Avery Hall, with Lady Noel and the others, it happened again. For a little while, I even thought she'd gotten better."

Olivia sighed. "That's of no use. We can't bring children to her now."

"What if..." Jarad said, then shook his head.

"What? Don't discard even the most foolish idea now, boy. We're out of options."

"Well, she always says, songs of praise draw the King near and are like a wall that stops the Thief of Souls. What if we all, I don't know, start singing?"

Olivia was silent a long moment.

"I've been telling them stories of the King's hand in our adventures," he said. "I think it's kept us safe. Maybe that's foolish, like you said, but—"

"No..." Olivia said. "It just might work. I leave you in command of the forces of song. From here, you and the children storm the realms of the enemy with voice and praise. Leave the rest to me."

Even as Olivia shot back through the window, Jarad began carrying out his duties. "Let's start with 'Halls of Wonder,'" he said. "Then, 'Our Hero King.'"

Olivia hailed one of her FAE subordinates from the air, then sent the russet-clad faerie to command her warriors to join in the children's song. Meanwhile, she stirred up a soft wind, then formed a little bubble, the opposite of a dome of silence. It left her hands, carried upon the breeze, ready to absorb and amplify the melodies.

"Yes..." Venefica's voice hissed through the fog of Lyssanne's pain. "Let go. Your struggles are useless."

Lyssanne's limbs trembled, even bound to stone. At least the Mist had come no closer.

Venefica's voice, a mere wisp of sound, circled Lyssanne's muddled consciousness. "Ask it, and I can end all this. Your existence—and with it, the pain."

Perhaps death was the only escape. Lyssanne could have welcomed it...almost.

"Ah, but there may yet be a use for you..." Venefica's words trailed off as if in speculation. "Give yourself to the Shadow Mist, and I may let you live."

No! Lyssanne clung to that one, clear thought. She must not open herself to the Mist.

Venefica's voice caressed Lyssanne's scalp. "I have the power to lessen your pain."

The pressure eased, becoming almost bearable.

"Or," the sorceress shouted, "to increase it!"

Pain slammed outward in all directions. For a moment, Lyssanne didn't even breathe. Then, she gasped, each heartbeat pounding further agony into her head. Had this intensified torment lasted more than a moment, she would have lost consciousness. If only she could.

As the pain ebbed, Venefica's poisonous words again reached her. "I offer you a choice. Die, or give yourself to my control."

"No," Lyssanne whispered. It was all the resistance she could muster.

"Are you so eager for death?"

"I'll never...give in...to the Mist," Lyssanne whispered through the ringing in her ears.

"I know your weakness, girl," Venefica drawled. "You are no match for my power. You do not, surely, still think you have the strength to resist me?"

Perhaps the sorceress was right; everyone would be better served if Lyssanne disappeared. A deadly thought, but she couldn't suppress it. Did that not prove her unworthy of the King's intervention?

The faeries would insist she command the Light, but she could summon neither the strength nor will. For that weakness alone, perhaps she no longer had the right.

The Mist's icy hand fisted around her heart.

A new sound broke through those lethal thoughts, faint, almost as if summoned from within her mind. Singing? The familiar melody, "Our Hero King," filled her with a sweet ache.

"Surrender," Venefica said, as the King's victory song flooded Lyssanne's tortured mind.

Surrender, a faerie's voice whispered from the past. *Surrender...to a loved one.*

Lyssanne's shoulders loosened, and she let out a slow breath. Only by surrendering to her King's power, had she commanded His Light.

King of All, she prayed, *I beseech you, by the power that first brought me to be, remake this vessel into which you've poured the living water of your Light. Reshape me as you would a broken vase, that I may withstand a little longer. Let me not shatter and spill out your gift unused and ineffectual. Seal me, lift me, and pour out your cleansing Light on this darkness.*

"Give me your will," Venefica said, "or watch your friends writhe at my hand before you die. Surrender!"

"None but the King of All Lands holds power over my life or my person," Lyssanne said, her voice gaining strength as she spoke. "To Him, alone, do I surrender."

The ever-present images melted from the surface of the Mist.

"Then," Venefica said, "you choose death!"

SHADOW'S TEETH

*B*rennus beat fists of smoke against the wall of magic Venefica had erected around him—the one surface in all the lands his nebulous body wouldn't penetrate. His innards boiled black as the Shadow Mist. He couldn't reach Lyssanne, couldn't attack Venefica with beak and talon to buy her more time, couldn't even offer what courage his words might have provided.

He leaned his brow against the hardened air and whispered, "You called her into this battle, oh King. Be her general and fight beside her!"

~

A burst of power slapped Lyssanne's face like an open hand, snapping her head to one side. Fighting for consciousness, she resumed her silent prayer. *Please, it is not the pain I ask you to remove, but the cause of this brokenness, which prevents me doing your will.*

All at once, the pressure within her skull deflated and her thoughts cleared, as if murky waters had drained from the surface of her mind.

"My curse!" Venefica shrieked.

Winds rose, plastering Lyssanne's skirts against her skin and stealing her breath.

"Where the King's Light is," Lyssanne shouted above the roar, "darkness must flee!"

The Shadow Mist recoiled, but only for a moment.

"I still have power over you!" the sorceress screamed. "You are nothing!"

Currents of air and Mist whipped at Lyssanne, slashing hair across her face. She closed her eyes against the stinging blows. Then, an invisible hand lifted her from the wall, only to bash her into it. Dazed, she hung limp within its unseen grip.

"The King is my shield," Lyssanne whispered. "His Light is my weapon; His hand, the strength that wields it."

The Mist receded again. This time, when it lunged for Lyssanne, a semi-spherical barrier blocked its advance. She hung suspended within a black bubble several paces in diameter.

"Your demise is at hand, feeble flame," Venefica said.

"Perhaps," Lyssanne said, "but even in death, it is the King who rules my path." She caught her breath. "Your power is an illusion, but I see clearly by the King's Light. You have no real power over me."

"Fool," Venefica said, "I *am* power!"

The Mist gathered in upon itself, deepening to an even darker blackness, then spewed toward Lyssanne in a concentrated stream. Like the juice of a punctured piquantine fruit spraying the underside of a glass bowl, the darkness spread out over the center of her invisible shield.

Lyssanne glanced to one side, at last able to see beyond the Mist, and gasped. She hung near the tower's high ceiling. Dizziness overtook her, and her shield wavered. She closed her eyes for an instant, imagining it was the King's hand holding her, rather than Venefica's power.

Venefica stood far below, arms raised, head thrown back, Shadow emanating from her body. The smudge of darkness near the tower wall at Lyssanne's left might have been Brennus, but she hadn't time to think on that. While the King's Light held the Mist at bay, she must wield the weapon of words He'd granted her.

"Even you, Lady Mortifer, are deceived by your mist of shadow," she said. "It is the Thief of Souls who wields this false power. See it for what it truly is." She flung her words wide to Earth and sky. "I loose the King's Light to reveal truth!"

The Shadow Mist writhed, then it contorted, its surface taking on living features and clawing appendages. The snarling approximation of a face continuously bubbled and reformed, always with empty pits for eyes and hideous fangs. Its jagged maw opened in a silent shriek.

Lady Venefica screamed.

"Not into the forest!" Olivia shouted.

Five villagers were fleeing jaw-snapping lizard-men. If they allowed themselves to be routed amongst the trees, it'd be nigh impossible for her forces to protect them.

"Stop them!" she said to the nearest contingent of FAE warriors.

Olivia executed an aerial S-twist to give herself a full view of the embattled valley and determine where she was most needed. Before she could complete the maneuver, a wave of the King's Light flashed across the landscape. Then, she caught a glimpse of the Shadow Mist and nearly fell from the sky.

All over the village, in the fields, and doubtless among the trees, humans and faeries stood transfixed at the sight of the Mist-spirits taking on tangible form.

As if the King had spoken a command, Olivia sensed her next duty.

She vanished her wand and cupped her palms together. Drawing them slowly apart, she formed another sound bubble. She filled it with her own voice, then sent it off above the heads of every living creature.

"Behold the Shadow Mist!" Olivia's voice echoed throughout the valley. "This is the weapon of your enemy, the enslaver of your hearts, the foe Lyssanne Caelestis warned you to beware. Now, will you not heed her words?"

Villagers and soldiers turned to one another, eyes wide, mouths agape. They pointed and shouted to friends and neighbors, seeing for the first time the shadow that had wrapped them in its dark embrace, many with its teeth sunk deep.

"Live in her likeness," Olivia's voice said, "and honor the King of All Lands with speech and heart. In His glory alone, can you shield your minds from this, the Thief's power."

Just as Olivia's sound bubble finished its work, Jada shouted, "Captain!" She pointed to the south of the village. "He'll get them all killed!"

Olivia spun around, and her faerie heart lurched.

Jarad marched at the head of row upon row of children. He led them, all holding hands, toward Market Square. Their little voices filled the air, as they stormed the streets of Cloistervale, singing praise to the King and shouting of His favor.

"What's that boy doing!" Jada cried.

"Winning this battle for us," Olivia said.

For, as if in terror, the Shadow Mist fled before the children.

One by one, the people of Cloistervale and warriors of Lyrya joined in. The Mist shrank and shriveled, slithering back toward the Lucent Mountains. Still, the battle was far from over. Venefica's willing servants and dark creatures redoubled their ferocity, fighting with more cruelty and malice than before. Without the Mist's influence to dull their wits, however, the allies of Light grew in strength and speed. They thought faster, reacted in reflex, and went on the offensive.

The tide was turning. Olivia only prayed the same held true for Lyssanne.

~

The spirit of the Mist reached for Lyssanne but couldn't puncture her protection. It snarled and snapped, its terrifying visage calling to mind tales of the Land of Lightless Fire from whence it was spawned.

Lyssanne had gone well beyond her threshold of fear, however. "Deception is the way of the Thief of Souls," she said, "but the mask is removed." As the King poured His words into her mind, she uttered them with growing strength. "Lady Mortifer, this power enslaves you as much as it does your victims. The Thief of Souls cares not for your concerns. He'll—"

"You know nothing, girl!" Venefica said. "I am slave to no one. It is I, who control the Shadow Mist. It matters not what face it wears. I, alone, am its master."

The sorceress drew a clenched fist to her lips then flung her hand, palm open, toward Lyssanne. New pain exploded behind Lyssanne's brow. What strength she still possessed leeched from her like water through a sinkhole.

"No," Lyssanne whispered. "I asked the King to remake me. The power of that curse is broken. He is my strength, no matter what you do to me."

The pain ceased as if it had never struck.

"Then, why does He not free you from my hand?" Venefica laughed. "He is done with you, girl. If ever He had use for you at all."

The unseen bonds pinning Lyssanne to the wall pressed harder, all but crushing her, as the spirit of the Mist snarled, prowling through its stream of shadow.

"Only in death, will you be free of me!" Venefica shouted

"Then," Lyssanne said between gasps, "I shall go to live…in His strength. You can't reach me there."

The Mist spirit raged, clawing at Lyssanne's shield of Light. This seemed to distract Venefica, for the pressure eased, and Lyssanne could again draw full breath. She took advantage of the respite and launched her next verbal assault.

"The Thief's bonds take the guise of power, while robbing you of the true might the King created in us all. Break free and embrace His Light."

"You dare?" Venefica whispered. "You dare invite me to serve your so-called King? My lands, my wealth, all but my title, were stolen from my family, and not by this fictional thief you fear. Your forebears usurped my birthright in your *King's* name! Their descendants' suffering is the gift I give myself for all He's cost me."

"And when the people of Cloistervale are all dead?" Lyssanne asked. "What will bring you joy, then? Pleasure born of vengeance can't sustain itself."

The Mist thickened and lunged, doubtless mirroring Venefica's wordless fury.

Flashes from the sorceress's life flitted like memories within Lyssanne's mind, filling her senses with an image of Venefica as the King must view her—A frightened, lost woman stumbling through the night, her sadness deeper than the Mist spirit's empty eyes.

"Where was your King's kindness when I was forced to live in squalor," Venefica said, "with nothing but an old servant for company and stale bread for food? Where was His mercy when my father attempted to use his family's magic to better our lot, costing my mother her life? Where was His protection when my betrothed was murdered?"

The Mist slowly retreated from Lyssanne's shield.

"Where was He?" Venefica said. "Luring me away for months to search for the child of His prophecy. Luring me *here*, where I'd be powerless to prevent my beloved's death. Here, where everything that mattered would be taken from me—by you!"

The Mist withdrew farther from Lyssanne. It was turning, turning toward Lady Venefica.

"These things were not the King's doing, nor mine," Lyssanne said, her heart crying out for the means to save her foe. "Acknowledge His goodness before it is too late. That will break the Thief's—"

"Silence!" Venefica shrieked, flinging her arms wide and slamming the breath from Lyssanne's lungs. "I am going to kill you, Lyssanne Caelestis," she drawled. Darkness pooled around her, a stain growing upon the flagstones, like ink spilled on parchment.

∾

Brennus dared not move or speak. Even his breaths grew silent. He must do nothing to break Lyssanne's battle focus. It blazed in her eyes, that fire which came over a warrior when every thought and sinew was honed to one purpose—survival.

She shimmered behind a half-sphere of transparent Light, bright as white-hot steel. She was a living rainbow, awash in the King's power. He'd never beheld anything more beautiful, more terrifyingly fragile. 'Twas a wonder her brightness didn't sear Venefica's eyes.

A sudden force gripped his nebulous form and pulled, hard. As if he stood before the maw of a great beast that had taken a deep breath, he fought the suction, clawing at Venefica's barrier for purchase.

The sorceress was preparing a deathblow for Lyssanne, drawing in every shadow to feed the Mist. Including Brennus. The magic pulled harder, flattening him against the barrier.

Through the swirling shadows, the battle played out in a tableau that stilled his heart—Lyssanne, radiant with holy power, yet helpless to save herself...Venefica, in the midst of a growing vortex of night, so black it threatened to swallow the world.

The hideous visage of the Shadow Mist turned its empty eyes upon its Keeper. It opened wide its jagged jaws, its phantom fangs snapping, ever ravenous for the taste of hate and rage.

In the last instant, Lyssanne tried to warn her, but Venefica fought the lure of Light with such ferocity, her renewed surge of power imploded upon her.

The Mist lunged.

Too late, Venefica saw her error. Her eyes, forever fixed on others with contempt, widened in terror. She took a single step back. Swathed in shadows she'd drawn to herself, she was powerless to break free of the enveloping spirit of Darkness.

Venefica's lovely face contorted into a visage more repulsive than the gargoyles Brennus had shattered. The Mist's jaws fastened over her body and...inhaled her.

Within a heartbeat, she was reduced to a wisp of vapor. The smoke of her essence dispersed, as if she'd never been.

In the time it took Brennus to blink, the Shadow Mist had ceased to be.

"Lyssanne!" he cried, his hollow voice echoing through the shock of Venefica's destruction at her own hands.

For a pair of heartbeats, Lyssanne hung against the wall like a shining portrait. Then, her honey-brown skirts and silken hair billowed out, as she fell from a height no human could survive.

A scream ripped free of Brennus's soul, and he plunged into the light.

RAVEN'S FLIGHT

*B*rennus leapt forward, his hopes as wispy as his body.
He reached for the sunlight. If he remained shadow, Lyssanne would fall right through him, to her death. He stretched his arms wide, willing feathers to sprout. Even if the light transformed him in time, her weight would crush his bird bones, perhaps ending in her death anyway and certainly in his. Still, if there was the slightest chance...

He flexed his hands. *Change!* Where was the magic he detested—now when, for the first time in his life, he needed it? He stood directly below her, flapping his arms, calling forth the raven within. She fell, closer, closer. Even if he shifted now, there was no time to save her.

No! Great King, bear her up! Else, take me in her stead.

He stretched out his useless shadow arms...

And caught her!

The impact of her slight weight jolted him to his knees, Lyssanne cradled in his solid arms. He crushed her to him, the rise and fall of her chest a gentle pressure against his. Her shallow, uneven breaths fluttered his tunic, tickling his skin.

She was alive. They both were.

He buried his face in her soft hair. He could *smell* her—a mixture of faerie dust and forest. Even the slight scent of her exertion was sweet to him.

She reached a shaky hand up to his face. "You're…you," she whispered, "real."

"Yes." He could say nothing more.

Her hand slipped. He caught it against his cheek and lowered his lips to hers. He breathed into her, around her own shallow breaths, to fill her with life, with his strength.

No confection could be sweeter; no pot of flyl or woolen cloak could warm a man so. She was liquid light in his arms. At last, a light whose touch brought not a curse consigning him to wallow in death, but the promise of new life.

After an age, he forced himself to lift his lips from hers. What would he see in those sapphire eyes? Anger? Fear? Revulsion? Almost, he did not care. He looked down into those Xavier-blue depths, and the breath left him anew.

She blinked up at him, eyes shining with new fire…and *smiled.* Then, her eyes fluttered closed, and she sagged in his embrace.

"Lyssanne!"

"Fear not," a melodious voice said, followed by a metallic crash behind him.

Brennus twisted around. Venefica had dissolved before his eyes. Who—?

Across the chamber, a fair-haired woman rose from a crouch, shaking out iridescent wings. "Lyssanne's body is merely taking its needed rest," the faerie said, violet eyes sparkling as she stepped over the remains of an iron birdcage. "I am Serena."

"Your Majesty," he whispered. "I should have freed you. Forgive me. You'd grown so silent, and I—"

"Had other concerns." Serena knelt beside him, her pink gown spreading like a flower.

Nodding, he drew Lyssanne close and dried the tears shimmering on her ashen cheeks. Her tears or his own? "Lyssanne," he whispered, over and over…her name, a song of praise, a prayer of gratitude to the greatest of all kings. "Lyssanne."

She lay still, her two watchers keeping soundless vigil, for once openly and without feathers—and, for once, with shared purpose.

Her fingers flexed within Brennus's. A hard shudder quaked through her body, and she inhaled a sharp gasp. Then, a soft whimper escaped her lips. "Please," she whispered, new tears leaking from her closed eyes.

"You're safe," he murmured. "It is over." A paralyzing thought struck him. What if it were he, she feared? "It was a lie," he whispered. "What she said, everything she said. I would never betray you. I...I would give my life for yours."

She blinked up at him, her haunted expression melting away. "I thought you a dream."

"Oh, love," he said, "I thought I'd lost you."

"Me too."

Brennus pulled her to him again, resting his lips against her brow, a kiss that wasn't a kiss. He needed a moment to compose himself. For her, he must be strong. Her whispered plea for mercy had nearly undone him. Never, he vowed, would she suffer as she had this day.

"Brennus?" Lyssanne's muffled voice stirred his tunic.

"Yes, love," he said into her hair. "I am here."

"I...I can't...breathe."

He loosened his hold. "Forgive me."

"How do you feel?" the faerie queen asked.

Lyssanne flinched.

"Fear not," Brennus whispered, running a thumb along her palm. "Lyssanne, may I present Her Majesty, Serena, Queen of Faeries."

Lyssanne gasped, then struggled to sit up.

"There is no need for ceremony," Serena said. "We are, after all, old friends."

"Yes, but," Lyssanne whispered, "I didn't know..."

"Rest, dear one," Serena said. "The time for haste will soon enough be upon us."

Brennus stared at the stone wall across the tower. Venefica had put this weakness in Lyssanne's voice, but he had brought her here to allow it.

"Self-loathing will profit you nothing, Prince of Navvar," Serena said. "Your vow to the King ended your blame in this affair. Lyssanne has forgiven you, as has He. Forgive yourself, else risk retracing the path you've forsaken."

"You read my thoughts, Your Majesty?"

The queen laughed. "No, they are clear enough in your eyes. And call me Serena, both of you. Friends need no formality between them."

"Friends," Brennus murmured.

"Your spell," Lyssanne whispered, again struggling to sit up. "'Tis broken...Serena?"

Brennus lifted her and leaned her against him, his arms encircling her, unwilling to let go.

"It died with the sorceress," said Serena.

Lyssanne looked up at Brennus. "She's..."

"Gone," he said, "Consumed by her own favored weapon."

Lyssanne covered her mouth, shivering again. "The shadows... swallowed her."

"Yes," said Brennus. "You saw it?"

She nodded. "Somewhat."

Moisture dripped onto Brennus hand where it clasped Lyssanne's at her waist. Then, another droplet joined the first. "What's amiss, love?" He turned her to face him. "Are you in pain?"

She shook her head. "I never wanted this, never wanted to hurt anyone."

"In battle, the King's Light is your weapon," Serena said. "Weapons wound, Lyssanne. Still, you did not cause her death. Venefica Mortifer was the victim of her own choices."

Lyssanne's tears flowed all the more.

"Why weep for her?" Brennus whispered, stroking her hair. "That witch murdered in her attempts to destroy you. And what she's done to you...you're limp as unbaked bread in my arms."

"She's forever lost to the King," Lyssanne said. "A fate far worse than any I've suffered."

Brennus's innards shuddered at how close he'd come to sharing that fate.

424

"We are free, love," he said. "Whatever else it means, her death has ended our curses."

"Her demise cannot be credited with that," Serena said. "It removed only the bonds she had placed upon me and the presence of the Shadow Mist in this place."

"But we *are* free?" He tightened his hold, as if his arms could protect Lyssanne from pain's return. "She no longer suffers? Venefica cast the curse; it must be over."

"Oh, yes, Prince." Serena rested a hand on his shoulder. "You are both free." She pulled away. "Lyssanne's curse broke before the sorceress fell to her chosen darkness. Did you not see the King's Light flare within her, burning away the sickly shroud encasing her head?"

"I saw the Light, yes. Filaments of it wove all over her scalp, as if—"

"Remaking her," Serena said. "When Venefica sought to rekindle the pain, Lyssanne denied the deception, forever breaking the curse's power and Venefica's to reinstate it."

"It can never return?" Lyssanne asked.

"Never," Serena said.

"Forever shall my thanks go before the King," Lyssanne whispered.

"And mine," Brennus said. "One thing I must know, Serena, if you can tell me."

"I shall do as I am permitted."

"Why is it, if not by Venefica's death, that I am free?"

"You have fulfilled the terms of the generational curse set upon your ancestor," she said. "You, at last, fulfilled a noble quest."

"How?" he asked. "This wasn't the first time I've saved a life, saved Lyssanne's, in fact. That never sufficed. Besides, today I was able to do so only *because* the curse had broken, not before." He pinned Serena with a direct stare. "Why this time?"

"That instant, alone, did not free you. When you pledged fealty to Lyssanne, forsaking the one thing which mattered most to help her fulfill the King's call, your true quest began."

Lyssanne squeezed his hand.

"In the end," Serena said, "when that quest succeeded at a price, you had not even the woman you…cherished…to gain. For, either she would live, resulting in your crushing death, or you would live, failing to save her. The King perfected the quest for you, who had given higher value to His will and purpose than to honor, family, or life."

"I begin to understand," Brennus said to Lyssanne, "your unwavering faith in His goodness. No knight ever stood more highly favored than to serve such a King."

"True words, friend," Serena said, "but we must leave at once. The dark creatures who survived the battle of Cloistervale will swarm this mountain within moments."

Lyssanne gasped. "Clark!" She struggled to stand.

"Careful," Brennus said, steadying her. "We know not what injuries you've sustained. We shall find Clark."

As they neared the door, Lyssanne glanced about the chamber, perchance seeking some sign of the struggle which had nearly cost them everything. Nothing remained but Serena's broken cage. Not even a wisp of ash marked the place of Venefica's passing.

They descended to the servant's hall then rounded the corner. The blacksmith met them at the foot of the grand staircase.

"Thank the King!" Clark said, engulfing Lyssanne in his burly embrace. "I bound the witch's loyal servants in the dining hall," he said. "Had to lock that Magda woman in a room alone. I sent the folks who were here under duress back to the village."

"Let us flee," Serena said. "Leave the prisoners. Take nothing from this lair of darkness."

"The only thing I wish to take from this place," Brennus said, "is Lyssanne. Follow close, I shall not wait for stragglers." He looped an arm around Lyssanne's waist and ducked into the passage to the river.

As they passed Murrough's Mill, Lyssanne stared ahead, only the motion of those beside her guiding her steps. She'd almost died, and her part in the Mist Keeper's demise couldn't be denied. She clutched her elbows as waves of cold washed over her.

Brennus caught her arm and raised a hand to call a halt, then pulled her to him.

She leaned against him, closing her eyes to recall the warmth of a similar embrace. He'd snatched her from certain death then called her *love*. How much of that had been real, how much a swooning dream?

She peered up at him. Her breath hitched at the dangerous beauty his countenance had taken on in the full light of the sun. In all the months she'd known him, how had she never realized she'd seen that face only by night?

"Come," Brennus said, lifting her into his arms, "I shall return you to the sanctuary so you may rest."

Lyssanne groaned as his arm pressed against her bruised back. "No, please, I must find Jarad and the others. Those images I saw in the Mist…"

"You can trust nothing you saw or heard in that tower. Venefica meant to torture you."

"Let us discover how her friends have fared," Serena said. "She will have no rest, else."

"As you wish," Brennus said. "Only close your eyes and allow me to carry you the remains of the journey. I suspect our battle is far from ended."

Lyssanne leaned against him and let his footfalls rock her into a fitful doze.

A sudden, earsplitting crunch startled her awake.

"Venefica's tower," Brennus murmured, setting Lyssanne on her feet.

"The darkness has consumed itself," Serena said, gazing toward the mountains. "The decay of years left the place susceptible to the violence of the Thief's creatures. It has fallen, crushing the last of them."

"Fitting end," Clark said.

"Indeed," Brennus said, keeping his body between Lyssanne and that sight.

Across Nettleworth's field, balls of jewel-bright color streaked toward them. Every hue Lyssanne could name, and a few she could not, whirled in a tightening circle around Serena, then the rainbow dance of lights ended, all but three of the colors streaking off in different directions.

Two green orbs and a larger, purple ball of light floated toward Serena. With a sizzle, the three faeries unfurled into their human-like forms.

Lyssanne gasped. "Captain Alvar?"

The purple-clad faerie nodded. "It is finished, then?"

"Yes," Serena said. "Venefica Mortifer is no more."

"Thank the King you are free, Majesty, and you all survived," Olivia said, leaf-green sparks pulsing around her. "Lyssanne, it is a gift to see you whole and safe."

"And you," Lyssanne said, "all of you."

"I see you've shaken loose your feathers, as well, Prince of Navvar," Jada said.

"The King's mercies are endless, it seems," Brennus said.

"We lost several good warriors in that battle," Alvar said, an edge to his voice. "Light is the swiftest force in all the King's creation, Lyssanne. What took you so long?"

Another wave of ice surged through Lyssanne, conquering her ability to speak.

Brennus's hand clenched at her waist. "Torture has a way of delaying one's victory, faerie," he said. "I don't suppose *you* can be expected to understand that."

Alvar shot between Olivia and Jada, growing larger as he moved.

Serena raised her palm toward Alvar, and he froze. "Lyssanne has brought great honor to the King, this day," she said. "As have you all."

Alvar diminished to his original size, then sailed back a pace. "Indeed, Your Majesty," he said, bowing. "The battle is won. We shall rejoice in that."

Brennus eased his hand from the hilt of his sword, but kept Lyssanne close as the two FAE captains and Jada gave their queen a full report of the battle for Cloistervale.

They had sustained some losses, both human and faerie. Several enemy prisoners had been taken, men who'd willingly served Venefica and continued to fight even after their defeat. The forest folk who had answered Reina's call had fought dark creatures at the fringes of the wood and ushered stray villagers to safety.

"Only one traitor to our ranks survived the battle," Captain Alvar said. "I've sent him, under guard, to await your judgment, Your Majesty."

"I shall see to that once matters are settled here," Serena said. "Lyssanne may yet have need of me."

"Will you put on feathers again, then?" Olivia asked.

"No, I shall assume a human guise." Stretching out her arms, Serena grew to Aderyn's height. The instant her feet touched the ground, her shimmering wings vanished. "Now, dear friends, I'm certain you wish to seek your rest and see to what duties remain. We must get our King's daughter to her people, so she may do the same."

Alvar bowed low, then streaked away in a blur of midnight purple. Olivia and Jada fluttered over to Lyssanne and clasped each of her hands.

"It has been an honor serving beside you, Child of Light," Olivia said.

"It was my honor, being allowed to know you all," Lyssanne said in a small voice. "Will I ever see you again?"

"That is not for us to know," Olivia said.

"But," Jada said, "you can be sure, we'll cherish that reunion if ever the King permits."

Lyssanne cleared her burning throat. "Until such a time, I shall miss you both."

Jada released Lyssanne's hand and wrapped miniature arms about her neck. The hug lasted less than a heartbeat, then she streaked off after Alvar.

Olivia squeezed Lyssanne's hand then she, too, backed away and vanished.

Lyssanne stared at the once neat row of cottages, her mind churning with a tumult of emotions. What would be the reaction to her return? She was, just by setting foot upon a single street of the village, breaking a law of her people.

She took that fateful first step into Cloistervale, and another mental blow assaulted her resolve. Had Captain Alvar been right? Might lives have been spared if she'd only been stronger? Bile choked her throat. With a supreme effort, she forced that line of thought down into the depths of darkness where it belonged. The King had been victorious; all else was secondary.

Even so, her steps faltered. This wasn't the Cloistervale she'd known. Her beloved village might have been a tomb, for not even birds or animals stirred the dead air. Debris and fragments of buildings covered the deserted streets. Boards, broken shutters, shards of pottery, and unrecognizable bits and pieces made her passage more a challenge than crossing Stupasce.

Lyssanne gaped as she passed boarded-up shops, burned out husks of homes, and building after building showing signs of decay and destruction. Lawns were overgrown or mottled with bare patches of dirt. Even the paving stones of the once smooth streets were, here and there, lifted out of place or broken into chunks.

"All this couldn't be the result of a single day's fighting," Lyssanne whispered. "Where is everyone? If they survived..."

She darted glances at her companions. Brennus's posture was rigid, his jaw set, gaze fixed ahead. Clark's silence was ominous. Even his lumbering footfalls made little sound.

"Do not give in to premature fear," Serena said. "My captains assured us the battle was won."

Near the end of a lane leading to the village square, Lyssanne tripped over a lump the color of the paving stones. Brennus caught her before she could fall. She stooped and picked up the book that had snagged her foot.

"One of Mr. DeLivre's," she said. She turned the book over, then gasped and flung it away. Its back cover was soaked in a dark stain that could only be blood.

Keeping a hand on her arm, Brennus led her onward. Lyssanne

paused at the entrance to the square. The smells were wrong. After a few more steps, she discovered why. A jagged, blackened hole and charred splinters were all that remained of Flora's candle shop.

"That damage is months old," Brennus said. "The shop burned before winter. Some boys overturned a vat of hot wax. Just one of many pranks that went awry before the Council fell."

The closer they ventured to the scribe's shop, more and more books and torn pages littered the square. Lyssanne fought back a sob. What had befallen Mr. DeLivre?

Except for a shutter hanging by one hinge, his shop appeared unchanged. She stopped in the open doorway and called in vain for her mentor then stepped inside.

"No, Lyssanne," Brennus said, pulling her away from the entrance.

"I'll look inside, if you wish," Clark said. He returned within moments. "Shop's mostly intact. No sign of anyone, alive or dead, on either level of the building."

"The old man is doubtless helping someone elsewhere," Brennus said.

Lyssanne could only nod.

They'd taken a few more strides when the wind shifted, wafting a flurry of torn pages into their faces, and with them, a foul stench.

Lyssanne covered her mouth and nose, fighting a gag. "What is that?"

"Eggs," Clark said, his voice muffled. "Burned ones, and… something else."

"The bakery," Brennus said.

Lyssanne swung toward the building across the street and a few shops down. A dark lump lay half in, half out, of the doorway. She gasped, inhaling more of the rancid odor. Swallowing bile, she lunged toward the bakery. It was burning, and someone was injured!

"Wait." Again, Brennus restrained her. "There's nothing you can do. Lyssanne, you…you don't want to see that."

"Mr. Whiskin?" The baker's name was a broken groan torn from her lips.

"No," Brennus said, "'Tis…not human."

She shivered. "What if there's someone inside?"

"The roof's collapsed," Brennus said. "It isn't safe. Once we find Jarad, I shall do what I can. Before all else, I must get you to a place of safety—in company I trust."

Lyssanne nodded. It was pointless to protest when his voice took on that steely edge.

"Where do you go in times of danger?" Clark asked. "For us, it's behind the inner walls."

"The meeting hall, of course!" Lyssanne pulled free of Brennus and rushed past Serena.

Chatter rang distinct through the hall's windows as she approached. Someone asked how Queen Stella had known Cloistervale would have need of the Starguard.

"We aren't with your queen's forces," a familiar voice said, halting her progress up the hall steps. "We hail from Lyrya."

Lord Duncan...he was alive.

She reached for the door handle. It grew slick beneath her hand, as memories of the last time she'd entered the hall froze her where she stood. Jarad, Aderyn, Mr. DeLivre...their faces swam before her as footfalls joined her on the steps. This time, she did not stand alone.

Taking a deep breath, she pulled open the door.

31

RECKONING

*L*yssanne blinked several times, attempting to focus on the dizzying swarm of activity filling the hall. Villagers rushed about, huddled in groups, or bent over the figures lying prone along one wall. Two men shuffled past, carrying a woman.

"More bandages over here!" Mistress Evlia shouted, hurrying to join them as they laid their burden on a blanket near the door. "What happened?"

"She was on her way back from Mortiferra Manor," Mr. Colby said. "Two of those creatures attacked her at the edge of the forest. Anything you can do?"

Evlia covered the woman with another blanket, then led the men a few paces away. "Her wounds are too numerous and have already begun to putrefy. Laced with venom, I suspect. Fever's raging, and her breathing's shallow. You'd best find her sons."

As they moved off in varied directions, Lyssanne slipped in and knelt beside the dying woman. Her own breaths constricted at the sight of that familiar, pain-etched face. "Madam Nettleworth?" she whispered.

Madam Nettleworth's eyes fluttered open, and a wheeze lifted her chest. "You were...right," she whispered. "That...fog..."

"'Tis gone," Lyssanne said. "It can't hurt you anymore. Nor can those creatures."

"S-so...sorry," Madam Nettleworth said. "For...give..."

Lyssanne clasped her hand. "There is nothing to forgive." Closing her eyes, she petitioned the King's mercy as she once had for Noel. Ringing filled her ears, and she grew dizzy.

"You!" a male voice shouted. "You brought this upon us, and now Mother is...is..."

Lyssanne glanced up at the man looming over her. Behind him, several people turned their direction. Evlia rushed forward and grasped him by the arm.

"Lower your voice," she said. "You'll only make matters worse if... Lyssanne?" Evlia flung her arms wide. "How in the Seven Lands—?" She gasped and dropped to her knees beside Madam Nettleworth. "Her wounds are changing. Their color, they hardly appear inflamed and, wait...now they're a healthy hue, as though they've had days to heal!" She looked up. "What did you do?"

"Nothing," Lyssanne said, dropping Madam Nettleworth's hand. "The King answered my plea. With enough trust, anyone may call forth His healing Light thus."

More and more townspeople swiveled to face them. Many uttered inarticulate cries, gasped, or muttered under their breaths.

"What is the meaning of this uproar?" Councilman Ratomer's voice shouted from the dais.

"She's back," someone said. "Lyssanne has returned."

People pressed together to form a haphazard aisle, revealing Ratomer's shape presiding from the center of the council table.

"You dare?" Ratomer said, his voice ominous in the hush that had fallen. "Lyssanne Caelestis, you dare return after bringing this evil upon us?" He waved a hand. "Seize her!"

Lyssanne pushed to her feet and backed away, as three men broke free of the crowd and moved toward her. Warmth brushed her arms, and she glanced around. Brennus and Clark stepped up to each side of her. The prince gripped the hilt of his sword. Clark, too, stood ready to strike, the handle of his massive hammer held across his chest, its deadly, business end hooked over his shoulder.

The three men of Cloistervale halted and staggered back a pace.

"You must come with us," said a burly man in a torn farmer's tunic.

"Like the chief said," one of his companions squeaked. "It...it's l-law."

Chief? Ratomer? Where was Aderyn's father?

"Give the word, Lyssanne," Brennus whispered, "and I shall take you from this place."

She shook her head. "I must find Jarad, and I cannot leave lest I know Aderyn and Mr. DeLivre are safe."

"As you wish," he muttered, "but should they make a move against you, we leave."

"What are you waiting for?" Ratomer shouted. "The law and safety of Cloistervale have been usurped! Take that woman to—"

"Lady Lyssanne!" called the most welcome of voices.

"Jarad!" she cried, her eyes welling. He was safe, this boy who was more brother than charge, more friend than student.

Jarad sidestepped the three motionless men who still eyed Brennus and Clark. "You're all right?" He grasped her hands. "Does this mean...is she...?"

"The sorceress is dead," Brennus said, his gaze fixed on the men.

"What happened?" Jarad asked. "Were you hurt? How'd she—"

"Later," Brennus said.

Lyssanne squeezed Jarad's hand then pulled him into a quick hug.

"Lyss?" a hesitant voice said.

"Aderyn?" Lyssanne's eyes roved the sea of faces and colors for her friend.

Aderyn stepped forward with a child in her arms, as a shock of white hair shone against the dimness of the crowd.

"Mr. DeLivre?" Lyssanne asked.

"*Fii*," he said. "Ah, but it gives these old eyes joy to see you, *Shirii*."

"Oh, thank the King, you're all safe!" she said over the clamor.

"Happy tidings indeed," Brennus said. "Now, let us depart. Jarad, if you wish to—"

A sharp bang cut off his words. The gavel rapped thrice more, calling for order.

"Citizens!" Ratomer shouted. "We have business to attend. Justice must be served, so we can get back to the task of setting our homeland to rights." He waited until all murmurs ceased. "In violating the terms of her exile, Lyssanne Caelestis has forfeited the mercy of banishment. Added to that, the crimes which led to our near destruction demand the highest penalty."

"Councilman, if I may." Lord Duncan's voice rang clear and strong. "You asked what prompted me to come to your aid, though you are neither my kin nor countrymen."

"What has that to do with—?"

"Mistress Lyssanne made it known to me that you faced a dire threat," Lord Duncan said. "It is for her, the friend of my brother-in-arms Prince Brennus, who stands at her right hand, that we intervened."

Murmurs swept through the hall, the comments now about Brennus.

"He's a prince?"

"*Her* friend?"

"A prince of Lyrya? Here?"

People began curtseying and bowing all over the hall.

"Pardon the oversight, Your Highness," Ratomer said. "We are grateful for your aid. Had I known of your esteemed presence, I would have welcomed you properly to our humble village. I shall be honored to do so, once this unpleasant business is ended."

Brennus huffed then lifted a hand. "That is unnecessary. We are comrades in arms, this day, and more important matters are at hand."

"Indeed," Ratomer said. "If you and your friend with the hammer will take your ease, we'll have this sorted momentarily."

"I think not," Brennus said.

"Your defense of the Caelestis woman is admirable, but you don't know her crimes. I'm certain you'd not wish to interfere with the enforcement of our sovereign law."

"You are mistaken," Brennus said in that icy steel tone which still sent a chill up Lyssanne's spine. "I know well the crimes of which the lady stands accused." He paused, and the hall grew still. "In the time I've known her, she has endured numerous perils most of you wouldn't have escaped with your sanity, including your *merciful* punishment. Not once did she turn from the impossible, but faced all with courage and grace."

"Regardless," Ratomer said, "her mere presence here warrants the death penalty."

Drawing his sword, Brennus stepped in front of Lyssanne. "Fools," he said, low and ominous. "After all you've seen, you persist in this? Her illness was a curse! The enemy who nearly destroyed you, one to whom you willingly gave control of this backwater village, attacked her and you banished her for it." He raked them all with his dagger stare. "She's suffered years of torture, a torture which came nigh to crushing her this very morn, all to save you!"

Lyssanne rested a hand on Brennus's steely arm and stepped up to his side. "I would never have disobeyed the will of the Council," she said, "but I discovered the cause of our woes, and that the village would soon be laid waste. I couldn't leave you at the mercy of sorcery."

"I knew it!" someone shouted. "She's a witch! She just did magic on Madam Nettleworth."

"Not I," Lyssanne said, but the chatter grew louder, and she had no strength to shout.

"Silence!" Brennus said, sounding every bit the prince he was. He rested his free hand at the small of her back. "Tell them."

"Lady Venefica Mortifer," she said, her cheeks aflame, "the last descendant of those we've long called the Noble Oppressors, was a sorceress of the darkest kind. She had lived, for two years or more, in her family's old estate on Mount Mortiferra."

"No, Lyssanne," Mr. Murrough said. "Lady Mortifer only arrived at the close of winter. She offered to help us, and I suppose she did, in many ways."

Grumbles echoed throughout the hall, not all in agreement.

"It was a ruse," Lyssanne said, "to gain further power over you." She had so much to tell them, but sensed her time was short. "The fog I saw before I left? It was a weapon of evil, her weapon." She took a deep breath. "Lady Mortifer was the Keeper of the Shadow Mist."

The room erupted again, people speaking of the Mist in frightened tones.

"We saw it," Jarad said, leaning around Clark's arm, "the Shadow Mist. Everyone did. We were singing, and it fled from us."

Her command for truth had reached as far as the village?

"*Was*, you say?" asked Mr. DeLivre. "Is this lady sorceress gone, then?"

"Yes, she…" Lyssanne swallowed. "She's dead."

Gasps filled the room.

"What have you brought down upon us?" the apparent new chief councilman said. "Lady Mortifer was a favorite of the queen!"

"There will be no reprisals." Serena's calm voice brought a brief return of silence.

"Your pardon, madam, but who are you?" Ratomer asked. "And how can you know this?"

"You may call me Lady Serena," she said. "I have connections in the highest courts. While Lyssanne's hand brought about the sorceress's defeat, her death was of her own making, and I assure you, no one in the Seven Lands will mourn her passing."

Aderyn gasped. "She took her own life?"

"She was swallowed by the Shadow Mist," Lyssanne said.

"Swallowed?" Madam Sewell asked. "It…*ate* her?"

"In a manner of speaking," Serena said.

"That may be," Ratomer said, "but Lyssanne has violated her exile and must face justice."

"Tell me, people of Cloistervale," Brennus said, his voice hard, "in her absence, did your troubles cease?" He waited a beat, but no one spoke. "Did they not, in fact, increase?" Murmurs coursed through the crowd. "Then, I ask you, how can it be her return which escalated them?"

"Remember the voice," Madam Sewell said. "We all heard it, that angel voice speaking of the Mist. It said we should have heeded

Lyssanne's warnings. Surely, that was the King letting us know she has His favor."

"I propose we vote to pardon Lyssanne for breaking exile," Mr. Murrough said. "Her motives warrant it."

"I second the motion," Mr. DeLivre said.

Ratomer huffed. "Gierre, you aren't on the Council."

"Neither are you," Mr. Murrough said, "until we're officially reinstated."

The hall erupted in shouts of "Here, here!"

Ratomer banged the gavel and called for a show of hands. Once again, Lyssanne's fate rested on a vote. This time, when the gavel sounded, it held the ring of freedom rather than the toll of death.

Ratomer's grudging pronouncement and the ensuing tumult set Lyssanne's head to reeling.

"Oh, Lyss!" Aderyn said, stepping around Clark and eyeing Brennus as he sheathed his sword. "You're really back! And you can stay."

"I'm just thankful you're safe," Lyssanne said, embracing her friend.

They had time to share little else, as the throng closed in upon Lyssanne. Well-wishes ranged from tearful joy at her return, to polite gratitude for her bringing those courageous soldiers to help. Lyssanne's hands were grasped, her arms patted, and occasionally her breath stolen by fierce hugs. Through it all, Brennus and Clark remained at her sides, ever vigilant.

Suddenly, dozens of little hands were reaching for Lyssanne. The children swarmed about her like insects to sweetbread, repeating her name. She staggered under the force of so many tiny bodies hugging her at once.

"Easy, little ones," Brennus said, stepping aside to accommodate them. "Give the lady room, else you'll push her over."

A ripple ran through the children like a current on the Esten. Little faces turned toward Brennus, transfixed. A few of the smaller children tried to burrow into Lyssanne's skirts to hide, while several of the boys wore wide grins and even wider eyes.

During a slight lull, in which villagers greeted Brennus and Serena,

Lyssanne beckoned to Jarad. "Has anyone seen Reina?" she asked, Venefica's words haunting her thoughts.

"Nobody's gone that deep into the wood," Jarad said. "Nobody who returned, at least."

Lyssanne shivered.

"But Reina wouldn't have let any of those foul creatures get close to her."

"I'm certain you have it aright," Lyssanne said, her throat tight.

"I'll go check on her," Jarad said, turning toward the door.

"No! Jarad, 'tis too dangerous. Dark beasts could still roam the wood."

"They all fled," he said.

"Jarad, you must not go into that wood alone. I...I forbid it." 'Twas ridiculous—she, acting the part of a guardian with this boy who had so often been her protector.

"But—"

"Heed her caution, Jarad," Brennus said, his tone more command than advice. "I, too, am concerned for our friend, but only a fool would venture alone into that wood."

"I shall accompany him, if you wish," Clark said.

Agreeing, Brennus assigned two of Lord Duncan's men to escort them, then he waved Duncan nearer. "Lyssanne needs safe lodging. She may be injured."

"Your pardon, Sir Prince," Aderyn said, shifting her child higher on her hip. "Kelyssa and I can tend her. Our cottage is rightfully hers, after all."

Brennus offered her a brief bow, then whispered to Lord Duncan, "Stay close."

"You expect trouble?" Duncan asked. "You don't trust these villagers, do you?"

"Not with her," Brennus murmured, his gaze weighing upon Lyssanne.

His vigilance was a comfort she wished she didn't need in this, of all places.

~

The moon, little more than a crescent shard, climbed higher as Brennus and Serena escorted Lyssanne through the wood to meet Reina. It would shed no light the following night. Serena, too, gazed at the sky, perhaps pondering the fate she'd so narrowly escaped. She glanced at Brennus, shifting shoulders that no longer needed fear the loss of wings.

Ironic, just ten months before, they three had made this same trek. Though, Lyssanne's feet alone had trodden the ground. Brennus might have jested with Serena about their aerial battle, had his thoughts not been heavy with all Lyssanne had endured since.

At Reina's whinny, Lyssanne rushed ahead and flung her arms about the unicorn's neck. Though she'd slept through the day and half the night, her pallor rivaled Reina's.

"Jarad said you were unharmed, but I had to be certain," she said.

"Fear not for me, child," Reina said. "The mud creature I slew wasn't truly alive—composed, as it was, of dead earth animated by corrupted magic."

"Your courage brings honor to your kin and your King," Serena said.

"You're certain you are well?" Lyssanne asked. "Your voice sounds strained."

"Little escapes your perception, child," Reina said. "I am no longer the carefree creature you first met. I've begun to notice the passage of time as never before."

"Oh, Reina!" Lyssanne cried. "Forgive me."

"I've gained more than I've lost, dear one. Including a deepened compassion for those who do not always act with the purest intentions." Her fathomless gaze rested on Brennus. "I have learned, from your ready forgiveness of your prince, that one cannot know what circumstance drives a creature to such actions."

Brennus doubted himself capable of ever extending that level of grace.

"Should the taint of the mortal realm grow too painful," Serena

441

said, "a place will forever remain reserved for you in Glenneirien." She caught Brennus's eye. "I sense Lyssanne desires a private word with Reina."

Brennus nodded and retreated to a discrete distance.

"You appear troubled, Prince of Navvar," Serena said, joining him.

"She's done all the King asked of her and more," he said, his eyes fixed on Lyssanne. "She nearly gave her life for theirs, and still these people hold her apart from them."

"It is often thus in wars of the spirit," Serena said. "Men's natural eyes fail to see the battles waged on their behalf in the secret place."

"It wearies her," he said, his voice thick. "The curse, you're certain, is lifted?"

"It is."

"Why, then, does her weakness persist? She speaks not of it, but I know the signs. With her smallest exertion, strength fails her."

"Only time can heal the toll years of torment have taken on her body," said the queen. "She must be patient, as should you."

"My sole wish is to see her safe and her suffering ended."

Serena tilted her head then stood silent for so long, Brennus thought their converse at an end. Then, she announced, "The King has just entrusted me with a message for you."

His gaze flashed to hers. "For me? Are you certain?"

"Quite," she said, her eyes glittering.

The King of All Lands considered him of sufficient worth to receive a personal message? It defied comprehension. "What message?" Brennus asked.

"For your courage in breaking free of Darkness and your selfless sacrifice, He has granted you a boon."

"Indeed," Brennus said. "With every sunrise, I shall offer thanks for His mercy in lifting the curse from my line."

"'Tis of a different boon He speaks."

"There is nothing more I could ask or wish," Brennus said, "lest it be assurance of Lyssanne's safety and happiness."

"Perhaps, but the King offers another reward. Should you wish it, you may retain the ability to transform into that avian form with which you are so familiar."

Brennus swung to face her, but Serena lifted a hand to forestall any protest.

"Not as a raven, which profits from the deaths of others," she said, "but as an eagle, a creature who brings forth new life from nests on high."

Brennus shook his head, refusal upon his lips, but with a wave of Serena's hand, his mouth sealed itself.

"Do not give your answer in haste," she said. "The eagle is a symbol of the King's power, grace, and majesty. As the King transforms the spirit, allowing the heart of man to soar above natural circumstance, He grants you this ability as a useful weapon in the wars you must wage."

Brennus shot her a hot glare that would have cowed many a man.

"I know well the relief of shedding those feathers," she said, "but this would be a transformation of your choosing. Take time to consider its advantages. In the hands of the King, what was a curse may become your greatest weapon."

Brennus nodded, and his lips fell free of their bonds.

"The King gives you several days to make your answer. Wherever you may be at the appointed hour, I shall seek you out and receive it for Him."

Brennus bowed. "Then, I shall await your prompting before voicing my decision."

"Six men, buried in one morning," Aderyn said, taking the stack of cloth strips Lyssanne had cut and dropping them into the tub of water boiling on the fire. "'Twill be passing strange, not seeing Mr. Cutler at his butcher's stall on Marketday."

"So much loss," Lyssanne said. She flexed her shoulders, then set to preparing more bandages. "I am thankful the children, at least, escaped that grim dawn unharmed."

443

"Yes, though we lost three while you were away," Aderyn said, settling at the dining table across from Serena. "One of the orphans got ahold of spoiled food. Then, Elward Murrough slipped and impaled himself on that broken shovel handle, trying to attack his own father."

Lyssanne rested her face in her palms. "Oh, Elward." She glanced up. "You said three?"

"You sure you want to hear this, Lyss?" At Lyssanne's nod, Aderyn continued. "Madam Blythe was murdered. Her husband's convinced Lady Mortifer had her killed because he voted against letting her rule. One of the twins witnessed it, we think. Poor dear went mad. Flung herself from the bell tower."

Was there no end to this sadness? Fighting for composure, Lyssanne shook out another bandage. How could Aderyn bear to sit in this room, where every surface or wall bore reminders of her slain parents? The uprising that overthrew the Council cost her more than anyone.

Like the promise of sun after a storm, Aderyn's daughter tugged at Lssanne's skirt and held out a piece of bread.

"Thank you, Kelyssa." Lyssanne took the soggy bread, smiling. "Such a beautiful name."

"She wears it in honor of the two people most dear to me," Aderyn said. "Kevan and you."

"Me? But we only name children for those who have died." She gasped. "You thought I—"

"Evlia sent me fer those new bandages," Mr. Whiskin said, stomping into the room. He poked at the blood-soaked cloth covering his arm. "That oversized lizard tried to tear this whole thing off. Evlia's a fair seamstress, but I suppose I'd best learn to knead dough one-handed."

"Allow me to assist you," Lord Duncan said, pushing away from the wall near the door. "It'll give me something to do until the changing of the guard." He lifted one end of a cooled, second tub of sterile cloths and helped Mr. Whiskin carry it into the next room.

Lyssanne watched them go, longing to ease Mr. Whiskin's

suffering, but Serena had warned her to use her gift only in the most dire cases, lest she, too, should become ill.

As if sensing her thoughts, Serena rested a hand on her shoulder and whispered, "Your faith, alone, would not suffice here. This man has knowledge of the King, thus his trust and expectation are required if he is to receive the gift."

Aderyn leaned across the table. "Lyss, you must tell me about this dashing prince. How did you meet?"

"That is a long and complex tale."

"Then, 'tis a good thing you are so fond of telling stories."

The door to the veranda burst open. "I found her!" Jarad shouted over his shoulder.

"Ah, I see my rest is ended," Lord Duncan said, reentering the room.

Brennus followed Jarad inside. "You're needed elsewhere, Duncan."

"Trouble with the prisoners?" Duncan asked.

"They're being moved from the mill. The village leaders ask that you explain their fate, once they're secured in the cellar beneath this house."

Lyssanne's stomach flipped at the thought of Willem, Teremiah Furin, and several others who'd so fully succumbed to the Mist that not even seeing the truth of its nature had restored their reason. "What is to be their fate?" she asked.

"They are to be guests of Avery Hall while awaiting judgment," Lord Duncan said.

The tower cell flashed into her mind.

"Duncan is a fair man, Lyssanne," Brennus said. "Even your learned scribe believes they will receive a more impartial hearing in his courts than they would here."

"*Fii*," Mr. DeLivre said, stepping around Brennus. "That, I do. How this village can ever repay you both for all you've done, I do not know."

"If you wish to repay me, sir," Lord Duncan said, "have someone prepare me a cup of that fine flyl I'm told is to be found solely in Cloistervale."

"Yeah," Jarad said. "We all need some flyl, especially Lady Lyssanne." He fixed his gaze on her. "You're so pale, I can almost see through you."

"What Lyssanne needs," Brennus said, "is more rest."

"So much remains to be done," she said. "How could I sleep?"

"Others will see to it," Brennus said, reaching for her hand. "You've done enough."

"Yes," Aderyn said. "Come, I shall brew flyl for our friends, and if you can't sleep, you can share with me that tale we discussed."

"And I have a pair of iron sculptures that want returning to you," Mr. DeLivre said.

Brennus pulled Lyssanne to her feet. "I shall escort you."

She nodded, too weary to resist.

A line of knights, herding men with bound hands, cut across their path at the foot of the veranda. Suddenly, one of the prisoners wrenched a sword from the knight in front of him. He lunged straight for Lyssanne.

With a flash of steel, faster than thought, Brennus leapt in front of her—and Willem lay on the ground. Dead.

32

CHOICE

*B*rennus took a slow sip of skyberry juice, his eyes sweeping the parlor of his temporary accommodations over the rim of his glass. He made the glance appear casual, just an outsider observing the village men who'd gathered for refreshment after the long day's cleanup efforts. Like a raven scanning the forest for wounded prey, however, he was on the hunt for the slightest sign of impending insurrection.

Most conversations in the room centered around the carpenter's attack on Lyssanne and the protests it had fueled against the Council's reinstatement. The pair of men nearest Brennus's chair debated whether it had been Lyssanne or Aderyn Clayton Willem meant to slay.

"The old Council couldn't keep us safe," one of them murmured. "This just proves the new one's no better."

Brennus tensed. He cared nothing for Cloistervale's political state, but Lyssanne's safety was one thing he would not compromise. He would use every weapon he possessed—including those peasants' nauseating acquiescence to his every wish—to ensure a peaceful transition.

A commotion drew his eye to the front door. Several men crowded a newcomer, who struggled to push his way into the room.

"Gentlemen, if you please," Duncan said, in polite but impatient tones.

"The new Council is eager to finalize that trade agreement you proposed," Ratomer said. "You truly believe there will be so great a market for flyl?"

"I've no doubt of it," Duncan said, "but if you'll excuse me—"

"What makes you so certain?" the baker asked, towering over the others.

"Lyssanne's version was such a favorite at my feasts," Duncan said, "King Luteson's own chef has demanded the recipe. Soon, every manor and merchant's house in Lyrya will be clamoring for your honcin. Now, I must—"

"Lyssanne, again," one of the men murmured.

Brennus smirked behind his cup, then leaned back in his hearthside chair, as the councilmen peppered Duncan with questions on fair pricing, means of transport, and such.

"We shall discuss these matters on the morrow," Duncan said. "I have urgent business to attend." He pushed between two men and hastened toward Brennus.

"What's amiss," Brennus asked, jumping to his feet. "Is Lyssanne—?"

"Safe," Duncan said. "Clark is with her. A messenger arrived with tidings for you. Said he rode night and day to deliver this." He held out a letter.

Brennus took it and broke its seal. A breath whistled out between his teeth as he read. "Has the messenger departed?"

"No," Duncan said. "My men are giving him food and a place to bed down for the night."

"Good. I must send an immediate response." Brennus beckoned Duncan to follow him into the deceased chief councilman's study.

"What's happened?" Duncan asked, closing the door behind them.

"Sorin found a Navvarish boy in the desert near Ravenshold," Brennus said, rummaging for parchment and quill. "Once he'd regained strength enough to speak, the child told Captain Tryggvi he's the sole survivor of his village."

"Disease?" Duncan asked.

"The Brotherhood." Brennus sank into the chair behind the desk. "Soldiers slew every man, woman, and child because, in the boy's words, 'our tribute was too small, including the people they required of us.'"

"People?" Duncan said.

"Slaves, perhaps," Brennus said, "or worse. Rumors abound of a magic so dark, it consumes life to feed its power. Some say Blackthorne wields such."

"Sounds like fodder for fireside tales," Duncan said. "Still, the Brotherhood's murder of its own people is nothing new."

"Sorin's tribe helped the boy survive the desert, Duncan. Blackthorne slew half their numbers, personally. If he dares invade the desert, Ravenshold could be next."

"Then, the time is upon us at last," Duncan said.

Brennus nodded and set to drafting instructions for his captain of the guard.

"Avery Hall stands with you, as promised," Duncan said, pulling up a chair. "Though, I must confess, overjoyed as I am that you are rid of the curse, your feathers would have proven most useful when it comes time for reconnaissance in Navvar. No spy in my service could ever match you for stealth, by day or night."

Brennus's jaw clenched, but he continued writing in silence.

Duncan chuckled. "When I think of how many times you saved my hide, warning me from the air of ambush or enemy attempts to outflank our forces during pitched battle…" He sighed. "Well, we shall just have to revise our strategies, eh?"

Brennus set down his quill and forced his gaze to meet Duncan's. "I have been offered a chance to retain the disguise of feathers." He explained every detail of Serena's proposal.

Duncan leaned forward, eyes aflame. "You accepted at once, I daresay."

"No."

"You...*No?*" Duncan stared. "Surely you didn't refuse such an advantage?"

"I've given no answer."

Duncan expelled a breath then slapped the desk. "Think of it, man, all the impenetrable strongholds you'll infiltrate! Blackthorne won't know which way to turn when we find holes in defenses never before breeched." He laughed as if their triumph were at hand. "Cursed your family with feathers, did they? Ha! They'll never suspect a bird of bringing their downfall!"

"It may not prove as effective a disguise as you hope," Brennus said.

Duncan shook his head. "Were you to remain a raven, sure, they might suspect you. But an eagle? They'll have not an inkling. It'll be akin to the battles of our youth!"

"You forget, my friend," Brennus said, "in those days, we were untested against sorcerers."

"What has that to do with—?"

"Venefica knew what I was from the first. What's more, even at the height of her power, she was nothing to what I've heard of Blackthorne's abilities."

"You think magic detects magic?" Duncan asked, sobering.

"Yes."

"But..." Duncan scratched his chin, a sign his brilliant strategist's mind was dissecting the problem. "She couldn't use magic to see Lyssanne, save through your eyes, correct?"

"That, or when Lyssanne was near a human under the control of the Shadow Mist."

"What if Lyssanne were alone in the presence of the Mist?" Duncan asked.

"She...could have gone undetected," Brennus said, "unless the Mist had a host to carry sight of her to Venefica." He peered at his friend. "What is it you're thinking?"

"Why do you suppose that was?"

Brennus shrugged. "I suspect, the King's Light shielded her from view, as from influence."

"Perhaps it will be so for you," Duncan said. "The sorceress couldn't see through the King's gift to Lyssanne. This eagle disguise is such a gift, is it not?"

Brennus nodded. "Lyssanne had similar thoughts on the matter. She said the Thief's darkness so blinds the hearts of the fallen, they can't see the King's Light or their need for it."

"She advised you to accept, then?"

"She wouldn't presume to offer counsel," Brennus said. "She only reminded me, the King sees what lies ahead and knows our future needs."

"Such wisdom would rival that of the most seasoned sage," Duncan said.

A soft rap at the study door punctuated that thought.

"Enter," Brennus said.

Serena sailed into the room. "I must take my leave," she said. "My guardianship in this realm is at an end, and I've long since been needed in my own."

Brennus rose and rounded the desk. "Have you spoken with Lyssanne?"

"She awaits me at the eastern end of the veranda."

He offered her his most deferential bow. "Then farewell, Majesty. May the FAE never lose sight of the honor which is theirs, to have so noble a lady as their queen."

"Farewell, fellow watcher," she said with a regal nod. "I rejoice that our vigilance now serves the same King."

The men followed Serena from the room, discussing plans for their own departure. Once Brennus had given Lyssanne ample time for her farewells, he slipped outside to join her. They'd spent not a moment alone since crossing Merchant's bridge, and he had much to say. Silent as shadow, he moved to the corner of the house.

She stood, small and alone, facing the unobstructed view of the River Esten. How often he had seen her thus, gazing out upon a world too large and fraught with peril for one so fragile to face alone. Yet face it, she had.

How had he ever thought watching her a chore? If time and the obligations of his birth would permit, he could have lived out his days doing just that.

～

Lyssanne turned to Serena. "How I shall miss the constancy of your presence."

"This battle may be at an end," Serena said, "but for the FAE, and for mankind, the war continues. Venefica Mortifer was but one pawn of the Thief of Souls. I must return to regroup my warriors and dispense justice among my people."

"Is it like this for you always?" Lyssanne asked. "So much loss and death?"

Serena chuckled. "No, we see far more good than bad." She took Lyssanne's hand, while shrinking to her true size and extending her wings. "Such as the privilege of your friendship. Lyssanne, you have done well. You had the courage to carry the King's Light into the very seat of Darkness in this land. Your parents' hearts would swell with pride, as does mine."

"I could have done none of this without you," Lyssanne whispered.

"You have come to the end of this path," Serena said, "but not the end of your journey. Your task, now, is to discover the first markers of your new road and follow it."

"Have you any counsel on where to look?"

"Your heart already knows."

Brennus's face filled Lyssanne's mind. She shook her head, but Serena spoke first.

"Don't pretend to daftness, daughter of the King. You know his heart as well as your own. Only one thing could turn a man who never breaks his word from avowed assassin to a champion willing to die for his intended victim. A love beyond the scope of legend."

Pearlescent sparks surrounded Serena, and her voice echoed as if she were already slipping into another realm.

"The need for my watchfulness is past," she said. "Others shall now take up that call. Farewell."

Lyssanne turned again to the view, until a sudden warmth suffused her back.

"How does the story end?" Brennus asked, his approach so silent, 'twas as if he'd been conjured from her thoughts. "When the villain is vanquished and the village saved, what does the brave knight do then?"

"I don't know," she said, glancing back at him. "I suppose he—"

"She."

Lyssanne smiled. "*She*...goes on to other adventures."

"And your next adventure, brave warrior of Light?"

She laughed. "It hasn't yet been written. Or, well, I suppose it has, but the Author hasn't shown me that page."

"I feel my own story began when first I saw you," Brennus murmured. "My life before was nothing but a shadow fallen across empty parchment."

"Had you not entered my book," she said, "it would have closed long ago, darkness blotting out its words." She smiled up at him, longing to bring back the playfulness of a moment before. "What is your next chapter to hold, oh slayer of shadows?"

"With my family's curse lifted and you safe," he said, "I must resume my first duty...that to my people." He spoke as if he must drag each word forth. "My battles have only just begun."

"Navvar," she whispered.

"Too long, has the land of my fathers suffered under tyranny."

"Then, you do intend to reclaim the throne?"

"Yes."

Lyssanne had to turn away, swept adrift on the current of images his words conjured. The heat of his nearness couldn't dispel the frost settling over her heart. He was leaving.

She'd known, hadn't she, that this must come? Certainly, he couldn't be expected to remain in this isolated village. She drew a tremulous breath, ready to give voice to all that she'd locked away in the secret parts of her soul. But now, when the storyteller must share the tale of her heart with the most important audience of all, words deserted her.

"Lyssanne," Brennus whispered, as if pained. His gentle hands turned her to face him. "Love, could I but rip that page from my story and never be parted from you, I would fling it into the fire, as though it had never been written. Alas, such is not in my power. To do so would dishonor the One who wields the pen."

"I wouldn't ask—"

"Please." He pressed a finger to her lips. "Allow me this chance to speak what I must."

She nodded.

"For weeks, I've struggled with all I need to say. I was prevented, first, by my own stubbornness, then events robbed me of opportunity. I dared not add to the burdens set upon your heart. Now, I find I have no more time."

"What has put this agony in your voice? Please, Brennus, let me help."

"'Tis only that I cannot possibly show you, in a few stolen moments, the wonder that you are, the truth I would spend the rest of my days proving to you." He rested his palm against her cheek and spoke as if in torment. "Lyssanne, I love you."

They were the most beautiful words in spoken or written language, holding the power to recreate life from cold ash. She drew breath to return them. "Brennus, I—"

"You promised to let me speak," he said. "Unlike you, I have no gift of weaving words, so I ask for your patience, as I blunder through this."

She nodded again.

"I thought I understood the meaning of love—duty, desire, affection." He sighed. "I was a fool. I knew nothing...Until you."

He turned to grip the veranda railing, as if it were the side of a storm-tossed ship. Lyssanne waited, keeping her promise with difficulty.

"I was born under not just one curse. The plague of self-interest was my birthright," he said. "Like Fescue's tower, I stood alone—cold, immovable. That, I thought, was strength. I needed no one, wanted no one." He sighed. "The disease was killing me, and I didn't even know it. You were its diagnosis and its cure."

He swung back to face her, then clasped her hands.

"When I thought you forever lost," he said, "I learned the meaning of fear. When the King gave you back to me, I learned a man can weep from joy." He lifted both her hands to his lips. "And when you look at me as you are now, I begin to understand I need no wings to soar." He bowed over her hands, saying, "my lady," and kissed each in turn. "To a soul once black with failed hopes, you are light. To a heart once cold as dead stone, you are life. To eyes gorged upon bleak despair, you are luminescent beauty. To this, the most unlovable of men, you *are* love."

Tears bathed Lyssanne's cheeks. "I…" She swallowed, certain she would drown in this well of emotion which had no simple name. "I love you."

A breath shuddered out from him, its waves trembling through their joined hands.

"Oh, Brennus," she whispered. "Words abandon me. They leave me desolate, with no way to tell you…" Her voice broke. "How can I tell you…?"

"Shh, love," he whispered. "There is no need."

"But I wish you to know my heart, what you are to me."

"I can see it, my lady," he said, his voice raspy. "The words are written in your eyes." Clearing his throat, he lifted her chin. "If I had anything to offer but a dangerous road and more battles at its end, I would ask, here and now, for the honor of your hand."

She gasped, then parted her lips to give him answer.

"No," he said. "Do not bind yourself with words. I will not condemn you to such a life, wife to a fugitive seeking to overthrow a tyrant."

"Must you do this?" she whispered. "You've saved your family line from the curse. Surely that is victory enough, without risking such danger."

"If this were for myself or the honor of my house," he said, "I would leave Navvar to its current rulers and gladly never depart from your side. But our borders are threatened. To abandon my people or those who stand in the Brotherhood's way, would dishonor everything I have so lately learned from the King…and from you."

"Me?" She shook her head.

He laughed. "Yes, teacher, you've taught even this reluctant student well. Evil's sway must be vanquished, wherever it is found."

"But why must it be you who overthrows this tyranny?"

"Because," he said, "I know what anyone who attempts it will face. The hereditary leaders of the Blackthorne Brotherhood are not mere warlords, Lyssanne. They are sorcerers. If my contacts can be believed, they are more ruthless and powerful even than Venefica."

Lyssanne shuddered and drew close to him. His arms wound around her.

"If I could see Venefica's power—can see the King's in you— perhaps I shall be given sight of what darkness Blackthorne wields." His arms tightened. "The Navvarish people are little more than slaves," he said. "I must free them if I can."

"When will you leave?"

"Sunrise, two days hence."

"So soon?"

"I wish to cross the Navvarish Desert by autumn's first chill. Sooner, if I could, but that wasteland is death to men in high summer. Thus, I have but a handful of months to assemble an army, see it outfitted, and form a plan of invasion. This campaign will require stealth, diversion, and misinformation. No war fought on so many fronts is quickly organized."

"I see."

As if on impulse, he said, "Come with me. At least to Lyrya. You should be where you are accepted and loved. You know Avery Hall would welcome you."

She looked past him, toward the square. "I don't belong at Avery Hall," she said. "I love its people dearly, but I am not one of them."

"You belong less here." He sighed and lowered his brow to the top of her head. "Had I the right, I would make it a command, simply to see you safe."

"The danger is past."

"To body, yes," he said, "but not in spirit. Duncan and MeMe value your words, your wisdom, your gift. These peasants—"

"I, too, am a peasant," Lyssanne whispered.

"Love," he said, his voice thick, "forgive me. 'Twas not my intent to demean your birth or theirs." He waved toward the neighboring houses. "But you are so much more than this. Those people are so dependent on their traditions, they have the sun in their midst and can't even see it. How long until they again accuse you of witchcraft or some other foolish charge?"

"Brennus—"

"I've heard the whispers," he said. "If Venefica singled you out for attack, they say you, too, must be a sorceress. The woman you healed has only added fuel to the gossip."

"This is my home," she said, "and at last I've been permitted to return. I need time."

"I have none to give." He took her hands in his. "At least return to Avery Hall until matters here have calmed. Let me venture forth into battle knowing you are safe."

Oh, the possibility tugged at her heart.

"Besides," he said, "that will allow Jarad room to ponder his decision."

"What decision?"

"I have offered him a position as my squire."

Her eyes flew wide as the doors of Avery Hall. "Do you mean, will he train as a knight?"

"If that is his wish."

"But he is not of noble birth. How—?"

"His standing as my squire will afford him what birth cannot. No lord in the Seven Lands would deny him spurs, once he has my endorsement."

"Thank you," she whispered. "It is all he could have dreamt, and more."

"Perhaps, but he feels his first duty is to you. He'll never leave you here unprotected."

"Here, he can have no life befitting his courage and intellect."

"No."

"He must accept your offer." She set her shoulders. "I shall speak with him and encourage him to do so. Strongly, if need be."

"Would that I held such influence with you," Brennus murmured.

Oh, but he did. He wielded more power over her choices than she dared admit.

"Will *you* not accept my offer?" His words hadn't held such hollow flatness since he'd made his vow to the King. "Will you deny me the comfort of knowing you are sheltered in what manner of protection I can give? Lyssanne…" His voice faltered on her name.

"Allow me the morrow, at least, to consider it?"

"I can deny you nothing," he said. "One thing more, I would request of you."

"What is it?"

He leaned so near, 'twas as if he swallowed all the air. "May I ask the favor of a kiss?"

For a moment she was too stunned to speak. "Yes," she whispered.

It began like a gentle summer rain, sweet, warming, life-renewing. Never had she known a heart could hold such joy and soul-searing sorrow intermingled. Then, as if his embrace could convey all the urgency in their hearts, the gentle rain became a storm. She forgot everything in the midst of lightning strikes of emotion, his leaving, dangers past and future, the choice she must make. A torrent of need for nothing more than his nearness swept her away.

When, at last and all too soon, he released her, Lyssanne clung to his tunic for steadiness. He pulled her close, and she rested her swimming head against him.

"I love you," she whispered. Why was she trembling?

"And I, you," he murmured into her hair. "I am a thief," he said. "I'm not certain how much you remember, but this wasn't our first kiss. Without your leave, I've taken another." With his lips brushing her hair, he whispered, "Forgive me."

She laughed. "I do remember, though I thought it a swooning dream. You have my consent, sir, be it after the fact." Suddenly shy, she lowered her eyes. "Should you desire a future occurrence, you have my leave for that, as well."

"No knight could refuse so sweet a favor," he said, then claimed his prize.

A moment later, footfalls broke into the blissful haze of their embrace. With more presence of mind than Lyssanne could muster, Brennus released her, save for one hand.

"Lyss! There you are!" Aderyn cried from the murky void of the world outside Brennus's arms. "Madam Sewell thought you'd returned to the cottage."

"No," Lyssanne said. "No, I've been here. We had…things to discuss."

"Ah, well…yes," Aderyn said, sounding puzzled. "Sure and I shan't keep you, then. I merely wished to bid you a good night. Kelyssa and I are for home."

"Doubtless, you are weary as well," said Brennus, squeezing Lyssanne's hand, "and I have matters to discuss with Duncan."

"A good eve to you, Your Highness," Aderyn said, curtseying. "Lord Avery and a few others are sipping flyl in the parlor."

"I thank you, madam," Brennus said. "For this and for opening your parents' home to us." He turned back to Lyssanne. "Rest well, and think on what I said."

"I shall think on nothing else."

As he backed away, his fingertips slid down the length of hers. "Until tomorrow."

"Tomorrow," she whispered, the word holding all the light and shadow of the future.

THE WATCHER

*B*rennus drove Duncan's war stallion toward Merchant's Bridge, allowing the other men to pull well ahead. He trained his mind on the impending battles and a strategy for seeing them won. It was the only way to maintain a hold on his slipping composure. He must keep as tight a rein on his thoughts as on his borrowed horse, lest either turn back to Cloistervale.

A sudden pounding of hooves beat a rhythm of impossible swiftness through the forest beside Trader's Road. The next instant, a flash of white streaked through the trees at his right. Without warning, that luminous shape darted onto the road in front of him.

Brennus jerked at his reins, and his mount reared. Once he could again see anything but sky, he gasped out an oath. "Reina!" he said, then swallowed, hard. If he hadn't stopped in time..."Shining One, what could possibly...?"

Words failed him, and his hammering heart sped up tenfold at the sight of what Reina carried, or rather, whom.

Waves of coppery hair lifted from the shelter of Reina's mane. Lyssanne shook the strands from her pallid face, her wide eyes searching. Her knuckles were as white as the mane they gripped.

Reina's panting breaths drew Brennus's attention, though his eyes would not be pried from Lyssanne's face. The unicorn was winded? She must have flown through that wood faster, even, than her magical nature would allow—with his purpose for life on her back!

"Shining One," Brennus fair growled, "I could have killed you. Both of you."

"Do you know me so little, still, Prince, as to think I would let you?" Reina asked. "I am not hampered, even at the speed of wind, by mere human perceptions."

Brennus dismounted and rushed to Reina's side. He lowered his love into his arms, his tunic replacing Reina's mane in her clasping fingers. When he set her on her feet, she was unsteady, so he held her a bit longer.

"What's amiss, love," he asked, "that you should risk such harm?"

Lyssanne parted her lips, her breaths coming in short bursts.

"I found her running through the wood behind her cottage," Reina said.

"Running?" Brennus asked, all senses in sharpest focus. He held Lyssanne apart to peer into her face. "Is there danger? Were you harmed?"

She shook her head.

"Fear not, Knight of the King," Reina said, chuckling. "All is as it should be. When I asked her reason for haste, Lyssanne gasped out your name. I understood at once." She whinnied. "It took all the considerable speed I could muster to catch you before you crossed that river."

"You've ridden to shame the wind, my lady," he murmured, smoothing Lyssanne's hair. "Why?"

"I...I had to..." Lyssanne said, still winded.

"Catch your breath, love. There is time." For her, he would create time, itself, if need be.

The faint thud of more hooves drifted to Brennus's hearing. He glanced back along Trader's Road. A lone figure galloped toward them.

"Jarad?" he called.

461

"Jarad?" Lyssanne said. "How? I left word…with Mr. DeLivre…not an hour ago."

"Followed you," Jarad said, reining in. "Figured you'd be sad today, so I started for the cottage. You rushed past me in the square but didn't see me. I heard you tell Mr. DeLivre you were going with Prince Brennus, so I ran to get my horse."

"Is he right, Lyssanne?" Brennus asked, hardly daring to hope. "Have you decided to accompany me to Avery Hall?"

"There and beyond," she said. "You've been with me through all my battles, how can I do less?"

"Beyond?" The word dropped upon his heart like the landslide in Stupasce. "No, I will not take you into harm's way. A battlefield is no place for you."

She lifted her fingers to his lips, stretching her arm to its fullest length to reach them. "I wouldn't presume to venture so far. I should only get in your way or endanger you and your men."

"Then, what—?"

"I propose," she said, "to travel as far as you deem safe, to remain close to you for however long I may. Brennus, 'tis my desire to be at hand when you've gained your victory, as you were for me."

"Such courage," he whispered, pulling her into his arms. "What of your home?"

"Home is the King's presence," she said. "Home is Jarad and Reina, and home is you." She rested her head against him. "You, who have watched me and watched over me far longer than I knew. I cannot imagine a life without your eyes upon me."

They stood locked in that embrace until Brennus could again find voice. "Have you come for Lyssanne," he asked Jarad, "or is it your intent to accept my offer?"

Jarad shook his head, fighting to steady his frisking mount. "I thought, since I said no…"

"Your reasons for refusal only prove you worthy. The position is yours, if you wish it."

"I—I do."

"Then," Brennus said. "You shall, henceforth, be named Jarad Stalwart, squire of Ravenshold."

"I've never had a proper surname," Jarad said, fidgeting nearly as much as his horse. "Didn't know being a squire made you worthy of one."

Lyssanne looked up at Brennus as if he'd just given her a palace. "That is a wondrous gift," she said, then turned to Jarad. "A name most fitting, but Jarad, our worth is not defined by what we do; rather, how we live."

Jarad ducked his head. "I know."

"You shall both accompany me as far as Ravenshold," Brennus said. "I must stop at my family's holding to gather additional troops and supplies before crossing into Navvar, and to inform my grandmother that her dearest wish has come to pass." He cupped Lyssanne's cheek. "You will be safe there until Jarad and I return."

"I shall be honored to meet your lady grandmother," Lyssanne said.

"She will adore you." He smiled down at her. "Once she discovers your role in removing the curse from Xavier blood, she'll doubtless loose all her formidable ire upon me, should I bring so much as a frown to your lips."

The corners of Lyssanne's mouth twitched.

"I shouldn't allow you to do this," he said. "There will be dangers, even along the way to Ravenshold."

"Things more dangerous than that Diornian? Or Lady Mortifer?" Lyssanne said. She rested a hand against his forearm. "More dangerous than you?"

A shaky laugh forced its way up through his chest. "I don't know."

"Well," Lyssanne said, "I shall have you to look after me. And this time, we are both armed with the certainty that you will be only my protector, not my peril."

"Never doubt it," Brennus said, tightening his hold.

"Two truths are forever unshakable in my mind," she said. "The love of the King and the goodness of your heart."

In a thousand lifetimes, were he to free a hundred lands, Brennus could never merit the favor of this woman. Light's Grace, indeed. He would gladly spend every moment left to him in the attempt to become worthy of her.

"One thing remains before we set out," he said, stepping back a pace. He drew his sword and let its tip hover just above her left shoulder.

"What are you doing?" Jarad shouted.

Lyssanne merely stared up at him with wide, trusting eyes.

Smiling, Brennus tapped her shoulder twice with the flat of his blade then repeated the gesture on the other side. "I, rightful Crown Prince of Navvar and knight of Lyrya," he said, "hereby declare you, Lyssanne, Lady of Ravenshold." He sheathed his sword. "All lands and property assigned to the title of Ravenshold are now yours in perpetuity, along with the standing of Lady of the Realm, both in Lyrya and Navvar. Such standing is recognized throughout the Seven Lands."

Lyssanne's eyes widened further, and her lips parted in a silent *o*.

He swept her a low bow. When he straightened, a shrug and self-mocking smile replaced the formality of the previous moment.

"In truth, Ravenshold isn't much more than a rock-strewn bit of land, bordering Lyrya and Navvar," he said, "but this will give you proper standing in both realms, regardless of my battle's outcome. Either way the war falls, you'll need it."

"Y-you cannot, surely, be offering me your lands, your birthright?" she said.

"My birthright is Navvar," he said. "Lyssanne, I offer what must fall to another, regardless this war's conclusion. If I survive, I shall make my home in the palace of Navvar, not Ravenshold." He took her hand. "If I do not—"

"Don't speak of it," she said.

"If I do not," he insisted, "my people will be left without a family to serve. If the title isn't passed on, the lands will be forfeit to whichever realm manages to take them first. My people will have no home, no livelihood."

Compassion filled her eyes, cementing his resolve. That she could experience such empathy for a people she'd never known, made his choice all the clearer.

"Lyssanne," he said, sensing her protest before she could utter it. "I can think of no other in whose hands I would entrust their welfare. My steward is an honest man and can assist you in the running of the household and lands." He lifted her hand by the fingertips in a courtly gesture of request. "Will you accept my gift? My people need you." He sighed. "*I* need you."

"Yes," she whispered.

"All I ask," he said, compelled to dispense with this one remaining formality, "is that my lady grandmother be permitted to live out her days at the estate."

"Of course," she said, one brow raised as if to question why he needed ask. "'Tis her home, not mine. Though, if it were otherwise, I would answer the same."

Brennus nodded. "You must understand, this is not yet a request for your hand. Nor shall I ask such until I have something more to offer you than battles. But know this," he vowed, "should I survive, I shall have no other as my wife."

"Then," Lyssanne said, her voice tight, "my heart and hand shall await your return and your proposal. For, both are yours, now and forevermore."

"Does this mean you're betrothed?" Jarad asked.

"Nothing so binding," Brennus said.

"I suppose," said Lyssanne, "it means we are engaged to become betrothed."

Brennus laughed, the rich depth of his joy filling the clearing and perhaps the whole wood. "Diplomacy, it seems," he said, "is as inherent in you as the King's Light. Should I be victorious, you will grace Navvar as a truly remarkable queen."

Jarad snorted. "I wonder what Councilman Ratomer would say to that."

Perhaps sensing a kindred spirit, the boy's horse imitated his snort. They burst into laughter, Reina's, loudest of all.

"And what is to be your path, Shining One?" Brennus asked. "We four have so long traveled together, it would seem amiss, were you not among us."

"Did you not say you'd left a carriage across yon bridge?" Reina asked.

"Yes," he said, "though I am not certain we shall find it awaiting our return."

"Then," said Reina, "I offer Lyssanne her accustomed seat. Should your carriage not be where you left it, the offer shall stand until she has no further need. Beyond that, none but the King can know."

Before taking up the reins for this, the final path they were certain to travel together, the four companions turned to face Cloistervale. The village had marked the beginning and end of the shared road that had changed each of them forever.

Rising morning light glittered off the River Esten, leaves swayed to the dance of spring air, and Reina's horn shone silver. Yet, Brennus's watchful eyes beheld nothing but Lyssanne. For, all other radiance, however it might dazzle, was the mere shadow of flame next to the Light of his beloved and her King.

THE END

FREE PREQUEL

JOIN THE QUEST!

Would you like to read *Tria*, the prequel to the Light-Wielder Chronicles...FREE?

Or perhaps you'd like to know what happened during Aderyn's wedding that sent superstitious townsfolk into such an uproar...

Then, visit https://bridgettpowers.com/free-book/ to join Bridgett on a journey through epic tales of light.

As an esteemed member of Bridgett's reader group, you will also receive exclusive content (deleted scenes, bonus material, book trivia, etc.) and be the first to hear about new releases, events, giveaways, and discounts.

Just visit
https://bridgettpowers.com/free-book/

For many of us, the most enjoyable part of reading or writing fantasy is the wonder...the chance to explore fictional words; to meet extraordinary, nonexistent creatures; or to share a character's adventures as he becomes empowered with superhuman gifts. However, many of these fantastical elements, while an invention of imagination, are based on some facet of reality.

This is true of magic's effects upon Lyssanne in *Keeper of Shadows*.

While the magic involved in Venefica's first attack and the curse she later cast on Lyssanne was, of course, fictional, its effects were based on the symptoms of two very real medical conditions: septa-optic dysplasia and intracranial hypertension.

Septo-optic dysplasia (a.k.a. de Morsier's syndrome) is a rare spectrum of symptoms and related conditions caused by issues with the development of the midline structure of a child's brain and optic nerves during pregnancy. Effects can include poor vision, diminished stature, lethargy, low stamina, and many other symptoms. The effects I have listed formed the basis for the results of Venefica's attack before Lyssanne's birth. For more information about this condition, visit: http://bit.ly/2hDcHDJ

Intracranial hypertension (a.k.a. pseudotumor cerebra) is a medical condition in which the body can't regulate the production and absorption of cerebrospinal fluid fast enough. This can cause pressure to build up around the brain, resulting in debilitating headaches, dizziness, nausea, sensitivity to light and sound, and—if untreated— damage to vision or brain function. This condition—along with a

form of neuralgia, which causes sharp pains along the nerve endings of the scalp—was the inspiration behind the curse Lyssanne endured. For more information about this condition, visit:
http://bit.ly/2muiP2S

One of my aims in writing this novel was to portray, in realistic terms, what daily life can be like for a person who lives with these medical conditions. While their symptoms can certainly shape our physical abilities and endurance—and even affect actions, choices, and careers—they do not define who we are.

ACKNOWLEDGMENTS

To God, Author of all life, first and greatest of creative thinkers…to Jesus, hero of my own story…to the Holy Spirit, wellspring of every worthy idea, true writer of this tale—I thank you for the gift of this novel.

My unending gratitude—and half my brain—belongs to Rebecca Bergren, my editor, partner in crime, coauthor on other projects, and dear friend. To our other critique partner and third member of WritingCraft Girls, Laura Smetak, you inspire me! To the rest of the Write Now writers' group, past and present, your encouragement and advice made this possible.

Special thanks to my first readers—Donna Endriukaitis, Curt Wellumson, and of course Ann Powers, a.k.a. Mom. It sounds cliché (sorry, Curt) to say I couldn't have done this without you, but that is the simple truth. You, brave warriors who helped me battle writer's block, insecurities, and long-windedness; motivators who kept me writing—often under threat if I didn't crank out that next chapter after a cliffhanger—I could fill another 500 page book describing all the ways you've helped me with this one.

Kirk DouPonce, most amazing cover designer in the realm, thank you for plucking a vision right out of my brain and making it far cooler than my imagination could dream up.

To Avery Powers, brilliant inventor of magical creatures, you rock, girlfriend! Who would imagine a nine-year-old could dream up Diornian? Thank you for giving him shape (the stuff of nightmares), for giving Bob a spine (er, shell), and for understanding why the jigglinerce must wait for her debut in a sequel.

Also, thanks to Xavier Powers, who kept the Seven Lands fresh in my mind for all those years and fueled spin-off stories through enthusiastic play of that world. Yes, Jarad is you in many ways, dear nephew.

To Colby Clark, another child collaborator, who gave Clark a voice and Sir Fizzil a purpose. Your drawings of the major players kept me inspired!

Heartfelt thanks to Dad, Brian, and KaWan for encouraging me during the journey. Brian, your supposed random nonsense broke through walls and fueled two of my favorite scenes. Thanks for being goofy! Also, thanks for sharing the moment, along with KaWan, when I wrote the last word of the story, a moment made sweeter by your celebrating with a song of praise to God.

ABOUT THE AUTHOR

Since Bridgett's journey began, light and words have defined her world. While defying the limitations of impaired vision and overcoming chronic pain, she learned a profound truth. Light shines brightest through cracked lanterns.

Words remain Bridgett's staunch allies and most powerful weapons in her continuing adventures as author, speaker, editor, and writing coach. By day, she runs Light's Scribe Writer Services in Minnesota. When she isn't slaying evil adverbs and rescuing lost commas in other people's stories, she's off exploring fantasy realms, futuristic worlds, and the deep places within the human spirit. She returns from these quests bearing the tales of cracked and broken beacons who courageously carry light into the darkness—never forgetting that the first such tale she discovered was her own.

For more information or to contact Bridgett, visit:
bridgettpowers.com

ALSO BY BRIDGETT POWERS

If you enjoyed *Keeper of Shadows*...

Check out these other Tales of the Seven Lands.

SHORT STORIES

Vinesinger

Shara's hopes of at last fitting in with her fellow Ehlief are as bright as the green and brown strands of her fanned tail, as high as the notes she can't stop singing. Until, that is, she learns the price of discovering her true destiny...

Set in the distant past of the Seven Lands, "Vinesinger" was published in *Havok magazine 1.3*, July, 2014.

LIGHT-WIELDER CHRONICLES

Tria: A Tale of the Seven Lands (prequel novelette)

Keeper of Shadows

Dark Prism (Coming soon!)

Dawn of Night (Coming soon!)

PREVIEW: DARK PRISM

PROLOGUE

Spring, year 1122 After the Dawning

*a*islin trembled, her lids clenching tighter against the vision. But, the truth of inner sight would not be so easily ignored.

"Tell me, Seer." The sorcerer's smooth, deep voice flooded the subterranean chamber.

The silence that followed pulsed a drumbeat in Aislin's ears, as if to hasten her answer.

"I—" She inhaled. The dank air did nothing to relieve her ashen throat. "'Twill not please you," she whispered, her voice holding all the steadiness of a guttering flame.

"Nor does your dithering," he said. He moved behind the cushioned stool on which she knelt, his heat only sharpening the gooseflesh crawling up her back. "Is it the raven?"

"Worse."

"Has he shed his feathers?"

She shook her head.

He leaned over her. His scent—rosewood, mulled wine with a hint of mint, and that unmistakeable whiff of bitter almonds—shrouded her senses. "That question is your sole purpose, Aislin." He stroked a

479

finger through her hair, curling a strand around his hand. "Three months since the Raven Prince dared publicly display the former royal crest, yet you squander the power on other matters."

"I seek only as you command, but I cannot control the answer."

His hands clamped onto either side of her head, encasing her scalp like the shell of the poisonous nuts he cultivated. "Show me."

"Master, please."

But it was too late. Power lanced through her mind, like a shard of tinted glass slicing through a beam of light, deflecting the vision to his sight.

A vine, green and bright as Aislin's eyes had once been, pushed its way up through the rock-strewn soil of a common field. It tore through weeds that fought to choke it down. The rocks fell away before it, its power growing as it rose.

The vine was truly an intertwining of three stalks. The centermost, a thin, smooth stem, was greenest of the three. The other two, thicker, a shade darker, and bristling with spines, wrapped the central stalk in protective embrace.

The vine glowed against the landscape as it spread across neighboring fields. Where it touched, new shoots sprang to life. Finally, it wound onto soil Aislin knew well. It swept the ground, the spines of its outer stalks ripping loose the dark thorns that covered the land. It came to a halt before a blackthorn bush, tall as a palace. The vine wrapped around that bush, its three stalks never separating. Round and round, it circled, until the bush was hardly visible. The stalks of the vine drew tighter together, crushing the bush.

"Explain," the master said, holding Aislin fast to the vision.

"Wherever it spreads, the three-fold vine uproots your hold," she said.

"The thorns."

"Yes."

"And the bush?"

"If unchecked, the vine has the strength to pull down your house."

"Then, I shall incinerate it," he said, his tone bored.

"It is impervious," said Aislin. 'The living waters of the King nourish it. Nor can it be cut down in the usual fashion. Its intertwining is its strength. As long as it remains thus, it will stand."

"Then, I shall unravel it," he said, "sever each stalk in turn. Beginning with the weakest."

"It will not be so simple a task. That one is the most deeply rooted. It feeds the other two."

"I need no seer to moan about what cannot be done." His words slid over her hair. "You live to show me solutions."

The shard of power piercing Aislin's mind twisted, spearing white pain through her very center. With each twist of his will, the faint light fueling her vision bounced back upon itself, intensifying. Her hands spasmed, clawing at the sides of the cushion. Then, the vision changed.

"There is a way," she whispered. "Only one."

The vine's centermost stalk lurched between its fellows. A blackthorn branch had stretched up from the bush and gripped its smooth, tender surface. The branch yanked the stalk loose. Its roots tore free of the soil, dripping living waters onto dry ground.

The two outer stems collapsed together, their spines impaling each other. The glow seeped out of them, brown replacing green around their punctures. Then, the decay spread, all the way to their bases. Roots slipped from the soil's shallow hold, and the stalks crumpled, nothing more than dried husks.

"Who is this weed I must rip from of the King's hold?" asked the master.

"I know not," Aislin said. "I cannot see."

"Look deeper."

His hands viced around her skull, but the vision was fading.

"I cannot. The light is consumed."

He released her, an angry severing nearly as painful as his taking of the vision.

"I know only this," she said, shaking a lock of brown hair from her eyes to peer up into his cutting, silver gaze. "The three-fold vine is your doom."

www.ingramcontent.com/pod-product-compliance
Lightning Source LLC
Chambersburg PA
CBHW030644120726
47905CB00001B/42